# PLAYING DEAD

1971, London gang boss Annie Carter is living the New York high life with the feared Italian godfather, Constantine Barolli. Then family tragedy strikes, signalling a major shift in mafia power. Annie flees to London with her daughter Layla, but someone wants her dead and the only way she can stay alive is to find out who's paying her pursuers, and to strike first. Then, the reappearance of an old East End face sparks a shocking suspicion. Is it possible that Annie's first and greatest love didn't die two years ago? Could he really just have been playing dead?

# PLAYING DEAD

# PLAYING DEAD

*by*

Jessie Keane

**Magna Large Print Books**
Long Preston, North Yorkshire,
BD23 4ND, England.

British Library Cataloguing in Publication Data.

Keane, Jessie
    Playing dead.

    A catalogue record of this book is
    available from the British Library

    ISBN    978-0-7505-3640-0

First published in Great Britain in 2011 by Harper
an imprint of HarperCollins*Publishers*

Copyright © Jessie Keane 2011

Cover illustration © Ruby Del Angel by arrangement with
Arcangel Images

Jessie Keane asserts the moral right to be identified as the author of
this work

Published in Large Print 2012 by arrangement with
HarperCollins Publishers

Magna Large Print is an imprint of Library Magna Books Ltd.

Printed and bound in Great Britain by
T.J. (International) Ltd., Cornwall, PL28 8RW

*To Cliff, with all my love.*

# Acknowledgements

To all my friends who help me in all sorts of ways to carry on the business of writing. To Lynne, Steve, Karen, Mandasue, Louise, Judith, Sarah, Wayne, Ryan – and if I've missed out anyone else, you know who you are, and thanks.

To the people of Majorca, who answered my seemingly stupid questions with endless patience, and to the girls at the hotel in Cala Bona – thanks for coming over and saying hello and asking me to sign the books. Thanks to John Follain for his excellent and informative *The Last Godfathers,* and to Thomas Reppetto for *American Mafia, a History of Its Rise to Power.*

And finally, thanks to all my dedicated fans and friends on Facebook and Twitter, whose kindness and encouragement lifts me every day and who have been clamouring for Annie Carter to stroll back into their lives – well, gang, here she is. Keep those lovely comments coming!

# America

# Prologue

## Montauk, Long Island, USA
## August 1971

Annie Carter-Barolli knew that there are some things you remember forever. Like your child's first cry. Or your wedding day – or *days,* in her case: she'd been married twice. Or like the moment you stare death in the face and it's not scary like you expected it to be, not a face of bones, not a reaper. Instead it's bright red ribbon on a big square parcel of sunny sky-blue, and your husband is picking it out from the front of the huge pile of presents. He is turning towards you holding it, smiling at you and saying, *Hey, wonder what's in this one?*

That moment stays with you. You want to rewind, replay, edit; take the hurt away. Splice the whole thing back together and make it come out another way. But you can't. Once the jack-in-the-box is out, he's out; there's no going back.

Annie was standing out on the big terraced deck overlooking the Atlantic Ocean. It was a hot August night but the breeze from the sea was cooling and sweet against her skin. Inside the house, Constantine's oceanfront house out here in the millionaire's playground of Montauk, there was the music of a mariachi band, and laughter.

Most times, this place was like a fortress,

15

guarded day and night by his men. Sometimes police cruisers drifted by the gates at the front of the Montauk estate and the cops took pictures, exchanged hard-eyed stares with the men on guard, and moved on.

But today was a happy day; it was the day of her stepson Lucco's wedding. The celebrations were likely to go on long into the night. Already she was tired. Layla, her little girl from her first marriage to Max Carter, was asleep upstairs at the back of the house, tucked in by her nanny Gerda. Annie clasped her hands over the bump of her pregnancy. Soon, there would be another child, *Constantine's* child, a new brother or sister for Layla. She was five months gone now and the morning sickness had – thank God – subsided at last. But the new baby was hungry, draining her energy levels, robbing her of sleep.

'Honey?'

She turned. It was him – Constantine of the sharp suits and the silver hair. Feared and revered Mafia godfather. Her husband, her lover, her friend. He had come to find her, knowing she loved it out here, that she liked to stand here sometimes, alone, and watch the sea at night.

*Hey, wonder what's in this one?*

The pulsating roar and suck of the tide, the music, and his smile. Some things you really do remember forever. He lifted the parcel – it seemed to her that it was heavy, that maybe he felt a little resistance as he did so.

The actual explosion was too sudden and shocking to take in. A huge flash of light, a deafening, mind-numbing *whumph*, then smoke and a

16

pushing out, a propulsion of hot air that made her ears pop as if she was on a mile-high flight, and brought with it the acrid smell of black powder.

She felt herself hit the balcony rail, but only distantly; her hearing was gone, everything was happening in some strange, detached, dreamlike state. Shrapnel sprayed. She felt a sting, distant pain in her arm, and then she was on the beach, lying on the sand, staring half-wittedly at a shell, her vision cutting in and out like a faulty light switch.

She could hear her own heart, that was all, beating very fast. The shell was ridged, pink, beautiful. A marvel of nature. Her brain felt scrambled. There were other things in the sand too, she could see that. Things charred and blackened, and she didn't want to look at any of that so she kept looking at the shell. She *would not* look at the black things. The sand was soft and her ears felt sticky. She felt more than tired; exhausted, ready to sleep.

But someone was touching her shoulder; someone was turning her onto her back on the sand. She looked up at a million bright stars with blank wonder. Then a face loomed over her, blocking out the stars. It was Alberto, Constantine's twenty-four-year-old son, her stepson. She loved Alberto, he was a total delight. Unlike Lucco, unlike Cara, Constantine's other children. Now Alberto's face was twisted in anguish. There were smears of soot on his chin. He was touching her cheek, checking that she was breathing. He was mouthing words but she couldn't hear them.

17

*Are you all right?*

She could read his lips. All right? She didn't know. She was alive ... wasn't she? Her ears were hurting now, really badly. She hoped it would pass. Everything did, in the end. Soon, she might even be reconnected to reality. A spasm of fear shot through her at the thought of that. She started to tremble.

She turned her head. *The black things.*

She screwed up her eyes, wished that she'd been blinded as well as deafened. She knew what the black things were. One of them was a hand, charred so badly it looked like a mummified claw, propped up in the sand not a metre from her head.

There was a ring on one of the bent, scorched fingers. The gold was tarnished, the diamond stars studding it were hidden beneath blackness. Somewhere inside her, she felt a scream building, but she hadn't the strength to release it.

# 1

## Two Months Earlier

'Hey, I'm home!' Annie called out as she passed the guard on the door and hurried into the penthouse apartment on Fifth Avenue with its spectacular views over the treetops of Central Park.

New York in June was stifling, hotter than the mouth of hell; but they had lingered. Constantine was doing business – among other things, he had bought a lease on a building in Times Square that by next September would be transformed into a new Annie's nightclub. Annie herself had just been killing time until today, when she'd consulted her gynaecologist.

Nico, Constantine's most loyal and long-standing foot soldier, was sitting on one of the huge couches, flicking through the *New York Times*.

'Hi, Nico,' she said.

'Hey, you see this? They say the Supreme Court's gonna clear Muhammad Ali of trying to dodge the draft. You know, Nixon's right. We got to come out of Vietnam.'

Nico's voice was deep, thunderous; it seemed to come from somewhere down in his boots.

She glanced over his shoulder at the headlines. It constantly amazed Annie how fascinated and involved with politics the Americans were; none of her English pals gave a stuff about it, and neither did she. But even she could see that Vietnam was a mess, and one that would have to be resolved soon.

She nodded in the direction of the study. The apartment was massive, and Old Colonial in its style of decor. It was one of only two apartments on this floor, with full-service white-gloved doorman, concierge and elevator operator.

'Is he free?' she asked.

'For you?' Nico rose to his feet with a courtly smile and a bow. 'He's free.'

Annie gave him a smile in return. She liked Nico. She felt he would throw himself under a ten-ton truck to protect Constantine, and she liked that; he needed good people around him.

Nico was a big friendly bear of a man with a thin scraping of darkish hair remaining on his big dome of a head. He had humorous and shrewd dark eyes, half hidden under thick eyebrows. In his gait and mannerisms he was shambling and casual, he always looked untidy. But he was loyal to the core and – this was the nailer for Annie – he had been hugely instrumental in recovering Layla when she had once been snatched away, and for that she was forever in his debt.

She went over to the closed study door. She knocked.

'Come!' came from inside, and she slipped in, closing the door behind her.

He was there behind the desk, replacing the phone on its cradle, looking up at her expectantly.

The silver fox. And he *was* a fox in every way. When Constantine Barolli was in a room, it filled with his presence. He was a man at the very height of his powers. Tall, broad-shouldered, slim-hipped, he had thick silver hair, an all-American tan, and armour-piercing blue eyes. Anywhere he went, a cloud of bodyguards swarmed around him like gnats. They swarmed around her, too, and she hated that – but she knew it came with the territory.

Now they had this to look forward to. She was going to give him his fourth child. His first three had been born to another woman – his first wife, Maria – who had died over six years ago. Alberto, Lucco and Cara were his grown-up children.

Now he was approaching fifty, and he would soon have a new baby to a woman not yet thirty. She was so much younger than him, and she knew that people talked, disapproved.

She was not from the old country – Sicily – and she wasn't even American. She barely spoke a word of his native language, but it didn't matter because he'd been raised in New York and his accent was pure Bronx. But he was the Don, Il Padrone, the godfather, so if people spoke of it, this scandalous second marriage of his, then it was only in whispers, never to his face.

Annie had heard some of those whispers. Caught the edge of them, before silence and watchfulness and fake smiles took their place. *Puttana,* she had heard them whisper. She'd looked it up in her phrasebook but it wasn't there. She'd asked Constantine what it meant, and he'd told her, asking where she'd come across a word like that.

'Oh, just something I overheard.' She'd shrugged it off.

He told her it meant 'whore'.

Well, she couldn't say she was surprised.

*Rich powerful men want young women, and young women are drawn to rich, powerful men,* she thought. It was a story as old as time itself. Some people derided it as mercenary or shallow. But even if beauty was desirable, even if power was an aphrodisiac, there was still – in her case, and in his – more to it than that. There was still *love*. Loving him wasn't always comfortable; frequently she was isolated, heavily guarded – and this ritzy apartment sometimes felt like a gilded

21

cage. But then, had she ever thought this was going to be easy?

'So what's the news?' he asked, pushing his chair back from the desk and beckoning her over.

'The news is that both baby and mother are doing well,' said Annie, coming around the desk, sitting down on his lap and linking her arms around his neck. She nuzzled into his shoulder, inhaling his own unique scent overlaid with Acqua di Parma cologne.

'Twelve weeks,' he said reflectively, putting his arms around her.

Annie nodded. He had wanted to tell the family at twelve weeks, when they could be sure the baby was safe, that it was truly *there*. And now here they were. Time up. 'Yeah. Twelve weeks.'

She wasn't overjoyed at the thought. She had loved it when the baby was their secret, just hers and his alone. Now it would be public knowledge; now things would get tricky.

More and more lately, she found herself thinking of her old London life. She missed her friends, Dolly and Ellie in particular. She hadn't even told *them* about the baby yet during their occasional phone conversations. Soon, she would.

She thought of Dolly there, running the three Carter clubs and swanning around town in a chauffeur-driven Jag. Even the thought of it made her smile. Once Dolly had been the roughest of all Aunt Celia's in-house prostitutes; now she was like the Queen. Wistfully, Annie thought of how good it had been, having her pals around her; but this was her life now, here with Constantine.

Sometimes she did get a twinge of homesickness, but she always suppressed it.

'We could call him Vito after my father, if it's a boy.'

Constantine's father had been killed in a hit from a rival family in Sicily. Although he rarely talked about it, she knew that he had lost his mother and brother the same way. It was said that Constantine's hair had turned from black to white overnight with the shock of losing his mother and brother in so brutal a fashion.

'What makes you think it'll be a boy?' she teased.

'Fifty-fifty chance.'

'Ha.'

'I'll tell them,' he said, kissing her dark brown hair. 'Okay?'

'Okay.' That was the deal. The family had to know *sometime*, after all. Annie expected ructions, nevertheless. She knew that – apart from Alberto – all Constantine's grown-up kids and even his sister Gina resented her.

Right now, Gina was babysitting Layla, Annie's daughter by her first husband Max Carter – not to please *her*, but to ingratiate herself with Constantine, as always. Alberto would be collecting Layla and bringing her home in an hour or so – because he liked her and Layla.

'There was something else I'd been meaning to talk to you about,' said Constantine.

'Yeah? What?' Annie cuddled in close to him, watching him with her serious dark green eyes.

'My will.'

'What?' Annie raised her head, stared anxiously

23

at his face. 'What do you mean? Are you all right?'

He gave a smile. 'Perfectly. But I have you to consider now. And our child.' He leaned in and kissed her 'I just want you to know that it's all in there. That this apartment's your home for keeps, and the Holland Park place in London...'

'Stop,' she said, shaking her head, feeling a nervous shudder, as if someone was walking over her grave. She didn't want to talk about this.

'...and if anything happens to me, then my forty-nine per cent share of the Times Square club passes in its entirety to you...'

'Stop it,' she said, and quickly silenced him with a kiss. His words were raising memories, fearful memories – because once there had been another man she loved, and she had lost him. 'Just stop it right there,' she murmured against his lips.

'Okay,' he said. 'Stopping.' He kissed her deeper, harder.

Annie clung to him. What was he doing, talking about wills? She didn't want to hear it.

When he made the necessary calls to the family, she decided she didn't want to hear *those,* either. She left the room.

# 2

It was mid-afternoon and Lucco Barolli was lying in the super-king-sized bed in his chic, ultra-modern Upper East Side condo with its red-lacquered walls and black Oriental furnishings when he took the call from his father. He put the phone down and lay there, staring into space.

'Wassup, sweetie?' asked Sophie, her lovely nakedness tangled up in the red silk sheets after their marathon lovemaking session.

Lucco stared absently at her. Sophie was as fair as he was dark. Unlike his father, Lucco truly *looked* Sicilian, with straight black hair, nearly black deep-set eyes and olive skin as fine as any woman's.

'My father's *puttana* of a new wife is expecting a child,' he said.

'Oh!' The girl propped herself up on her elbow, her delectable tits swinging in his face. She was an English model and beautiful – he could afford the best and Sophie Thomson was renowned. He had pulled strings, got her the plum jobs using his connections. Nobody said no to a *caporegime* of the family. Now, with her tall athletic body and the face of an insatiable fallen angel, she could command ridiculous fees worldwide.

'Well that's good news.' She smiled engagingly. *What the fuck's a puttana?* she wondered. 'You'll have a new brother or sister.'

Lucco looked at her as if she'd taken leave of her senses. 'The child will not be my brother or sister,' he said coldly.

'But ... the kid'll be your father's, like you,' she said.

Lucco suddenly sprang up and struck her hard across the face. Sophie fell back amid the tangled sheets. Lucco pinned her down there. He glared into her shocked eyes from inches away.

'The child is *not* my brother or sister,' he roared.

'All right, okay,' said Sophie hurriedly, tears of pain spilling out from her eyes. He'd slapped her once or twice before, just love play, but this time he was frightening her. She knew all about his connections, she knew he'd used them to help her up the ladder of fame, and she liked that. Or at least, she had. But now ... her face hurt from the blow. She hoped he hadn't marked her. She had work tomorrow.

'You understand me? This kid is nothing to do with me.'

'Yeah. Got it,' said Sophie, and suddenly he released her and lay back.

She looked at him warily. She reviewed all that she had been about to say, and decided against saying any of it. Silently, she watched him. He had a big erection jutting up from between his thighs; hitting her always seemed to turn him on. She adored Lucco, but she was coming to realize – not to put too fine a point on it – that he was a bit of a shit.

Lucco saw her looking, and glanced down his

26

impressive body. 'Mount me,' he ordered.

Would he hit her again if she refused? Sophie decided not to risk it.

Lucco lay back, sighing restlessly as Sophie straddled him and guided him smoothly inside her.

Everything he had feared since the day Annie Carter had come into his father's life was coming to fruition. He tried to consider it all logically, furious though it made him feel. Constantine was forty-seven while his new English wife was twenty-seven – twenty years his junior.

The Carter woman – Lucco couldn't bear to think of her any other way – was closer in age to him, his brother Alberto and his sister Cara than to their father. It was *obscene*. And now the worst had happened. Marrying the whore had been bad enough, but now his father had impregnated her; there would be a baby.

Why hadn't his father just had her if he wanted to – she was just a cheap English gold-digger after all; she'd have been grateful to receive the attentions of a man like him. He didn't have to go and *marry* her.

Lucco thought of Annie, his father's new wife. Her glossy, cocoa-brown hair, her dark green eyes, her intriguing body, always discreetly hidden, but ... oh yes, guessed at by Lucco. He didn't doubt that she was *hot* between the sheets, to have snared his father so easily. And now she was going to give him a child; a new child who would supplant his grown-up children in his affections. He felt sick at the thought, furious.

'You know what? My father's right. It *is* time I

got married,' he said aloud. It was all arranged, anyway – not that he'd confided that to Sophie. Why the hell should he? The wedding was only two months away now. Of course it was expected of him, part of the process that would see him assuming control of his father's empire one day. Already he was *caporegime* like Alberto, joint second-in-command beneath their father; but he, Lucco, was the eldest son, the rightful heir. It was good to appear settled, married, *respectable;* there would be children, his *own* children; family life.

Sophie stopped bouncing up and down on Lucco's cock and raised her head. She looked at his face, her blue eyes wide with surprise and a sliver of hope; all right, sometimes he lost it, but so what? She adored him, and she was excited by his powerful family with its dubious links to the underworld. Was he proposing...?

'Not married to *you,* obviously,' said Lucco, correctly interpreting her gaze.

His marriage had been arranged ever since he was eighteen. He was going to wed his dull little second cousin Daniella. He'd been reluctant before, dreading the day, but now he could see it might be a good thing. Now he appreciated the need to get some kids off Daniella at the earliest opportunity. If anyone was going to inherit his father's considerable fortune, he would make sure that it was *his* line, *his* sons – not hers. And not Alberto's, either.

'Harder,' he said, and Sophie obeyed while Lucco closed his eyes and thought of Annie, his father's wife.

# 3

Cara Barolli Mancini, Constantine's daughter, got the news just as she was finishing lunch with her girlfriends and her second cousin, who was fresh off the boat from Sicily. They were in the plush uptown apartment that Cara shared with her husband Rocco.

The second cousin, Daniella, was her brother Lucco's intended, a laughably rough-around-the-edges girl with long frizzy black hair, big frightened eyes, lamentable dress sense and nothing of any interest to say for herself. She had been sitting there like wood all through the meal, her hands folded in her lap, her head bowed, the conversation of the assembled Park Avenue princesses buzzing around her.

'What's the matter?' asked one of Cara's friends, looking at her face when she came back into the room.

Cara shrugged and sat down again. Her pretty mouth twisted. 'Apparently, my father's wife is going to have a baby,' she said.

'Oh! Well ... congratulations, darling,' said the friend, looking at Cara's stormy face with uncertainty.

Even Cara's closest friends knew you had to treat her with kid gloves. The dreamy-eyed quality Cara possessed was a thin veneer. She was very beautiful, with her tumbling blonde hair, her heavy-lidded blue eyes and her voluptuous mouth, always half open, pouting, inviting. But she could be touchy and arrogant. Daddy was an important man in this city, and she never tired of letting everyone around her know it.

Cara couldn't trust herself to speak, not yet. She was crazed with rage. How dare he get that *tramp* pregnant; how dare he foist a filthy half-sibling on his three truly legitimate children?

'When ... is the baby due?' asked Daniella in her stumbling English.

Cara looked across at her with irritation. Poor stupid sacrificial lamb, shipped over here to marry elegant, arrogant Lucco with the razor-sharp tongue. Lucco would demolish the girl, Cara didn't doubt that.

'I don't know that yet,' she said.

'She'll have a baby shower, won't she?' another friend asked as the maid cleared their plates away.

'She's English,' said Cara. 'I doubt she even knows what that *means*.'

The friends were silent for a long, awkward moment. Cara's own marriage had so far proved fruitless, and they all knew she wanted a child. It was whispered covertly among them that Rocco might even have some problems in the bedroom department. Which wasn't surprising, really; Cara had a strong, vocal character, but Rocco was quieter – too quiet to put her in her place some-times, which was what they all secretly thought she really needed in a man.

Cara was staring at Daniella. Lucco had met Daniella at the age of eighteen when he visited Sicily with Constantine. She had been sixteen

30

then, virginal and shy, socially inept. She still was. The marriage had been agreed between Constantine and her father, and there had been celebrations, countless bottles of fiery yellow Strega consumed and many a tarantella danced because it was a huge honour for any daughter to receive a proposal from the son of a great Don.

Now Cara watched Daniella sourly. *Lucco is going to eat her alive,* thought Cara. She knew her brother.

Not that she much cared about the fate of this little *paisan* from the old country. She had her own problems.

# 4

Alberto, the youngest son of Constantine Barolli, received the news when he went to collect Layla, his stepmother Annie's bright and adorable five-year-old from her first marriage, from his Aunt Gina's that afternoon.

Layla ran to him; she loved her big brother Alberto. He swept the giggling child up into his arms while Gina looked on sourly. She was putting the phone back on the cradle and she looked as if someone had just told her something really, really bad.

'What's the matter?' asked Alberto in concern.

'Your father's wife,' said Gina, her mouth pursing even as she uttered the words.

Alberto knew that Gina despised Annie. Gina would have despised *any* woman who came close to her brother. She had hated Alberto's own mother, Maria – and after Maria's death, he knew very well that Gina had hoped there would be no more women; but then along had come Annie Carter with her 'whore's tricks', bewitching his father – according to Aunt Gina.

Privately, Alberto believed that his aunt was too possessive, clinging to Constantine in a way that was both selfish and faintly perverted. He for one was delighted that his father had found happiness with his second wife.

'Annie? What about her?' Alberto glanced at Layla.

'Your father tells me she's expecting a child,' said Gina. She didn't look overjoyed about it.

Alberto's attention sharpened. 'And it's fine? She's fine?'

Gina nodded tensely.

'Well, that's good news.'

'Good? How can it be good?'

Alberto stifled a sigh. He knew Gina would never soften towards Annie, and he knew she thought him a fool for liking his father's second wife so much. But, to him, Annie was family now. He could be the hard man, the tough *caporegime* when it was required of him, but at heart he was a family man, and both more reserved and more reflective than his elder brother Lucco.

Sometimes, he had to do bad things, *difficult* things, for the family good. Quiet and polite though he was, he had been responsible for many deaths while carrying out his father's orders. But he could never delight in the pain and suffering of others, as Lucco did.

'You hear that, Layla?' Alberto bounced the little girl in his arms, smiled into her dark eyes. 'You're going to have a new little brother or sister to spoil, how about *that?*'

'Yay!' said Layla.

Gina watched her nephew with a glacial eye. Alberto was a good boy, but he was too amiable, too soft. Couldn't he see how this would affect his own standing in the family; how it could affect them all? Constantine's English wife had up until this point been an unwanted, isolated interloper with little say in the running of things. Now her status would radically change. She would be the mother of the Don's baby; her position would be assured.

'Are we going to go home and see Mommy now?' asked Layla, watching her big stepbrother's handsome face and not seeing the expression on Gina's.

Alberto smiled. *Mommy.* Layla was sounding more American every day. 'We sure are. And we'll stop off on the way and get her some flowers, okay?'

Gina watched them, her expression surly. *Flowers,* for the love of God. She turned away, irritated. Personally, she would rather see flowers laid on the Englishwoman's *grave.*

# 5

'Well,' said Rocco Mancini reluctantly, signalling to the waitress for the check, 'I must go.'

'So soon?' his dining companion pouted. They were tucked into a corner table beside the window at a seedy little diner on Lexington and Third, where neither of them would be known. It was a cheap place, tacky, charmless; full of losers and fat, contented mothers with shrieking infants. It wasn't what either of them would have chosen, but that was simply the way it had to be. Snatched moments in random places.

'Yeah, Cara's got plans for this evening.'

Cara *always* had plans for the evening. Dinner with the Vanderbilts; the Nixons' charity ball in aid of the Third World; the invitation – which had filled Cara with wild-eyed joy – to fly to Washington for the September opening of the Kennedy Arts Center, with the premiere of Bernstein's *mass* for the late president.

There was always *something* – some silly social engagement they just *had* to be seen at. Rocco was not interested in any of it, but still he had to go.

The waitress came over, chewing gum and wearing a grubby white apron. Rocco paid, his aesthetic face pinched with distaste. The waitress withdrew. Rocco stood up, shrugging into his jacket. He was tall and very thin, with dark curly hair, bright lime-green eyes and a big sensuous mouth. He looked at his dining companion's expression and sat down again, sharply.

'Look, you know it has to be this way,' he said, grasping the pale hand on the table.

'I hate her,' said his companion. 'Cara has you all the time, at her beck and call. And what do I have? Just the dregs.'

There was nothing Rocco could say to this. It was true. But he knew he couldn't afford to make waves. He had the lifestyle he had always craved, the cars, the apartments, everything. He summered in the Hamptons, wintered in Aspen, lived a life of ease and plenty. And that was all thanks to his marriage to Cara Barolli. If he tried for separation, or – God forbid – *divorce,* then all that would be over.

And he had no wish to make so powerful an enemy as the Don. Would Constantine Barolli just accept his daughter being dumped like so much excess baggage? Rocco didn't think so. Already, Rocco was aware that he had been tested and found wanting by the Don. He wasn't a made man, he wasn't even a *capo* in his father-in-law's organization yet, and he resented that. But he knew he had a lot still to prove.

And what about his own father, Enrico? He would be exceedingly angry if Rocco made waves. Constantine and Enrico Mancini went way back. There would be hell to pay.

'My darling,' said Rocco, 'you know it's you I love.'

'But you're with her.'

Rocco stood up. They'd had this same conversation many times; it never got them anywhere. 'I'll see you here on Friday. We'll take the boat out on the Sound, how's that?' he said hopefully.

His companion was hard-eyed for a moment. 'What, and you'll screw me again in the cabin, where no one can see?' Then the look faded to a faint smile, remembering... 'Ah, all right. You got me, you know you have.'

Smiling, Rocco moved out of the booth. He looked around and then dropped a quick kiss onto Frances Ducane's almost effeminately smooth cheek.

'It's you I love,' Rocco repeated, against Frances's skin. 'Goodbye, my darling.'

And then he was gone, leaving the young man sitting alone at the table, wondering why he always, *always* had to play second fiddle in life. Now it was to his lover's wife, but before that he had lived in the long shadow cast by his father, Rick Ducane.

# 6

## 1938

Before Rick Ducane became a big Hollywood star and household name, he'd been Lionel Driver, a struggling British actor. Frances had inherited his russet hair; he had the identical penetrating grey eyes. Lionel had looked like an aristocrat. He had his own father to thank for that, a good-looking chancer who had married and then cheerfully abandoned his mother with her bad nerves and her whining little voice.

Lionel's voice was the first obstacle of many he had to overcome. Born within the sound of Bow bells, he had a pronounced Cockney accent, and it was a bugger to lose. But lose it he did, practising his vowel sounds hour upon hour in the stone-cold and stinking privy in the backyard behind their tenement building.

'Fuckin' *toff*,' his schoolmates snarled at him.

They'd shoved him against a wall, kicked him, then stolen his meagre pocket money.

Lionel didn't care.

He had *plans*.

He worked in a series of dead-end jobs until his twenties, then, without regret, he left his mum and the slums of the East End to go to Stratford-upon-Avon and start trying his luck in auditions. He worked hard, even if it was mostly unrewarded, painting backgrounds, helping with props. But then he got a small break, and started treading the boards in walk-on parts, and was approached by an agent.

On the advice of his new agent, he then abandoned the stage and went to try to make his name in Hollywood. Once or twice he even hung out hopefully around the constellation of bright stars that haunted every party. Lana Turner, Spencer Tracey, Clark Gable – they were all there, and all far too high-powered to acknowledge the existence of a handsome starstruck stranger from quaint little England.

'What we need here is an angle,' said his agent.

*Or for you to get me some fucking work,* thought Lionel. But he asked, 'What do you mean?'

'Well, you've been a Shakespearean actor. A real *thespian.*'

'Only in walk-on parts though.'

'Who cares?'

So Lionel's résumé now stated that he'd played the lead in *King Lear* to rave reviews. But even *that* didn't get him off the breadline. Nobody wanted an English hero right then, and he was too good-looking to play the part of the hero's chubby best friend.

One day he was waiting with around twenty other hopefuls at yet another audition, this time for a small part – a destitute man – in a Warner Brothers movie. It was only a walk-on, but he was desperate and bloody near destitution himself.

As usual, his bowels turned to liquid at precisely the wrong moment – he was next but one up – and he had to go off to find the toilet. He passed two men fiddling with one of the new smoke machines. A crowd of people hurried past. Was that brilliantly stylish blonde at the centre of them Barbara Stanwyck...? He walked on, looking back, entranced by the allure of stardom, the way that cluster of people stuck to her like iron filings around a powerful magnet. He *wanted* that. But was he going to get it?

He was starting to seriously doubt himself. Maybe these endless rejections were a sign that he was *never* going to make it. And Warners were a bunch of slave-drivers anyway. Everyone in the building called the place San Quentin after the notorious prison. Did he want to work for people who drove their staff – even their stars – so hard?

Well ... yes. He did. Anything they wanted, he'd do. He *had* to get there. But this was getting to be the last-chance saloon now. This was his last audition, he'd promised himself. If he didn't succeed today, then he was going home. Not to his old mum in the East End, sod *that;* but back to England, to try his luck again there.

He missed England. There'd been trouble there, he knew, rumblings from Europe over a jumped-up little German leader – Führer, he called himself – Adolf Hitler. But now Chamberlain had the new Anglo-German accord in his hand, everyone was relieved and peace was guaranteed.

But maybe – just this once – he'd break the mould, get the part...?

'No fucking chance,' he muttered, and found the john, did what he had to do, and then emerged. He might have missed his place, but if he hurried...

'I don't care what you say, a deal's a deal,' said a tearful female voice from further down the corridor.

Lionel hesitated and peered into the dimness. A vivid blonde was standing there with a man, and for a moment he thought it was Stanwyck herself, but he quickly realized it wasn't; this was a red-nosed, teary-eyed kid, no shining star.

'And *I* don't care what *you* say.' The man leaning over her was a big bruiser, dark-haired and red with fury, shouting into her upturned face. 'There's no job. There never was.'

'You *said* there was,' she insisted.

'You got proof of that?' He let out a bark of

laughter. 'No? Thought not. So why don't you just fuck off, sweetheart. Don't come around my place of work making accusations again or you'll be sorry.'

'You *bastard*,' she sobbed. 'You promised...'

'I promised nothing.' Now he was grinning down at her. He slipped one hand inside her blouse and roughly squeezed her tit. The girl let out a yelp of pain. 'But if you want to try and read through again, be my guest. The last reading was shit, but baby, you were *hot*.'

Lionel stepped out from the dimness of the corridor. 'What the hell's going on here?' he asked loudly.

Stupid question. It was clear as day what was happening.

'What's it to you?' asked the man, instantly pushing the girl away from him.

Lionel found himself going forward, even while his brain was saying: *The audition, you'll miss the audition...*

'Are you all right?' he asked the girl.

'She's fine,' said the man bullishly. 'Just sore 'cos she didn't get the part.'

'He *promised* me a part,' said the girl. She was pretty, Lionel saw. Her tears had dried and now she just looked furious. 'If I ... *you* know.' She went red and stopped speaking.

'What we have here is a little misunderstanding,' said the man. 'We had some fun together and the lady thought that meant–'

He didn't even finish the sentence before Lionel hit him, hard. He went crashing back against the wall, and slid to the floor.

'Come on,' said Lionel, grabbing the girl's hand.

'Is he going to be all right...?' They were walking away, but she was glancing back, worried.

'Do you care?' asked Lionel, hurrying away.

'No.' A smile appeared briefly on her face.

'I'm Lionel Driver, by the way,' he said.

'Vivienne Bell.'

'And I think I've probably missed my audition...'

Having failed spectacularly at the Hollywood dream, Lionel took Vivienne home to England with him and married her there. She was a chatty bottle-blonde and tired of being pawed over by fat old producers on the casting couch, tired of being wild at heart while presenting a carefully virginal image to the outside world, tired of the coke-fuelled merry-go-round that Hollywood truly was.

Vivienne was charmed by his English gentility, thinking that here was a real gentleman. He'd played at Stratford, for Chrissakes. He quoted the Bard's love poems to her, and she melted. Accustomed to encounters like the one Lionel had interrupted, lifting her skirts for quick, sweaty couplings in draughty backstage corridors on the promise of a part – after which the part *always* failed to materialize – Vivienne was entranced by his old-fashioned charm and amazed that he actually took the trouble to woo her. Before a year was out, she was pregnant with Frances.

It was such a touching story, such a happy tale, it should have ended with bliss everlasting. Lionel and the lovely Vivienne waltzing off into the sunset together. But Vivienne quickly got bored with daily life in England. She was a good-time girl; she

41

loved the bright lights. And Chamberlain's famed 'piece of paper' had been proved worthless. War was declared on Germany, so Lionel went off to fight.

Feeling lucky to be alive and not maimed when so many of his comrades had died or had their lives altered forever at the hands of the Nazis, Lionel returned home when it was all over and thought, *What the hell?* He would give the acting dream one last shot.

He ditched his old agent and acquired a new thrusting one called LaLa LaBon, who was bursting with energy and unscrupulously single-minded in the pursuit of a deal. LaLa was a rampaging, cheroot-puffing dyke with black bobbed hair and a vulpine, predatory face. She appreciated beauty in her male clients and was now pushing him westwards with manic enthusiasm.

'Think of it! Hollywood! You heard of an actor called Archie Leach?' she asked him one rainy day in her poky little London office.

'No,' he said, feeling dubious but finding her enthusiasm infectious. He'd already told her he'd tried Hollywood before, but LaLa was not to be deterred. 'I've never heard of him.'

'And you fucking well won't,' she said, busily puffing on her cheroot. She stabbed the air with it, making her point. Her eyes gleamed diabolically through the smoke-haze. 'You know why? Because he changed his name to Cary Grant and look what happened to him. He's English, he's charming, he's handsome. And so, Lionel my pet, are you – and your time is now.'

So he went back to Hollywood not as Lionel Driver ('My God – so dull!' said LaLa) but as Rick Ducane.

He was back on the party circuit again in no time. LaLa went with him and worked long and hard to get him into the best places. He was rubbing shoulders with people like Frank Sinatra and Ava Gardner now, and the dirt was they were having a *hot* affair, with Sinatra singing and shooting out streetlights as he walked her home.

As for Rick's affairs – well, he had taken Vivienne and sulky little baby Frances with him; he owed them that much, surely? The gloss had already gone off the marriage thanks to Viv's drinking, but he couldn't just *abandon* them, now could he? LaLa insisted he could. Rick insisted he couldn't.

Finally, LaLa won the vote. And she laid down the ground rules. Rick rented a modest house in the hills and Vivienne had to stay there with her little boy. To the outside world, to Hollywood, Rick Ducane must be a single man. There must be no mention of any marriage, none at all – not unless he wanted to fuck up his career before it had even started. He needed to be free to escort older ladies, the fading stars who needed 'walkers' and could thereby get him into the most desirable parties.

'Jesus,' complained Vivienne. 'That fucking woman dictates our whole *life*. What, are you ashamed of me? Ashamed of your *son*?'

Vivienne took a lot of placating, but she agreed in principle to just keep her head down and later, *much* later, when he'd made it, LaLa promised that the announcement would be made and wife and son could begin to appear in public.

He'd be paid to schmooze the movers and shakers, an opportunity that many a struggling actor would kill for. *What more could LaLa do for him?* she demanded. *Hold his fuckwit little* hand?

So Rick Ducane started schmoozing. He schmoozed so hard he felt as if his head was coming off. He chatted with directors, producers, gofers and lighting men; he attended so many auditions that he became bewildered about which part he was reading for.

He resented it. He was back here again, chasing bit parts and walking old female farts who usually got falling-down drunk or hopped to the eyeballs on drugs, and groped him. After a year of exhausting failure and domestic discord he was all but ready to call it a day.

'You're never going to make it,' Viv told him in one of her drunken rages. She was hitting the bottle harder than ever. 'You're a *loser.*'

But the war had taught him endurance in the face of adversity and so he went on, sparkling, entertaining, handsome, until one night he exerted his charm on the right person and then ... well, next day on his dressing-room door they hung a star. They really did.

# 7

## 1971

Saul Jury watched Rocco Mancini and Frances Ducane from his car, which was parked across the street. *Idiots,* he thought. They were sitting there in a window seat in the diner, thinking themselves unobserved. Touching hands all the time – Jesus, he hated faggots.

*A woman's instinct,* he thought grimly. Hadn't his own mother told him it was lethally accurate, whenever he'd tried her out with some scam or other? Didn't his own *wife* tell him it was infallible, when he tried to get away with his own little minor indiscretions?

And look at this; they were both right. And so was Cara Barolli Mancini. Only she was right in a way that was unexpected; probably it was going to shock her. However, he took the pictures, particularly pleased with the one that clearly showed Rocco Mancini kissing his little fag friend Frances Ducane's cheek as he left. If Mrs Mancini was going to snoop on her ever-loving husband, then she had to accept that the consequences might not be pleasant.

The private detective knew the identity of Frances Ducane because he'd already trailed him twice, once to Rocco's cruiser out in New York Sound, and had even given Mrs Mancini his name. She was paying him plenty for all this work; he was a happy man. Frances was a good-looking kid, an actor – and, like ninety-five per cent of all actors, he was spending a lot of time 'resting'. His father Rick had been a big noise in Hollywood in the Fifties, before a spectacular fall from grace. Saul hoped little Frances wasn't going to go the same way, but the way things were shaping up, it didn't look so good for him.

Rocco had married a whole heap of money – apparently the Barolli family were huge importers of wine, olive oil and fruit from all around the world – and Frances was reaping the benefits, happily accepting not only Rocco's manhood in places where Saul didn't even like to *think* about, but accepting expensive presents too.

Of course it was the presents that had given him away.

*Woman's instinct.*

Yeah, his mother and his wife were right. If a woman got a feeling about something, probably there were some grounds to it. Cara had been going through Rocco's pockets for weeks, looking for evidence to back up her theory that he was playing away from home; finally, Rocco got careless and she found receipts. Incriminating stuff. And then she had hired Saul. And Saul had done his work, and now ... now he was going to spin this out just a little longer, bump up the tab. She could afford it.

Rocco got back to the apartment at six. He'd wasted as much time as he could, walking around, just kicking his heels, but finally he *had*

46

to go home.

'Where have you been?' Cara called from the bedroom the instant he walked through the door.

'I had some business to attend to,' said Rocco, coming to stand in the open doorway. His expression was closed-off, guarded. She was sitting at her dressing table, brushing her hair, wearing a raspberry-pink silk negligee and matching peignoir.

'Oh.' Cara stared at him in the mirror until he looked away.

Did she suspect anything? No, he was sure she didn't. She turned away, yanking the brush through her long blonde hair and Rocco took the opportunity to stare at his wife. Her hair was beautiful; *she* was beautiful. But there was an unsatisfied pout to her mouth, and an avaricious look to her dreamy blue eyes that said, *Whatever it is, I want it. Right now.* Her body was splendid: tall, statuesque. He ought to be a happy man. But he wasn't.

'Annie's going to have a baby,' said Cara, her lips growing thin.

'Oh?' Rocco sat down on the bed. 'Your father must be pleased.'

'Pleased?' Cara gave him a disgusted look. 'Really, I think he must have lost his mind, marrying that foreigner.'

Rocco said nothing. He was indifferent to his father-in-law's second wife, but she seemed to make the Don happy, and wasn't that what counted most?

Cara put the brush down and stood up with a hiss of silk. She came over to the bed and sat

47

down next to him. 'My lovely husband,' she said, smiling, and leaned in and grasped his lightly stubbled chin in one elegantly manicured hand. 'You need a shave,' she purred, rubbing her fingers over his chin. 'We're going out tonight.'

*As usual,* thought Rocco.

'To visit the expectant mama,' said Cara.

Rocco looked at Cara in surprise. She shrugged. 'We have to keep my father sweet.'

Of course. Rocco knew that the Don's family hated the Englishwoman, but they had to be seen to fawn over her. Cara's face was inches from his own. She *was* beautiful. He leaned forward a little, lightly brushed his lips over hers. Cara gave a smile.

'So you were busy with work?' she murmured against his mouth. 'All day?'

Rocco nodded.

*Liar,* thought Cara.

She'd already taken a call from Saul Jury. Cara knew exactly where Rocco had been today, and with whom. That woman called Frances Ducane again. Hadn't there been a film star once, Rick Ducane? Maybe some relative, but who cared? What concerned her now was that soon, very soon, Jury would have all the information she needed to hang Rocco out to dry.

# 8

## 1950

Rick Ducane was the toast of Hollywood, an action hero with a Brylcreemed slick of British smoothness who could hold his own alongside Flynn and Lancaster. The audiences loved him, like they loved to hear about the young Princess Elizabeth having her second child, a daughter named Anne.

'The Yanks love all things English,' said LaLa. 'We have to capitalize on that.'

Rick knew she was right.

The studio loved him too. He wasn't beset by women trouble like Flynn, he wasn't egotistical like Lancaster; he was easy to manage, a workhorse. He arrived promptly for his read-throughs, learning his lines with punctilious care.

Born in poverty, he adored and quickly became adapted to the high life – the private planes, the twenty-four-hour limos and bodyguards, the great house and the swimming pool high up in the Hollywood hills; he'd *earned* it.

The only slight shadow upon his otherwise dazzling life was his wife, Vivienne – and his son, Frances – now installed in a wing of his palatial house in the Hollywood hills. Vivienne drank to while away the time in her comfy Hollywood prison. She had started having drinking buddies in – Christ alone knew where she met them. That disturbed Rick. Suppose Viv got legless and told one of these wasters who she was married to? The studio would string him up by the balls. But Rick was away so much on location that he frequently – and blissfully – forgot that his wife and son were there at all.

When he did come home he was harangued by Viv for being late, absent, uncaring.

'You've got a child,' she ranted at him, gin bottle swinging from her hand, her bleached-blonde hair showing an inch of black untended roots and her once-pretty eyes slitted and mean with drunken rage. 'Don't that mean a thing to you, you cocksucker?'

Rick cast a look at the child. Nearly ten years old now, and watching them with hunted eyes as they shouted and swore over his head.

Actually, it didn't mean much to Rick. He'd been brought up by a chilly, unmaternal woman, and as a consequence he didn't feel particularly bothered about kids. He'd had her, she'd got pregnant: the luck of the draw.

Or not, depending on your viewpoint.

His viewpoint was that he wished he had never met her, wished he had never stuck his dick up her in the first place; then there would be no Viv staggering around the place night and day giving him earache, when all he wanted was peace and quiet after a hard day's work, and no kid skulking in corners watching him with hostile eyes.

'You *bastard*,' she was shouting. 'We're just your dirty little secret, aren't we? You'd rather we didn't exist at all – wouldn't you!'

Frances looked on the verge of tears.

Viv was raging.

'Fuck *this*,' said Rick.

He turned on his heel, left the house, got back in his car – she followed him out, shrieking and cursing at him as he started the engine and then drove away.

Rick called one of the older, dimming stars he'd once been a walker for at the Oscars. Chloe Kane was no old fart. She was still beautiful, but calls from screenwriters and producers and the press had all but dried up. What the hell – she was forty and everyone knew that once a woman hit the big four-oh in this town, she was done for.

But Jesus, she was still so beautiful, even if her allure was waning. Thick glossy red hair – which must be dyed, but who cared? – and a mouth that still invited trouble. A body that would make a bishop kick a hole through a stained-glass window, even if she had let her personal grooming slide and her bush was a tangle of red and grey that extended down her thighs and up to her navel. But so what? She was stacked, and last time they'd spoken she'd said call me – please.

So here he was, calling her. And she liked that. It soothed his sour mood, how pleased she was to hear from him. When had his wife ever sounded like that? She invited him over. Poor cow had nothing going on except an evening in on her own with her pet pooch for company; he was doing her a favour.

'Darling,' she greeted him at the door in that famous, breathy tone she had used to such good effect up on the silver screen. 'How lovely. Come on in.'

There had followed a wild night in which they had made out in the hall, on the stairs, in her huge, imposing bedroom ('Strictly for press shots, darling; actually I sleep in a teensy little room down the hall'), much to the pooch's annoyance.

It was gone two in the morning by the time he got home. He crept in, fearful of waking Viv. The last thing he wanted now was another argument. He was exhausted. Chloe was very demanding.

In the lounge he found empty bottles and up-turned bowls of nuts and nibbles that crunched under his feet as he walked. *A thousand-dollar rug and she treats it like this,* he thought. Nat King Cole was stuck singing 'Mona Lisa, Mona Lisa' over and over again. He went over and switched Nat off.

Then he went through to the master bedroom. The coverlet was perfectly in place, the bed still made.

Now what the hell?

Had she gone out somewhere? He hoped not. She was a crazy driver in her too-visible red Corvette at the best of times – oh, and the arguments they'd had about that – but today she'd had a skinful. What he didn't need was her wrapping her damned car around a tree and the press getting wind of her existence. She was just a nobody.

He hurried along the hall, past the closed door of Frances's room.

That kid. Strange little fellow: he wanted to be an actor when he grew up like his dad, and Rick was flattered by that, but – for fuck's sake – the

52

kid didn't have the talent; all he could manage was a few lines of amateurish mimicry. He would deter him from entering the industry if he could – do the kid a favour. Bad enough when you had that special touch of stardust; it was still hard, gruelling work all the way. But without it ... Hollywood would break your heart. No doubt about that.

He opened the bathroom door.

Maybe she was ill? Puking up all that gin, no doubt. He heard water flowing.

'Viv? Honey?' he said softly.

Through the half-open window the moon cast its silvery light into the room. He could see the bath filled to the brim and overflowing. Something was lolling in there, arms akimbo.

Shit! Had she fallen asleep and fucking well drowned? How the hell were they going to hush that up if she had? He felt a spasm of fear at the thought. His career, his fabulous career, in ruins, and for a gormless whore he'd been stupid enough to get the hots for, and marry.

He flicked on the light with a movement that was half panic, half anger, and fell back instantly.

Vivienne was in the bath, but her head was above the water. Her eyes were open, but they weren't going to see anything, ever again. There was a long gash across her forehead. Her face was a blanched, vacant mask. The water in the bath was bright red.

He made a noise in his throat, horrified.

No. She was just playing dead or something; he couldn't believe what he was seeing.

But ... it was true. He reached out, picked up

53

one limp, cold hand. Felt for a pulse and found none.

She was dead. Now how the fuck were they going to keep this quiet?

He heard a movement. Letting out a half-strangled shriek, he turned and saw Frances standing silently in the hall, watching him.

# 9

## 1971

Constantine Barolli's estate on Long Island's stylish Montauk peninsula would be a stunning location for Lucco Barolli's marriage to Daniella Carlucci. The house itself was massive, clapboarded in soft duck-egg blue-and-white trim; it was fronted by huge decks and terraces that overlooked and led down onto the long white beach and into sand dunes thick with the billowing fronds of marram grass.

Cara had told the men on the gate to expect Saul Jury at four, that he had business with her, and that they were to show him straight in; she'd be waiting in the waterfront lounge. The roar of the Atlantic breakers pounding the beach was a throaty, ominous counterpoint to her black mood.

Saul Jury arrived promptly at the agreed time. He always did; with high-end clients you learned early on not to fuck around too much. Shame her *husband* hadn't learned the same lesson, because

Saul suspected that this was not a lady who'd take betrayal lightly; she didn't have the look of a gentle, forgiving sort of girl.

As he was shown in to the huge lounge with its big expanse of glass that displayed the ocean out there beyond the white stretch of the beach, Saul felt overawed. He'd had wealthy clients before, but these folks lived like the Rockefellers. Schlepping home to his little apartment in the Bronx, he had often glanced up and wondered about the flashy Manhattan types and the rarefied air they breathed – that special, radiant space they occupied. He knew he was in the presence of great wealth here. But seeing the scary people on the gates and patrolling the grounds, he *also* knew that these were not the sort of people you would ever want to upset. Olive oil and fruit importers, for fuck's sake. Saul knew what *that* meant. He was starting to feel more than a little sorry for the erring Rocco.

When she'd first taken him on they'd met up in Central Park, neutral territory, but now Saul was seeing Cara in her natural environment, and it made him feel like the small fry he was. Hell, he was *happy* to be small fry. He didn't want to be up too close and personal with people like this.

She looked vindictive and trigger-happy; he'd thought that the very first time he'd seen her: *Here is a woman who won't take prisoners.* What if she now decided to shoot the messenger?

Cara stood up as he was shown in by Frederico, who waited around the house when he was not driving for her father. Frederico – or 'Fredo' as he was affectionately known by the family – was

55

the son of one of Constantine's gardeners and a cook. He was her own age and she knew he adored her – he had been making cow-eyes at her ever since kindergarten; but he was beneath her and they both knew it. It was Fredo who had driven her to the meeting with Saul in Central Park. He had asked no questions, but she had seen the curiosity in his eyes. *Idiot,* she'd thought, *as if I would tell you anything.*

Dismissing Fredo with a wave, Cara swept imperiously towards Saul – dwarfing him in will and in size too. Cara winced as she shook his limp, ineffectual hand. She hated using the services of this cheap little man, but he was a nobody, he was outside her family's normal circle of influence, and that was good: she didn't want any of this getting back to Rocco's ears before she was ready. 'What have you found out?' she asked.

For a split second, Saul thought of saying that he'd found nothing, that Rocco was clean, and high-tailing it out of there; fuck the money. But the thought lasted a split second only, because he *needed* that money. He had a bit of a gambling habit, and yes, both his mother *and* his wife knew about it and nagged him day and night.

There was some professional pride involved here, too. He had caught Rocco red-handed doing the dirty with his fag boyfriend. He had pictures, dates, information, everything gathered together; he'd done a good, thorough job, like he always did. But now, being here, seeing this place, these people, the look in Cara's eyes, he thought he would just as soon not get involved because what he might be doing by staying out of it was saving

56

Rocco Mancini from a whole heap of trouble.

Professional pride won. Saul fished out the photos and the neatly typed information; he handed them to Cara. And as Cara looked at them in growing disbelief, slowly her face emptied of colour, her hands tightening on the sheets of paper and the damning photos until her long, beautifully manicured nails dug in.

'But...' Cara glanced up at him. 'What *is* this? You said he was seeing someone called Frances Ducane...'

Saul nodded. 'That's him. That's Frances Ducane.'

'But ... for God's sake! I thought you meant a *woman*.'

'No. A man. I'm sorry if you misunderstood, Mrs Mancini. That's Frances Ducane. His dad was a big Hollywood star; then there was a scandal and...' His voice trailed away. Cara was silent, staring at the pictures of her husband betraying her with a man. Finally, she said: 'You can go.'

'I'll send the bill on,' he said.

She said nothing. She was still staring at what he'd shown her: her husband of only a year, kissing a handsome young actor. Not even a woman. Her husband was cheating on her with a *man* called Frances Ducane, son of the more famous Rick.

# 10

## 1950

Mud sticks. Oh, so true. Rick knew it. The first thing he'd done when he'd found Viv's body was to phone the studio, tell them. They would know what to do; they would help him.

Only, they didn't. He couldn't get hold of anyone.

As he was going apeshit trying to figure out what to do, Frances came into the lounge and said, 'I phoned.'

Rick stopped his anxious pacing and stared at the boy. '...You what?'

'The ambulance. I phoned.'

Oh *shit*.

He could see it all caving in on him. Could see it all hitting the fan.

He phoned the only one he could truly count on. He phoned LaLa.

'Rick? What the fuck? It's four o'clock in the morning.'

'LaLa. You've got to help me. Viv's dead.'

'She's *what?*'

Rick was standing in the hall. 'She's dead,' he said again. LaLa would help. She would know what to do. 'Looks like she slipped or something getting in the tub. Cut her head open. Either that or one of her drinking cronies whacked her.

Either way, she's dead.'

'Oh.'

'Oh? Is that all you can say? LaLa, the woman's *dead... Shit a brick...*'

The ambulance was pulling up, and the police. Frances opened the door to them.

'Oh dear. Are the police there?' asked Lala.

Then the press were crowding into the hallway, flashbulbs were popping in his face.

'Yeah. *And* the press. Some bastard must have tipped them off.'

LaLa hung up.

'LaLa? Hello?' He redialled, but she didn't answer. Anyway, the police wanted to talk with him...

Within days – hellish long days when the press camped outside, trapping him inside his own home with nobody but Frances for company – the studio heads wrote and very politely told him that he should consider his contract terminated, with immediate effect.

He phoned LaLa, but her secretary said she was in a meeting. The day after the studio heads dumped him, LaLa dumped him too.

The papers came, and he flinched at the headlines.

'*Secret wife of dashing movie star Rick Ducane in suicide drama*', they shrieked.

'*Mystery death of Mrs Rick Ducane.*'

'*Did he do it?*' Beneath *that* one, there was a picture of him standing in his hallway, white-faced with shock, holding up a hand to fend off not only the photographers but also disaster. But he couldn't stop this.

Vivienne had killed him. Killed his career,

killed his life.

The police questioned him endlessly, but his alibi was watertight. They hauled in a couple of her drinking buddies and questioned them, too, but nothing stuck. Finally, they seemed to be satisfied that Viv's death was nothing but a tragic accident.

Within a month he fled back to England with Frances, and he never acted again.

# 11

## 1971

Once she had recovered from the shock of it – for Christ's sake, a *man?* – and had stood there for several minutes, staring out with sightless eyes at the sunlit sea and wondering how he would *dare* do that to her, Cara went quickly to her father's study. He was busy of course; Nico, his right-hand man was there, standing beside him as he sat at the big walnut desk, and there were other men with him too. Her father was doing business, but there was no business that could be more urgent than this.

Constantine looked surprised at the interruption, but he quickly read her expression and apologized to the three men who were there with him and asked them to wait outside while Cara spoke to him.

'Nico, can you go too please?' Cara said, and

flung herself down in a chair.

Nico looked at Constantine. He nodded, and Nico quietly left the room.

'So what's so important?' asked Constantine mildly.

Cara flung the brown envelope containing the photos and the reports onto her father's desk. Constantine looked at his daughter's face for a long moment, then picked up the envelope and tipped out the contents. Cara watched him as he looked through them, giving each document and each photograph his full attention. Finally, he put the items back in the envelope and pushed it back into the centre of the desk.

'I'm sorry, Cara,' he said.

'Not as sorry as *I* am, Papa,' fumed Cara. 'I knew. I just *knew* he was up to something.'

'You used an outsider for this?'

'I used a private detective. I didn't want all the family and their friends knowing my business.'

Constantine gazed at her levelly. 'But now you don't mind, uh?'

'Only you, Papa. I only want you to know this. I couldn't stand to be made to look such an idiot.' Cara stared at him and her eyes filled with tears. 'He has *insulted* me, made a fool of me.'

'So now you bring this to me. Why?'

'*Why?*' wailed Cara, red-faced with temper, the tears flooding over and running down her cheeks. She looked like a large, angry child – which, he thought, was effectively what she was.

Constantine loved his daughter. He loved *all* his children. But he wasn't blind to their faults. Since her mother Maria's death, Cara had taken on the role of only daughter with an almost missionary zeal. She had clung and cuddled close to her father, fawned over him; and maybe, to be fair, he had fawned over her too – rather too much, in fact. Annie Carter had come as an unwelcome shock to Cara, but maybe it was partly his fault that she was so hostile to Annie.

Now she thought ... what? That he was going to solve her problematical marriage with a magical wave of his hand? He had warned her against Rocco before she rushed into wedlock with the boy. A few background checks had quickly shown that Rocco was lazy, feckless and inclined to fuck around. He'd warned her of this. But Cara, so used to getting her own way, had been obdurate. She wanted to marry Rocco; no one else would do.

*Now* she was coming to him for help. He had many, many problems – the Cantuzzi family was trying to muscle in on some of his businesses, and they were going to have to learn the hard way that this was unacceptable behaviour. Always there were concerns.

He was the protector of many Italian families in New York, shielding them from the worst excesses of the American legal system by employing many useful people in the judiciary and the Police Department.

The Barolli organization had a system of payoffs in place, and a large 'sheet' or list of officials on a monthly wage, so no friends of the Barollis would ever face the trauma of prosecution.

The whole operation was unbelievably slick; Constantine had over many years made it so, and now it was an empire with him at its head and many layers of power beneath him. His sons had, of course, followed him into the business; Lucco and Alberto were *caporegimes,* or captains, and everyone beneath them was a soldier. He had his legal counsellor, or *consigliere.* It was a smooth, well-oiled system. He gave his orders to Lucco and Alberto, and those orders filtered down and were carried out; rarely did Constantine have to issue a direct order to anyone.

But such a complex business didn't run itself. There were always problems to be resolved. Added to *that,* he had a gorgeous pregnant wife, and no time to spare for rescuing a silly situation that should never have arisen in the first place.

'He's insulted me. He deserves to *die* for it,' said Cara.

Constantine sat back in his chair and stared at her.

'The Mancini family are old friends to us,' he pointed out. 'Rocco is their youngest boy and he's been spoiled. He wasn't a good choice for you. As I told you, when you decided to marry him.'

'I want you to do something to him, Papa,' said Cara, sobbing now, nearly incoherent with rage. 'I want you to hurt him. Break his legs. *Do* something.'

Constantine shook his head slowly as he looked at her. 'You're missing the point here. I told you. The Mancinis are friends of ours. We have reciprocal arrangements going all over town, all over the *country.* And you expect me to wound, maybe kill their youngest boy?'

'If you love me, you'll do it,' hurled Cara.

Constantine leaned forward. His blue eyes held hers in a hard, laser-like gaze.

'You know I love you. That isn't in question here. What *is* in question is your choice of husband and what's to be done about him if he's looking elsewhere for his enjoyment.'

Cara jumped to her feet, overturning the chair. 'Well you are *obviously* going to do nothing,' she spat out.

Constantine sighed and leaned back. 'I'll talk to his father. Maybe between us we can come to some sort of arrangement.'

'So you think all this is *my* fault?' shouted Cara.

'You made a bad marriage.' He shrugged. 'It happens.'

'You don't understand *anything*,' she complained. 'You're too wrapped up in your new little cosy domestic setup. You don't care about the fact that your daughter is being humiliated, that all my friends will laugh at me.'

Constantine rose to his feet in one swift movement. The look on his face shut her up in an instant. She'd gone too far; she knew it.

'I understand *this*. My domestic arrangements are my business,' he said coldly. 'And if your friends laugh, then d'you really think they're friends at all? And I also understand that only a *fool* shits on his own doorstep. Do you? The Mancinis are good people and I will *not* be damaging their youngest son to gratify your injured pride.'

Trembling, Cara nodded. She brushed angrily at her tears and glared at him. Why couldn't he see that she had every right to be affronted? But she knew she'd hit a nerve; he was so totally absorbed

64

with that English whore and her brat that he was neglecting his own family, his *true* family.

She felt that no one was on her side now, that *everyone* was more appreciated, more valued, than she was. Lucco was getting married to a girl of his father's choosing and so he was, for once, very much in favour. Alberto was *always* in favour – that went without saying. And now – and this was the worst thing of all – the English bitch was going to present Constantine with a brand-new child. And as for Cara ... well, she used to be the apple of her father's eye. And then along had come Annie Carter, and all that had changed overnight.

God, how she hated that bitch.

And right now, how she hated *him,* her father.

Whatever he said, she was going to get her revenge on Rocco, one way or another. If her father refused to punish the bastard, *she would.* She was going to find a way to do it. She thought of Rocco and his fag lover, and vowed that Frances Ducane was going to *pay* for this. She wasn't Constantine Barolli's daughter for nothing.

# 12

## 1960

'What you need, my boy, is an arsenal,' Rick Ducane told his son over and over again.

Frances was thirteen when it first occurred to him that his father was ... well, more than a little screwy. He missed his mother. He couldn't talk to his father about anything.

When they'd come back to England, Rick had become a bitter recluse. He'd bought a house called Whereys, an old red-brick Victorian pile with a big cluster of barley-twist chimney pots soaring high above its gabled roof. It was impossible to heat – Frances always felt cold there – and it was deep in the Kent countryside, miles from anywhere. Secretly, to himself, Frances called the house Where-The-Fuck, Kent.

He could still remember that wild night when his mother had been drunk, reeling, strange men drinking on the sofa, cavorting naked with her in and out of the bedrooms in the house; and then the next thing, Dad was home and there were police and ambulance men and press swarming over the place like ants.

That was the last time he ever saw his mother. Now, all he had in the world was dear old Dad, and Frances strongly suspected that Dad was Looney Tunes. Had a screw loose. Was barking mad.

That worried him.

And this thing his dad had about weaponry. He'd built up a vast collection of arms. A bayonet knife that – he never tired of telling Frances – he'd taken off a dead Nazi during the war.

'Rigor mortis had set in,' said Rick. 'Had to break the bastard's fingers to get it off him.'

*Nice,* thought Frances.

There was also a Prussian officer's dress sword. And guns, he was a maniac for guns.

'People will try to hurt you in life, people will

pull you down,' he told Frances.

Yeah, you got that right, thought Frances. No one could ever hurt him as his dad did, mocking his efforts at amateur dramatics, saying he didn't have 'the ear' when he attempted accents, telling him that stardom was a false mistress and would always break your heart, grudgingly listening to Frances's readings of Shakespeare's soliloquies and then telling him that his diction was poor, that he didn't 'enunciate' or 'project' enough.

Oh, Frances knew he could never be the star his dad had once been. He knew he was lacking. But he tried hard, and he hoped he could get somewhere – with or without his dad's blessing. And it would be without, he knew it.

'So what you've got to do, son,' said Rick, his eyes wild with enthusiasm, 'is protect yourself. Get a store like I have. Because if you've got anything worth having, people will resent it and try to snatch it away from you. Friends, colleagues – even loved ones. You can't trust a living soul. You understand?'

Frances nodded. Sure he did. He understood his dad was cuckoo; he understood that all right. He understood that he was always delighted to get back to school, away from the crazy old coot. He understood that he preferred to huddle in his freezing-cold bedroom listening to Elvis Presley crooning 'It's Now Or Never' on his Dansette, rather than spend time with him.

Jesus, he so missed his mother. There was no way he could tell Rick that he was getting these feelings for boys and not girls. Maybe his mum would have understood, maybe not. All Frances knew was that he had to keep his particular sexual leanings to himself. He'd read Oscar Wilde's 'Ballad of Reading Gaol' and knew Wilde had been put in the slammer for consorting with men; and if any of his friends knew or even suspected he was homosexual, he knew they wouldn't be his friends for much longer.

Now it was a dreary Saturday morning, raining hard, and Frances was dreading the weekend to come, closeted here in the backside of fucking nowhere with his dad when he would rather have been somewhere – anywhere – else.

But he couldn't escape. Dad had said he had something to show him, something exciting, and Frances had thought, yeah, big news, another fucking handgun.

But it wasn't a handgun this time.

Maybe a sword then?

No. His dad's eyes were dancing with merriment as he made Frances guess, over and over, as they trudged out to the workshop. Frances saw that his dad had hung a horseshoe over the door. Rick saw his son looking at it.

'For luck,' he told him with a grin. 'Go on then. Keep guessing.'

'A Buffalo Sharps?' hazarded Frances. His dad had enthused about the rifle; it could pick off a target a quarter of a mile away.

'No. I said. Not a gun.'

'What then?' asked Frances, slightly intrigued despite himself.

His dad was going to give him a demonstration of something he'd picked up during the war, he told him. Something really exciting.

'Come on then. What?'

Frances was smiling so hard his jaw was aching. And his dad said he was a bad actor? He thought he was good. After all, he acted as if he could stand the loopy old goat. And he couldn't.

Frances had already decided that once he left school he was off, back to America. He was half-American after all; he loved it there. But his dad's dire warnings about the toughness of Hollywood had penetrated, and his mum had been desolate and lonely there, he knew she had; so he'd decided he was heading for New York, and Broadway. Just as soon as he could.

'So come on,' he said to his dad. 'Give. What is it?' Like he cared.

Dad winked. 'Explosives,' he said, and showed him a box full of...

*Oh shit. Were those live grenades?*

Yes. They were.

It was then that Frances really knew his dad had flipped.

But it wasn't going to happen to him. No way. He was *sane*.

# 13

## 1971

Cara stood alone in the hall while Nico and the others filed back into the study. The door closed behind them, and it was like a door slamming shut on Cara's damaged heart. She felt diminished, dismissed out of hand. She went outside onto the drive, feeling thwarted, furious, bitter; she walked until she found herself outside the multiple garage block.

That idiot Fredo was there in his shirtsleeves, polishing the bonnet of the limo in the hot midday sun. It was a huge, heavy, armour-plated car, bulletproof and grenade-proof. Her father's car. Sometimes – not often – Fredo drove Constantine; but more often it was Nico who took the wheel when the Don was in the car. Still, Frederico was as proud of this large heap of black metal as a mother with a new baby, cleaning it – and the other cars in which he ferried various members of the family around – constantly.

He didn't see her standing there, but Cara watched him, and slowly she began to formulate a plan. She walked over and tapped him on the shoulder.

'Oh!' He whirled round, startled.

Cara smiled. 'Sorry, did I surprise you?' She came in closer, close enough for him to smell her perfume. She saw his eyes dip to the deep V neckline of her white cotton shirt. 'I think I left my purse in the other car. Is it in the garage?' she asked, walking that way.

Frederico followed her, frowning; he was thinking that she was beautiful and that he adored her. He found his eyes resting on the enticing swell of her buttocks beneath her tight-fitting cream-coloured pencil skirt. Ah, if only ... but she was married; she was the Don's daughter; she had no feelings for him. It could never be. And he had cleaned the car two or three times since her trip to Central Park; if the purse had been there, he would have found it.

'I don't think it's there,' he said as they passed from the hot glare of the sun outside into the cool, dark shadows of the garage.

'Oh, maybe I've just put it somewhere,' she shrugged, then looked at him intensely. 'Fredo,' she said, using the baby-name that everyone used for him, the name she had never used, not once. 'I've got to talk to you about something,' she told him.

'Oh?' Now Fredo was confused. Cara *never* wanted to talk to him; she barely grunted a civil word to him in passing.

'Yes, something important. Can you close the doors? Lock them?'

'What is this...?' He was frowning.

'*Please*, Fredo.'

'All right,' he said, and turned away and went to the doors. He locked them and turned back.

His mouth dropped open.

Cara was standing there wearing only her skirt

and high-heeled shoes. She had removed her blouse and her bra and was clutching both garments in her hands in front of her tits. He could see the soft upper swell of her skin there, paler skin, not tanned. Fredo's eyes bulged in his head.

'Wha...?' he started to say.

'Do you want to see them?' she asked him.

'I...' Fredo was lost for words. He'd adored her for so long, and now she was here, flaunting herself in front of him. It was like a miracle. He felt so unbearably aroused that he was afraid he was about to come in his pants.

'I'll show you, if you want,' said Cara.

*If* he wanted? There was nothing on God's earth that he wanted more.

'Only you have to say please. And ... you have to promise to help me with something, something *special.*'

Fredo gawped at her. 'I would do anything for you,' he said at last. 'You know that.'

'You promise?' Suddenly Cara's eyes were sharp as they rested on his.

'Of course I promise.'

Cara seemed to relax then. 'Say please.'

'Please,' said Fredo unsteadily.

Cara gave a small, secret smile and tossed her shirt and bra onto the grubby garage floor, while keeping one arm across her chest to conceal her treasures.

'Please,' said Fredo, a little more desperately.

'You give your word,' said Cara sternly.

'I swear.'

'Then...' said Cara, letting her arm fall to her side, exposing her voluptuous naked breasts to his view. They were much fuller than he had imagined – and he had imagined Cara's breasts a *lot*. The skin there was as silken and white as snow, giving a startlingly erotic effect against her slender tanned arms and belly. Her nipples were small, hard and rosy-pink.

Fredo made a half-strangled noise in his throat.

'Next time,' said Cara, putting her hands brazenly on her hips, 'I'll let you touch them. Would you like that?'

Fredo could only nod. The front of his trousers was tenting up so much it was painful.

'And when you've helped me with the secret thing,' said Cara, 'I'll let you do more. Touch me *anywhere*. Here on my breasts, or even *down there*. Fredo, I'll let you have sex with me. When you've done it. You understand?'

Fredo nodded again, then clutched desperately at his groin. He came in his pants.

# 14

Rick told Frances about blowing up German emplacements with the grenades, then he set up a little demonstration and blew up an old tree root in the garden.

The noise of the explosion was one Frances would never forget. The old tree had rocked and then collapsed sideways, revealing a tangle of blackened root.

'See? Easiest thing in the world,' said Rick.

It was. Frances could see that it was, but he wasn't greatly interested. He just wanted to be *gone*. His father was a deranged egotistical monster, twisted first by fame and then by a spectacular fall from grace.

As soon as he'd finished school at eighteen, Frances picked his moment and told his dad that he was going to New York to try to get an agent, try to get some parts on Off Off Broadway if he could.

'You're going back to that place?' said Rick, hearing his son's words with disbelief. 'It'll kill you, boy. I'm telling you.'

'I'm not talking about Hollywood, I don't want to go there. I was never happy there, I don't have good memories of it. I'm talking about the Big Apple. Broadway.'

Rick was watching him, his mouth moving querulously, his eyes astonished.

'But do you think you have the talent?' he asked.

'Yeah. Actually, I do.' Frances felt his face colour as his father smashed his ego yet again, with his usual casual indifference.

But this time he was fighting back. He *did* have talent; he knew he did. It wasn't as great a talent as his father's, but what could you do? Stay at home and weep? He wanted to act. He was going to do it.

'I'd like to think I have your blessing,' said Frances.

'Well you haven't,' said Rick, eyes darting. 'I think you're mad.'

*Ha! Coming from the fruitloop of the year!*

'Next time I come home, I'll show you. I'll

74

prove you wrong.'

And maybe even make you proud of me, thought Frances, but he doubted such a miracle could ever occur. Frances knew that he could come back here with a bunch of plaudits from the critics, with a sodding Oscar, and his father would still dismiss his son's achievements with a shrug of his shoulders. In Rick's eyes, Frances knew that he would always be a failure.

Broadway wasn't an easy nut to crack. Frances had to work long hours in delis and restaurants to make ends meet, to pay for the modest – actually pretty tatty – apartment in Lower Midtown.

He loved New York. He found an agent – not the best, but Solly was the first agent in a list of twenty who would even meet him. He told him he was Rick Ducane's son. He didn't *want* to, but he knew that agents and PR firms always craved an angle and, if you had one, you'd be damned stupid not to use it.

Solly's hawklike eyes sharpened to pinpricks over his squashed nose.

'You're Rick Ducane's boy? Hey, that's good.' Solly wrote it down. Then he looked up with a frown at his new client's face. 'Wasn't there a scandal with him? A dead woman, something like that?'

Frances nodded. 'My mother.'

'Oh – hey, sorry.' Solly paused and delicately cleared his throat. 'Would you mind if I mentioned it?'

'What?'

'After all, there's no such thing as bad publicity.

Did you see anything...?'

'No. I didn't.' *Hey, why don't you just cut a hunk of flesh out my arse, you fucking hyena?*

'I have to ask these things,' said Solly.

'Of course.' Frances smiled.

Solly worked hard for him after that, pushing the name forward, Rick Ducane's son, getting him bit parts. It was a start. It was the most fun he had ever had in his life, although it was – admittedly – tough. He worked the years away and tried to believe he'd make it big one day. And he had his admirers: the critics were kind and people loitered at the stage door sometimes, pretty young girls, hormonal matrons, stylish young men, to say how much they'd loved his performance, he had pitched it just right, and would he just sign this...?

When Frances signed his first batches of autographs at the age of twenty-four, he felt powerful, delighted. The two-week run was slow to start, but eventually packed out by people who'd read favourable reviews. He'd even got a mention from one of the critics best known for his harsh, unforgiving words. So what if all the posters proclaimed him to be the son of Rick Ducane, the once-great Hollywood star? He had got a good review.

Time went on. The admirers still came, and he was easy now about signing the autographs – he was casual, he smiled and was charming. He noticed the tall, thin, sallow-skinned and handsome young man waiting outside the theatre for three evenings on the trot, and when he moved forward to shake the man's hand, he said: 'Good grief, you must really like this play.'

The stranger went red in the face. 'I do like the

play,' he said earnestly. 'But your performance was the thing that drew me back. You were wonderful in it.'

'Oh! Well ... thanks. You're very kind to say so.'

'Just truthful,' said the man. He looked down. 'Can I buy you a drink?'

'Oh, I don't...' said Frances nervously. He'd met his fair share of crazies since coming to the city; he didn't know this man from Adam.

'Just a drink,' the stranger persisted, and he looked up and smiled straight into Frances's eyes.

He was very handsome, almost Latin in appearance. Frances distinctly felt his stomach do a little back-flip of excitement.

'Well ... I don't see why not.'

'Excellent,' said the man. He held out a hand. 'I'm Rocco Mancini, by the way. Is it true you're Rick Ducane's son?'

Within days they were lovers, meeting up at every opportunity. Frances even found he could forgive Rocco for the Rick Ducane question. It seemed to Frances that Rocco avoided the more populated areas of the city whenever they were together. But he didn't care. They were together, and delighted in the time spent strolling in quiet places, or eating bagels bought from a street-corner vendor. When they were in bed together, it was as if it was always meant to be.

It was bliss.

'I love you,' said Frances, as Rocco and he lay entwined in a hotel room one afternoon.

'I love you too,' said Rocco, although he didn't. He had a real weakness for beauty both in men and women. His own wife Cara was exquisitely lovely and he'd fallen in 'love' with her on sight. Only later had he discovered what a spoiled, controlling bitch she was.

If he saw another beautiful boy, another lissom woman, in the next week or so, then – Frances or no Frances – would he have the willpower to turn it down?

Rocco didn't think so. He knew he was weak. He knew he was an emotional lightweight. He hoped Frances wasn't expecting too much. Frances had told him about his uncaring father and his mother's unfortunate death.

'That's so tragic,' said Rocco, thinking of his own doting mother and how awful it would be to lose her.

'If you love someone, you're open to all sorts of hurt,' said Frances. Dad had been wrong about nearly everything else – he was crazy, after all – but he'd been dead right about that. But Rocco had said he loved him.

And right now, right here, maybe he really did … although Rocco was growing tired of Frances and finding him clingy.

They took lunch together in the diner on Lexington and Third next day, and Rocco was, for once, a little careless. They sat in the window, smiled and laughed and joked a lot. They looked like what they were – lovers. Rocco knew he'd have to end it soon, but for now, what the hell? It was just fun.

Meanwhile, Saul Jury, the private detective hired by Cara, watched them, and took photographs, and sealed both their fates.

# 15

## 1971

'I'm not sure about this,' said Fredo. There was sweat beading along his upper lip, although the air conditioning in the car was on full blast to counter the humid summer heat of New York.

Cara looked at him coldly. They were sitting in the front of the car watching customers going in and out of the diner. It was evening, and Rocco had told Cara that he was playing poker with friends, and she'd thought, *Ha! You're certainly poking* something, *my friend.*

They had followed him twice before. Fuelled as she was by her need for revenge, still Cara was sick of this. She felt humiliated beyond belief that her husband should do such a thing. Oh, she knew their once passionate marriage had quickly dissolved into mere tolerance on both sides as she discovered that Rocco was pure Jello at the core: vain and stupid and with an almost girlish appreciation of all things beautiful. Maybe that was why he'd married her. Cara knew the value of her own looks; after all, hadn't she used them to get her own way ever since she'd learned to bat her eyelashes? And she'd used her beauty to ensnare Fredo, because she wanted – *needed* – his help with this.

But shit, she hated it so much. Following Rocco

and persuading Fredo to do what had to be done had stretched her almost to the limit. Fredo had quickly realized that she needed him for the first time ever, and he had sensed an opportunity.

'I want more,' he had said when they'd first followed Rocco and she'd explained to him what was to be done.

'More?' Cara had stared at him. What was the idiot talking about? Did he want money now?

But Fredo was nodding, smirking. 'I want sex now. Full sex. *Before* I do it.'

'That wasn't the deal,' said Cara.

But Fredo – and this was the Fredo she thought she knew; the one who had followed her around like a puppy-dog since childhood; the one whose chain she yanked on a regular basis – only shrugged and smiled.

'Hey, it's nothing to me if the bastard cheats on you. But it is to you, and I'm willing to help you, so what's in it for me?'

'I *told* you. When it's done...'

'When it's done you'll say thank you very much, Fredo, and get lost,' he said.

Which was precisely what she had been intending to do. And if Fredo by some chance got named by anyone, and incurred any heat over this from her father, she was going to look all wide-eyed and innocent and say, No, Papa, what, me? No, Fredo must have realized how much Rocco had upset me, and decided to do this on his own. You know how he's always adored me, the silly thing. *I* had nothing to do with it.

And who would Constantine believe? Her, or Fredo? She knew the answer to *that* one.

'How can you think that?' she demanded, feigning a hurt expression.

Fredo looked at her and he didn't seem like an adoring boy any more.

'I *know* you, Cara, remember? This is Fredo you're talking to, not some stranger who'll be taken in. So I want sex first, not after. When we get back tonight, I want it. Or the deal's off.'

So what could she do? After the first time they'd followed Rocco, seen him there in the diner with what was obviously his male lover, discussed what they could do, Fredo drove them back to the Montauk estate in her father's car, drove it into the garage, then got out and locked the garage doors.

'In the back,' he said to her, and Cara wondered how it had happened that Fredo, of all people, was ordering her about like this.

Still, she knew she had to comply if she was to get him to help. It was semi-dark in the back of the car, and quiet but for the ticking of the engine as it cooled down. Fredo got in the back too and closed the door. He was up close to her – Jesus, he was trying to kiss her. Cara turned her head away.

Fredo pulled back, uttered a low curse. Suddenly his hands were on her, pushing her skirt up and reaching under, scratching her, bruising her, grabbing her pants and pulling them down, and off. Quickly he got between her legs and then with a groan he unzipped himself. Cara looked away, trying not to feel even his breath on her, but she felt the big hot tip of his penis parting her flesh, felt the hard jolt as he drove it all the way

81

into her cringing body, was pummelled by every manic thrust of it as he had her.

He was finished very quickly. He moaned as he came, and lay there for a moment against her. Then he withdrew, zipped up, flopped back onto the seat beside her. Cara sat there, feeling his disgusting wetness on her thighs. She was trembling, sore, aware that she'd just been raped and that she had brought it entirely on herself.

'Now,' said Fredo imperiously when he'd got his breath back. 'Get your tits out. I want to touch them.'

Shivering and nearly crying, Cara unbuttoned her blouse, unfastened her bra. When she was naked to the waist, Fredo fell upon her, pinching and pulling at the tender flesh of her breasts until he was too aroused to stop. Then he raped her all over again.

The second time they trailed Rocco and finally agreed how the thing would be done, this pattern repeated itself. Fredo drove them home, locked them in the garage, and had Cara forcibly in the back of the car.

Now, it was time for him to keep his part of the bargain. And he was saying: *I'm not sure about this.*

After all that she had done, all that she had *let* him do, he wasn't sure?

She had to breathe deeply to keep her voice from shaking, so ferocious was her hatred of him at that moment.

'You're not *sure*? What do you mean?' she asked, and she was surprised to hear her own voice emerging from her body with that cool, calm

82

sound to it. Inside, she was raging. She wanted to *kill* him, she was so angry.

Fredo was silent for a moment. He had the upper hand and he knew it. She would never want her father to know she planned anything like this. Rocco was a Mancini. The word had got around among the boys; they had overheard a shouting-match between Cara and her father, with Cara threatening all sorts. Constantine had said the Mancinis were not to be touched. And okay she *wasn't* touching them, but it was a moot point. She would still be doing Rocco harm, if only indirectly.

'I'm not sure you love me,' said Fredo, and turned his head and grinned at her. *'Joking,'* he said.

Cara had to look away or she was afraid she was going to throw up all over the bastard.

'Look,' she said, swallowing hard. 'You know what you've got to do, yes?'

'I know,' said Fredo.

Cara glanced at her watch. 'They should be out soon.'

*And then it would be over,* she thought.

But, she wondered, would it? She felt she had descended straight to hell to wreak her revenge on Rocco. Maybe the price had been too dear. Maybe not. Only time would tell. Now all she wanted, all she was here for, was to be absolutely sure that what she needed Fredo to do, was done.

'There's Rocco,' said Fredo.

They watched silently as Rocco came out of the diner and walked quickly away down the block.

Minutes passed. Fredo casually laid a hand on Cara's thigh. She let it stay there, but only by an extreme act of will. God, he disgusted her.

'There he is,' said Fredo, and left the car.

Frances Ducane was walking back to his car, thinking happily about the coming weekend. Under the pretext of a golfing break with the boys, Rocco and he were going to take off alone to a cabin in the Rockies. Frances loved Rocco and he wanted more time with him, but he understood that Rocco's witch of a wife came with the money, and the money was what they enjoyed, so she had to be tolerated.

*Cow,* thought Frances in disgust. Swanky Upper East Side Princess with her nose in the air, busy spending Daddy's money. And he knew from Rocco there was plenty of it. Why else had Rocco married her? For love? Frances didn't *think* so.

'Hey – faggot,' said a voice behind him.

Frances felt a shudder of fear jolt up his spine to the top of his head. He half turned and then felt the first stinging lash of the blade as it struck the edge of his mouth. Blood splattered out and gushed down over his clothes. Frances screamed with pain. He staggered back, half running, desperate to get away, and Fredo came after him, shoving him back against a building wall, slashing in with the knife that glinted in his hand.

*'No!'* Frances wailed, hardly able to speak now, raising his hands to protect himself.

Fredo waded in, slicing fingers and palms indiscriminately. Two digits spun off into the gutter, blood spurting, and when Frances lowered his hands to stare at them in horror, Fredo came in close again and slashed the other side of Frances's mouth wide open.

Frances fell to his knees, groaning. The crimson slashes on either side of his mouth looked like a clown's painted-on smile: grotesque.

Fredo knelt down too, grabbed a handful of hair and yanked Frances's head back.

'That's a present from Rocco and Cara Mancini, you little shit. Now *back off*,' he hissed. Then he wiped the knife on the front of Frances's once-pristine shirt and left the man there, blubbering and bleeding.

Fredo slipped the knife back in his pocket and made his way back to the car. He got in.

'Well?' said Cara. 'Did you...?'

'Yeah, I did.'

'Show me the knife.'

'Jesus,' said Fredo. He'd already wiped it clean, what the hell, didn't she *trust* him?

But there were traces of blood still on the blade. Cara sat back, satisfied. 'And it went okay?' she asked.

Fredo slipped the knife into his pocket and grinned at her. 'It went fine,' he said. 'Let's go home and fuck.'

# 16

When Annie left the massive master suite with its sprawling ocean view, she walked straight into Cara.

Annie groaned inwardly. Her relationship with

her stepdaughter had never got off the ground. She had tried hard to befriend Cara, but she found her snobbish, vain and unlovable. She spoke to Annie hardly at all, and Annie thought that was just *fine*, if that was the way Cara wanted it.

But today, something about Cara seemed different. She looked ... well, Annie wasn't exactly sure *how* Cara looked. Usually, Constantine's daughter exuded an icy poise that left no room for even an attempt at civility. But today, Cara looked *shattered*. She looked as though someone had just given her a scare that had rocked her world. She looked sick.

'Cara?' Annie caught her arm as Cara was about to pass right by her without a word. 'Are you all right?'

Cara's eyes met hers and in that instant before her guard went up, Annie saw something there; something bruised, something covert and uncertain. But then the shutters were in place again and Cara just stared at Annie coldly.

'Like you care,' she said, and looked pointedly at Annie's hand resting on her arm.

Annie removed it. 'I wouldn't ask if I didn't.'

But Cara was right: Annie's words were a lie. There was just something about Cara's own personal fuck-you demeanour and the swanky peabrained friends she hung around with that put Annie's back up.

'I told you. I'm *fine*.'

*Yeah, and I'm the Queen of Sheba*, thought Annie. But fuck it. Did she really want to know what petty concerns went on in the life of someone so vacuous, spiteful and vain?

Answer: no.

Cara hurried on by. Annie heard her go into the bathroom at the head of the stairs, slamming the door behind her – and then she heard retching.

Annie paused there on the stairs, frowning. Maybe Cara was pregnant? But Annie sort of doubted that. So maybe Rocco had upset her ... but then, Rocco was so mild, so practically invisible as a personality, that Annie couldn't imagine him upsetting *anyone*, far less his notoriously difficult wife.

In the downstairs hall, Annie found Nico sitting patiently on guard outside Constantine's study.

'Is he free?' Annie asked him.

Nico rose to his feet and gave her a smiling half-bow. 'For you, yeah – he's free.' He turned and tapped at the door.

'Come!' came from inside the study.

He looked up as she came in. She stood there leaning against the door. He pushed himself back from the desk and stared at her.

'Mrs Barolli,' he said, his eyes playing with hers.

'*Mr* Barolli,' Annie greeted him.

'And to what do we owe this unexpected honour?' Constantine made a 'so come here' gesture with his hand.

Annie went over to the desk.

'Closer,' said Constantine.

Annie stepped nearer.

'Not close enough,' said Constantine.

Annie went around the desk, sat in his lap and put her arms around his neck. 'Close enough now?' she asked.

'Barely,' he complained, nuzzling her neck with his lips. 'Something bothering you?'

'Not really.' Annie thought briefly of Cara's face, but then it was gone, forgotten.

'The baby?' said Constantine, anxiously. He glanced down, concerned, at the small neat bump beneath her light lilac shift dress.

'I just wanted to see you.'

'Mrs Barolli, I love you very much,' he said, and kissed her, and Annie found herself remembering her *first* pregnancy, when she had been expecting Layla; and Max had been so delighted, just as Constantine was now.

A sharp pang of sadness and regret struck her heart as she hugged her second husband and whispered her love for him, because once there had been Max, owner of the East End streets around Bow in London; Max Carter, gang lord, lover – and her first husband, her first true romance. And she had loved him too. Oh, so much.

She shivered, and clung to Constantine.

# 17

Rocco got called to the hospital at two in the morning. Cara was asleep beside him when the phone rang. He flicked on the bedside light. She stirred sleepily and looked at him as he spoke into the phone. When he put it down, his face was ashen.

'What's wrong?' asked Cara.

'It's...' Rocco paused, shook himself. His eyes were distant. He looked like a man who had seen a brief glimpse into hell. 'It's one of my friends. He left the poker game and he's been attacked in the street.'

Now Rocco was throwing back the sheets, getting out of bed, hurrying to pick up his trousers and put them on.

'Is ... is it bad?' asked Cara innocently. She knew exactly how bad it was. Here was the reward for all her suffering; here was her revenge. Fredo had slashed up Rocco's little fag friend ... before driving her home and then forcing himself on her once again in the garage. She shuddered to think of it.

She had told Fredo that this would be the last time. And, chillingly, he had laughed and said fuck *that,* not unless she wanted her father to hear all about what she had *made* him do to her husband's fag boyfriend.

Now she was in a mess and she knew it. She despised Fredo for all that he'd done to her, but worse than that was the fact that she despised her father too, for making her sink to such levels of depravity with his refusal to help.

Would Fredo really dare tell her father? She didn't know. And if she told Constantine first, blaming Fredo rather than carrying the blame herself for the attack, would her father believe her? She couldn't take the risk, because Constantine would be so angry if he discovered she'd wormed her way around his warnings and found another way to get to Rocco.

'This don't stop until I'm ready,' Fredo had told her, crudely slapping her on the arse as she emerged once again, shaking and abused, from the back of the car.

*The bastard!*

But the deed was done. And here was the result. Wasn't it worth it? Yes, she knew it was.

Now Rocco was fastening his shirt and almost running for the door.

'I hope your friend's all right...' Cara called after him, but he was gone, slamming the door closed behind him.

Cara lay down, a catlike smile playing over her pretty features.

So Rocco Mancini thought he could make a fool of his wife, did he? He was about to discover how horribly he had miscalculated her capabilities.

Rocco got to the hospital at nearly three a.m. They let him in and Rocco had to hide his shock at the state Frances was in. His face – oh, his beautiful face! – was a mess of stitches and bloody smears and bandages. His mouth had been slashed almost neatly on both sides, widening his lips so that they were hideously elongated. Two of the fingers on his right hand were missing.

Rocco tried to cover his disgust at the sheer ugliness of Frances's appearance, but he couldn't quite conceal it from his wounded lover. He sat down beside Frances and, while Frances sobbed, each sob muffled beneath the wadding and stitches around his mouth, Rocco asked him who had done this to him, who *could* have done such a thing?

'You're saying you don't know?' said Frances indistinctly. His eyes were red and accusing. 'It was *you*, you fucker.'

Rocco looked aghast. His eyes went to Frances's face, and he had to look quickly away.

'What? No, I swear–'

'It was a man,' said Frances. 'You must have paid him. He said it was from Rocco and Cara Mancini. For the love of God, you only had to *say* if you wanted to end it. You didn't have to do this.'

Rocco sat back in his chair, feeling dizzy from the shock.

Cara must have instigated this. Cara must have known about their affair. He felt his insides clench with fear. If Cara knew, had she told her father? My God, if the Don knew...

Clearly, she had somehow discovered his secret. He felt consumed with horror at that thought, at the dangers inherent in this situation for him. Again his eyes strayed to the damage she'd wreaked on his once-exquisite lover, and again he had to look away, frightened that he might actually be sick. He was no good in hospitals. His grandmother had been an invalid for much of her life, languishing in bed; he had a horror of sickness. And as for any sort of disfigurement ... well, he knew it was shallow. He *knew* it was bad. But he couldn't help it. Just to look at Frances, the repulsive state of him, was making his stomach heave.

And he could see – oh, and wasn't this the worst bit? – he could see that Frances's beauty was comprehensively wrecked. These wounds were too severe to be anything other than permanent. Frances was *ugly* now. And if there was one thing Rocco couldn't stand, it was ugliness. He only liked beautiful people around him. Men or women, he didn't much care which, but they had to be *flawless*.

'It's going to be all right,' he told Frances.

'But *look* at me,' wailed Frances. 'You vicious fucking *bitch!* How am I going to find acting work now? I'm a *freak*. And this is all down to you.'

Frances stared with hate-filled eyes at his lover. Self-pity flooded through him and he flopped back against the pillows in despair. In his heart he knew that this was the end of it. Tears splashed down his cheeks, soaked his bloodstained bandages.

'I didn't do this,' insisted Rocco, patting Frances's unbandaged hand and wondering when he could decently leave. He wouldn't be coming here again. It was over.

'Yeah,' said Frances, snatching his hand away. 'Right.'


# 18

Rocco said nothing to Cara, except that his friend was recovering and would be fine. He wanted to grab her, to break her stupid head against a wall for damaging something so exquisitely beautiful. All right, he *had* been tired of Frances. But what she had done was like smashing a Ming vase or defacing a Renoir: a crime against a work of art.

But he bit his lip and said nothing, although he felt sick with a mingling of loss and terror. If she had told her father about this, then he believed he was a dead man. Only last week that sadistic bastard Lucco had been laughing about Roy Giancana, who the Barolli mob had sent out to Vegas to handle business and who had tried to cheat them on the skim. He'd ended up in an oil drum at the bottom of the sea, just off the coast of sunny Florida.

And there had been others, *many* others Rocco knew of; men who had once been called friends and had been dispatched to meet their maker for stepping out of line in one way or another.

Now *he* had stepped out of line and he knew it.

Cara, the daddy's girl, would run weeping to Constantine with any trouble, he knew that, and what would the Don do? Let it rest? No way. Rocco knew that once the word was given by the Don, his life was over. He was wracked with terror. Frightened of Lucco, who could in an instant switch from charming to deadly; and equally frightened of Alberto, whose urbane politeness concealed a businesslike efficiency when it came to conducting his father's business.

Brother-in-law or not, he knew that *neither* of them would baulk at giving the word for an enforcer to take him out. He *had* to make moves of his own, to preserve his own safety.

He drove up to New Jersey to pay a visit to his father, Enrico Mancini.

His mother greeted him with all the usual hugs and cries and kisses.

'You've lost weight!' she tutted, fluttering around him, pinching his sallow cheeks.

It was true, he *had* lost weight, such had been his

93

anxiety over the mess he had gotten himself into. He'd been under so much stress: keeping out of Constantine's way, tiptoeing around Cara, and worse, much worse, fielding the unwanted and increasingly desperate calls from Frances, yelling accusations and wild declarations of love down the phone at him. He felt as though he was under seige. Food had been the last thing on his mind.

'Son.' His father greeted him without enthusiasm. He was watching the Boston Red Sox play the Yankees on TV. He glanced up, waved Rocco into an armchair and looked back at the screen.

Rocco glanced at it too. He had no interest in sports. His older brothers, Jonathan and Silvio, did, they were always in their father's favour, but Rocco was the youngest and had clung to his mother's apron-strings as a boy and even – yes, he admitted it – as a young man. He didn't doubt his father loved him, but it was in a remote and dispassionate way.

Enrico Mancini shot a sideways look at his son. 'Is your mother fetching us something? You look thin.'

'Had a virus,' lied Rocco.

'Bad things,' said Enrico, shaking his head, and returned his attention to the game.

Rocco looked at his father. He was balding and relaxing into old age in a beige cardigan and carpet slippers. His heart was bad, too; he couldn't do too much these days. His father had no style, but Rocco understood that even so he was a great man. Rocco had a lot of style, but he knew in his heart that he had no real substance at all.

His mother came in, carrying a tray of *verdure*

*fritte, arancini,* olives and cheese. She set the appetizers down on a low table in front of them, along with strong coffee laced with anisette, tweaked Rocco's pallid cheek once more and left the room.

'So, what's the news?' asked Enrico. 'You don't phone home much. It upsets your mother. Now suddenly you do, so what's the beef?'

Rocco swallowed. This was very delicate, very embarrassing; he wasn't quite sure how to start.

'I've ... been having an affair,' he said.

Enrico looked at him. 'And this is news?'

Rocco paused. Both his elder brothers were married, and both had their fair share of little popsies on the side: it was expected. What the hell, they were men, weren't they?

'Cara found out about it,' said Rocco.

'And? You telling me you can't keep control in your own household, Rocco? Give her a sweetener or two and lay it on the line; you do what you do. Who's the man of the house, you or her?'

Rocco was sweating; this was even more difficult than he had imagined it would be.

'She found out and she had this person worked over – really badly – as a warning to me.'

Now he had Enrico's full attention. '*She* did?'

'Her name was mentioned when it happened.' *And so was mine,* he thought, but didn't say it.

Enrico paused for a beat. Then he picked up an olive and popped it in his mouth. Chewing, he looked at Rocco and said: 'Don't sound like any woman *I* know, to do that. And for sure this ain't Constantine.' Then he spat out the stone.

'We can't know that.'

Enrico gave a laugh. 'You kiddin'? I've known

that man thirty years. He's a good friend to this family. A thing like this, over his son-in-law having a little fun outside wedlock? He wouldn't stoop so low.'

'Cara wouldn't act without his approval.'

'You think so?' Enrico's old eyes stared at his son in disbelief. 'I think you're wrong. She's been over-indulged since her mother died – she's become too headstrong. I told you so when you married her, but would you listen? You would not. Now you see the sort of woman you married. She thinks she's too special to have her husband playing around. I did warn you. I *told* you you'd be pussy-whipped for the rest of your life if you married her.'

Rocco thought about that. His father was right; but it was Cara's looks that he had fallen for. He had been stricken by her blonde beauty and, before they married, she had curbed and con-cealed the worst excesses of her spoiled and dominating nature. Once they were wed, she had dropped her guard, let it show who was the boss; and that was *her*.

'Men have women on the side,' Enrico shrugged. 'We all do it. Why should the girl take offence at an affair? It don't affect her standing as your wife and that's what matters. You got to keep the wives sweet, Rocco, that's what I'm telling you.'

Rocco's heart was thumping in his chest. His mouth was dry. He knew Cara had taken the whole thing badly because it was a man he'd slept with; had it been a woman, she would probably have ignored the situation, even accepted and eventually maybe welcomed the focus of his sexual attentions being elsewhere.

'It... Papa, it wasn't a woman,' he managed to say.

Enrico was silent. The teams were rampaging around the pitch to the cheers and shouts of the crowd. Slowly, Enrico levered himself out of his armchair with an elderly grunt of effort. Then he leaned down and struck Rocco, very hard, across the face.

Rocco recoiled in pain and surprise. His cheek stung. He sprang up, furious.

Enrico looked him dead in the eye.

'Oh, you think you want to hit me back, uh?' he scoffed, his eyes running over his son with contempt. 'You ain't hard enough to even try it. Now I understand. You *deserved* that. And Rocco, you *deserved* to have your fag boyfriend worked over. I always *knew* there was something off about you, you little...' Enrico looked disgusted. He flicked his ear in the Italian sign for homosexuality. 'How's any woman going to take that, her husband playing away with another *man?* You know Cara's nature. And you're surprised she did this?'

Rocco was almost crying with humiliation. 'I think the Don himself ordered it,' he panted. 'If he knows, I'm as good as dead.'

'Yeah, maybe he did. For this? Maybe he'd feel his daughter had been insulted; maybe you're right.'

'Well, what are you going to do?' demanded Rocco.

'*Me?*' yelled back his father. 'I'll tell you what I am going to do: precisely *nothing*. You think I'd raise a hand against one of my oldest friends over a little fucker like you?'

Rocco's mother came into the room and stood just inside the door, looking anxiously from one to the other. 'What's going on here?' she asked.

'What's going on is that your milksop little baby has had his nose smacked and he don't like it. Well, he had it coming,' Enrico told her sharply. He turned to Rocco. 'Now get outta here. I got a game to watch.'

And he sat back down in his armchair and gazed once more at the screen.

Rocco's mother stood there, staring at her son. After a second, Rocco managed to get his legs working, and he pushed past her, out of the door, out of the house. He heard her concerned cry drift after him but he ignored it. He got in his car and drove back to the city.

His father was going to do nothing to help him – so what else was new? His father never had. Cara *must* have told the Don about this. After all, who among Constantine's soldiers would dare do her dirty work for her without first securing her father's permission? No one would do that, would they? No one would risk incurring Constantine's wrath by acting without his say-so. The Don *must* know. And if he knew then he was just waiting to pick Rocco off at his leisure.

# 19

Cara was shopping, as she often was, when the man with the scarf hiding the lower part of his face came up to her.

'Cara Mancini?' he asked, his voice muffled.

Cara was both startled and puzzled. How did he know her? He sounded English. And why the hell was he wearing a thick knitted scarf on a summer's day? He looked cloak-and-dagger, like a spy in one of the old movies. Now she wished she'd had Fredo come in with her today, but she hated his guts, hated him anywhere near her; she hadn't wanted him trailing after her.

'You're married to Rocco Mancini, that's right?' he said, and she was struck now by how attractive his clear grey eyes were, how thick and glossy his chestnut-coloured hair. But the scarf...

He saw her looking at it.

'Neuralgia,' he said, patting it. 'I'm a martyr to it, sadly. I'm an old friend of Rocco's. Can we go somewhere and talk for a moment?'

Cara suppressed an impatient sigh. She didn't want to sit somewhere with this weirdo and talk about the cheating yellow-bellied shit she was married to.

'Look, I'm sorry, but I really have to go.' She was moving past him, moving away.

He stopped her with a hand on her arm.

'Please,' he said desperately. With fumbling

fingers – two of them were no more than stumps, she noticed in horror – he pushed the scarf aside.

'Oh my God,' whispered Cara as she saw the puckered purple slits on either side of his mouth.

She pulled back, revolted. And then she thought, oh shit, it's him. It's Frances Ducane, that actor Fredo cut up, Rocco's lover.

All the blood left her face and she felt as if she was going to faint. He'd found out she'd instigated that. He knew she'd set Fredo on him. She started to pull away, to flee. He was going to hurt her, scar her too. She'd been through so much, had to tolerate Fredo pawing at her, sliming over her, and for what? Now it was all backfiring on her, it was all going bad. She opened her mouth to scream, but she was so terrified that she couldn't even draw breath.

'Please don't go,' said Frances, and something in his voice arrested her, made her freeze to the spot. She looked into his eyes, which were brimming over with tears.

'You see what he did to me?' he sobbed. 'You see what that son of a bitch Rocco had someone do, just because he'd had enough of me?'

Cara took a breath as his words sank in. He didn't think she was responsible; he was blaming *Rocco*.

Cara gulped in air, composed herself, tried to get her racketing heartbeat back under control.

'How could he have done anything so awful?' she demanded. 'Look, there's a café over there. Let's go get a drink, and you can tell me all about it...'

# 20

Annie Carter-Barolli was slipping on a pale blue silk shift in front of her dressing-table mirror. She turned sideways, slid a hand over her full belly.

'Shit,' she said as she glanced at her reflection.

'What's that for?' asked Constantine, coming through from the dressing room shrugging on his jacket, shooting his cuffs. His tie was hanging loose around his neck.

'I won't be able to wear even these slightly fitted things soon,' she sighed.

The day of Lucco Barolli and Daniella Carlucci's wedding had dawned bright and clear, as if the gods were smiling upon Long Island. The bride, with her mother, her sisters and her cousins, was up in the guest wing, putting the finishing touches to her ensemble. The house was in happy chaos, with the garden being set out for the ceremony with elaborate rose arches all the way up the pathway leading to the altar, where the priest would perform the ceremony. Small gold chairs had been set out in neat rows; florists were hurrying around. The caterers had arrived and taken over the kitchen. At the side of the house, long trestle tables were being covered in pink damask. Elaborate floral arrangements were placed down the centre to form a cascade of white, cream and lemon. The best silverware was being laid out with military precision; glasses were being polished by uniformed waiting staff until they sparkled in the sunlight.

By early afternoon the guests were taking their seats for the ceremony. As Annie checked her appearance, Constantine came and stood behind her, his eyes meeting hers in the reflection.

'You look beautiful,' he said. 'You'll look beautiful when you're as big as the side of a house, too.'

Layla came running in. She was wearing a long pink taffeta dress with a matching headdress of pink and white roses. She was going to be flower girl today, scattering rose petals beneath the feet of Daniella the bride. Her dark green eyes, an exact match for Annie's, shone with excitement. 'Mummy, I've lost my flower basket!'

The nanny, Gerda, a thin, solemn-faced Nordic blonde, came dashing in after Layla, looking embarrassed. 'I'm so sorry, Mrs Barolli. Come *on*, Layla, I know where it is.'

'You like my dress?' asked Layla, twirling around.

'Spectacular,' said Annie, and Layla sped off with her nanny.

The door closed behind them. Annie turned to Constantine with a slow smile. 'Do you think they'll be happy?' she asked, knotting his tie for him.

'Who? The bride, Layla...?'

'The couple.' Annie completed the knot and smoothed her hands down over his chest.

Constantine's mind was suddenly full of an image of Cara, in tears over the state of her marriage. He sighed. 'I hope so.'

'But you don't think so?' she asked.

He linked his arms around her waist, nuzzled her neck. 'I know you haven't found Lucco the easiest person to get on with.'

There was an unspoken world in that simple sentence. Lucco hated her: always had, always would. She tolerated him, no more than that. Constantine was no fool; he had seen the friction between them – he could scarcely fail to.

'I hope they'll be happy,' said Annie. *For Daniella's sake.*

'Have you considered the diplomatic corps as a career?'

'Since marrying you? About once a day.'

'We met on Cara's wedding day,' he said. 'You remember? In London.'

Annie thought of the grey rainy streets, the old Palermo club that was now called Annie's. She thought of Dolly running it, with Tony ferrying her around town, and Ellie in charge of the Limehouse knocking-shop where once she herself had reigned as queen. A hard pang of homesickness hit her. She was having a baby in a foreign country with a Mafia boss. Her friends were far away and her new husband's family had not welcomed her – well, Alberto had, but that was all.

Oh, she kept busy here. She was going to launch the club in Times Square next year, and meanwhile she saw to the running of this household, and to the elegant, sprawling New York penthouse by Central Park where she spent a greater part of her time when Constantine was busy. She'd made many acquaintances but no real friends. In fact, she felt she was viewed more as a temporary curiosity than a permanent fixture, accorded politeness and respect because she was Constantine's wife, certainly; but the warmth was only a veneer, not truly felt.

'I remember,' she said. London was a world away. *This* was her life now. She sighed and put her head against his chest. He kissed her hair, inhaling the clean, sweet scent of it.

'What?' he asked. 'Something up?'

'Nothing.' She looked up at him. She was the luckiest woman in the world. She had Layla; she had this stunning man in her bed; she was carrying his child; she had her own business interests – funded partly with Mafia money, but so what? – and she lived in comfort and security. What more could any woman want?

Constantine glanced at his Rolex. 'It's time we were downstairs,' he said. He turned her in his arms and kissed her mouth.

'Ruining my lipstick,' she complained against his lips.

'Yeah? Sue me,' he said, and kissed her harder.

# 21

Lucco made an impressive bridegroom. He was as smoothly, slickly handsome as always, his dark hair gleaming, his elegant bearing showing off his white jacket and bow tie to its best advantage. Daniella, an averagely pretty girl, looked almost beautiful today, her face flushed with happiness.

She had many gifts of money pinned to her bridal gown, in the Sicilian tradition.

'She looks gorgeous,' said Annie at one point to Cara as they were standing beside each other. 'So happy.'

Cara turned her head and gave a tight little smile to her stepmother.

'That won't last,' she said. 'Not with Lucco. She'll soon learn.'

Annie went to ask her what she meant – she thought she *knew*, anyway – but when she looked at her stepdaughter's face, Cara was staring across the garden at one of Constantine's men. Annie recognized him as one of several drivers who ferried the family around, a tall young man with a sullen look to him. Cara's face was set in an expression of extreme dislike. The young man – Annie thought his name was Fredo – gave a sneering half-smile in return.

Before Annie could speak again, Cara moved away. 'Stepmom,' said a male voice behind her.

Annie turned. It was Alberto. She smiled. Alberto was so like Constantine to look at; nothing like him in character. Constantine was an authoritarian with an edge of fire; Alberto was smoother and, if he had aggression – and she knew he must – it was more rigorously controlled than his father's.

'Stepson,' she greeted him.

He kissed her cheek. 'Having a good time?'

'Oh, spiffing.'

'*Spiffing?*' He laughed. 'What the hell does that mean?'

'It means great.' They stood side by side,

looking at the happy couple at the high table.

'Isn't she lovely?' marvelled Alberto, watching the bride. 'Just think of it – Lucco, married. You know what, that's scary. It'll be me next.'

'Anyone in mind?'

'Would you divorce Papa and marry me instead?'

'That's a tempting offer, but no, I don't think so.'

'Then I don't have anyone in mind.'

Annie smiled at him. She liked Alberto's ways. In business he was polite and efficient. In his social life, she had found him to be the same. When he had women in his life – and there had been a few – he treated them well and somehow always managed to part from them on good terms.

'Is Cara all right, do you think?' she asked him.

'Cara?' Alberto looked over to where Cara was now standing, deep in conversation with Aunt Gina. 'Why? Has she said something?'

'No, nothing at all. It's just a couple of times she's seemed ... I don't know, sort of upset.'

'She hasn't said anything to me. I think maybe Rocco and she have been going through a rough patch again. Happens a lot, believe me.'

That probably explained it. Or did it? Annie thought again of the look that had passed between Cara and the young driver. Sick and furious on Cara's part; sort of *gloating* on Fredo's.

'Well, better mingle,' said Alberto, and was off among the crowds again. He met up with Rocco. *And there's another miserable face,* thought Annie.

Rocco was more than miserable. He soon made

his excuses to get away from his brother-in-law. He was feeling too tense and unhappy to socialize, but he'd had to come today. It was expected of him; there was no way he could back out. Frances was making a thorough pest of himself. He'd only phoned at first, and then, when Rocco had blocked all his calls, he'd written letters, pouring out his heart, saying that he still loved Rocco, why had Rocco hurt him like that, why didn't Rocco love him any more?

Rocco certainly did not. He ripped up all the letters and didn't bother to reply. And *then* Frances had shown up at his door.

'What the fuck do you want from me?' he'd screamed at him, distressed by even *looking* at him.

My God, the *ugliness* of his face now. His mouth looked as though it reached his ears. There was purple mottled scarring, and the marks where the stitches had come out, and two of his fingers ended in stumps. Jesus, he was a mess!

'I wanted to see you. That's all,' said Frances, trembling with the force of his love and desire for this heartless son of a bitch.

'Well *I* don't want to see *you*,' said Rocco coldly. 'And I'm warning you...'

'*What?*' Frances couldn't believe it. The man he loved, the man he'd thought loved him, had defaced him, and was now threatening him again?

'You heard. Try to come anywhere near me again and you'll be sorry.'

Then, shaking, Rocco had slammed the door in that repulsive face. Frances had stayed there for almost half an hour, hammering on it, begging, crying, pleading. Rocco had stood there listening to it all, trembling all over, chewing his nails, wondering how the hell he could get rid of this *monster*.

But finally Frances had gone. And – so far – he hadn't come back. But Rocco's biggest fear was that he would. And he blamed his wife over and over in his mind, cursed her name, because *she* had caused this thing to be unleashed upon him – her and her father. As for his own father – well, nothing new there. His father didn't give *that* about him.

Annie saw that the light was going now. A cool evening breeze was coming in off the ocean. Gerda came over, ushering a tired-looking Layla in front of her.

'Say good night to your mama, Layla,' said Gerda.

'Night-night, Mommy,' said Layla, holding up her arms for a kiss and a cuddle. Annie happily delivered both.

'You had a good day, sweetie?' she asked, hugging her tight, inhaling the sweet scent of her skin.

'Yeah, good.' She grinned.

'I'll be up later to tuck you in, okay?'

The evening stars were winking on up in the blackening heavens. The mariachi band struck up and the bridal couple took to the floor to cheering and clapping. Other couples started to drift onto the dance floor. She saw Constantine in a huddle with several other men, talking intently.

She watched him, concerned. She'd heard the rumbles about the Cantuzzi clan; there had already been trouble. Shit, there was *always* trouble. But he seemed to handle it well; nothing ruffled

108

him. At least, nothing *appeared* to. Sometimes she found it hard to equate the two strands of his personality – the cool, controlling Don, and the tender, considerate husband. Sometimes he seemed like two different men entirely.

She went to slip upstairs but, as she passed the doors onto the terrace, she saw that there was no one out there. She went outside onto the decking, and was instantly enveloped in the rush and thunder of the ocean, the stiff breeze riffling through her hair. She walked to the edge of the terrace and looked over the deserted beach, breathing deeply of the fresh, tangy air. The presents were piled up on the table at the end of the terrace, ready for the Don to present them to the couple at ten o'clock.

God, she was tired! The pregnancy was taking a toll on her energy levels. She gripped the rail and looked up at the nearly full moon. It was so weird to think that men had walked up there; that *Apollo 15* was in orbit right now, gliding through space.

'Honey? What are you doing out here all alone?' asked a voice behind her.

'Just taking a moment,' said Annie, turning to smile at Constantine as he stepped out onto the deck and closed the French doors behind him. He looked at the pile of presents and picked up the one at the front of the table, the biggest, with a red bow over sky-blue paper. 'Hey, wonder what's in this one?' he asked, walking towards her.

Then her whole world exploded.

# Majorca

# 22

## February 1970

The first thing the man knew was pain. Pain, then blinding light. Something was moving through the light. Shapes. Maybe birds.

Buzzards?

They were circling overhead, like in an old Western movie when the gunman's been laid out to die by the Sioux or the Apache. He'd been laid out to die too, and die he would, because for sure he couldn't move. Everything was pain. Any movement – oh, and how he had tried to move – hurt like a bastard. So he'd just lie back and let it all unravel. He had decided that was the best thing to do. Let the buzzards come down and pick him clean. Get it over with. No more struggling, no more fighting.

Thoughts, though. His thoughts said move. His guts said move.

Couldn't. No good.

Images too, drifting through his brain. A shot. A man falling into the pool, a spreading stain of crimson tinting the water. A girl, screaming.

Move, you sod. Come on.

But his body wouldn't listen to the urgings of his mind. It said no. You kidding? Lie there and *die*, man, we are all out of alternatives.

His mouth was so dry. His lips felt cracked. The

sun was burning him. Burning him up. He closed his eyes.

Bells.

Tiny tinkling bells – now he was hearing things. Maybe this was what it was like, dying; maybe everything went blank, like his mind was blank right now. Why couldn't he think straight, what was wrong with him...? Maybe the blankness came first, and then the bells. They were getting louder. He'd be hearing heavenly choirs next and, frankly, that would be nice. He could just give up, and die.

But for now, it was just bells. Getting louder and louder. And now ... a little movement, a little wetness nudging at his neck. Something was there. An angel, must be. Bringing him water. He forced his eyes to open.

He looked into slitted eyes, devil's eyes.

Ah shit.

Not heaven then, and no angel coming to fetch him. He was bound for hell. This was an imp, a tool of Satan, here to bring him home to eternal damnation.

He tried to move again then, to protest, to say no, I've been a good man.

But ... had he?

He didn't know. Couldn't think. Again, there was that frightening blankness, pressing upon his mind like a white wall of fog.

The thing's face was brown, hairy. The eyes were yellow. The face loomed over him, terrifying. Leaned closer, closer, touched his neck again. Coldness, moistness. An icy brush of metal.

Bells.

A bell on the neck of the thing: jangling, deafening.

A groan escaped him and the thing twitched back, startled by the sudden noise.

A goat. He was looking at a goat, not a devil.

He could almost have laughed at that, if he'd had the strength. But he didn't. All he could do was lie there. Exhausted. Damaged. His eyes fluttered closed, and he hardly even heard the soft footsteps of the boy coming closer. Damned goat nudging him again. His eyes came open, the glare of the sun, buzzards, a nut-brown human face coming in close, blotting out the unbearable heat and light.

'¿Señor?' said the face. '¿Se cayó?'

He closed his eyes. He understood. *Did you fall?* the boy was asking him. But he couldn't answer. He didn't know. He didn't know anything.

The goatherd gave the man water, then went to alert the monks at the nearby monastery. The boy was shaking with fright because he thought that by the time he returned with the help of the brothers, the man might be dead. But, when they got there, the brothers having struggled and panted and sweated with effort as they traversed the uneven and, in parts, treacherous rocky ground, the man seemed still to be clinging to life, even though his injuries were horrendous.

The brothers looked him over while the boy watched them nervously. They'd brought a stretcher from the monastery's small sick room, but one look at the man – who wore nothing but a brief pair of swimming shorts – made them doubt he would survive the journey back up to the monastery.

Both ankles were shattered into bloody pulp.

His left arm was broken, the bone protruding through the skin, so bad was the break.

There was a deep, nasty-looking gash on his head. Flies buzzed there, feasting on the drying blood, laying their eggs in the open wound. His lips and the skin on his face were cracked from the extreme heat of the sun. He was feverish. God alone knew how long he had lain there on this precarious rocky platform above the sea, because the man was making no sense. He needed water, and shelter. And even then, the brothers warned his young rescuer, there was every chance that he would die.

'Be warned, child, he might not get through this,' one of them told him.

The boy, distressed, looked at the man. He had found him, rescued him. He felt an attachment for him, of course he did.

'I don't want him to die,' he told the monks.

'God may spare him,' they said, and they looked at the man and thought that perhaps it would be better if God took him. He looked athletic, fit; he would not, they felt sure, relish a half-life. And they could already see that, if he survived, he was going to live out the rest of his life as a cripple.

# 23

The monks had a long, hard and perilous job getting the man stretchered off the cliff and onto the nearest dirt track of a road. Once there, one of the younger brothers ran ahead to take the one battered old car the monastery possessed down to the village so that an ambulance could be called to take him to hospital in Palma. There was no phone at the monastery.

Brother Benito went with the poor wretch, who seemed to be drifting in and out of consciousness, murmuring foreign-sounding words under his breath.

'Who is he?' asked the medics.

'I don't know,' said Benito, his kind eyes watching as they attended the man. He was hot and dusty himself from the climb on the dangerously exposed rock face; he couldn't imagine what the man had gone through, lying out there in the boiling sun. For how long? That thought tormented him. To think of the man out there in agony for hours, perhaps even days.

It was a shame, but perhaps death would be a release for him. Brother Benito knew that death was hovering very close to this poor stranger; perhaps it would be a mercy if he was taken.

The medics were glancing at each other. The man seemed to be a foreigner from what he was babbling, and he had no clothes with him. Who was going to cover the cost of his care?

'The monastery will pay for his treatment,' said Brother Benito, seeing clearly where their thoughts were straying. He was a lost soul, poor man; it was an honour to play the Good Samaritan, to offer whatever little help might be of use.

The man's dark blue eyes were opening, and the medics hovered more closely over him, asking him who he was, where he was from.

The man's eyes stared at them with blank pain. Then, slowly, he said, in English, 'I don't know.'

His eyes closed again.

The medics looked at Brother Benito.

'He says he doesn't know,' the brother told them. Benito was a learned man; he spoke five languages, including English, which was clearly the man's native tongue. 'Perhaps the blow to his head or the lack of water has made him confused.'

They nodded. The man seemed to have lapsed back into unconsciousness; and Benito thought that those brief, bewildered words would probably be the last he ever uttered.

The man was in a very bad way; the doctors all agreed on this as they pored over the X-rays of his feet. They put him on a drip at first, because he was so severely dehydrated. When he occasionally regained consciousness, he seemed to have no idea who he was or where he came from. More X-rays were taken of his head, his ribs, his arms, his legs.

He'd suffered a severe blow to the head, but there were no fractures in his skull, no dangerous build-ups of blood pressing on the brain. Two ribs were broken but had – by good luck – punctured no soft internal organs. They would be strapped up, and would heal. His arm was a bad break but a clean one, and it was quickly set, plastered, sorted.

His ankles, however, were quite another matter.

The man was lucid sometimes, then suddenly not. Sometimes he was hearing the rapid Mallorquin tongue being spoken as the medics clustered around the end of his bed; sometimes he was not even aware they were there. He knew – from the snatches he heard – what they were saying, though.

It wasn't good.

One ankle was very badly broken. And the other – and here there were mutterings of *Madre de Dios* – the other ankle was so severely damaged that amputation might well be in order. There was little hope of this man ever walking again. Even after the necessary surgery, the outcome would be doubtful.

He heard that, but couldn't believe it. Not to walk again?

He closed his eyes, felt a spasm of intense fear. He couldn't feel the pain any more – they'd drugged him, he was sleepy and confused; and now he was also really, really afraid.

*Who the fuck am I?* he wondered. *How did I get here?*

But when he managed to ask a question, they just gave him some pile of shit about no damage to the temporal lobe of his brain, where language and memory were stored. They were more concerned with his ankle injuries.

*Jesus! Is this right what they're saying? Am I going to be a cripple?*

But they just smiled reassuringly at him when he asked that and, fuck it, he was anything but reassured. He wanted to leap up and shout, tell them they weren't making sense, but he couldn't. He felt limp with weariness. Then there was the light sting of a needle entering his arm, and he was being wheeled down corridors, passing lights, nurses walking alongside him, smiling reassuringly.

No, he wasn't reassured. They were going to cut his foot off, that was all he was sure of.

'Don't take it off,' he managed to mumble, feeling stupid, thick-mouthed, barely able to force the words out.

'*¿Qué?*' asked one of the smiling nurses.

'Don't smile at me, you cunt, just listen to what I'm saying, don't take my foot off,' he shouted, or at least he tried to shout, but it came out in low garbled English, and the nurse looked at him blankly, not understanding.

'Don't take off my foot,' he was still saying when he saw the big lights, the surgeons all gowned up, rows of gleaming silver saws and hammers lined up at the ready. A mask came down over his face.

'Don't–'

And then he was gone.

# 24

When he came round he was by a window, and the sun was beaming through onto the bed where he lay. He was very hot. He lay there drowsily for long moments, staring out of the dusty window, seeing rooftops, chimneys, a brilliant blue sky.

Then he remembered, and the fear clamped hold of him all over again.

Oh Jesus, his foot.

They'd cut it off.

He couldn't face it, not life as an invalid, not him.

He whooped in a panicky breath and felt the compression of his ribs beneath their robust strapping. He tried to sit up, but he couldn't: his arm was in plaster and he couldn't get a grip on anything. There were pulleys, ropes, things tying him to the bed.

He daren't look down. He couldn't. Some things were just too fucking awful to face head-on.

He kept his eyes on the rooftops, the blue sky. Easier to look out there. Pigeons soaring along, flying free. He envied them that. Here he was, tied to a bed, unable to move. He had a sense then that he was a very fit man in everyday life. His body was well-honed, muscular; obviously he looked after himself.

*Yeah, but who am I?* he thought again.

He didn't know.

Maybe he was just a miserable, stinking coward, because he couldn't look at what they'd done to him.

He ought to look. Whatever had been done was done, what was the point in averting his eyes?

He steeled himself. He was going to look. He had to look.

He looked.

Both feet were still there.

All the breath left him in a rush and a half-hysterical laugh burst from him as he stared at what they'd done to him in surgery. There were huge bolts through both his ankles – right through. The bolts protruded by three inches on either side of the mangled flesh of his feet. And hooked up to the bolts were pulleys, with weights attached. The weights were pulling his legs out straight, to prevent atrophy. The bed itself was sloping upwards at the end, so that his feet were higher than his head. It felt strange. And ... there was no pain.

After discovering he still had both his feet, that was the best part: no pain.

He lay back, and his eyes closed. He slept.

Brother Benito came in to visit.

'My friend, you look better,' he said in near-perfect English. Seeing the man's confusion at the arrival of this stranger he said: 'One of the goat boys found you on the rocks. I came with you to the hospital. Do you remember?'

The man in the bed didn't remember much at all. He just stared at his saviour. Brother Benito was a big man, dressed in plain, coarse monk's robes, with a tonsured head of grey hair, bushy white eyebrows and a big-featured, almost lumpish face. It was not a patrician face by any means; in fact, the monk looked if anything like an old trooper, battle-scarred and buffeted by wars, but his clear grey eyes were astonishingly gentle and good-humoured.

The man in the bed stretched out his one good hand. 'Thanks.'

Brother Benito shook it. He was surprised at the strength in the man's fingers. Here was a grip that could crush, easily.

'Who's paying for this?' asked the man. He hadn't been asked for cash and he was grateful for that – he didn't think he had any – but he was anxious that there was going to be a huge bill waiting for him upon his eventual departure from the hospital.

And then where would he go? He had no idea where he lived or what he did in life. His mind was as clear as a blank sheet of paper. How did he earn his living? He hadn't a clue.

'The brothers are paying,' said Brother Benito.

'I can't let you do that,' protested the man.

But Benito only smiled serenely. 'My son, it is our duty to help our fellow man. You needed help – you still do – and so it is an honour to provide whatever is needed.'

'You say you come from the monastery,' said the man. 'It can't be rich.'

'It is rich enough,' said Brother Benito.

'Then thank you again.'

The doctors were coming on their rounds, and the man asked that Brother Benito should stay

123

and hear what they said to him. Their faces were grave this morning. But why, he wondered? They'd done the work on his shattered ankles; now it was just a case of letting them mend – wasn't it?

They began to speak to him in Mallorquin and he understood them. Maybe this was progress; maybe the fog in his brain was going to clear soon. He knew he was English, and that he spoke Mallorquin too.

They asked him how he felt and told him that they had made an attempt to reassemble his ankles, but it was no more than that; he must prepare himself for the possibility that he would not walk again.

The man exchanged looks with the doctors and with Benito.

'You what?' he asked angrily.

They'd carved him up, turned him into something resembling Frankenstein's bloody monster, only to tell him that it was an experiment, a gamble, and one that probably wouldn't work?

'We have to prepare you for the worst,' said the doctor.

He was going to be in a wheelchair. He could see it in their eyes. What had they done all this for, the money? Bastards!

'Just fuck off the lot of you. Leave me alone,' he snarled.

The doctors left.

Benito remained in his chair.

'And what the fuck are *you* hanging around for? Piss off!'

Benito rose and quietly left the room. The man knew he'd seen the last of Brother Benito now.

He'd cursed, shocking him no doubt, and told him to get lost. Somewhere deep inside himself he knew that he wasn't good enough for such a holy man to bother with anyway.

He turned his face away from the sun, unable to bear the sight of the sky and the free, swooping birds, while he was in here, confined, calling for bedpans, having to pee in a bottle, having no more power or say in anything than a babe in arms; trapped within his own ailing body.


# 25

The physiotherapist came by a month later. She was a large, brown-eyed brunette in a white uniform, and she told him that now the healing process was under way, they would devise a programme of exercises to strengthen his ankles.

The man gazed at her with cynicism. Why were they going through the motions like this, attempting to deceive him? He knew he wasn't going to walk again, that all he had to look forward to was a half-life: why were they tantalizing him with false hopes?

'Fuck off,' he told her.

Her olive skin flushed brick red, and she quickly left the room.

Next morning, the doctors came again. 'So,' they said, 'you are not even going to try to help yourself get better?'

The man gazed at them with dark, steel-blue eyes. He was an imposing man, they thought, with his blue-black hair, his piratical hook of a nose, his grim, determined mouth. He didn't seem at all intimidated by them, as some people were.

'What's the point?' he flung back at them. 'You've told me I'm not going to walk again. What the hell's the use of exercises to me?'

'There is always hope,' said the doctor.

'Piss off out of it.'

The doctors left. Days dragged past and turned into weeks. The man didn't eat, he was too sick at heart for that. All his meals were sent back. The nurses bathed him, attended to his needs, adjusted the weights on his ankle, but he was detached, uninterested. Then, finally, bored to tears, he saw the tall brunette physio passing by his half-open door.

'Hey!' he called out to her. 'You!'

She stopped and came into his room, her pretty face blank with dislike.

'What's your name?' he asked.

For a moment she just stared at him, not speaking. Then she said, coldly: 'Marta. Did you want something?'

'Yeah,' he said. 'Show me some of these bloody exercises, Marta. I'm sick to death of lying here like a fucking invalid.'

She showed him how to flex his ankles against the weights on the pulleys. The left was not too bad. Just about bearable, at least. But the right was agony. After the surgery, there had been no pain. Now, there was pain so intense he felt sweat break out on his brow.

126

'Jesus!' he complained.

'A little pain, a little gain.' She shrugged.

The woman was obviously a sadist.

'Keep doing that. Fifty on each ankle,' she said, and left him to it.

She came the next day. His ankle had throbbed like a bastard all night, keeping him awake. He always refused sleeping pills; he hated the damned things. He felt confined, bitter, furious at the world, and even more furious with his brain, which refused to give him any information whatsoever about who he was, or how he had come to be here on this big Spanish island.

'How do you feel?' she asked, watching him steadily.

'How do you think?' he snarled.

'Do you know, there are people in here *dying* who are politer than you,' she said.

'Yeah? Well go and harass those poor bastards, then.'

She left. At the door, she paused. 'Fifty,' she said. 'Both feet.'

He did a hundred, groaning and swearing and sweating through the agony of it. In the afternoon, he awoke from a restless doze and found Benito sitting at his bedside.

'Oh,' he said rudely, wincing as the pain hit him again. 'You.'

'How are you?' asked Brother Benito.

'Fucking wonderful. There's this girl keeps coming in here saying give me fifty, and then I feel like my feet are going to drop off.'

'You need to work at it, to get better.'

The man glared at the monk. Whatever you

said to this god-botherer, you couldn't seem to shake him. 'Look, I thought I told you to *fuck off.*'

'So you did.' Benito smiled. 'Yet here I am, back again.'

'So take the hint and do one.'

'Is there anything I can bring you next time I call?' asked the brother, standing up with a serene smile.

'Yeah. Whisky.'

Benito frowned. 'I don't want to save your feet at the expense of your liver.'

'Then don't fucking well bother,' snapped the man, turning away.

Benito brought the whisky. It was cheap, raw stuff, almost bitter, but it helped dull the pain. The man did the physio day after tortured day, sweating and cursing, and then drank the whisky at night so that he could sleep.

After six months, the agony began to ease. After seven, it was manageable; he could sleep without the deadening effect of the liquor. After eight, two nurses came and said it was time for the bolts to be removed. They removed the left one okay, but the right one had fused itself to the healing bone.

'Fuck's sake,' he said, irritated by their fluttering efforts.

He reached down and yanked the thing. They squawked out objections. A moment of searing agony, and the bolt was out. He felt like he'd pulled out most of his flesh with it. He looked at the metal bolt lying, bloody, on the sheets, and felt a surging upswell of sickness. He fell back onto his pillows, panting.

They cleaned the exit wounds on either side of his ankle, bandaged them, then cleared away all the paraphernalia of pulleys and levers. They cranked the bed down so that the bottom of it was no longer elevated, but flat.

'Whoa,' said the man, clinging to the edges of the thin mattress. 'You've tipped it too far, I'm going to slip out the bottom.'

'You're lying flat,' they said.

'No I'm bloody not.'

'Yes you are. You've been tipped up for so long, it just feels as if you're tipping downwards now. You're not.'

After that, they left him alone.

Next day, Marta was back.

'Fuck's sake,' he moaned. He'd had a rotten night again: he'd felt the whole time as if he was going to slide straight off the end of the bed; the pain had been extreme – and where the hell was Benito? He needed more whisky.

The physio looked at him with jaded eyes. 'Today we step it up to a hundred flexes,' she told him. 'And tomorrow we get you out of that bed.'

'Bitch,' he muttered, but the prospect of getting out of bed was tantalizing.

That was, until he tried it.

When he lowered his feet to the floor they went blue, then black, then brilliant red as the blood surged back into them. He screwed his face up and endured it as the pins and needles danced under the skin of his feet like a marauding army of soldier ants.

'Shit a brick,' winced the man, sitting on the edge of the bed and wondering what had hit him.

His head spun with the shock of being semi-upright. His feet were acutely painful. His newly healed ribs throbbed. So did his left arm and his head.

'Easy, yes?' asked Marta with a teasing light in her eye. She was holding a pair of crutches.

'Piece of piss,' he said, sweating with the pain of it. Still, he almost smiled back at the bossy cow. She wasn't so bad after all. And she had a *terrific* arse on her.

'Now, you walk,' she said, and held out the crutches.

But they'd said he wouldn't walk again.

He looked at the crutches. He reached out and took them from her, tucked them under his arms. 'This is a waste of time,' he told her.

'Walk,' she repeated firmly.

He levered himself to his feet. Felt instantly giddy, unreal. The weight hit his feet and they throbbed out a hot, heavy complaint. He gasped and stood there, supported by the crutches, swaying a little, wondering if he was going to pass out.

'Walk,' she said again.

'Oh hell, all right,' he muttered, and gingerly put one foot in front of the other. It hurt. He stepped forward again, and again. The pain was excruciating. 'Fuck that,' he shouted, and threw the crutches aside in sudden, impotent fury. Having done that, he collapsed to the floor in an ungainly heap.

'*Shit!*' he bellowed.

He wasn't going to be able to walk again, what the hell was she tormenting him like this for?

'Patience,' said Marta, bending and putting his

arm across her robust shoulders. She started to haul him upright again. With her help, he was able to flop back onto the bed. 'We'll try again tomorrow.'

# 26

They tried the crutches again the following day, and the day after that. On the fourth day he fell sprawling to the floor, every cramped and aching muscle screaming a protest. The physio simply helped him up and said: 'Again.'

Within a fortnight he was able to make it to the door. For the next two months he stomped along the hospital corridors. Brother Benito came back several times, bringing whisky and that benign, infinitely tolerant smile.

'Didn't I already tell you to fuck off?' asked the man.

'I believe you did,' said Brother Benito. 'But you didn't mean it,' he added, and sat in the chair in the man's room with almost Buddha-like patience, until the man had completed his physio for the day and returned to his bed to rest.

'That bitch,' complained the man when Marta had left, promising more torment tomorrow. 'What the hell's the point of all this? I'm never going to walk, the doctors said so.'

'Indeed,' said Brother Benito, and handed him the whisky.

A month after that, she presented him with a flat circular board about two feet in diameter, with a six-inch plastic ball set in the centre.

He was walking with two sticks now. It was painful, laborious, but he no longer needed the crutches. He stared at the board with extreme suspicion. Marta had no doubt contrived yet another way to torture him.

'What is it?' he asked, as she sat on the side of the bed next to him.

'Balance board,' she said. 'It's going to strengthen your ankles.'

It did. It hurt like hell, but it did. Now he was down to one stick, stomping along the corridors with the physio at his side, saying, faster, come on, *faster*.

It was a relief to get back to his room, back to his bed, sip some of Brother Benito's whisky, and rest.

'You're a slave driver,' he complained, flopping back onto the pillows while Marta put his sticks neatly in the corner by the door.

He watched her. She had a slender waist and good breasts beneath the unflattering concealment of the white uniform. Her thick dark hair was neatly tied back into a ponytail. She turned, caught him staring at her arse and went red.

She came over to the bed where he was sprawled out. 'How's your memory coming along?'

'Badly,' he said, his half-smile dying on his lips. He still could remember nothing. And it worried him. How was he ever going to get back into the world if he didn't know who he was? The doctors had said there was no neurological reason for this blankness where his memory should be; their suggestion was that some psychological rather than physical trauma – maybe the shock of the fall? – had triggered the loss of his memory.

'It will come back,' she said. 'When it's ready.'

She touched his hand. He grasped her fingers, twined his into hers. She didn't pull away.

'Shut the door and come and sit down here, Marta,' he said.

Marta went and closed the door and came and sat on the side of the bed. The man leaned forward, grasped the back of her glossy dark head, and kissed her, snaking his tongue into her mouth.

'Oh,' she murmured against his lips, but once again she didn't pull back. Her tongue met his and played with it.

After a few seconds she did pull away, and he let her.

'We shouldn't,' she said, her cheeks red now, her eyes bright.

'Why not?' asked the man. 'We both want to.'

He kissed her again, trailing his hand down from the back of her head over her collarbone and down to the buttons on the uniform. He unfastened them quickly as he kissed her, pushed the edges of the coat back, then he drew back a little.

She was wearing a thin, blue-sprigged summer dress. More buttons, running all the way down. He undid these, too; a black sensible bra and panties underneath. It was like trying to break into a fortress, but somehow he did remember how this was done. He leaned in again, kissing her more deeply, his hands busy unfastening the bra behind her back. She had pale skin on her belly, and a few moles here and there, like beauty spots.

133

The bra came loose and her heavy breasts fell free of their confines, her large dark nipples already hard with desire. The man brushed his hands admiringly over them and she cried out. His hands dropped to the pants. She lifted her hips and he quickly got rid of them. A thick black bush there, hugely erotic to him. He felt his cock stir to new heights at the sight of it.

*When did I last have a woman?* he wondered. He didn't know. He didn't know anything except that he needed this now.

Sitting on the edge of the bed, he pulled her across him so that she was straddling his lap. He freed himself, paused long enough to kiss and lick her nipples, then guided his cock up into her cavernous wetness. She was hot and panting now, and he was desperate for this, rock-hard with lust.

He thrust crazily into her, holding her tight in his arms, lifting her so that her thighs slapped against his belly in a rocking motion as his penis plunged in and out of her. He wanted it to last, it felt so good, but it couldn't; it had been a long time since he last did this, he knew that, and his orgasm was approaching, stealing over him, making him shudder and gasp with delight.

'I'm not on the pill,' she gasped, her arms around his neck, her lips beside his ear.

He did the decent thing and withdrew – not that he wanted to. The hot pulse of his loins told him orgasm was just a beat away, and almost the instant he pulled out of her he came. In the same split-second of orgasm there was another woman in his head. Dark-haired like this one, but not merely pretty: beautiful. This woman was thinner and with larger, tauter breasts. He saw her face in a sudden flash – serious dark green eyes, sculpted cheekbones, a wide, laughing mouth ... and then it was gone.

They stayed like that for several long moments, breathless; then Marta flipped her leg back over, picked up her panties from the floor, set about refastening her bra. She rebuttoned her dress, then her uniform. Then she stood there and stared down at him.

'So, who were you fucking?' she asked, her mouth curved in a cynical half-smile.

'What?'

'Who was it?' she asked. 'It certainly wasn't me.'

Again, he saw her. Green eyes dark as tourmalines. Thick, flowing, cocoa-brown hair. Who the hell was she?

He stared at Marta, hardly even seeing her. *Who was that woman...?* Marta's face was thunderous.

'I don't know,' he said. He didn't. It was the truth.

She slapped his face, hard, and stormed from the room.

After that, it was strictly business with her. She was cold with him, remote; and he accepted that. He mastered the balance board with an effort, and walked the corridors with his sticks, sweated through the physio, ate, grew stronger – wondered what the hell was going to happen to him when the day came that he had to leave hospital.

But Benito had an answer for that. The doctors were talking about how pleased they were with him now, that his memory should return to him given time, that he had made a most remarkable recovery – but they couldn't let him out of hospital unless he had a home to go to, and someone to care for him as he completed his recuperation.

'Of course you must come and stay at the monastery,' said Brother Benito.

The man looked at the brother, sitting there as he had so many times before, patient, kind; he remembered that this was the man who had in all probability saved his life, who had taken no notice of his surly refusal to accept comfort and companionship, who had come back again and again and again, with whisky and quiet conversation, when all he got in return was anger and abuse.

'I couldn't do that,' said the man. He stared at the monk. 'You know, I don't know a damned thing about you, do I? Except that you saved my life. Have you *always* been like this?'

'Like what?'

'Kind. Giving your arse away, taking nothing in return.'

'Ah! No.' Benito was smiling, lighting up his craggy features. 'I wasn't always one of the brothers, you know. Once I was a bastard.' His eyes twinkled with mirth as he said it. 'Just like you.'

The man was intrigued. 'A bastard? You? Come on.'

'Oh yes.' Now the smile drained from Benito's eyes and they looked sad. 'I was a soldier once. A Falangist volunteer. I fought in the Battle of Majorca during the civil war in Thirty-six. We drove the Republicans back into the sea.' He

136

paused. 'We won.'

'You say that as if you *lost*.'

'What I lost then, my friend, was my taste for bloodshed. I saw things ... terrible things. And did them too. We won, yes – but at such a cost.' Benito shook his head and then brightened again. 'So come and stay with us. No one will bother you. You'll be left in peace. I promise.'

'I couldn't.' Benito had already done so much.

'Oh? Why not?' Brother Benito looked at him. 'Where else would you go? The doctors won't release you until they are certain you can manage alone, and, to be honest, you can't. You need somewhere to stay so that you can recover properly. The hard work's done, now it gets easier. Accept the invitation. Come and stay.'

The man stirred uneasily in the bed, aware that he owed the brothers an enormous debt of thanks. And what choice did he have? He had no idea where his home was; all he could do was wander the streets if he turned down the offer. And he had been churlish enough to this good man, he knew that.

'Then ... thanks,' he said.

And it was agreed.

# 27

The monastery was a haven of calm, perched high upon the edge of the Tramuntana mountains where they dipped down to the sea. As the monks went about their daily business of prayer and work, the man started to walk outside the monastery walls, going further and further every day.

Nurtured by good food and sunshine, he grew strong. Months passed peacefully by and he felt shielded from the world, content with his lot, sheltered within the cosy rhythms of this spiritual hideaway. The endless cycle of prayers and the daily singing of the choir in the little Renaissance church were a soothing backdrop to his daily life. He even threw aside the sticks and walked unaided, wearing shorts and a thin shirt, which he stripped off when the day grew too hot.

His ankles still gave him some pain; occasionally, one or the other would lock solid, and he had to sit down in the pink Mallorquin dust and swear and groan until the crisis past. But he persevered, and grew fitter, until finally he was able to jog along the precipitous pathways with the ocean crashing onto the rocks far below him. When he was able to do that, he knew that his body was back to normal.

But his mind ... that was another matter. It frustrated him badly, the weird flickering images that drifted in and out of his brain. The dark-eyed woman. An occasional feeling of urgency, of tension – as if he had missed something vital, that there was something he had to do ... but what? He didn't know.

'Come into the town with me, I'm going to get provisions and go to the bank,' said Benito often, but the man always refused. He felt safe in the monastery, as he had in the hospital. The world could not intrude here.

He said no so many times that, finally, Benito's patience snapped.

'There's a word for this,' he said.

'For what?'

'For what you've become. It's institutionalized.'

'What?'

Benito was looking at him sternly as they stood in the garden. The man had been digging up vegetables for dinner, he was happy – why wouldn't Benito take the hint and piss off?

'First you wanted to stay in the hospital.'

That was true enough; he had.

'Now you're barely going outside these walls except to walk alone. You've been living here for a year my friend. You can't hide away from the world like this.'

The man stared at his friend and saviour. 'Are you saying you want me to go?' He felt hurt and angry at this unexpected attack.

'No. What I am saying is that you must start to get back into the real world. For the sake of your health. That's all. So next time I ask you to join me, just come. All right?'

Benito left him alone. But the following week

he came back.

'I'm going down to the town,' he said. 'Come with me.'

'I'm busy,' said the man. Benito was right and he felt ashamed but he *did* feel apprehensive about venturing out.

'No you're not. So you're coming.'

It wasn't a request, it was an order.

'Well fuck *you*,' said the man. But Benito was right. This was ridiculous. 'Start the bloody motor up,' the man said. 'I'll get washed. Ten minutes, okay?'

The first time out was the worst, but after that he did sometimes go with Benito when he went down to the nearest small town. He drove a battered, wheezing old Renault; it looked as if the journey back up might kill it stone dead. Benito always went on market day to get provisions and do any banking.

At first, the crush of people and the noise felt strange to the man. But Benito moved confidently among the stalls, filling bags, chatting to the stallholders while the man held back, uneasy among this teeming mass of life. He was usually glad when they got back to the car and started back up to the monastery; but every time he accompanied Benito on these trips, he felt a little more comfortable with it all.

This particular day, he was sitting there in the rickety passenger seat of the old car as Benito drove them back up to the monastery after their shopping expedition, when he had another flashback; vivid and sudden. He saw himself in the back of a sleek black motor, and someone else was driving him.

It was there, and then it was gone.

'I think I'm starting to remember things,' he told Benito.

Benito glanced at him with a cheerful smile. 'Are you? Like what?'

'There's a woman,' he said. 'And a car.'

'That's good. Don't force it, my friend. Let it happen as it will.'

*As if there's anything else I can do,* thought the man gloomily.

They turned a sharp bend in the road, and the way ahead was blocked. There was a fallen cork oak lying across it. Benito wrenched on the handbrake and turned off the engine.

'Look at that! Sometimes this happens, they just die of old age.' Benito got out of the car and walked towards the fallen tree. 'Come on, I'll need a hand with this,' he said.

But the man held back. The oak hadn't been there to impede their passage down the mountain, but now here it was. The man looked at the base of the trunk of the tree; to his eyes it looked as if someone had hacked at it to give it a helping hand.

He felt tension take hold of him, some sixth sense telling him something was wrong with this. The man knew that Benito made this journey every week on the same day and at the same time. And if he knew it, maybe others knew it too.

Warily, he got out of the car. Brother Benito was already standing beside the oak, pulling up his cumbersome robes to get a good grip on the thing and heave it out of the way.

141

'Benito...' said the man, moving forward, looking left and right, wanting to say: Wait; be careful.

Then two men emerged from the shrubbery on their right.

*Fuck it,* thought the man. Benito had seen them too – and the man could see that he was instantly thinking the best of people, as he always did; that these kind strangers had been passing and were now going to help them move the obstruction.

'You need help, Brother?' shouted one of the men, moving forward, his grin a bit too wide, a bit forced.

'Thank you, we do,' said Benito, and then he bent over the oak and one of the men, young and wearing a sweat-stained red shirt and shorts, ran forward and struck him across the head with a branch. Benito fell forward.

The other one, who looked older, his dark hair flecked with grey at the temples, wearing a torn grey vest and jeans, was watching the man, who had started forward with a warning shout just before Benito was hit. The older one pulled out a knife.

The man came from the car at a run, straight at him, then he stopped a yard away, his eyes on the knife. Grey Vest grinned, and lunged, expecting the man to fall back. Instead, he jumped forward, catching the arm with the knife in both of his hands, then launched himself furiously at Grey Vest, hitting him square in the nose with his forehead.

Grey Vest staggered back, blood pouring down his face. The man dug his elbow hard into his solar plexus and when he started to topple he kicked his knee and heard a satisfying crunch as it broke. Grey Vest screamed with agony and dropped the knife.

The man picked it up; Benito's young red-shirted attacker was running at him now with the stick raised. He threw the knife, and it thwacked hard into the join of the man's elbow. He shrieked and fell to the ground, the stick bouncing away from him, The man came in fast and kicked him in the groin.

*Get them down and keep them down,* shot into his brain. He turned, ready to inflict more damage. The two men were grovelling in the dirt now.

*Finish them.*

He yanked the knife free of Red Shirt's arm. Red Shirt yelled, cursed, but the man ignored him. With the dripping knife in his hand, he stepped towards Grey Vest.

'My friend!' Benito was there by the oak, tottering a little on his feet, clutching at his bruised head. 'No! Don't. Enough.'

The man paused, breathing hard. Looked at the two writhing men, looked back at Benito. 'Are you all right?' he asked after a couple of beats. The blood was singing in his ears. He *wanted* to hurt them.

'Just a sore head,' said Benito, but he looked ashen.

'Get back in the car, in the passenger seat, I'll drive,' said the man.

He glanced at the knife in his hand, then at the two men who were watching him with abject fear and anguish in their eyes. Suddenly he hurled the knife out over the cliff. Then he approached the oak and, keeping a careful eye on their fallen assailants, he grunted and lifted the thing to the side of the road.

He went back to the car, got in.

'But what about...' began Benito, his anxious eyes on the two men, still prone in the dust.

'They'll live,' said the man roughly. 'Not that they deserve to. Benito, you have to vary the days for your trips to the town. Don't just go down on market days, it's not safe. And always make sure you have someone else with you, an escort, all right? Take more care.'

Benito was staring at him. There was a large blue lump coming up on his tonsured head. He seemed shaken, but not – thank God – badly hurt. 'Um, my friend?'

'Yeah, what?' He was restarting the engine, shoving the gear into first, taking off the handbrake. The car started to move, past the men, up the mountain road once more.

'My friend ... you're driving. Did you know you could drive?'

The man took a breath. Seemed to become aware. He flashed a shaky grin at Benito.

'No, I didn't. But obviously I can.'

'So ... you can drive, and you remember a woman, and a black car...'

'A Jaguar,' said the man suddenly.

'A Jaguar.' Benito nodded, then winced and clutched at his head.

'You all right?'

'It's nothing; it was just a glancing blow. I turned away just as he struck me.' Benito was still staring at his companion.

'What?' asked the man.

'You seem to know how to defend yourself. With more force than is strictly required.'

'He had a knife.'

'Still ... you broke his leg.'

'How can you know that?'

'I heard it snap.'

'Ah. Well, he deserved it,' said the man, grim-faced as he steered the car up the dusty road.

Benito was still watching him. 'You have a talent for violence.'

'Maybe I'm a soldier,' said the man. 'Like you used to be.'

'Do you think that's what you are?'

The man thought about it. 'No. I don't.'


# 28

Several times when he was running along the pathways in the mountains, he glimpsed a boy herding goats, and he wondered if this might be Jaime, the boy who had found him and, with Benito's help, saved his life. He tried to get near enough to find out, but it was difficult; Jaime was as agile as the goats he herded, and always seemed to be away in the distance, inaccessible. This had become the norm: spotting the boy but being unable to do more than raise a hand to him and have him raise a hand in return. So when he rounded a bend in the track one day and came face to face with the boy and his goats, he was both surprised and delighted. He slowed to a walk, then a stop.

'Are you Jaime?' he asked with a grin.

The boy nodded warily.

The goats milled around the man, nudging his legs with their hard little noses.

'You found me,' said the man, pointing. 'Right down there somewhere. Didn't you?'

Jaime's darkly tanned face split in a bright, white smile. 'It's you!'

'Yeah, it's me. I want to thank you.'

Jaime was shaking his head in wonder. 'You look so different! So ... better.'

'I have you to thank for that.'

'*De nada.*' It's nothing.

'Can you show me the spot? The exact place where you found me?' He wanted to see it; maybe it would jog some hidden memory, who knew?

'*Sí,*' said Jaime, and headed off down the path to where it grew rockier, more difficult to traverse. The man felt his freshly healed ankles twinge in reproach as he scrambled after the boy, going off the main path and out over the crashing dark blue ocean to a small ledge.

At last, Jaime stopped, pointed. 'Here. Here is where I found you.'

The man looked at the place where he had almost lost his life. It was a narrow ledge, rocky, treacherous. If he had fallen from above, he could so easily have missed it altogether, and gone straight down onto the rocks and then into the ocean far below.

'Do you think you fell, *señor?*' asked Jaime, holding up an arm to squint against the sun.

'Must have done,' said the man.

'From right up there, at the top,' said Jaime. 'You think?'

'Maybe.'

The man looked up too; the sun dazzled him. He raised an arm, peered upwards. He thought he could see a low wall, way up there above the crags and rocky outcrops, but the blinding intensity of the light made it difficult to be sure.

'What's up there?' he asked Jaime.

'I never go up that far,' said Jaime, shrugging.

The man decided right then and there that he would.

It was days later when he managed to find the time to go up the track where it continued into the more mountainous terrain beyond the monastery. He was busy helping the brothers with the digging in their vegetable garden, wanting to pay them in kind since he had no other way to earn his keep.

When he got a spare hour or two and the brothers were at prayer, he washed, slipped on clean shorts and a shirt, and started walking up the track. It was a hot day, baking; the heat haze shimmered on the rough road ahead of him. One of his ankles gave a twinge, but behaved itself. He breathed in the fresh mountain air and felt liberated, at peace as he strode along. Yet still there was that niggling feeling of suppressed urgency, of something missing, something that should be found.

It took nearly three-quarters of an hour to reach a closed set of intricately fashioned, high wrought-iron gates. They were padlocked and there was a thin strand of barbed wire across the top of them. He stared at the gates; seemed in some unplumbed part of his brain to know them. He looked to left and right. All was still and silent. A lone buzzard circled lazily overhead, but no other living thing disturbed the peace of the place. He was alone.

The man took off his shirt and threw it over the top of the gates, then scrambled up and – using his shirt as protection against the barbs – levered himself over the top and down the other side.

He pulled the shirt down, put it back on and started to walk down the driveway. Into his brain, sharp as the scent of lemons, drifted a name: Rufio.

There was a small gatehouse on his left.

Rufio lives here, he thought. With ... with *Inez*.

Now he had a picture in his mind of Rufio, middle-aged and beaming smiles in all directions, shinning up the date palms with his machete to make them neat and pristine every year.

And Inez ... gently smiling Inez, gabbling away in fast Mallorquin while she prepared lunch for ... but there the memory stopped.

He paused by the little *finca*. *Jesus, I know the people who live here. Rufio and Inez.*

He stored the names away like a pirate storing treasure, adding them to the bank of memories – the luxurious Jaguar car, the beautiful dark-haired girl – that he was beginning to accumulate.

Then he stepped onto the terrace under the rickety old pergola at the side of the *finca*. A vivid magenta bougainvillea was tumbling over the tired-looking structure, shading the terrace beneath it. After a moment's hesitation, he tried the old door, which was painted a faded sky-blue. It was locked.

'Hello?' he called, and knocked on the door.

Only silence answered him.

A car – shouldn't there be a car? Rufio had driven one, he somehow knew that, but he couldn't remember the make. There was no car here. He stepped out from the terrace and walked on down the drive, each step giving him the weird feeling that he had trodden this path before, that everything about it was familiar ... and yet now so strange.

There was a big villa down here, way down around a bend in the drive, hidden from the track. As he approached it he could hear the rush and suck of the sea far off down the mountain-side. He could see the big freeform swimming pool, which was empty of water. He stepped onto the terrace between the villa and the pool, looked at the four sun beds set out so neatly. All empty. The whole place was empty. There was no one here, except him.

Suddenly he felt dizzy. He sat down on one of the beds, clutching his head. Images swirled into his brain with nauseating force. He looked up, his eyes watering, across the empty pool to where there was a low wall. He staggered to his feet and went over there, looking over the wall at the rocks below, the sea battering them far down there at the base of the cliff.

*A big man, very strong, dark eyes. Implacable. Set on killing him.*

There had been two of them, grabbing him, throwing him over. His hands clutching wildly at the wall, his feet dangling in space. Heavy feet crushing his fingers so that he fell ... and fell ... and fell.

He remembered the fall. Oh shit, he remembered the fall. Hideous, never-ending. And then the impact; the bone-crushing collision of flesh on rock. Shattering pain shooting up his arms and his legs, and then blackness followed by hours of baking, merciless sun. How long had he lain there? He couldn't even guess.

The world spun. He sat down on the wall. Looked around him. The pool house, there had been a pool house, but now it was missing. There had been an explosion. Screaming. A shot. More pictures thundered into his mind, a crazy ghost-whirl of faces and scenes and bodies. A blonde girl, shrieking. And...

He sank his head into his hands and a loud sob escaped him.

Jonjo.

*His brother.*

Jonjo had died here. He could see now how it had been: the shot fired, the red flower blooming between Jonjo's rapidly glazing eyes. Screams and shouts and a child singing a French song.

The man stiffened and shot to his feet. A child, there was a child, a girl, his girl.

*Layla.*

He looked around him wildly, his cheeks wet with tears. 'Layla!' he roared at the top of his voice.

And there was a woman. There was that woman again, in his brain. He half fell and half ran over

150

to the door of the villa and beat upon it with his fists.

'Annie!' he shouted.

Then he stopped hammering at the door and stood there, amazed, staring at the tiles of the terrace and thinking, with total clarity, *Annie Carter*. My wife. Layla. My daughter. My brother, Jonjo, and there was a blonde with him.

And I ... oh fuck, I'm Max Carter.

*'I'm Max Carter!'* he shouted to the uncaring world.

He wasn't a soldier, although commanding troops was meat and drink to him. He knew who he was, he knew where he'd come from. He thumped the door again, uselessly. He knew there was no one here. But they should be here ... shouldn't they?

But time had passed. So much time.

*What the fuck happened?* he wondered crazily.

Annie, Layla and the blonde.

The men had killed Jonjo. They thought they had killed him, too. The blonde? Who knew? The little girl, his daughter, Layla ... where was she?

And Annie. The woman was there in his mind again, beautiful, alluring ... *his* woman. And where the hell was she? What could have happened to her? Over two years had passed, so now where was she? Where was his child?

With a bellow of rage and frustration, he shoulder-charged the door.

# 29

Inside the villa it was so cool, so quiet. Every step he took filled him with an eerie sense of déjà vu. He knew this place; he had lived here. He could be blindfolded and he would know where the kitchen, the bathroom, the bedroom was.

It was to the master bedroom that he went first, pausing inside the door to stare at the double bed. Images again. His body locked in love with a woman, his wife: Annie.

He went over to the bed and sat down on the side of it, running a shaking hand over the re-membered silkiness of the purple bedspread. The colour was familiar too, he knew it; knew how luminous her skin looked against its jewel-like darkness.

He sat there and thought about all the time that had passed. In February 1970 he had been thrown to his death. Now it was 1972. *So much time*. Where was she? Had the men killed her, killed Layla? If they hadn't, if she was somewhere whole and well with his child, had she searched for him and been unable to find him?

There was so much he didn't know.

He reached out for the drawer on 'his' side of the bed. There would be...

There would be a gun in there. An old Smith & Wesson revolver, with a box of bullets.

It wasn't there.

Keys too. There should be keys, and a ring – he remembered the ring he had worn now, gold with Egyptian cartouches on either side of a square slab of lapis lazuli.

The keys weren't there. Neither was the ring.

Had the men taken all that? Robbed them, killed them all – and believed they had killed him, but by some miracle they had failed to succeed in that.

*Annie and Layla could be dead.*

He faced that, felt a howl of anguish building at the back of his throat even at the thought.

He got to his feet, went over to the wardrobes. Empty.

He slammed them shut again.

Robbers, killers.

He pushed the thought of Annie and Layla suffering, being hurt, being abused, being killed from his mind; it filled him with impotent, gut-churning anguish to contemplate that. Time had passed, so much time. What had become of them?

He'd been an invalid for far too long, unable to even think, let alone act. And now ... oh Christ, now his brain was full of horrific imaginings, his wife and child in pain and torment.

*Don't think about it,* he told himself. *You mustn't think about it.*

He relaxed, tried to focus. Breathed deeply. Steadily. In, out, in, out. Slower, slower. He looked down at his hands and realized that the nails were digging into his palms so hard that there were small crescents of blood rising there.

As he calmed down, it came to him. Quickly, he

153

left the bedroom and went back outside.

Around the side of the building there was a short, narrow stretch of concrete pathway, and set into the centre of it was a circular drain cover. He knelt down, and levered the thing up, pushed it aside.

Musty air wafted up, but no one had been in the property recently; there was no fresh stink of sewage. He lay down on the concrete and reached down inside the drain to a depth of six bricks. Stretching hard, he got a grip on one of the bricks lining the right-hand side of the drain and yanked at it. It hadn't been moved for some time, and it crunched against fragmented mortar as he eased it from side to side, edging it out inch by inch, until he held it in his hand. Then he pulled the brick out and lay it on the grass nearby.

Again, he lay flat on the path and stretched down into the drain, his fingers searching. They found what they were looking for and he pulled out a sealed transparent plastic bag. He sat up on the pathway and placed it on the concrete beside him. His fingers ripped impatiently at the bag, tearing it open; inside was a white cloth, wrapped around a big wedge of English bank notes, pesetas, keys and a passport. He put all the items back inside the cloth; the bag was beyond saving. Then he carefully placed the brick back down in the drain, and replaced the drain cover.

After that, he walked all around the property to be sure they weren't here. He knew in his heart they weren't. The barbed wire on the locked gates, the sad abandoned air. No one was here. But

where would Annie go, if she had escaped whatever mayhem had occurred that day?

He thought he knew the answer to that one. He
thought he knew the answer to everything now.
She would go back to London, where Max
Carter's boys ran the streets of the East End,
where they could give her shelter.

'I know who I am,' he told Benito when he found
him two hours later, quietly reading his Bible in
a shady corner of the physic garden.

Benito looked up with the same calm, un-
troubled expression he always wore. 'Oh? And
who are you, my friend?'

'I'm Max Carter,' he said, slumping down beside
Benito and staring out over the sun-dappled
shrubberies with unseeing eyes.

'At last we've got a name for you. That's good
news.' Brother Benito gazed at him thoughtfully.
'It suits you. And what does Max Carter do?'

Max turned his head and gave Benito a crooked
little smile.

'I'm not a good man,' he said regretfully. Into
his mind came more memories, crowding for
space. It seemed now that the memories could
not get into his brain fast enough. His head was
aching with their speed and their impact. Gang
fights, characterized by vicious interaction. He
could hear cries, screams, could hear the whirr of
bicycle chains, see the glitter of knives lit by
moonlight.

'I don't believe that,' said Benito. 'Are you a
soldier, as I thought?'

'No.' Max shook his head. 'I'm afraid you're

155

going to be shocked.'

He was a gangster. A mobster. He had ruled the East End and people had quailed with fear and grovelled with dread and respect because he had power of life and death over them. He'd run rackets. He'd pulled heists. He'd provided protection and come down hard on those who had baulked at paying it. He told Benito all this, and told him too the things he had remembered up at the villa.

'So you have a wife and child ... and you have no idea where they are right now?'

Max shook his head. 'I have to find them. Benito, I have to leave. The sooner the better. I'll need to borrow the car, go down into the town and use the phone.'

'Of course. When?'

'Now.'

Max drove down the hill. He found a phone booth and made the call to the airport, then he went through all the rigmarole of phoning Jimmy Bond, his most trusted lieutenant, in England, but there was no answer. He drove back up to the monastery and joined the brothers for their evening meal.

He was surprised to find that he felt genuinely sad to leave. There was such a peace to this place, he found himself suddenly reluctant to rejoin the outside world. But he had to.

Next day, wearing borrowed clothes and with a small package of bread, meats and cheeses from Benito to sustain him, he said his final farewell to the monk who had become his friend.

Benito shook hands warmly with Max, and

Max handed him a large wad of pesetas.

'I can't–' started Benito.

'Shut the fuck up,' said Max, pressing the money into his hand. 'Buy some new tools for the garden, or whatever you need. And,' Max fished in his shirt pocket and pulled out more cash, 'give this to Jaime, will you? He saved my life.'

'He was happy to do it. He doesn't need a reward.'

'He's got one anyway,' said Max, and refused to take any of it back. Without Jaime, without Benito, he would be dead and he knew it.

Benito clapped him on the shoulder. 'You take care now, my friend.'

'Too right,' said Max. 'And you.'

Having made his farewells, he set off for London, his heart full of dread, to find his family.

# Long Island

# 30

## Montauk, Long Island, USA
## August 1971

After the explosion, the weirdest thing was, Annie couldn't hear anything. People wearing yellow were bending over her, mouthing words, their faces taut with concern. There was no screaming, there was just this *impression* of people panicking, milling around, shouting for help.

Inside her head, there was only silence. She hugged it to her, trying to ignore the sour sickness that held her chest in a tight grip, the horrible cramping pain in her belly. If this was reality – this bewildering, frightening world of smoke and dust and the scent of cooked flesh – then she wanted none of it.

Strange, dreamlike impressions moved across her vision. Alberto, kneeling in the sand beside her, his face anguished and soot-stained, his mouth working but no sound coming out.

*Oh fuck this.*

She had to get up, had to rejoin the living. But she couldn't. All her efforts to rouse herself came to nothing more than the twitch of a leg, the faint, troubled movement of a hand.

*A hand.*

Had she really seen that, lying in the sand – that blackened, clawlike thing?

161

She turned her head. The thing was gone. Maybe she had never seen it at all.

But she knew she had.

She knew she had a world of pain coming to her.

She closed her eyes, tried to shut it out. Felt her stomach clench again, sharply, and bile surged into her throat. She felt terribly cold and started to shiver. Which was odd, because she knew the deck – what was left of the deck at the back of the house – was alight with hot, leaping flames, its blackening timbers split and ragged, shattered into disarray. Finally, the darkness welcomed her with open arms.

'She's coming round,' was the first thing she fully heard.

Days or weeks could have passed since she lay in the sand, catapulted there by the force of the blast. Annie opened her eyes. Saw white all around, a nurse, and Nico sitting there at her bedside, his thin straggly hair sticking up on end as if he had been dragging his hands through it, his face riven with tragedy. He was still wearing the fancy DJ that he'd had on at the wedding, but the fabric and even his face were smeared with soot. He smelled like a bonfire.

The blast.

The fire.

*The blackened claw.*

Annie closed her eyes again, but she couldn't close her ears.

'Annie? Mrs Barolli?' the nurse was asking her insistently.

*No. Go away. I don't want to face this. I can't do this.*

'I saw her eyes open just now,' said Nico.

'We'll give her some more time. Let her rest,' said the nurse. There was a pause. 'You ought to go home, get some sleep.'

'Nah,' said Nico. 'I couldn't sleep anyway. I'll stay.'

Darkness again. Annie clung to it. The darkness was her friend.

But she had to wake up in the end, and wake up she did – feeling sick to her stomach, hurting in every part of her body – to dull morning light. Something was making a loud snorting noise. She looked cautiously around. It was Nico, fast asleep in the chair at her bedside.

'Nico,' she tried to say, but her mouth was dry and her lips didn't seem to want to form the words.

She licked her lips and tried again. 'Nico.'

The snorting stopped. He jerked, his head lifted suddenly from his chest, his eyes opening. He stared at her, then looked around, as if wondering where the hell they could be. Then he remembered. She could *see* him remembering. He ran a huge, unsteady hand down over his unshaven face.

'Ah, fuck,' he mumbled, then he heaved a heavy sigh and sat forward, his bloodshot eyes resting on her face for an instant before sliding away. 'How ya feeling, Mrs Barolli? I'll ring for the nurse.'

He was reaching for the button, but Annie shook her head quickly. It hurt; made her feel as if her brains were about to leak out of her ears.

163

'In a minute,' she said, and her voice was a croak, not like her voice at all.

'She'll want to check you over...' He wasn't looking at her eyes.

'Nico,' said Annie. 'What happened? Was it a gas leak or something?'

Nico sat back, swallowing. Shook his head. 'Looked like a bomb,' he said.

Annie lay back. God, she felt dog-rough. For a moment after waking there, she had felt as if maybe she was tied down, restrained. But now, looking down her gowned and bandaged body, she could see an IV drip was attached to her left arm, and that arm was bruised and abraded. There was a pressure dressing over her right arm, indicating burns.

'They said you were concussed,' said Nico.

Annie saw it again in her mind: Constantine walking towards her with the parcel.

*Hey, wonder what's in this one?*

She winced with pain and stared at Nico. 'Is he dead?' she managed to get out, her voice breaking on every word.

Nico's eyes met hers at last. He nodded and compressed his lips. Tears spilled over and ran down the lines of his face.

'No,' whimpered Annie, her face screwing up in denial. Then she had another terrifying thought. 'Layla?'

'She's safe,' said Nico. 'Her and the nanny were way out of it, at the other side of the house. I'll ... I'll get the nurse.'

Annie was staring down at her stomach. She moved her right arm painfully, laid a hand on her belly. It was flatter. A spasm of terror and misery shot through her.

*No...*

Nico pressed the button and they sat there together in dazed silence until the nurse arrived. She was brisk, professional. She smiled a lot and said she would fetch the doctor. The doctor turned out to be female, white-coated, dark-haired, yellow-skinned, Eurasian.

'You want me to go...?' asked Nico, lumbering awkwardly to his feet.

'You're a friend of Mrs Barolli's?' the doctor asked.

'Yeah. A good friend.'

'Then if Mrs Barolli doesn't mind, I'd like you to stay for a while.' The doctor turned her attention to Annie. 'You've been very lucky,' she said.

Funny how Annie didn't *feel* lucky. She felt as though her insides had been scooped out. There was a solid lump of anguish occupying that space now. Constantine was dead.

The doctor did something very surprising to Annie then. She took Annie's right hand and laced her fingers through hers. Annie stared at their conjoined hands.

She had to ask the question. She was very afraid of the answer, but she *had* to know.

'Is the baby okay?' she asked with lips that felt numb.

The doctor's face grew grave. A million times she must have delivered bad news to patients, she did it so well.

'I'm sorry, Mrs Barolli, but no, it's not. I'm afraid you've lost the baby.'

165

# 31

The police came – two plain-clothes detectives –
and interviewed her the next day. Nico had gone
home, shattered, to change and wash and try to
get the stink of the explosion out of his hair and
off his skin.

'Mr Barolli died instantly,' said one of them; he
had corn-gold hair and looked more like an Iowa
farm boy than a city detective. 'He didn't suffer.'

Annie took some comfort from that. She felt
shaky, weepy; not herself. She was a tough nut –
everyone who knew her said so. Born in the East
End of London to a drunk of a mother and an
absentee father, she'd had to grow up fast. She
had learned to fend for herself, fight her corner.
But this was all too much. As the detective spoke
those words, she could feel her control slipping,
could feel her throat begin to close, her eyes
starting to fill with tears.

Her baby was dead.

Her husband was dead.

And what had that doctor said yesterday? Oh
yeah. *You've been lucky.*

'Do you feel strong enough to answer a few
questions?' asked the other detective – a tall, ath-
letically built man who looked both older and
more world-weary than the golden farm boy.

Annie got a grip, and nodded. A single tear
escaped and slid down her bruised cheek, but

that was all.

'The parcel containing the bomb – did you see it?' he asked.

Annie could see it even now. Constantine walking towards her with a smile, shaking the damned thing, saying, *Hey, wonder what's in this one?*

His last words on earth.

Her throat closed again. She reached unsteadily for a glass of water, sipped it, could barely swallow a drop. But it helped. Gave her a moment to compose herself.

'It was blue,' she said hoarsely. 'Sky blue. With a big red ribbon.'

They both nodded. The farm boy was taking notes.

'The techs are cataloguing the evidence,' said the dark-haired one.

*Evidence?* she thought. *Was there enough left of it for that?*

'But it looks like a booby trap,' he went on. 'A cluster of grenades with the pins wired through to the table, so that when it's picked up ... boom.'

She thought again of Constantine, picking the thing up and starting to come towards her. Dying instantly.

'Your husband was in business, is that right?' asked the dark-haired one.

Annie looked at him and instantly she could see it in his eyes. These two knew what Constantine was. They wouldn't *say* it, but they knew.

'Imports and exports,' she said. 'Olive oil, mostly.'

'Olive oil,' said the farm boy, and wrote it down.

'Why would he pick up that particular present?'

asked the dark-haired one, watching her face. 'There was a table full of presents for the happy couple, according to some of the guests we've spoken to. Why that one?'

Annie forced her addled brain to *think*. And when she did that, she realized that Constantine had just hurried his death along by an hour or so by picking up the thing when he did. Because at ten o'clock it had been agreed with the party planners that Constantine would present Lucco and Daniella with the wedding presents. By doing what he did, Constantine had spared the lives of his son and his new bride, and of many of the guests too, because they would have all been out on the deck to watch and applaud and cheer.

'It was the biggest gift. The most brightly wrapped,' said Annie. 'The most eye-catching. And it was right at the front. Almost out on its own.'

*As if it had been deliberately placed there.*

And Constantine was being playful with his wife; he was so happy because all the family were there on that special day. But she wasn't about to tell that to these two cynical men with their knowing faces and their notebooks. *Fuck* them.

She knew she ought to co-operate. These two might be doing more than going through the motions; they might actually be able to find out who had left that bomb there. But she didn't believe they'd try too hard. She simply didn't. They knew Constantine was Mafia – she had seen the patrol cars loitering outside the Montauk estate entrance, watching who came, who went. Taking pictures. Taking notes. Their attitude to the death of a Don would be *Good. One less to keep an eye on.*

Annie leaned over and pressed the button to summon the nurse.

'You know what?' she croaked out. 'I don't think I feel up to this right now. I'm sorry.'

The nurse came.

'If you think of anything...' Farm Boy was saying, closing his notebook.

'I'll call,' said Annie, closing her eyes.

'Anything at all,' said the dark-haired one.

*Yeah. Like you give a flying fuck.*

'She's very tired. If you can go now...?'

They left.

So did the nurse.

Annie lay there in her hospital bed, alone and exhausted. Of course the police would do nothing. It was for the family to find out who did this thing to Constantine and to dish out appropriate punishment. She should know that. She had been married to a king among men; she had been a Mafia queen. She ought to know by now how these things worked. Lucco was head of the family now. He was the Don. It was for him to seek revenge for the death of his father.

As for her, she was too tired to think any more. Her eyelids were drooping. Without even being aware of it, she drifted off to sleep.

She came awake with a start and with the clear realization that she couldn't breathe. There was something smothering and relentless pressing her head inexorably back into the lumpy hospital-issue pillow, clogging up her nose and her mouth so that every panicky attempt to draw

169

breath ended in a no-show.

Spots were dancing in front of her eyelids. But it was dark. This big, soft, deadly thing was compressing her airways, and someone – *someone* – was trying to squash the life out of her.

She tried to cry out, but her mouth was full of cotton fabric and she was drowning in the stink of antiseptic, and all it did was make that someone push down harder.

*Jesus, she was going to die.*

And would that be so bad? She was weak and bloodied and bruised, she had lost her baby and the man she loved. Would it *really* be so bad to join them?

But the urge to survive, the urge to *kick ass* was so strong, and what she actually felt along with the panic was rage. Rage that someone could have shattered her life so comprehensively, and now they were looking to finish the job off. And what was she going to do? Give them that satisfaction; just lie here like some limp dick and *let* them?

But she couldn't stop them. Her arms were flailing around; she was trying to strike at some solid body that was lying upon her, crushing her, smothering her, but she was making no headway and she knew it.

Spots dancing in front of her eyes ... and a new feeling, a sensation of detachment, of the whole world spinning away, that air didn't matter, that there would be something else, something better.

And then, voices.

God, she felt so weak. Wondered if she was imagining all this, if it was just a result of the trauma of the explosion, her mind playing games. Once in the long restless night she had awoken to see Constantine sitting in the chair beside her bed – Constantine alive and well, smiling at her ... and when she reached out for him he began rotting, became a corpse, melting like wax into the fabric of the chair. She had been too weak even to scream, and she had been crying and retching as she drifted back off to sleep.

This was just another nightmare. That was all. She would wake up, and it would all be okay. *She would be okay.*

But in her gut she knew that she wasn't going to wake up from this.

And there were voices now, and those voices weren't imaginary.

The voices were *real.*

And then the pressure was gone. Annie was aware of quickly receding footsteps as she threw the damned pillow away from her, onto the floor. She whooped in air, heaving, gasping. Tried to get up, tried to haul herself from the bed. She was too weak. She fell sideways, her arm hitting the floor, her legs still pinned beneath the bed-clothes. The drip flew loose from the arm with a sting of pain and spurted liquid. She was twisted sideways, staring at the stark hospital flooring, upside-down, gasping. Noticed the door was still swinging on its hinges.

*That was real,* she thought. *That wasn't a dream.*

Nico and the nurse arrived at a run. They looked at Annie, lying there, half in and half out of the bed, red in the face, in clear distress.

'Mrs Barolli?' The nurse's tilted upside-down

face was taut with concern as she dashed forward, but Annie's eyes were on Nico.

'Someone just tried to kill me,' she wheezed. 'With the pillow.'

Nico was off like a shot, out of the door, dashing along the corridor.

*He won't catch them,* she thought. *He doesn't know who he's looking for. And neither do I.*

'Are you all right?' the nurse was asking, easing her back into the bed, refastening the drip, touching Annie's brow. Ten seconds longer and she wouldn't have been all right at all.

Someone had tried to kill her.

Someone had wanted her to join her baby and her husband in death.

But for fuck's sake – *who?*

# 32

The burial of Constantine Barolli was as lavish and as full of pomp and ceremony as the burying of an emperor. His remains were grandly interred in a heavy and elaborately gilded casket strewn with mounds of red roses. A procession of limousines carrying hordes of mourners followed the hearse into St John's Cemetery in Queens, and in the first of these was his widow, only recently released from hospital.

Layla cuddled up against her mother as they stared out from the limo at the thundering sheets of rain that fell from the heavens like tears. Annie

172

had done her best to explain to Layla that Constantine was with the angels in heaven – like Daddy Max – and she was filled with pity for the little girl's bewilderment.

Layla had now lost two fathers. She'd doted on Constantine – the more so since she had lost Max – and now the poor little cow had lost him, too.

Annie hugged her daughter tightly and tried not to give in to the despair and the rage she felt flooding her like a cold, bitter tide. Someone had intended that Constantine should die. Had they intended that she should die too? They had managed to kill her unborn child, hers and Constantine's. Layla's little brother or sister would never draw breath, never know the sweetness of life.

Annie still felt ill. To find one great love in a lifetime was extraordinarily lucky; to find two was nothing short of a miracle. The gods had smiled on her despite the fact that she'd been bad, borderline crooked; but now she was being punished for her luck; what the fates had given, they had decided to snatch away again.

The burns on her arm had not been serious, and had healed well. But her mind was a mess. She had long since stopped bleeding from the miscarriage, and the doctors had assured her that there was no reason, no reason at all, why she should not go on to have more children.

*Nothing other than the fact that my husband's been blown to fucking bits,* thought Annie.

Wearing a severe black skirt suit and with her head swathed in a thick black veil, Nico holding

173

a huge umbrella over her and Layla, she stood at the graveside and watched Constantine's coffin being lowered into the ground.

Whoever had done it, she wanted them to pay.

Standing beside Lucco and his new bride Daniella, Cara and Rocco, Alberto, Aunt Gina – all solemn-faced and properly mournful, she knew they all wanted whoever had done it to pay.

Annie looked around at all the mourners. So many of them had come to pay their respects to a great man. She recognized heads of other families, *capos,* foot soldiers. And she looked around her at all the people there – hundreds of them, packed together and getting drenched by the rain – and wondered who could have done this thing.

Somehow she got through the day, clutching Layla to her for reassurance that good things did exist in the world, that not everything was blackness and death.

'It's for the Don to decide what will be done,' Nico said when she was finally strong enough even to broach the subject.

'Yeah,' said Annie. 'I understand.'

The world had shifted; *her* world had changed, irrevocably.

It was for Lucco to pursue his father's killers, to hunt them down. The cops wouldn't do it. And she couldn't. She wouldn't even know where to start, and right now she hadn't the will to even try.

The Don wasn't Constantine any more. The Don was his eldest son: Lucco.

She went to the little bolt hole on Martha's Vineyard, where she and Constantine had shared happy times together. Nico drove Annie and Layla, and stayed with them there. She walked on the beach, sometimes with Layla but mostly alone, staring at the sea, her heart like a stone in her chest. Nico and the housekeeper and Gerda kept the house running, kept Layla amused.

She couldn't.

Grief gripped her and wouldn't let go. She barely ate, although the others encouraged her to do so. Food choked her. And she was having terrible, painfully real nightmares; she couldn't even sleep for fear of them.

Time dragged on.

Alberto phoned, anxious about her.

'Tell him I'm fine,' she told Nico. 'Just resting.'

She couldn't speak to anyone, not yet. Day after day she walked the beach, picked at food, suffered and churned through the nights, until it was February, *months* had gone by and she knew, painful and hard though it was, that she was going to have to try to pick up the threads of her life – if only for Layla's sake. Spring was coming; she saw it happening all around her but she could feel no leap of happiness, no promise of renewal. Her husband and baby were dead; that was all she knew. But she *had* to rejoin the world, and so she did.

They returned to New York, to the Fifth Avenue penthouse. As she made to pass the front desk in the lobby of the palatial building, the concierge, Michael, called Annie to the desk.

'Mrs Barolli.'

'Hello, Michael,' she greeted him, steeling herself against the words she knew were coming. I'm so sorry for your loss. Is there anything I can do? Empty, meaningless words.

He looked awkward and unhappy, of course he did – people would cross the street rather than talk to the bereaved, but this poor sap had no choice.

'I'm sorry, Mrs Barolli, I've been told you're not to go up.'

'*What* did you say?' she asked faintly.

He looked away from her. This was a man who had seen her coming and going for well over a year, had joked with Layla, told her all about his big Irish family in the Bronx. Now he was looking at her as though he didn't even know who she was.

'Um, the owner ... Mr Barolli ... he said no one's to go up to the penthouse.'

Annie felt dizzy with the shock of it. 'Mr Barolli?' she echoed. She had expected sympathy, not *this*.

'Mr Lucco Barolli ... the new owner.'

Nico was silent at her side. Layla was cuddling in against her, oblivious to the fact that her mother was being denied entry to her own home.

Annie felt something stir in her gut: a sick, consuming flare of anger. After all she'd been through, Lucco was still playing his cruel games and she'd be *damned* if she'd stand for it.

'We'll see about that,' she said, and stormed over to the lifts.

Nico followed with Layla. Ignoring Michael's shout, they all three bundled inside the lift and ascended to the top floor.

Annie took the key from her handbag and, with

fingers that trembled with rage, she put the key in the lock. The door wouldn't open. She tried the other key, the spare. That wouldn't open the door either.

'He's had the locks changed,' said Nico.

'Thanks for stating the bleeding obvious,' snapped Annie. She kicked the door in fury.

*That jumped-up little shit,* she thought. *He's cutting me out. Well, we'll see about* that, *too.*

# 33

Annie had Nico drive the two blocks over to Lucco's place. She was certain he would be there. For the new godfather, it had been very much business as usual since Constantine's death. And if he *wasn't,* by some chance, then she would wait. However long it took, she was going to speak to Lucco today, thrash this out.

She left Layla in the car with Nico and went into the plush brownstone building. Another concierge, beautifully turned out and briskly polite. She gave her name, said she was here to see Mr Barolli but that he wasn't expecting her.

'I'm his stepmother,' said Annie, revelling grimly in the announcement. She had always tended to flaunt the title 'stepmother' whenever she could, knowing how much it rattled Lucco.

Now she thought that maybe she shouldn't have taken such delight in putting in those tiny barbs, because Lucco was being obstructive.

Maybe she should have tried to charm him.

*Ha! Frankly, I'd rather charm a snake.*

She waited patiently at the desk as the concierge phoned up to Lucco's apartment. Probably the bastard wouldn't see her. But she was surprised when the concierge directed her up to the twenty-fifth floor. She went over to the lifts, and pressed the button for twenty-five. The doors closed on her and the lift went up.

As the lift doors slid open, Lucco was standing there flanked by two heavies. As usual she was struck by how handsome he was, staring at her with his hooded black eyes. Also as usual she found him oily and offensively slippery – not attractive.

'Welcome,' he said, and she noted that, as always, he avoided using her name. And as for 'stepmother' – forget it.

*Welcome, my arse,* thought Annie. *I'm as welcome here as typhoid.*

'Hi, Lucco,' said Annie, and followed him and his guards across the hall. They took up station outside the door, while she and Lucco went into the apartment that looked out over the stunning skyline.

She followed him over a large tan-and-white cowhide rug between two vast terracotta-coloured sofas that stood in front of the huge picture window. New York was spread out there like a multi-faceted jewel, bathed in warm spring sunlight.

'Some view,' she said, as Lucco joined her there.

'Of course, you haven't been here before, have you? May I take your coat?' he asked, icily polite as always.

*Yeah, he'd never say a thing to my face,* thought Annie. *Everything this bastard does, he does when you're not looking. And of course I haven't been here – I've never been invited.*

'No thanks, I'm not stopping,' said Annie.

'This isn't a social call?' He was watching her, sneering at her. He knew damned well why she'd come here.

'Is Daniella here?' she asked.

'Cara's taken her shopping.'

Well, that was good. Annie thought of Daniella, with her frightened, naïve eyes, and was glad that she was going to be spared a front-row seat at this particular shindig. She hoped that Cara was being nice to the poor little cow – but she doubted it.

'You've had the locks changed on my apartment,' said Annie. 'Why? What right do you have to do such a thing?'

Lucco gave a slight smile. 'Ah, that. Are you sure you won't take a seat so we can discuss this in a more civilized fashion?'

'I'm sure.' Really, she would have loved to sit down. She still felt weak, she was still grieving, but she didn't want to show that in front of Lucco. 'Why, Lucco?'

'I own that apartment now.'

'No you *don't.* That's my home.'

Now Lucco was smiling. 'It may have been your *home,* but it's my *property.* I own it.'

Annie stared at him. 'Constantine told me that the apartment would be mine. He said it was all in his will. The apartment, and the London house, and his club shares.'

'You're mistaken,' said Lucco.

'But ... the will hasn't even been *read* yet.'

'Yeah, it has.'

*'What?'*

'Sorry, did no one tell you? The family gathered and the will was read.'

The family. Not her. They hadn't even told her it was happening, far less invited her to attend. Not even Alberto!

'But I'm your father's next of kin,' she said, her words stumbling over one another with shock. 'I'm his *wife.*'

Lucco stared at her. 'You're nothing. *I* am his heir, and things have been changed around to make sure I get all that I'm entitled to. But I'm not an unreasonable man – you can keep your controlling share of the new Times Square club.' He gave a smile full of venom. 'We'll be partners. How's that? Everything else passes to me,' said Lucco, his dark eyes glittering as they held hers. *'Everything.* The Montauk house. Which is still a crime scene at the moment, but I will see that it's rebuilt, if only as a sad memorial to a great, great man. The penthouse apartment you've been living in. The olive groves in Sicily. The vineyards and chateaux in the Dordogne. The orange and lemon groves in Majorca. The Barbuda mansion. The stables in Kentucky. You know how much Papa loved his horses.'

Annie knew. Constantine had kept racehorses both here and in England, had attended race meetings all over the world; he'd loved best of all to go to Ascot and Goodwood.

'Then there's the house on Martha's Vineyard.

All the properties my father owned all around the world. They're all mine now, as he willed it.'

*As he willed it.*

But Constantine would never have left her out of his will. She knew he wouldn't.

This was all *bullshit.*

'You sneaky little arsehole,' said Annie through gritted teeth. 'What have you done? Thrown a scare into the lawyers? *What have you done?*' she shouted. But of course she knew the answer to her own question. He had control now; he could do whatever he liked. And what he *liked* was to cut her out of his father's life, and his family's life too.

Lucco gave a light shrug. He looked very sure of himself, very smug.

'All I have done is taken over my inheritance,' he said. 'I understand how bereft you must be feeling at this sad time, and it was tragic – really tragic – that you lost the baby you were expecting...'

Annie stood there feeling sick and powerless.

'You bastard,' she hissed. 'Don't you *dare* mention the baby to me. You must be absolutely fucking *delighted* I lost it.'

Lucco looked wounded now. 'Delighted? No, I don't think so. Of course it would never have been a proper member of the Barolli family, that's out of the question.'

Now Annie was spitting mad. 'That baby was a Barolli. Your half-brother or half-sister. Your father's child.'

Lucco cocked his head to one side and stared at her.

181

'Yes, but can we be entirely sure about that? You have to admit that your history is colourful in the extreme...'

Annie flew at him, wanting to wipe the smirk off his face. He grabbed her and held her. She struggled, crazy with rage, needing to inflict damage, but she was as weak as a kitten.

'You *shit*,' she gasped out, her face inches from his.

'Shh,' said Lucco, and he was smiling, really smiling now.

*His father's dead and he's standing here looking like he's won the lottery. And guess what? He has.*

'Hush now,' he insisted, holding her tightly against the front of his loathsome body even while she struggled and squirmed, trying to get free, trying to kick, trying to hurt him any way she could. She raised a knee, but he turned his thighs sideways so that she missed his groin.

She was wearing herself out, what little strength she had evaporating. Finally, she just stood still, filled with hate for him, wishing he was dead so she could stamp on his grave.

'Now listen,' he said close beside her ear.

Annie gave a desperate heave; but it was no good. She couldn't break free.

'Hush! Listen. Life has to go on and I'm afraid that apartment where you spent your time here has only very sad memories for me following my father's death. So I've decided it's to be sold. Sorry.'

'You bastard,' said Annie, her voice hoarse with fury.

'But listen,' he said, and she could feel his

182

breath tickling her cheek now, he was so close. 'If you're nice to me ... then we'll see, yes?'

Annie's eyes glared into his. 'You little runt.'

'I'm sure you could be nice to me ... if you tried.'

'Yeah,' sneered Annie. 'If I could be *arsed*. Which I can't. Sorry.'

'I like the fact that you fight me,' he said, grinning happily at her. 'You know what? I really like it.'

'Make the most of it, sunshine,' said Annie coldly. 'You won't get away with this. I'll contest the will.'

'Oh yes?' He gazed at her for a moment. She felt his hands tighten, just for an instant, on her waist. 'I know you're angry now, but take a step back. Think about what you're doing. Think of your daughter.'

Then he pushed her roughly away from him. Annie staggered, taken unawares. She righted herself, stared at him like he was something nasty she'd stepped in. He was threatening her. Threatening Layla. A woman, and a *child*.

'You're not even fit to lick your father's boots,' she told him in disgust.

His smile dropped. 'Careful,' he warned.

'Or what? I've had the crap kicked out of me, Lucco. I've lost the man I love. I've lost my unborn child. You've shut me out of my home. What next?'

His smile was back in place. She longed to smack it straight off, but she had already tried and failed to do that. No use pushing against the tide when it was clearly too powerful for her to cope with.

'If you were so foolish as to try to contest the will? Oh, I don't know. Try it. And then ... let's just wait and see, shall we?' he asked her, his smile loathsome and gloating.

*No,* thought Annie. *Let's not.*

She'd had a shed-load of shit dropped on her head. Someone had already tried to smother her in the hospital. Maybe one of Lucco's people. Who knew? Lucco was the Don now. She was out of her depth here.

The only thing she *did* know was that she felt frighteningly alone.


# 34

She was still in the hospital bed, a drip attached to her arm. Just waking, feeling heavy with all the bandages and the cramping in her stomach; ah, God, she felt so weak, so drained. And there was Constantine, standing at the end of her bed ... only it wasn't Constantine at all, it was a black-ened shell of a human being; there was *smoke* coming off this poor semi-incinerated thing, this monster. Its mouth opened, and dust and ashes poured from it.

She tried to scream; couldn't.

*Hey, wonder what's in this one?* it said in a voice like gravel, the words echoing around inside her head; and then the awful thing seemed to fall apart, its form disintegrating, breaking down, twirling into nothing but skeins of black smoke. She could smell it, the burning, the powder, it enveloped her where she lay, choked her.

'Constantine!' she shrieked, and all at once she was awake.

'Mrs Barolli?' Nico's big face loomed in front of hers.

There were bright lights behind him, there was a background hum going on; they were in a machine, in a plane, they were ... oh God, now she knew where they were. Light grey leather seats in front of her. A small, cylindrical cabin. People turning, looking.

'Mummy?' Layla was sitting beside her and her face was white with anxiety.

'You all right, Mrs Barolli?' asked Nico. 'You've been asleep. Think you must have been dreaming. You cried out.'

They were flying back to England.

After the run-in with Lucco, she'd retreated; rented a place in the city and tried to get her head around all that had happened to her. She'd felt that Nico's stoic presence, and that of Gerda, Layla's nanny – who looked after Layla when she felt too weak, too grief-stricken to do so – were the only things keeping her sane.

She'd wanted to talk to Alberto, to phone Dolly or even Ellie, but she couldn't do it. There was no way she could talk about losing Constantine and the baby without crumbling, without shrieking aloud. Her pride was all she had now, and stubbornly it wouldn't let her break down in front of anyone, not even her closest friends.

Nico had tried his best to jolt her out of it. He'd driven her over to Times Square one day to look at the new Annie's club venue, but she could only stare blankly at it, without interest.

'You want me to have one of the boys get some staff on board – site foreman, a manager...?' he'd suggested.

She'd turned to him with a sigh. 'Yeah, why not? That would be good.'

'You still going to open in September? Have you talked to the boss about it?'

Annie had given a shrug. 'No. I haven't. Maybe I'll go ahead with the September date, I don't know.' She hated that Lucco was co-owner, even if she did have the controlling share. She didn't want to see him, or speak to him, or even know the bastard was *breathing*.

'So what would you like to do now?' he'd asked, watching her with concern.

Annie looked at him and all at once she knew what she wanted.

'I'd like to go home,' she'd said.

'Home?'

'To England.'

Nico had said he'd get one of the Gulf Stream company jets organized, but Annie had said no; she didn't want the potential embarrassment of turning up at the airport and finding that Lucco had blocked that, too. So instead she'd asked him to book them on Concorde, which he'd done; and furthermore he'd said that he would travel with her, Layla and Gerda.

'There's no need for that,' she'd said.

'Bullshit,' retorted Nico. 'Constantine told me

186

that if anything ever happened to him, I was to take care of you. I mean to do that.'

Annie felt almost weak with gratitude. Even from beyond the grave, Constantine was looking out for her. She'd thought of the penthouse then, the place where she and Constantine had made a life together.

Oh, he had often been away on business. So often he had arrived home weighed down by the worries of the world, to find her waiting for him, ready to make him smile. She never asked him about his business; she always kept it light; she was used to doing that. She had been married to another powerful man, another man with dubious connections; she knew how to play that particular game. You asked no questions and were told no lies.

She thought of the penthouse. She'd loved that place, been happy there. All right, she'd been homesick – *horribly* homesick – when she had first gone out to the States with him; but she had settled into life there because he was with her. Maybe she would even have stopped there, given the choice. But she'd *had* no choice at all. Lucco had seen to that.

'I had to tell him what you're doing, you do understand that, Mrs Barolli, don't you?' said Nico.

Annie had nodded. Of course Nico would have to tell Lucco what was happening, that she was going back to England, because Lucco was the boss now. To do otherwise would be both disrespectful and dangerous.

187

'We're just coming in to land,' said Nico, and Annie gave Layla's hand a reassuring squeeze. She looked out of the window. Loads of scudding grey clouds, they were flying blind ... and then – suddenly – there was mild sunshine, a brilliant patchwork of small fields in tones of green, yellow and ochre. They were home, in England. It was only then, seeing the sweet little fields, the changeable skies, that Annie realized how much she'd missed it.

'Take your seat sir, and put on your seat belt, please,' said the stewardess, hurrying up behind Nico.

He patted Layla's cheek and sat down across the aisle beside Gerda.

The stewardess went off to the front of the plane. They heard the aircraft's wheels lower into place with a resounding *clonk*.

Annie stared out of the window.

All right, she had to start again. Find her feet. She felt a little better now, just a bit stronger. Her life in the States was over. She would go back to open the Times Square club in September; she was still the majority shareholder, so technically she was still in charge of *that*, if nothing else. Maybe she'd even take her old mate Dolly with her for support, because, oh shit, she hated admitting this, even to herself, but the idea of coming up against Lucco again scared the crap out of her. He was right. There was nothing left there for her, not any more.

Now she was home. And suddenly, she was so glad of that.

# 35

She was betting that Lucco wasn't quite as thorough as his father. That he would forget little things, little loopholes that he maybe ought to have closed up. Like ... oh, like she still had the keys to the Holland Park mansion. Although Lucco had closed her off in New York, maybe he hadn't thought it important enough to shut her down with quite such thorough ruthlessness across the pond in England.

The fact was, he thought she was whipped, finished. Well, maybe he was right. Nico had told him she was going home to England, and she could imagine the pleasure that had given him. But maybe here he would get careless.

*What the hell,* she thought as their cab pulled up in front of the big, red-brick William and Mary house where she had first met Constantine. They piled out with their cases, Nico paid the driver and the cab roared off.

Annie paused there, looking up at the impressive frontage of the house, the identical bay trees in terracotta pots on either side of the elaborately stepped entrance where the door was painted a discreet and glossy dark blue and furnished with a big brass lion's-head knocker.

*Shit, I'm never going to see him again,* she thought with a stab of familiar anguish. *Only in my nightmares.*

189

But Layla was tugging at her hand, hauling her up the path, Nico and Gerda following close behind.

*Well, here goes nothing.*

If everything was as it should be, the staff would be here. Maybe she should have phoned ahead, but she felt that might have given Lucco a tip-off. At which point the little slime-ball would quite likely have the locks changed and instruct the staff that she was not to be admitted.

Annie walked up the steps to the front entrance.

She remembered so vividly standing here once before, coming to petition Constantine for his help when Layla was snatched. People staring at her, wondering what on earth she was playing at. Cara had been getting married that day. But against all her expectations, that had worked out. Constantine had helped. Layla had been safely recovered. And ... she'd fallen in love with him. Expecting never to fall in love again, not after Max. But she had, and it had been a kind of miracle.

*And now look how it's ended.*

She got out the key with a shaking hand, inserted it in the lock. Turned it.

*Oh please,* she thought. *Just this one break. Please.*

There was a moment's resistance.

*He's changed them, he's already done it...*

Then the door swung open.

She shot a look at Nico. He was watching her, his big friendly avuncular face carefully devoid of expression. Layla jumped and twirled between them, oblivious to the tension above her head.

Gerda grabbed Layla's hand and started talking to her.

Annie stepped inside and came face to face with Rosa, the squat Spanish maid, her greying hair scraped back in a bun, her dark eyes wide with surprise when she saw Annie standing there.

'*Señora* Barolli!'

'Hi, Rosa,' said Annie, pushing into the hall before the maid had time to change her mind about the warm welcome. She didn't know *what* to expect here. But she feared the worst.

'But what you doing here?' Rosa's face clouded with sadness. 'So sorry, *Señora,* about *Señor* Barolli. So sorry.'

Annie swallowed hard past the lump in her throat. Nico had phoned ahead, explained. And probably told Rosa to tell no one else Annie was coming. Not even Lucco. 'Thanks, Rosa. We're going to be staying here for a while.'

Rosa nodded and started fussing around with the bags.

It was as easy as that.

Lucco had dropped a stitch; she was in.

# London

# 36

'You know what?' said Ellie. 'If I'd known there was such a good living to be made out of galloping the maggot, I'd have started up my own place years ago.'

Chris, eighteen ugly, bald-headed stone of meaty muscle, put down his paper. They were sitting in the kitchen at the Limehouse knocking-shop, where Ellie – formerly prostitute and cleaner – now held sway as Madam. She *liked* being Madam. It was so much more fun dishing out orders than taking them. But Chris looked at her and knew this was all hot air; Ellie didn't have the business nous to have launched her own place. Ellie was a worker who'd got lucky by being kicked upstairs.

To be fair, though, she'd made a pretty good job of it so far. This place – first under the command of Celia, then Annie, then Dolly – had always done a roaring trade in punters, and it was continuing to thrive with Ellie at the helm.

There had been major changes over the years, of course; brasses came and went, punters fell off the twig and new ones came in to have the old man given a polish or a whipping. Life went on. Now, he was doorman here once again and it was a job that suited him better than his last one, on permanent nights in security at Heathrow. This job kept him more fully occupied, since he'd lost his wife – who had also been a working girl, God rest her.

'Yeah, but it's not all profit, is it?' he reminded Ellie.

Ellie shrugged. No, it wasn't. Once this busy establishment had paid protection to the Delaney mob; now they handed a weekly wedge over to the Carter boys. The Carters kept the lid on any trouble, so it all ran like clockwork.

And today was party day! Friday. Her favourite day of the week. There were eats and drinks laid out ready for the clients in the front parlour, the music was playing, there were willing trollops aplenty, a new dominatrix occupied the Punishment Room upstairs; the whole place was abuzz.

The doorbell rang.

'First punter of the day,' trilled Ellie, and hopped to her feet to check out her appearance in the mirror behind the door. Once, she'd porked up like a mini barrage balloon, neglected herself, fed her anxiety and misery with biscuits and cakes. Now, she saw reflected there a still curvy but well-groomed woman of medium height, wearing a red skirt suit, her dark hair neatly coiled up in a French pleat, her skin pale and pearlescent, her pretty hazel eyes alight with the challenge of a new day.

'I'll get it,' said Chris, and walked off down the hall.

Ellie watched him go with a sigh of longing.

All right, she still had a few problems. She was head over heels in love with Chris and she *still* couldn't bring herself to tell him so. And she thought one of her prossies was meeting clients on the side, working out her own rates with the bastard outside somewhere and bypassing the knocking-shop.

However...

Apart from all *that,* things were good. She was still in regular touch with her old mate Dolly, who ran the trio of Carter clubs. Back in the day, they'd been called the Palermo, the Blue Parrot and the Shalimar; they'd been old-fashioned nightclubs, then seedy strip joints, now they were all called Annie's and the clientele were decent people out for a night's clean, wholesome entertainment; the dirty-mac brigade was long gone.

She hurried out into the hall after Chris, fixing her bright professional smile in place to greet the first punter.

Chris was blocking the doorway, and Ellie noted with a little irritation that he wasn't saying hello, come in, kiss-my-arse or nothing. He was just *standing* there like a lemon. She came forward and peered around his bulk, smiling broadly.

'Hello, do come...' Her voice – her best *posh* voice, the one she always used on the clients – died on her in an instant.

She felt all the blood drain from her head and plummet down into her elegant patent-leather court shoes as she saw who was standing there.

'Holy *shit,*' she said instead, forgetting to sound posh in the extremity of her shock.

There was a ghost standing on her doorstep.

# 37

Dolly Farrell put the phone down and wondered what the fuck was going on. It was a warm evening and she was up in the office over Annie's, one of the three clubs that Annie Carter had put her in charge of before shooting off to America to discover love's young – well, maybe not so young – dream.

She could see the lure of that lifestyle. Endless amounts of money, couture clothes, a swanky home in the Hamptons, exclusive Caribbean hideaways, olive and orange and lemon groves in the Med, racehorse studs in England and sunlit vineyards in France, all peppered around the world like a string of precious jewels that could be picked up and put down at a moment's notice. Even if the guy had been plug-ugly, Dolly might have considered going for it.

Or maybe not.

Personally, she was now wondering if Annie had dropped her wits along with her underpants. All right, Constantine was gorgeous. She'd been pretty smitten herself when she'd met him at the club opening – the silver fox. That aura of power, the dazzling white hair, those snazzy silver-grey suits, that fit tanned body of his and those blue, blue eyes ... oh yes, she could have gone for that, she could *understand* that. But he was also trouble with a capital T. Mafia. Dangerous.

But then – Annie had always pushed the boundaries. Ever since Dolly had first met her, when Annie had been in disgrace for snatching her sister's man and Dolly had been a working girl at Aunt Celia's place in Limehouse; ever since *then*, it had been clear that Annie would never, ever play by anyone else's rules. Try to confine Annie Carter, and she'd kick the door down and boot your arse right up between your armpits.

Dolly loved being manager here at Annie's flagship London club; she loved directing the staff, seeing that everything ran smoothly, swanking around town in the long black Jag with Tony – once Annie's driver, and before that Max Carter's – at the wheel. Dolly sat at her desk with the boom-boom-boom of the sound system thrumming up through the floorboards and knew that she had come a long, long way. From tart to Madam to nightclub manager, acquiring a little gloss, a *soupçon* of polish, along the way. Oh, she could still curse and drink and smoke along with the best of them when she was off-duty, but Annie had taught her a long, long time ago that in the work environment you had to behave in a certain way to make people respect you.

She'd learned her lessons. Been bumped up the ladder to success. Left tarting behind and embraced the life of the boss lady – as had her mate Ellie, who was now running the Limehouse knocking-shop, ruling the roost there as Madam. She was pleased for Ellie and they had remained great mates, meeting up for a voddy and tonic and a laugh whenever they could find the time.

Now, Dolly sat there and stared at the phone.

Ellie had just called her, gabbling at top speed. She'd *thought* Ellie had phoned to suggest a meet, but no; Ellie had been in a right state, nearly gibbering like a lunatic with the need to impart her news. And impart it she had, after Dolly had told her several times to calm down, what the hell was the matter?

Ellie had told her the most incredible thing.

Now Dolly let out a heavy breath and leaned back in her chair.

'Fucking *hell*,' she murmured.

She felt like someone had punched her in the gut, knocking all the wind out of her.

Jesus. *Such* news. Unbelievable news.

With a trembling hand she reached out and picked up the phone, listened to the dial tone and wondered how you were supposed to break news like this. She gulped and thought she didn't know *how* she was going to do it. But she knew she had to. She opened the top drawer and pulled out her notebook with all her telephone contact numbers inside. Went through all the business of phoning the operator and finally getting a connection to the New York penthouse. She was roughly working out the time zones as she did so. They were five hours behind England. She checked her watch. Nearly nine o'clock here, so about four there; Annie should be home. Dolly almost hoped she *wasn't*.

How was she going to say this?

Dolly was sweating, her thoughts tumbling over themselves. She really, really didn't want to do this, but friendship dictated that she must, and as quickly as possible.

200

The phone rang.

Endlessly, it rang.

'I'm sorry, would you like me to keep trying?' asked the operator.

'No. Don't bother. No wait. In half an hour, can you try it again?'

So she tried again half an hour later, then half an hour after that, and so on until with relief she accepted that she wasn't going to get an answer. Well, she'd done her best. She went to bed shortly after midnight. She couldn't raise Annie, although she had tried.

A cowardly part of her was glad; and she went to bed in her cosy flat over Annie's nightclub feeling relieved that she'd put off the evil moment for now and wouldn't have to think about it again until tomorrow. As she drifted off to sleep she thought of Ellie's frantic call again, and she wondered: how *did* you tell someone that their first husband, the one they believed to be dead, was in fact alive?

How did you tell your best mate in all the world that Max Carter was right here, in London, and that he now knew what she had done – cleared off to America with another man and married him (and didn't that mean Annie was a bigamist? Dolly thought it did).

What she also thought was that Max Carter wouldn't take very kindly to his wife – even if she *did* believe him to be dead – scarcely waiting for his supposed body to rot before fucking off with another man.

She didn't know how she was going to break any of this to Annie.

She turned over, thumped the pillow.

*Fuck it.*

Like Scarlett O'Hara, she was going to think about it tomorrow.

# 38

Annie had breakfast in the dining room with Layla, Gerda and Nico and then she went into Constantine's study at the front of the house and gratefully closed the door.

Gerda was taking Layla over to the park to feed the ducks; Nico was taking a walk. Apart from two staff, she was alone in the house. The effort to be cheerful for Layla was exhausting her now. She didn't want to be cheerful; she wanted to lie down and die.

She couldn't even sleep any more. Lying in the big bed upstairs last night she had tossed and turned, unable to rest. She had always slept soundly until last year's disaster, but now she had lost the knack of it. She kept *seeing* him. Waking in the night to dimness, she could see his outline across the room, standing beside the window. She would scramble out of bed, half asleep, half awake ... but then he would vanish.

And then, in dawn's first light, he had been there again when her eyes flickered open. Sitting across the room in the Louis Quinze chair. Constantine, watching her with those laser-blue eyes. She could see the dim light forming a halo of silver on his hair, could see how tanned he was, how healthy. She could see the diamond ring winking on his finger as he breathed. He was *there*.

But now she knew how this went. Now she didn't hurry from the bed to embrace him. Now she just waited ... and it happened. His skin, his hair, the bright diamond ring; everything faded to black with a grim inevitability. A charred corpse was there now, not Constantine, not any more. And Annie had to bite down hard on her knuckle to stop herself from screaming. She didn't want to frighten Layla. She didn't want Nico thinking she was losing her mind.

But she was. Wasn't she?

Thank God, the next time she looked – the next time she *dared* – the chair was empty. And now ... now she sat in Constantine's study, at Constantine's desk, and wondered – seriously – if she was going mad.

She looked around the study with its rows of books, the bankers' lamps, the big tan Chesterfield sofas and costly rugs, the elaborate marble fireplace. Here was where she had first met Constantine, on the day of Cara's wedding to Rocco. Here was where he had helped her find Layla, and here was where he had told her he wanted her for the very first time.

Now it was nothing but an empty room. She let out a sigh and became aware that her eyes were wet. Angrily, she wiped at them with her fist. She *never* cried. She was tough.

*Dig deep and stand alone.*

That was the credo she had always lived by.

But now ... now she just wanted it all to be over for her. She didn't want to go on, she was too weary, too beaten.

She could hear voices out in the hall; Gerda's, raised and shrill.

A bolt of anxiety shot up through her midriff. She stood up and hurried over to the door.

*Please,* she thought, *no more...*

Not more trouble. She couldn't take it. Not now.

She hurried across the big hallway with its black-and-white chequered tiles and huge dazzling chandeliers. Crime didn't pay? You only had to look around this place to know that was *bullshit*.

The front door was open. Nico was standing there, alongside Gerda and Layla and Rosa the Spanish maid. Gerda was waving her arms around and the maid seemed to be remonstrating with her. Nico was listening attentively as Annie crossed the hall and joined them. With a brief glance at her, he went outside and they could see him going out onto the roadway, looking left and right.

'Mommy...' Layla was reaching out for Annie.

Annie grabbed her hand and pulled her in close. 'What's going on?' she asked quickly.

'There was someone following us in the park,' said Gerda. 'A man.'

*Christ.* 'Did you get a good look at him?'

Gerda shook her head. 'Only that he was tall. And dark. Everywhere we went, *he* went too. So I came back right away. We ran ... didn't we, Layla? And then when we left the park he followed us right up to the end of the square.'

Gerda looked frantic. Annie could see that she had been really, really scared. And Gerda normally wasn't the type to panic. But who would be following Layla and her nanny in the park? All right, Gerda was a beautiful Nordic blonde – men were attracted to her.

'There's no one out there now,' said Nico, coming back in and closing the door.

Annie looked at him. Maybe just some oddball. Maybe not.

'Next time Gerda takes Layla out, you go with them, okay?'

'Sure thing.'

The Spanish maid was taking Layla off to the kitchen; she had cake there, she said...

Annie stood there in the hall and looked at Gerda and Nico.

'Maybe just a false alarm,' she said.

'Maybe,' said Nico.

'Maybe,' said Gerda, but her nervy, faltering smile said otherwise.

# 39

'Oh, holy shit – *there* you are.'

Dolly opened the main club door wide and sagged against it with relief. Annie Carter-Barolli stood there, blinking in the morning light on the doorstep, and Dolly thought she looked about as rough as a bear's behind. Annie was dressed all in black, her hair looked uncombed, her cheeks sunken, her eyes hollow and shadowed with pain.

*Looks like she hasn't slept in a week,* thought Dolly. *Or maybe a year.*

Annie frowned. 'What?' she asked vaguely, pushing past Dolly into the club.

'I've been trying to *reach* you,' said Dolly, closing the door and hurrying after Annie up the stairs to the flat.

Annie gazed around the cosy little living room, which had once been where she lived but was now very much Dolly's abode. There were lots of fluffy touches in the room now that shouted *Dolly,* lots of pale blues and pinks; it was a blonde's room now, not a brunette's.

'Sit down, sit down,' said Dolly, bustling around, switching on the electric fire.

Annie sat down. Or rather, she seemed to collapse onto the sofa like a sack of shit, Dolly noticed. There was none of Annie's usual elegance in the movement. She looked as though she'd had the stuffing knocked out of her.

'What do you mean, you've been trying to reach me? What for? Something up with the club?' asked Annie, but Dolly didn't think she looked particularly interested. If Dolly had said the place was about to collapse around their ears, she didn't think she was going to get a reaction.

Annie was still looking distractedly around the room. She felt as if her life was on some weird, ever-spinning loop. She was here again, back home in London, but it felt alien to her. She was here with Dolly, her closest friend – but she had never felt so alone as she did right now.

She passed a weary hand over her brow. Dolly

sat down on the sofa. Annie stared at her friend. From rough brass to Madam to nightclub manager, Dolly certainly had progressed. Now she looked every inch the successful business-woman in her strawberry-pink Chanel rip-off skirt suit, her poodle-perm nicely tinted to a gentle shade of ash-blonde, her make-up and nails faultless, her pale tan leather court shoes buffed to a high shine.

'Fuck it, look at the state of you,' tutted Dolly, her blue eyes anxious as they swept over Annie. Jesus, she was so skinny! 'Why didn't you *tell* me you were coming over? I've been trying to reach you because I've had some news. I was phoning you all day yesterday and the night before, couldn't get an answer.'

Annie let out a weary sigh. 'I was on my way back here,' she said.

'I can *see* that, you daft mare.' Dolly hesitated. 'Annie Carter, you look like shit. You really do. What's happened? Don't tell me he's dumped you! He wouldn't – would he? But mind you, bearing in mind what *I've* heard, it could be a good thing. I *said* it was rash, didn't I, you going off with him to the States? You didn't even–'

'Doll,' cut in Annie harshly, clutching at her head. 'Shut the fuck up, will you? I've got a head-ache like someone's sticking a knife in me and waggling it around in my brain. So just *shut up*. Let me think.'

'Well, excuse *me*,' sniffed Dolly, put out. She was quiet for a while, staring at Annie who was just sitting there, gazing at the rug on the floor. Finally, she said: 'So ... what's happened? Why've you come back?'

Annie heaved a sigh that shook her entire frame. 'He's dead, Doll,' she said quietly.

Dolly's jaw nearly hit the floor. 'He's *what?*'

'Constantine. There was an explosion at the house last August. Killed him, Doll. If I'd been two feet closer it would have killed me, too.'

'What, was it an accident...?' Dolly was flailing around for the right thing to say, but coming up empty. Constantine, *dead?*

Annie was shaking her head. 'It was no accident. Someone wanted him dead.'

'Shit, but you said ... holy *shit*, are you all right?'

'Oh, I'm still here,' said Annie, and she turned her head and looked at Dolly, who thought that looking into Annie's eyes right then was like looking into hell. 'Spent a while in hospital. Had a few minor burns on my arm, but they're almost healed now.'

*Lost our baby.*

*Lost my husband.*

*Now I'm fine, only I keep seeing a corpse at the end of my bed, and smelling the smoke and the stench of a burning body.*

She didn't want to tell Dolly any of that. She couldn't bear to. She felt that if she started talking about it she would either shriek or sob – maybe both.

Dolly was silent. Didn't know what to say. Then at last she managed: 'Did they get who did it?'

Annie shook her head.

'Do they *know* who did it?'

She shook her head again.

'You should have called me. I'd have come

straight over, you know I would.'

'I couldn't even think straight, Doll. I was in hospital, and then there was the funeral... I can barely even remember anything about that, only the rain coming down ... and then ... I just *couldn't.*'

'So ... for God's sake, what are you going to do?'

'Lucco snatched the rug from under me, Doll.'

'Lucco? Ain't that the grease ball who's the eldest son?'

Annie nodded. 'Lucco's in charge now. He changed the locks on the Manhattan place so that I couldn't get in there. I went to see him, and he pretty much said that if I stayed around or played up, I'd go the same way as his father.'

'That fucker,' breathed Dolly.

'So I'm back. I'm staying at the Holland Park place; he hasn't closed the door on *that* one yet. I suppose it's just a matter of time.'

'If he does...?' Dolly was looking around, her eyes flitting anxiously from her cosy electric fire to her frou-frou decorations. She loved living here. But Annie was the boss, and if Annie wanted her flat back, what could Dolly say but yes?

'I'll find somewhere else,' said Annie, reading Dolly's expression. 'Don't worry, Doll. I've got money, I can buy another place. I won't be trying to muscle back in here.'

'Oh.' Dolly looked a bit shamefaced at that. She reached out and grasped Annie's hand. 'You poor cow. I'm so bloody sorry.'

Annie gave a taut smile. 'Well, shit happens.'

'You got *that* right.' Dolly thought about what

she'd heard, what she had been so desperately trying to relay to Annie – and all the while, Annie had been in deep trouble. Now she was in even *deeper* trouble, it seemed to Dolly. Right up to her *neck*.

'So ... what was it you were trying to reach me for? I know you were having problems on the refurb at the old Blue Parrot – haven't the contractors turned in again?'

As if she'd bother Annie with something so piffling as that.

Dolly shook her head. Now that she'd heard about Annie's shed-load of trouble, she didn't feel she wanted to pile yet another ton on top of the poor mare. And yet ... she had to. She couldn't let her wander around the damned town not knowing that a storm was about to break over her head.

'What then?' Annie gave a grim, tired smile.

'I'm sorry,' said Doll, biting her lip. 'I really am. To be the one who has to tell you this.'

'Tell me *what?*'

'It's Max,' said Dolly.

'Max?' What the hell was she talking about?

'*Your* Max. Max Carter.'

'What...? What about him?'

'Fuck it all, Annie, I can't believe it but I have to. It's true.'

'Dolly, would you spit it out? Come on.'

'He's not dead. I'm sorry. I know this is a bloody awful shock, but *he ain't dead*. He's *alive*.'

# 40

An hour and a half later, Chris opened the front door of the Limehouse knocking-shop to a tornado in human form.

'Where the fuck is she?' it demanded, shoving past him and roaring off along the hall to the kitchen.

In her haste and distraction, Annie didn't even see Rosie, one of Ellie's little blonde working girls, halfway down the stairs with a semi-dressed punter. She wasn't aware of the parlour door standing open, music drifting out, the sound of giggling and moaning, the heaving shapes inside. She didn't even notice that one of the panels on the kitchen door had been damaged, knocked through. She just threw it open and found Ellie sitting there, a cup of tea halfway to her lips.

'What the f–?' asked Ellie.

Annie lunged at her. The cup fell to the table, splashing the contents everywhere, including over Ellie's neat red suit, before rolling off onto the floor and smashing. Before either Ellie or Chris, who had followed Annie in her flight up the hall, could react, Annie had Ellie by the throat.

'You've played some dirty horrible cruel tricks in your time,' shouted Annie full in her face, spittle flying. 'But this one? This takes the fucking biscuit.'

'Annie...' Chris was saying, trying to pull her off

211

without inflicting harm. 'Come on. Enough!'

But Annie was shaking Ellie by the throat, half throttling her. She was weak but the sheer force of her anger was stunningly intense. The much more robust Ellie was sitting there like a sacrificial lamb, too shocked and terrified by this unprovoked attack to even begin to fight back.

'I said *enough*,' said Chris, and he grabbed Annie around the waist and bodily hauled her away from Ellie.

Now she started fighting Chris. Flailing about madly. He was lifting her clean off the floor but she was still shrieking and shouting. Ellie stood up slowly, her eyes fixed on this mad banshee who'd just come crashing into her lovely, peaceful, well-run house. She raised a trembling hand to her neck. Then, slowly and deliberately, she moved around the table and approached Annie. She pulled back her arm and slapped Annie once, very hard, on the face.

Annie's head was whipped sideways with the force of the blow. She stopped swearing, stopped struggling. Stared at Ellie for a stunned moment. Became aware of where she was, what she was doing.

'Fuck's sake,' muttered Ellie, as girls in various stages of undress came crowding into the kitchen doorway to see what was kicking off. She turned an angry glare on them. 'Get off out of it,' she snarled, and stalked over and shut the door on them. She leaned against it, breathing hard, watching Annie.

'I had to do that,' she said. 'Sorry. You were bloody hysterical. It's all right, Chris, think you

212

can let her go now.'

Chris gave her a dubious look. But he released Annie. She gulped in a breath and dragged a quivering hand through her hair. Then she pulled out a chair and collapsed onto it. She leaned on the table, shaking, her head in her hands.

Chris gave her a long, uncertain look and then he went over to the door and back out into the hall, closing it quietly behind him.

Ellie went over to the worktop, grabbed a cloth and dampened it and applied it to the tea-stains on the red suit before they set. Then she started mopping up the spilled tea from the table and the floor. She picked up the broken bits of crockery, and chucked them in the bin.

Finally, she came back to the table and sat down opposite Annie and looked at her. A red mark was coming up on one thin cheek where Ellie had struck her. Her hair looked as if it hadn't even been washed; it was all over the place. There wasn't a scrap of make-up on her face. Her clothes looked dishevelled. This wasn't the Annie Carter she'd known.

'What the hell happened to you?' asked Ellie in wonder. 'You look fucking terrible.'

'What happened to *me?*' Annie let out a harsh croak of laughter. 'What happened to *you,* you cow. What do you think you're doing, telling these bloody awful lies? Oh, I knew you could always stretch the truth. But *this?* This is beyond a bloody joke.'

Ellie folded her arms on the table and stared at Annie.

'Dolly said you'd never believe it. But listen. It

213

ain't a joke,' she said flatly.

Annie drew herself up. She looked like a cobra, mad dark eyes and a grim mouth ready to spit venomous rage.

'Listen, you malicious mare. Max Carter is *dead*. He died two years ago when he was thrown down a mountain. The kidnappers *told* me he was dead. Why would they have lied about that?'

'Maybe they weren't lying. Maybe they believed they'd killed him, but he survived.'

Now Annie was shaking her head quickly. Ellie thought she looked jittery, deranged.

'No! He's dead. They *told me he was dead*.'

Ellie leaned forward and spoke in low, measured tones now.

'Annie. He's *alive*. I've seen the bastard, he was right here. Chris saw him too. He was looking for you, and Layla. He didn't tell us the full story, but he was looking for you both.'

Annie was still shaking her head, crossing her arms over her body, her lips pursed in denial. 'No,' she said. 'No.'

'What should I have done, Annie?' asked Ellie. 'We've known each other a long time, we're friends, ain't we? Come on, what would you have done in my place? I thought about it long and hard, I can tell you. You were in the States. You were happily married to another man. And when we told him *that* ...' Ellie's face clouded.

'What?' Annie was watching Ellie as if *she* was the crazy one. Because this couldn't be true. It *couldn't* be.

'Well, I got in touch with Dolly as quick as I could because I didn't have your number and she did. He was asking about you and Layla. Then ... well, Chris broke the news to him. Right here. He was sitting right where you are now. And when Chris told him ... he went real quiet. I tried to defend you; I told him that you had *believed* he was dead. And you know what he said?'

Annie shook her head slowly. This was all crazy. This was *mad*.

'He said, what the fuck? You thought he was dead and so you cleared off with some other man before he was even *cold*? That's what he said.' Ellie shivered slightly. 'Christ, he was angry. Not hot, not excitable, no shouting and screaming. Just real cold and controlled and bloody scary.'

'Did he say anything else?' asked Annie. This couldn't be true, but that ... that sounded like Max when he really lost it. He went quiet. And that was when he was at his most dangerous.

Ellie shook her head. 'He just stood up and went over to that door. He looked calm. And then he punched it. Knocked the ruddy panel straight out. There was blood dripping off his knuckles but I don't think he even felt it.' Ellie drew in a shuddering breath. 'He's a hard scary bastard that one. So I phoned Dolly straight away, the minute he'd gone. I told her. And she's told you, and that's why you've come back I suppose? Fuck me, I don't think *I'd* have come back to face him if I'd gone off with another man. I'd stay clear, that's what I'd do.'

Annie shook her head. She felt so weak, so tired and bewildered. And now this. Ellie didn't seem to be making any of this up. Annie's eyes drifted over to the damaged door. Could it be true? Had

215

he really been right here?

'You don't know why I've come back?' she asked.

'Well ... to see him, I thought. To face him down. Tell him you've moved on.'

'I didn't know anything about any of this,' Annie told her wearily. 'I was on my way back when Dolly was trying to reach me to break the news. I came back because it's over for me in the States. That's all.'

Ellie nodded slowly. *Over in what way?* she wondered. But she didn't say it. She'd ask Dolly, she'd have all the dirt. This poor bint looked as though she'd had enough talking for now.

'Let me make some fresh tea,' said Ellie, standing up and moving over to the kettle. 'You want something to eat? You look like you could do with a feeding-up.'

But when she looked round, Annie was over by the door. She was fingering the splintered wood, looking at it as if it might be a dream, not reality.

'Annie...?' said Ellie when she didn't answer.

Annie glanced at her. Her hand dropped away from the damaged door. She shook her head.

'I'm off to catch up with Kath and Ruthie.'

'Well, mind how you go,' said Ellie, but Annie had opened the door and was already hurrying away down the hall. 'Take care...' said Ellie to the empty kitchen. Annie didn't hear her. She was gone.

# 41

The word was spreading around the streets like wildfire now. Max Carter was back. Steve Taylor and Gary Tooley, who had once been – along with Jimmy Bond – his most trusted foot soldiers, heard it but didn't believe it. And then one night they went to Queenie's as usual for a meet with the boys, and there he was, inside, sitting at the head of the table, waiting for them.

'Fuck me,' said dark, squat, powerful Steve, stopping dead in the doorway, thinking he was seeing a phantom. Max had been his friend forever, both his boss and his mate; maybe he just *wanted* to see the old bugger sitting there and his eyes were playing tricks.

Gary shoved him aside and he too stared in disbelief.

'Oh, you're having a bloody *laugh*,' said Gary, six feet seven inches tall, blond and whip-thin.

'You greasy old bastard, how'd you pull *this* one off?' asked rat-faced little Jackie Tulliver, chomping on his usual massive cigar, finding a gap in the crowded doorway to shove his ugly little beak through.

Max stood up. Steve came forward and hugged him hard. Then Gary. Then Jackie. Then all the other boys. For a while the room was full of shouts and laughs and general excitement, then they all settled down and Max told them what had happened to him.

They listened attentively.

'Shit a *brick*. We thought you were brown bread for sure. When we offed Jimmy we thought that was the last of you, too,' said Gary.

'Your old lady took over for a while,' said Steve.

'She's a tough girl,' said Jackie.

'Yeah.' Max sat back in his chair and they thought they had never seen him look better, fitter. 'That was before she pissed off with the Barolli boss.'

The room was silent.

Then Steve said: 'Dolly Farrell said she's back in town. Got some trouble over there in the States.'

'She's got some fucking trouble *here* too,' said Max, frowning. 'What d'you mean, Dolly said that? She wouldn't grass up her mate – they're tight together. And that whorehouse is on the Delaney patch.'

'Ah yeah,' said Steve. 'About that...' And he explained all that had happened, and that Dolly's establishment now paid protection – as did the rest of Limehouse – to the Carters, not the Delaneys.

Silence again.

'So ... you want us to bring her in?' asked Steve.

Max shook his head slowly. 'No. I'll catch up with her when I'm ready. Tell me more about Jimmy.'

Jimmy had been Max's right-hand man; he still couldn't believe what they were telling him about Jim. But Jimmy was gone, and Steve and Gary had taken over the running of the firm.

'Fill me in on the business. How's everything going?'

'Pretty fair,' said Gary. 'We got a lot of security work going now, right out to Essex. Christ! You wouldn't know, I suppose, but back in April there was a big police raid. Didn't touch us, but a few faces went down. The Bill grabbed a shit-load of arms from around the East End.'

'None of ours copped it?' asked Max.

'Nah. See, we're *legit,* more or less. All the arcades, shops and restaurants are coughing up on time, no problems.'

'Billy still doing the milk run?' asked Max. The milk run was gang slang for collecting the protection money.

Gary broke the news about Billy.

'Fuck,' breathed Max, taking it all in.

He'd lost Jonjo, Jimmy, and even poor bloody Billy. He'd been laid up in a hospital bed with busted ankles and his head shot in all directions, not even knowing who the hell he was, while his ever-loving *wife,* who should have been prostrated with grief at his loss, had been busy doing a bunk with his daughter and committing bigamy with a Mafia Don. Making him look like yesterday's news; like a fucking fool. He was spitting mad about it all; too mad to trust himself to be within a mile of her just yet.

'What about the clubs?' he asked.

'Paying good,' said Jackie. 'Mrs Carter turned 'em around, put that Dolly woman in charge...' His voice tailed away.

*And then fucked off for pastures new,* Max finished in his head.

'We can bring her in if you want. Just say the word,' Steve reminded him delicately. He couldn't imagine how Max must be feeling. But he knew that if *he'd* been declared dead he'd want his old lady to be so grief-stricken that she'd chuck herself into the hole after him, at the very least – not just fuck off with some other man.

But Max shook his head again.

'Or the kid? We seen your kid with a blonde woman, a nanny; they've been out walking near the Barolli place in Holland Park.'

'Nah. I'll sort this out myself. In my own time.'

# 42

'That man's still loitering around in the park, with his collar turned up', said Gerda. 'I saw him, watching from a distance. But when Nico went to have a word, he vanished.'

Now why should anyone be watching Gerda and Layla in the park? Annie wondered. Of course, someone had already told the Carter boys that she was back. She sat in Constantine's study and phoned her sister Ruthie, who had a place over in Richmond; then she called Dolly.

'Have you told the Carters that I'm back?' she demanded.

'Course I bloody well have,' said Dolly. 'What you think I am, barking mad? I'm sitting here running a Carter club. Ellie's paying them for protection. We're both up to our necks in Carter business – of *course* we had to tell them you're back, with Max Carter showing up alive instead of dead as toast.'

Annie still couldn't believe that was true. She thought of the man, trailing Gerda and Layla. It made her deeply uneasy, even if Nico *was* with them wherever they went now. Maybe a Carter foot soldier, maybe not. She thought of how she had nearly lost Layla once before, how Layla still bore the scars of that ordeal. She couldn't let that happen again. No way.

'Fuck's sake, did you really have to tell them?' she asked.

'You know I did. That's how it works, Annie. You know the score.'

Yeah, she did. In the days when the Delaney family had been running Limehouse, Dolly had answered to them, tipping them off to anything happening on their turf. Now she answered to the Carters: it was a simple fact of life.

'What the hell are you going to do?' asked Dolly.

Annie had no idea. If it was true that Max was still alive, they would have to talk. But so far she hadn't even encountered him. She thought of Ellie's kitchen door, knocked in – Ellie claimed – by Max in a rage when he had heard she'd left for the States with Constantine. *Had* it been Max, her Max, who had done that? She couldn't believe it. She had to see him to know that it was, and so far she hadn't. She was chasing ghosts, demons and dead men around town, and finding no evidence of their existence at all.

'I don't know what I'm going to do, Doll,' said Annie with a heavy sigh. 'If everything you and

221

Ellie have told me is true–'

'It *is*.'

'Then the ball's in his court. If he wants to find me, he can. Meanwhile, I ... I just have to try and get over what's been happening.'

That man trailing Layla and Gerda. If Max was as mad about what she'd done as she imagined he *would* be, might he not have Layla snatched and brought to him? She thought he might do that, to spite her.

The idea made her go cold with fear.

The notion of him being somewhere here in London, somewhere close by, with his men watching her movements, was weird beyond belief. But he could do it. She knew he could. He could take Layla, declaring her an unfit mother out of revenge for her having defected to the Barolli camp. And how would she ever get her daughter back then?

While Gerda and Layla went off upstairs to play, Annie called Nico into the study. They sat down on opposite sides of the desk and Annie got straight to the point.

'I'm worried about this man in the park,' she said.

Nico sat back and stared at her face. 'You got any ideas who it might be?'

She shook her head. 'Nico, I've been hearing some really strange things.'

'What things?'

Annie dragged her hands through her hair. 'My friends are saying that my first husband ain't dead. That he's alive and he's in London.'

Nico's eyes widened. 'No way.'

'They're saying it's true. They're also saying that he's furious with me for clearing off with Constantine. And... I think maybe the man in the park is one of the Carter boys. And maybe Max thinks Layla would be better off with him, and he's planning to snatch her away from me.'

'We can't let that happen,' said Nico.

Thank God for Nico. He understood instantly where she was coming from; he was a clever man with a quick brain. Also, he was her last link – her only link – to Constantine. Just having him around was a comfort.

'We won't,' said Annie. 'Nico, I've spoken to my sister. She's got room for Gerda and Layla for a while, until all this is sorted out. I want you to take them over there.'

Annie's heart ached even as she said it. Once again, she had to be separated from Layla because being with her, being *near* her, could be putting Layla at risk. And yet, who would care for Layla better than Max? He wasn't a danger to Layla; he had doted on his little girl.

Maybe she was being overcautious.

Or maybe the follower in the park wasn't one of Max's boys at all?

But then – who else could it be?

If it *was* Max behind this, then she wouldn't give up her daughter without a fight. She was determined on that. All right, he was seeing her marriage to Constantine as a betrayal. But it wasn't. For God's sake, her only crime had been to believe that her husband was dead, to mourn him bitterly and then to fall in love again. What had he expected – that she would withdraw from life altogether simply because he was no longer a part of it?

If she had sinned at all – and she didn't believe she had – then she had been roundly punished anyway. Constantine was dead now. Max might have come back, like Lazarus rising from the tomb, but Constantine would not. Constantine was lost to her forever.

'I'll talk to Gerda and Layla, get some stuff packed,' said Annie, pushing her chair back and standing up.

'You're sure about this?' asked Nico, his brows drawn together in a ferocious frown.

'I'm not sure about anything,' said Annie. 'But I know that Layla will be fine with Ruthie. All this... I can't have her here, in the middle of it all. It's not fair.'

'Maybe all she needs is to be close to you,' said Nico.

'No.' Annie shook her head firmly. 'That's not an option. I want her somewhere safe, so I want you to take her and Gerda over there this afternoon.'

'Wouldn't that be the first place he'd look for her? With your sister?'

'With our history?' Annie raised a grim smile. 'I don't think so.'

'You think he's gonna cut up rough? Really?'

Annie put her fists on the desk and gave it some thought.

'Max Carter? Oh yeah. I think so.'

When Gerda and Layla had gone with Nico that afternoon, Annie phoned Kath, her cousin.

'Holy fuck, this is all so *interesting*,' Kath said the minute Annie said hello. Annie could picture her beaming smile all down the line. If Annie was getting shit, Kath was always pleased about it. The kids – little Jim and Molly – were shouting and wailing in the background as usual. Annie could imagine the scene round at Kath's. Unwashed crocks in the sink, dirty floors, kiddies' toys strewn everywhere, and Kath sitting, hugely fat, in the middle of it all in a mucky T-shirt and elastic-waisted skirt, puffing on a scraggy roll-up and laughing her arse off at Annie's woes.

'What's interesting?' asked Annie.

'What I been *hearing*. They're saying Max Carter ain't dead; that he's back here and he's gunning for you.'

'News travels fast.'

'Fuck *me*, girl, you're in big trouble now. I mean, let's face it, he was barely cold before you were getting the old pork sword off that fancy Mafia bloke. Gawd, I should think *any* man would want to lynch his wife if she did that.'

'And how are you, Kath?' asked Annie, gritting her teeth to choke back the angry words that wanted to come out of her mouth.

'Bloody marvellous. Kids are a nightmare, as always. Really cheered me up, hearing that Lady Muck's got troubles too.' Kath was actually laughing now.

'Kath.'

'Hm?'

'You're a cow, you know that?'

But Kath only laughed.

Annie slammed the phone down. That *bitch*.

225

Her stomach was clenched up in a knot of unease. Layla was out of the way now; it was safer, far safer, that she should be with Ruthie. But already, Annie missed her so much. She felt weak tears prickle behind her eyes as she sat there alone and painfully bereft in the big grand house.

The show had to go on – didn't it? Broken and devastated though she might be, she had to keep going, keep things normal if she could – and then maybe, one day, they would start to *feel* normal again too.

Tonight, she was going to pay Dolly another visit, get a proper look at how the club was running when it was open and packed with punters. Maybe on the way there she'd stop off at Queenie's and see if Max was there. She doubted he would be. She thought that this was all one long nightmare, and that at any moment she'd wake up, and Constantine would be there with her, saying hey, what's up? Think you've been dreaming.

But Constantine was dead, *truly* dead.

Not like Max, who had just been playing at it.

*He's gunning for you*, she thought. Kath's words. Well, Layla was out of the way now. *So just bring it on*, she thought. She'd done nothing wrong. She had nothing to be ashamed of.

But would he believe that? She didn't think so.

# 43

Max wasn't at Queenie's when she called in there that evening. She still had a key, so she opened the front door and walked around the echoing, musty-smelling rooms. Nothing much in there except a few sticks of tatty Utility furniture and the big table upstairs where the boys met. There was a faint odour of cigar smoke hanging in the air. *Jackie Tulliver,* she thought.

She left the old terraced house and got back into the hire car, with Nico sitting there patiently at the wheel.

'Let's go on over to the club,' she said wearily.

Nico steered the car out into the traffic. 'I wanted to talk to you about Layla,' he said.

'Oh God, Nico, not now,' said Annie. Her head was pounding; she felt exhausted. Layla was safe with Ruthie; she didn't need to know any more than that. She couldn't *take* any more than that.

He shrugged and drove on in silence.

When they got there, Nico parked up in a side street, grumbling about right-hand-drive cars and tiny roads not fit for purpose as he man-oeuvred the car into a space. They got out and walked the short distance to the club, its bass back-beat keeping time with their footsteps. Punters were swarming into the club as they ap-proached.

Annie paused and looked at the red neon sign

over the scarlet-painted doors. Annie's. If Max was really and truly back, really alive, what would he make of *that?* He had known this as the Palermo Lounge. Right now, the workmen were over at the old Blue Parrot, gutting it, tearing that old sign down too, replacing it with another one of these, the red neon Annie's.

'Hi, Paul,' she said to the doorman, and he nodded as she passed inside with Nico trailing behind.

'Knock Three Times' was blasting out of the massive sound system as they went down the stairs and into the main body of the club. There were gyrating bodies out on the circular glass dance floor, the strobes beneath it flashing up yellow, orange, red, blue. On the tiny up-lit podiums the go-go girls danced and twirled in their fringed white bikinis and white boots.

'Jeez, the noise in here...' complained Nico, leaning close to Annie's ear to make himself heard.

Annie cast an appraising eye over the club's dimly lit interior. Chocolate-brown banquettes lined the walls; cosy little spaces where people could chat, eat their chicken or scampi in a basket, drink, watch the dancers.

Annie went over to the bar with the duplicate neon-red 'Annie's' sign glowing warmly above it. Dolly was behind the bar, complaining to the barman about there being no mixers as per bloody usual, then she turned and saw Annie and her face fell.

'Pleased to see me?' asked Annie with an attempt at a smile.

'Daft bat, I'm always pleased to see you,' said

Dolly, coming to the bar and leaning over so she could make herself heard. 'But ... fuck it, he's *here,* Annie love. He's bloody here, over there in the corner.'

Annie felt as if all the blood had left her head and shot straight down to her feet. She swayed for an instant and Nico caught her arm.

'You okay?' he asked.

'Did you hear that?' Annie asked him.

'Yeah. I heard.'

Annie peered among the crush of bodies, but she couldn't see anything. She felt the blood singing in her ears and wondered if she was about to pass out cold. She gulped down a breath. It steadied her a little. But she could feel herself shaking, literally *shaking.* Because ... he could really be here. Max Carter, the man she had loved so passionately once; the man she had won, lost and mourned; the man she had thought she would happily spend the rest of her life with.

But it hadn't worked out like that.

'I'm going over there,' she said through lips that felt numb with shock. 'I'm going to talk to him.'

Nico still had hold of her arm. 'Is that the smart thing to do? Bearing in mind what everyone's told you about how he took the news of you and the Boss?'

'I don't give a shit whether it's smart or not, I've got to know if it's true. I've got to know if it's really him.'

She pulled her arm away. Nico stared at her face. 'You want me to come over there with you?'

Annie shook her head: no.

Aware of Dolly standing there tensely behind

229

the bar watching her, aware of Nico's worried expression as she moved away across the room, still Annie felt that she was in some sort of awful twisted dream as she pushed through the fug of cigarette smoke and the crush of bodies.

Would she get there and see Constantine there, not Max; Constantine charred and grinning at her, lolling dead and incinerated on the banquette?

*Oh God, please let me wake up now,* she thought, aware of her heart thudding away in her chest, of the unsteadiness of her legs, of the sick tension in the pit of her stomach.

She pushed on through the punters, their laughter grating on her ears, their curious looks at this demented-looking dark-haired woman glancing off her like darts off a rhino's hide. Yeah, this was a dream. She would just go on and on walking, trying to find him, and she would never get there. She would wake up, and the dream would be over.

Then the crowds seemed to part at last, and she stopped walking. She was looking at a banquette with a group of people sitting around it. There were half-full glasses on the table, the remnants of a meal. Baskets and red napkins, knives and forks.

The first person she saw was Steve Taylor; dark-haired, muddy-eyed, he was looking up at her in surprise. The other people at the table were talking, but soon Steve's silence infected them as they saw what he was looking at, *who* he was looking at. Steve had a woman with him, but Annie didn't recognize her.

Gary was there too, with another girl; his blond hair was catching the light of the whirling strobes, his pale eyes were pinning her where she stood. Beside the girl who was with Gary was another woman: a small, succulent blonde in a sugar-pink Dusty Springfield get-up, who was draping herself over a dangerous-looking dark-haired man sitting right in the corner, his back to the wall.

Annie stepped forward until she was standing right in front of their table.

Her eyes were fixed on the dark-haired man, the one who seemed to be the centre point of the group. He had a deeply tanned complexion, a predatory hook of a nose under black brows, and thick black curling hair. His face was sharp, sharper than she remembered, hardened in some fiery crucible she knew nothing about, but his eyes were the same – a dense, dark navy blue – and they were staring at her right now, sweeping up over her body and then back down again, with a chillingly cold disdain.

'Who the fuck's this?' the little blonde was asking.

'That's his *wife*, dingbat,' said Gary, stubbing out his cigarette in the ashtray but not taking his eyes off Annie for a minute.

'His...?' The blonde was looking between the dark-haired man and the dark-haired woman now, her expression thunderous.

'Holy shit,' said Annie. 'It's true. You're *alive.*'

Now there could be no more doubt. She was looking at Max Carter.

# 44

Annie stood frozen to the spot. She didn't feel
that she could have moved, even if she'd wanted
to. The last time she had seen him he had been
diving into the pool in Majorca over two years
ago – and then the nightmare had really begun.
The kidnappers had told her he was dead, that
they'd thrown him down a mountain.

Yet here he was. Alive.

Now Steve and the girl beside him were moving
out of the way. Max was shrugging off the em-
bracing arm of the Dusty Springfield lookalike;
he was coming off the banquette and walking
towards her with that same fluid, panther-like
way of moving he'd always had.

He stopped walking two paces away. It was
him. More compact and more powerfully muscular than Constantine. Shorter, but only by a
couple of inches. It was *him*.

'Jesus...' said Annie.

'You fucking *slut*,' said Max.

Annie recoiled as if he'd slapped her. 'What?'
she could only whisper, blinking with surprise.

'*What? What* do you mean, *what?*' he went on
angrily. He was staring at her as if she was filthy.
'My God, I should have known. Getting into bed
with your own sister's fiancé? That should have
told me all I needed to know about you.'

'What the...?' Annie was trying to gather herself.

He was attacking her, wading into her, and – for God's sake – *he'd* been a part of that too, every bit as guilty as she was. She felt a stirring of fury deep in the pit of her stomach. She'd done nothing wrong. Nothing at all. He had *no right* to slag her off like this.

But now he was grabbing her left hand, staring at it. She was still wearing the wedding ring Constantine had slipped onto her finger, and the big vulgar diamond engagement ring he'd bought for her at Tiffany's in New York.

Max stared at the evidence for long moments, then dropped her hand with a disdainful flick of the wrist.

'You know what?' he said, and now his eyes were boring into hers. 'Constantine Barolli's fucking well welcome to you. Of all the cheap tricks!'

'I thought you were dead,' said Annie numbly, aware of Dusty back there sneering at her and enjoying this put-down, aware of the others watching, taking it all in. 'I was *told* you were dead.'

'Yeah? And instead of going into mourning, what did you do? You shagged Barolli and left the country with him. *That's* how grief-stricken you were.'

'That ain't true,' she whispered.

'Yeah it is. You couldn't *wait* to get another man in your bed, could you?'

Annie could only stare at him, overcome.

'*Could* you?' he demanded.

She took a deep breath, steadied herself. She felt on the verge of collapse, on the verge of shrieking and being unable to stop. But she wouldn't let him and his cronies see her fall apart. She drew herself

233

up to her full height and looked him dead in the eye.

'You know what, Max Carter?' she said, and her voice was firmer now, louder. 'You can just *fuck. Right. Off.* You got that?'

And she turned on her heel and walked away from him, pushing back through the crowds until she reached Nico, who was still standing at the bar with Dolly.

'You see him?' asked Dolly, her face worried.

'Oh yeah,' said Annie on a trembling laugh, breathing hard with the effort of maintaining a calm front. 'I saw him. Come on, Nico, let's go.'

# 45

Outside, Annie breathed in the fresh night air and felt that she wanted to just get in the car and tell Nico to drive to the ends of the earth; she just wanted to get away from the torment of it all, the confusion in her brain, the hideous images that kept flashing through it, the nightmares that would not let her rest.

'You okay?' Nico asked her as she hurried along, hands in pockets, trying not to even *think* any more.

'Fine,' she lied. The car was up ahead; she just wanted refuge, she wanted it all to *stop*.

They reached the car, and Nico was now fumbling with the key on the passenger side of the car to let her in out of the misty rain, while she waited. There was a loud noise, stunningly loud, a car backfiring. Annie jumped and looked around, up and down the street. She could see nothing, only shadows, only the wet gleam of the tarmac after the evening's early rain, the lines of cars, the cold yellow glare of the streetlights.

Nico was leaning in against her, heavier and heavier.

She looked at him, actually focused on him for the first time since they'd rushed out of the club. In the dim light she could see he wasn't trying to open the car door any more; his eyes were closed and he was slowly keeling over onto her.

'Nico!' she screamed.

But he didn't seem to hear her. He was toppling like a tree. She was falling beneath him, trying to support his weight and failing. She sagged to the pavement with Nico's huge bulk pinning her there. She felt the hard, cold surface hit her shoulder, then her knee. Oh Christ, he was so heavy!

'Nico,' she gasped out. He was smothering her, crushing her ribs; she could barely get her breath. *'Nico.'*

He'd had a heart attack. She was certain of it. All that they had endured together over the last months had finally proved too much for the old soldier. She lay there, pinioned. She tried to move, tried to shift him even an inch or two, and she couldn't. She slumped back. Tried not to panic. Help would come. There were other cars here; someone would sooner or later come and free her, get Nico the help he needed.

Someone was coming now. She heard footsteps, saw a dark shape standing over them.

'Thank God,' she wheezed. 'He...' And then she stopped talking as she saw the gun.

*That wasn't a backfiring car.*

Nico hadn't had a heart attack. He'd been *shot*.

'Holy *shit*,'she muttered, pushing desperately at Nico's bulk, trying to move him, desperate to get free, to run, while all the time her eyes were fastened upon that dark shadowy figure above her – she couldn't see its face – and the icy glint of the muzzle as the figure raised the gun and pointed it with slow, easy deliberation, straight at her head.

*Oh shit, was this Max? Was this Max, disgusted with her, wanting her dead?*

It would be quick, anyway. An end to all the pain.

But still she pushed at Nico's body, tried to get free. She wasn't succeeding. She was going to die. She slumped back onto the pavement and the figure took aim.

*Here it comes.*

She was almost glad.

Then there was a shout; the figure stopped, the gun lifted. The shadowy figure stepped back, started to run, was gone. Suddenly there were men surrounding her where she lay, people tugging at Nico, heaving his senseless body off her. Someone pulled her roughly to her feet She staggered, feeling the swell of sickness, the aftermath of terror – and then realized that she was leaning against the hard, reassuring body of her 'dead' first husband, Max Carter. Horrified, she pulled herself quickly away and sagged instead against the side of the car. Gary Tooley was there, squatting over Nico, Steve Taylor looking on.

'Any good?' asked Steve, glancing down at Nico and then skipping around to scan the streets all around them.

Annie looked where they were all looking now – at the dark spreading stain on the left of Nico's chest. The sickness swelled up into her throat. She swallowed hard, turned away.

Gary shook his head. 'Clean shot. Straight through the heart.'

'Take care of it,' said Max to the two men, and grabbed Annie by the arm.

'What the f...?' she asked, as he dragged her off along the road. She peered back over her shoulder. They were manhandling Nico. Hefting him about as if he were no more than a piece of meat. 'No. Nico!' she wailed.

'He's had it,' said Max roughly, hurrying away and taking her with him.

*But that's Nico,* she thought desperately. *That's not just any thick-headed thug lying there, that's Nico.* Constantine's friend for all of his life. Her last true link to the man she'd loved.

'Another few seconds and you'd have joined him,' said Max, stopping by a black Jag, opening the passenger door and pushing her inside.

'You bastard, that's *Nico,*' she told him as he got in the driver's seat. She was furious, devastated, shaking. She sagged back into the seat and buried her face in her hands. Nico was dead. Oh God. Not Nico, she couldn't stand it.

'One of Barolli's boys, right?' he sneered, and started the engine and pulled out. 'Holland Park, yeah?'

Annie dropped her hands and stared at him.

237

She wasn't going to cry. No matter what he said, no matter what he did, she wouldn't cry in front of him. Just a few moments ago she had been afraid that he intended to kill her. She wasn't about to show weakness. Not over Nico, not even over Constantine. She was determined to do any crying in private. 'Well you should bloody well *know,*' she told him. 'You've had someone watching the house, watching Gerda and Layla when they walk in the park.'

He glanced at her as he steered the Jag through the traffic. 'I haven't,' he said.

'Oh please,' said Annie wearily, 'don't *lie.*'

After that, he was silent and she was glad of that, all the way back to Holland Park.

# 46

Back at the house she went into the study and straight over to Constantine's desk. She sat down in the place where he'd always sat and crouched there, shivering. Nico was dead. She couldn't take it in. And he wasn't even going to get a Christian burial. She knew how the boys dealt with things like this. Nico's body would vanish; bold, loyal, brave Nico, to who she owed so much, would end up in the concrete foundations of a motorway, or deep in the English Channel.

'Here, get this down you,' said a voice.

She looked up, startled, thinking that Constantine would be there, blackened, charred,

238

dead, reaching out his ruined arms to her. But it
was Max. She thought she'd left him at the front
door, but he must have followed her in. She
hadn't even noticed. He was holding out a glass
of brandy.

'Take it.'

'I can't...' she said numbly. Talking was hard.
Thinking straight was almost impossible.

'You're in shock. Drink it.'

Annie reluctantly took the glass and sipped the
stuff. It burned her all the way down, and she
started to choke.

'Shit, you never could take a drink,' he said, and
poured himself one from the tray and threw it
back in one hit. He turned and stared at her.
'Unlike your pissy-arsed mother.'

'Leave my mother out of it,' she said, eyes
watering, although he was right. Connie had died
of the drink. Once, she had been frightened her
sister Ruthie would go the same way, but thank
God she'd pulled herself back from the brink in
time.

*Ruthie*.

Suddenly she had a desperate need to hear
Layla's voice.

Annie reached out shakily and picked up the
phone. Max was wandering around the study,
eyeing the books, the couches, taking it all in.
Annie watched him in disbelief. It was really him.
She couldn't believe it, but it was. Her husband.
She told herself that. *Her husband*. But she
couldn't feel a thing; all she felt was numb.

'You've done well for yourself,' he was saying.
'From a crappy little East End two-up-two-

down, to a fucking great mansion.'

She longed to say that it wasn't *her* mansion, Lucco had seen to that, but the words stuck in her throat.

'But then you always were the ambitious type. Trust you to aim straight for the top.'

'Hello?' said a female voice on the other end of the phone.

'Ruthie? It's Annie, I just wanted to check that Layla's okay.' Max turned and stared at her as she said his daughter's name.

There was a brief silence.

'But ... I thought you'd changed your mind...'

'What? What are you on about?'

'Well ... she's not here. When we spoke on the phone I got her room ready, but when you didn't show up with her, I thought you must have changed your mind.'

'What?' Annie gulped down a breath. For a moment, the whole room spun. Her head felt as if it was about to implode. 'You mean ... she's really not there?'

Ruthie gave a slight laugh, but then her voice grew tight with concern. 'Of course she's not. Isn't she ... isn't she with you?'

'No,' said Annie weakly. 'She's not.'

Now she was remembering Nico's words. He hadn't been happy about her choice of Ruthie to care for Layla. And he had tried to tell her that, earlier today. But she had cut him off. *He had been trying to tell her where he'd put Layla.*

But Gerda was with her. And Nico wouldn't have put either of them anywhere he wasn't completely sure they were rock-solid safe. But

Nico was *dead*. And there was no way she could ask him the question now, no way he could tell her the answer.

*Fuck it.*

'What's going on?' Max was asking.

'Who's that?' asked Ruthie.

*Shit, did she recognize his voice, after all this time? And how was she going to break this particular bit of news to Ruthie?*

She couldn't face that conversation, not now.

'Nobody. It's okay, Ruthie. Just a mix-up. I'll phone again later.' She put the phone down.

Max was staring at her. 'Where's Layla?' he asked.

Annie swallowed hard. 'I don't know.'

He moved before she even had time to blink. Suddenly he was across the room. He grabbed the front of her coat and hauled her bodily to her feet. 'You don't fucking well *know?*' he snarled at her from inches away.

'I told Nico to take her and Gerda to Ruthie's. I thought there was cause for alarm. *Stop shaking me, will you?*' Annie tried to draw breath. 'The man in the park. I told you about the man in the park.'

'And *I* told *you* that it wasn't me. It could have been one of the boys. Or someone else, who the fuck knows?'

'And Nico was trying to tell me earlier today, he was trying to tell me that he didn't think Ruthie's place was a good idea and so he'd taken them somewhere else, but I wasn't listening...'

'Are you trying to tell *me* you've lost my kid?' said Max through gritted teeth.

'She's *my* kid too. And I'm *telling* you that Nico's put her somewhere safe, but I don't know where. But Gerda's with her. Gerda will get in touch.'

Gerda *had* to get in touch. But what if she didn't? What if she *couldn't?*

'Jesus, this is a nightmare,' said Annie, shutting her eyes, trying to blank it all out.

'This Gerda – she trustworthy?'

Annie's eyes opened. Oh God, he was still there, it was Max, it really was. Looking at her with such angry disdain; looking at her like she was shit on his shoe.

'She's trustworthy,' she managed to get out. Her mouth was dry, and the brandy had given her heartburn.

She was afraid she was going to vomit. She was sick to her stomach of all this – sick of constantly having to be apart from her little girl because the life she led was too fraught with dangers. She knew that sometimes it was the only possible option, the only *sensible* thing to do. But she hated it; it ripped the heart out of her, every time she had to do it.

'Then this Gerda will get in touch.'

'Yeah. She will.'

'And *then* I'm taking Layla.'

Annie stared at him, open-mouthed. She couldn't believe her own ears. 'You *what?*'

'You heard. Better with her own father than with a sorry excuse for a mother who can't keep her legs together for two minutes at a time.'

'You *bastard,*' hissed Annie, wild-eyed. 'You're not taking Layla away from me.'

'Watch me.'

'I'll fight you in every court in the land,' she spat.

'Really? Try it. See how it goes down with the legal system. You've committed bigamy, after all. You seriously think they'll overlook that?'

'Bastard!' Annie was struggling against him, trying to get free, but his grip was like iron. 'My God, I can't believe I loved you once. I can't believe I actually wasted *tears* over a cruel, despicable piece of *nothing* like you.'

'Yeah? Now I suppose you're going to tell me Constantine Barolli is twice the man I was? And where is he, exactly? I'd like a fucking *word* with him.'

Annie froze. All the fight went out of her in an instant. 'He's dead,' she said flatly. She saw the shock of it register on his face. She let out a cracked, bitter laugh. 'You know what? I nearly died too. But I lived. I wish I'd died, but I didn't.'

'Why?' Now he was staring into her face from inches away. 'Because you loved him so much?'

Annie's mouth was a quivering bitter line of hate as she stared into the face of the man she had once loved, once married, once had a child with; and once mourned.

'Yeah,' she said, wanting to hurt him as badly as he was hurting her. 'Because of that. Yeah.'

Now she felt so empty, so spent. Constantine was dead. Nico was dead. Max despised her. She sagged against him and instantly, roughly, he pushed her away, stepped back, glared at her. His eyes swept contemptuously over her. 'Don't come the helpless little woman act with me. I don't buy it. And you're not *that* irresistible. In fact, you look like something out of fucking Belsen.'

Annie recoiled. She thought she heard the doorbell, but she couldn't have. It was too late in the evening. It was only his words she heard, flung at her like weapons, clanging around her head. It was true, what he was saying. She knew it was. Her hair was unwashed, her clothes were shabby. She hadn't been eating. Food had only made her gag in these past horrendous months since the explosion. She had barely even been drinking. She was a mess, inside and out.

'I...' she started to say, and then there were voices out in the hall. It *was* the doorbell. She frowned. 'Who the hell's that?'

She glanced at the longcase clock ticking steadily away in the corner. It was after midnight. Who would come calling in the small hours; *what* would come calling except trouble?

*Oh my God – Layla...?* she thought, and rushed to the door and threw it open.

Rosa, in dressing gown and slippers, was ushering in a group of people.

Annie's mouth dropped open as she stared at the back of the tall man standing there.

It was Constantine. Constantine alive and well, not blackened, not burned and blown apart.

Then the man turned.

It was not Constantine.

It was *Alberto,* taking Aunt Gina's coat, and she was moaning on – as usual – saying oh this English *weather,* and Cara was depositing all her hand luggage into a man's arms, a man who looked like one of the drivers Annie remembered from Montauk. Fredo. That was Fredo.

'Take that up to my room, will you?' Cara told him. 'First left on the landing.'

Rocco was there, quiet and long-suffering as always, and there was Lucco's new bride Daniella, looking around in awestruck silence at the grandeur of her surroundings, and there – oh shit – there was Lucco, smiling silkily as he saw Annie standing there watching the scene.

'Annie,' he said, his eyes cold as black ice. 'How surprising to find you here. And how *nice*.'

# 47

Lucco was striding across the hall towards her. God, you had to hand it to the creep; he really was handsome as hell with his glossy black hair glinting in the lights of the chandeliers, his good height and his almost girlishly smooth olive skin; but his eyes were hard and pitiless as stones.

'What are you doing here?' Annie asked, wondering if she was finally going mad.

He was holding out his hand to her. He expected her to kiss it – because of course he was the Don now. He was in charge. She thought of Constantine, so regal, so intimidating, in the days when she had first known him. She had refused to kiss his hand, and she *certainly* wasn't going to kiss this jumped-up little scumbag's.

When she didn't take it, kiss it, Lucco gave a twisted little smile and moved in and instead kissed her on each cheek. Annie repressed the urge to wipe her skin clean afterwards. She stared blankly into his eyes as he drew back.

'I'm so pleased to see you making yourself comfortable in my house,' said Lucco smoothly, his eyes moving past her to fasten on the man lounging in the doorway. 'And who is this?'

Annie half turned and her eye caught Max's. *Fuck, what could she say to that...?*

'Mark Carson,' said Max, moving forward and extending a hand to Lucco. 'Security.'

Lucco reluctantly shook Max's hand, but Lucco's expression was bemused. He glanced back at Annie.

'I would have thought Nico would have provided all the security you need – *if* you needed any at all, which surely can't be the case any more.'

He was saying that she was no longer worth bothering with.

Annie gulped. *What* had Max said? Security? What the hell was he playing at? 'Nico's gone back to the States,' she said.

'Really? We haven't seen him over there.'

'Just today,' Annie managed to blurt out.

'Ah.'

Now Alberto came forward, smiling warmly at her. 'Stepmom,' he said, and embraced her. He drew back a little, holding her arms with his hands and smiling into her eyes. She stared at him, shaken. Sometimes, he could look so much like Constantine that it freaked her out. One moment, Constantine's strong image was there, but then it was gone as if imagined. 'Where'd you get to? You left without saying a word to any of

246

us.' His eyes lifted and rested on Max. 'I hope you're taking good care of her.'

'I am,' lied Max.

'Good.' Alberto paused, eyeing Max assessingly. 'I'm Alberto Barolli, this is my brother Lucco ... and,' Alberto smiled at the hesitant-looking girl who stood there in the centre of the hall, not knowing quite what to do, 'this lovely thing is Daniella, his wife. That's Aunt Gina.'

The regal older woman, clad in funereal black, gave Annie and her 'security' a sour look and a little nod before going silently up the stairs.

'And that is my sister Cara and her husband, Rocco.'

Beauteous blonde Cara gave the group by the study door a brief glance and said: 'I'm going on up, I'm tired. Come on, Rocco.'

And they followed Gina up the stairs.

'But what are you all doing here...?' asked Annie dazedly.

Alberto shrugged and his face grew serious. 'After what happened, we thought, maybe we shouldn't ... but then, what would Papa want us to do? So we've come, as we usually do, for Goodwood. But it feels so sad, without him.'

'Yeah,' said Annie. 'It does.' In her heart she felt outraged that they could do that, even *think* of enjoying themselves when what was left of Constantine was lying dead in a New York graveyard. But in a way she understood; they wanted to carry on the family tradition, maybe as a tribute to his memory.

She'd forgotten that the Barolli clan always came over for the races when they could. She'd forgotten that, and perhaps she'd forgotten other things, *important* things she really ought to have remembered. Maybe she'd had some sort of breakdown.

'Well, we're exhausted, we're off to bed. I'll see you in the morning, sweetheart,' said Alberto.

He went over to the stairs, passing Daniella and kissing her on the cheek, then he had a brief word with Rosa, and went on up.

Lucco gave Annie an ironic little bow, gave Max a nod, and then followed, taking his wife by the arm and ushering her up the stairs.

When the hall was empty, Annie turned to Max.

'What the fuck are you playing at?' she demanded.

'Shut up,' he said, and grabbed her arm and drew her back inside the study, closing the door behind them.

Annie angrily shook herself free.

'Don't *do* that,' she snapped. 'I want to know what all that was about. What the hell do you mean, security?'

Max stared at her. 'Listen, you're my only link to my daughter. So until I know where Layla is, until I've *got* her, then I'm not letting you out of my sight, understand?'

Annie was shaking her head. 'No. They've seen you before, they'll *know* who you are.'

Max shrugged. 'They saw me once, briefly, in a gallery years ago. They don't know me. No, listen. You ain't getting rid of me as easily as that. I'm sticking to you like *glue,* lady, until I have Layla with me.'

'You're not taking her away from me,' said Annie fiercely.

'Watch me,' he said. 'Now – where do you sleep?'

Annie's jaw dropped. 'You're *not* staying here. And you are *not* staying in my room.'

His mouth curved in a sour smile. 'I'm not interested in sleeping in your room. Fuck me! I wouldn't touch you with someone else's, much less my own. I want to know which room's yours, that's all.'

Annie felt weary under this onslaught. He hated her. She understood that. But for God's sake, did he have to keep driving the point home?

'I'm staying in the master suite, the one at the top of the stairs – that is, unless Lucco's had all my stuff moved out, which could happen.'

'Well, supposing the oily little git *don't* start chucking his weight about first chance he gets, is there a room adjoining it?'

*So he's got Lucco's number too,* thought Annie.

'Yeah. There is,' she said tiredly.

'Then I'll sleep in there.'

'The door between the rooms will be locked,' said Annie coldly.

'Don't fucking well flatter yourself,' said Max.

# 48

It was a long night. All nights were unbearable for Annie now, but this one took the prize. She lay sleepless, staring into the darkness for what felt like hours, her mind a jumble of confusion.

Layla, where the hell was Layla? She had to make herself believe that she was all right, that Gerda was with her and that soon, very soon, Gerda would make contact. But when she did, Max was going to take Layla away from her.

*Max was asleep in the room next door.*

Max, alive and well and breathing fire and fury because he felt she'd betrayed him. Now she could remember how she had wrestled with herself over her attraction to Constantine. It hadn't been an easy decision to make, getting involved with him after losing Max, but she could never, ever regret it. She had *loved* Constantine. How could she have known that Max had somehow – how? – managed to stay alive.

She turned over, hugging the pillow. Couldn't get comfortable, couldn't *rest*. In the half-light cast by the streetlight filtering through the drapes, she stared at the dim outline of the door leading into the other room. Max was in there. She couldn't even begin to believe it. But this wasn't *her* Max; he wasn't the Max she'd known. *This* Max was a hardened stranger, one who was going to snatch her daughter away the first chance he got.

*She couldn't let that happen.*

But for fuck's sake – how could she stop him?

She reached out and switched on the light, to chase away the shadows. She put her head in her hands and thought of Nico, her loyal and trusted friend, lying dead on the pavement, shot through the heart. And then the gun pointing straight at her head.

If Max, Steve and Gary hadn't come along just then, she would be dead now too. But why would anyone want to kill Nico? Or her? What possible threat could she be to anyone?

She got out of bed and went over to the dressing table, poured a glass of water. Her nude reflection stared back at her.

*You look like something out of fucking Belsen.*

He was right. She was thin and pale, almost gaunt, with big mauve shadows under her eyes and a look in them that said she had seen straight into hell. She hadn't attended to her hair in a long time; it hung in a wild, dark tangle almost down to her waist. Every day of pain and torment she'd endured after losing Constantine and then his baby was etched on her face and body.

She turned away from the mirror, not liking what she saw there, and went to the window, lifting the drape to peer out. The square was quiet, apparently deserted. But away up at the end of it, a match flared. Someone was there, in the darkness. Annie felt her heartbeat accelerate. Was someone watching the house, watching *her?* She dropped the curtain quickly and hurried back to the bed, crawling back under the covers. She snapped off the light, oh *God,* she wanted to sleep, to rest, to just sink into oblivion.

But her eyes were open and as her night vision returned she found herself staring at the chair beside the dressing table again, and he was there. Constantine was there, sunk in shadows, Constantine dead and charred, *incinerated,* but somehow watching her.

This time she didn't run from the bed, throw herself into his blackened arms only to find that he wasn't there at all. This time she *knew* he wasn't, her head was just playing tricks on her.

*It's true,* she thought. *I'm losing my mind.*

She turned over, clutched at the pillow, a single weak tear escaping and sliding down into her disordered hair. Finally, she slept. Her dreams were dark, and troubled.

# 49

Frances Ducane stood at the end of the square. He saw the light go out, the last light in the house. Now it crouched there like a dark monolith, full square, imposing, an exquisite William and Mary red-brick mansion that spoke of great wealth, extreme comfort, security. The London night was cool, damp, and he was wearing only a jacket, but Frances didn't notice the weather. He didn't feel the cold.

Inside there was Rocco – his love, his pain, his betrayer.

So close.

He finished his cigarette and threw it to the ground, grinding it out beneath his heel. Once, he wouldn't have smoked. He would have guarded his voice, his precious actor's voice.

But not any more.

He had no career, thanks to Rocco.

All he had were the crumbs *she* fed him from her table. And tonight she was probably going to withdraw even them, because he had failed, let her down.

He stared up at the house. Rocco was in there. So close, and yet so far away.

Rocco, sleeping in comfort, having forgotten all about Frances Ducane. Everyone forgot Frances Ducane, while everyone remembered his father Rick. His *late* father.

Frances's disfigured face twisted as he loitered there in the shadows.

His father, who for two years had – in Frances's opinion – been clinically insane, had finally succumbed to the frailties of old age, and died. His funeral had taken place last week, and Frances had attended, standing alone in the crematorium and rejoicing in the fact that Rick Ducane, once famous, was now so unknown that no one even came to his funeral except the son who despised him.

*So much for the great Shakespearean actor, the great Hollywood star,* thought Frances with bitter satisfaction.

Tomorrow he would go to the house, the much-hated place in Kent, which had been his father's and was now his. See his inheritance – before he sold it lock, stock and barrel.

Then maybe he could begin to forget the hand that fate had dealt him. Forget that he was the one who stood in the shadows, the one who was abused, overlooked, forgotten. Finally, he could forget.

Now he could see her, stepping out through the front door of the house, hurrying over to where he stood. When she drew near, her eyes were cold.

'She's still alive,' she said.

'I know.'

'What happened?'

'The old guy got in the way.'

'Listen, you said you could do this.'

'I *can*.'

'Yeah?' She looked sceptical. 'Well now she's got another minder, and he's sharp. So next time, no mistakes – okay?'

Frances nodded.

'Or no money,' she said.

Frances nodded again. Very soon now he would have his own money, and she could go fuck herself.

'Good.' And she turned and hurried back to the house.

Next day, he took the train down to Kent, catching a taxi from the station to the solicitor's office. He easily assumed the grave air of the grieving son – he was an actor after all – and pretended not to notice the old man's flinch of revulsion as he saw Frances's face for the first time.

They sat in the gloomy wood-panelled offices of Treacher, Burton and Quaid, and old man

Quaid, after many harrumphs and much fidgeting, finally settled himself, put his reading glasses on and unfolded the will.

'Coffee?' he asked, shooting a glance at the abomination sitting across the desk from him.

'No, thank you,' replied Frances. *Just read the damned thing,* he thought.

The old man's eyes returned to the will. He started to read it, and Frances waited confidently to hear his name mentioned. His father had no other living relative, so he knew that he was sole heir.

'...so I bequeath my estate in its entirety to Dubrow Pines,' concluded the old man, and refolded the will.

Frances leaned sharply forward. '*Dubrow Pines?*' he spluttered. 'Who the hell is Dubrow Pines?'

'Rather, it's a *what,*' said the man with a dry half-smile, removing his glasses and placing them neatly to one side. 'Dubrow Pines is a home for badly injured ex-servicemen. I believe your father fought in the war...'

'You mean he's left me nothing? Nothing at all?'

'I'm afraid that is the case.'

Frances sprang to his feet. 'Are you *serious?*'

He had been sure that he was going to be comfortably wealthy from this day on. He had planned to tell the woman that she could stuff her orders, that he had means, he had funds – but now, he didn't.

'I'm sorry,' said the solicitor.

'Well fuck *you,*' said Frances, and he turned and rushed from the building.

That afternoon he went to Whereys, the grand rambling Victorian house out in the countryside where his father had slowly lost his wits and where he, Frances, had been so inconsolably miserable.

He kicked in the front door into the panelled hallway with its big sweeping mahogany staircase. Then he stood there, the door open, sunlight streaming in behind him so that dust motes danced all around him.

The place smelled musty, full of mould spores and years of neglect. But it was worth a fortune and his father had squandered it, tossed the whole damned thing away. He closed the door and listened to the silence in the place. No more would he hear his father's booming actor's voice hectoring him, deriding him. The old man was dead. And this place ... this place was dead too.

He moved into the hall and past the mirror where he'd always paused before, paused to check his appearance, his faultlessly handsome face ... and now he saw himself in it, the scars on either side of his mouth making a mockery of his memories. He saw a *monster*.

*People will try to hurt you,* he heard his father say.

And the mean, crazy old bastard had been right all along – people *did* try to hurt you, and sometimes they even succeeded. Like dear old dad had hurt him, cutting him out of his will without a thought for how he would manage without the money the house would have brought him.

He turned away from the mirror and went on through the hall to the kitchen at the back of the house. He kicked his way out of the back door and stumbled outside, into the overgrown garden. The lawn was knee-high and thick with brambles; it hadn't been touched in years.

He waded through the weeds and detritus, burrs catching his trouser legs and dew dampening them right up to the knee. He went to the workshop, where the horseshoe still hung, rusty and decaying now, above the door.

*For luck,* he heard his father's voice say.

Well, it hadn't brought Rick Ducane any luck and it *certainly* hadn't brought Frances any either.

He opened the door and moved inside.

Looked around at the guns, the knives, the boxes stuffed full of instruments of death.

*What you need, boy, is an arsenal,* said Rick Ducane's voice.

And look at this!

He had one. Even better than the one he'd been gathering together in the States.

# 50

'And where is my favourite girl?' asked Alberto.

'What?' Annie asked, startled. She was sitting with her chin propped on her hand, stirring her coffee, glad that the night was over, that it was morning, that the sun was bright outside and the forecast promised more hot weather to come. Not that it mattered to her, not really. Rain or shine, it was all the same.

Layla was somewhere with Gerda, not here with her, and the knowledge of that, the absence of her little girl when she craved her so badly, was like a hard gnawing pain in her belly.

Soon, surely, Gerda would get in touch? She *had* to.

Annie had already gone to the room Nico had occupied, and turned it upside-down searching for some clue to Layla's whereabouts; she'd found nothing. Nothing except the contact details for the management team at the new club in Times Square, the one Nico had put in place before they left the States. She was still the majority share-holder of the new Annie's, and she knew she ought to be doing something about that. She owed it to Constantine, who had set up the purchase in the first place. To just let the whole thing go to hell, to let it fall in its entirety into Lucco's clutches, would be an insult to his memory.

And now his family were here, and she was wondering whether it would be best to go some-where else, *anywhere* else; but her innate obstin-acy had kicked in. Lucco would love to see her run for cover. Spiting him was reason enough to make her stay.

They were at the breakfast table in the dining room – her and Alberto, Aunt Gina and Daniella. Cara and Rocco hadn't yet put in an appearance, and neither had Lucco. Neither, much to her relief, had Max.

'Layla,' said Alberto patiently. 'Where is she?'

'Oh.' Annie jolted upright, thinking quickly. 'Gerda's taken her out to stay with my sister for a few days.'

'And how are you, since the...?' he asked, looking at her with Constantine's eyes.

*He means the baby,* thought Annie. *Since the miscarriage.*

'I'm fine now,' said Annie.

'You don't look it. Come on, eat something.' He pushed some toast and conserve towards her.

Annie started slathering the red goo onto the toast. It looked like congealed blood. Alberto was watching her, so she took a bite anyway, but nearly choked on it as Max came into the room and sat down beside her.

'Morning,' he said to them all, while the maid poured out coffee for him.

Gina nodded sourly. Daniella blushed then smiled shyly at him before returning her attention to her breakfast. Annie looked at the toast and determinedly took a few more bites. Alberto was right. She *had* to start eating again.

Alberto nodded a greeting to Max. 'I know it's hard,' Alberto said to Annie. 'It was bad enough losing Papa, but then to lose the baby too ... any woman would buckle under the strain.'

Annie wished she could just sink into the floor and disappear. She was hotly aware of Max sitting right there, taking all this in.

'Look, the plan is that we'll spend a few days here, then we'll all shoot off to Sussex for the races. You can just rest until then, but you will come with us, won't you?'

'Oh, I...' Annie started. Winding Lucco up by being here was one thing, but joining the whole bunch of them on a family outing was the last thing she wanted to do.

'Papa would have wanted us to carry on the family traditions,' said Alberto firmly.

*Oh shit,* she thought. He was right. Constantine would have wanted it, she knew that. She took a breath.

'Okay,' she said. 'Why not?'

She could think of a thousand reasons why not.

'And Annabella's running,' added Alberto.

Annabella had been Constantine's last equine acquisition, a stunning and speedy filly he'd named after Annie. Annabella was stabled at Newbury, at Josh Parsons' yard: Josh was the trainer who'd handled all Constantine's horses here in the UK. Now Annabella and the other horses, like nearly everything else, belonged to Lucco.

'I know you will probably want to be alone until then, but we won't get under your feet – will we Aunt Gina?'

'No,' said Gina with a tight smile at Annie. 'Of course not.'

'Excuse me,' said Annie, jumping to her feet and quickly leaving the room.

She went into the study, trying to find a quiet corner, but Lucco was sitting there at the desk, talking into the phone and smiling.

''Bye, Sophie,' he said when he saw Annie there.

He put the phone down and stared at her as she came in and shut the door behind her.

'Oh – sorry,' she said, and was opening the door again when he said: 'No – stay.'

Annie let the door close. *Sophie?* she thought.

'I wasn't expecting you to be in here,' she said.

'You weren't expecting me at *all*, were you?' Lucco smiled. 'You looked so shocked when we arrived last night. You know, the risks you take, you really *do* need a bodyguard. I hope this Mark Carson comes highly recommended?'

'Yeah. He does.'

'I'm surprised Nico just left you here, un-attended.'

Annie shrugged. 'He said he had business back in the States.'

Lucco sat back in his chair – in *Constantine's* chair – and eyed her speculatively.

'You know, I'm sorry we parted on such bad terms.'

'Forget it,' said Annie.

'I know you were upset when I refused you entry to the Manhattan penthouse.' He smiled. 'It's sold, by the way.'

'Oh? Good for you.' Annie's jaw was clenched so hard she could hear it creaking.

'It's just business,' he went on. 'Nothing personal. Just as when I leave here – *my* house – I will expect you to hand your keys back and not to come here again unless it is with my express permission.'

'Yeah,' said Annie.

'Unless we can come to some mutually acceptable arrangement...?' he said smoothly. His eyes were crawling over her.

Annie shuddered but forced herself to give him a twisted smile. 'I don't think so,' she said.

'No? That's a shame.'

'Ain't it just,' she said, and opened the door and

261

stepped back out into the hall. She was crossing to the stairs when Max came out of the dining room.

'So,' he said, 'at what point were you going to tell me that Barolli got you up the duff?'

Annie glared at him. 'At *no* point. Since it's none of your bloody business. And can you *keep your voice down?*'

Max squared up to her and hissed: 'You think it's not my business when my wife's pregnant by another man?'

'He was my *husband*. And the baby's not a problem any more,' said Annie, her voice nearly breaking with the effort to remain calm. 'As Alberto said, I lost it. It's *dead*. Just like its father. Happy now?'

Max folded his arms and stared hard at her face.

'What?' she demanded.

'Oh, I'm just wondering how it could have worked, you and him. I knew Constantine. He *always* had to be the boss. And you're such a bloody handful, such a bolshy cow at the best of times.'

Annie glared at him. All right, maybe he had a point. Maybe she *had* suppressed her true personality just a little with Constantine. But she'd be damned before she'd admit it to Max.

'This "Gerda" woman been in touch with you yet?' he asked.

Annie shook her head. She so wished that Gerda would call, and yet, if she *did*, she knew she would lose Layla in an instant. Her guts were knotted with hope and terror every time she heard the phone ring. She was frantic for news and at the same time scared to death that she would get it.

The dining-room door opened and Daniella came out, saving her from the necessity of dredging up an answer. Daniella looked lost; the poor little bint *always* looked lost. Annie felt so sorry for her, married to a nasty piece of work like Lucco. She left Max and went over to the girl.

'Hey, shall we go out?' she asked.

'Sorry...'

The girl's English was improving rapidly, but it still wasn't the best.

Annie made hand gestures. 'You. Me. Out?'

Daniella's face split in a wide smile.

'Go get ready, then,' said Annie, and Daniella hared off up the stairs. Half smiling, Annie watched her go. She liked Daniella very much.

'I'd better get ready too,' said Max.

'What?'

'Wherever you go, I go too, remember?' He gave a humourless smile. 'I'll drive you.'

'That's not...'

'Button it, *Mrs* Barolli. As I said before, I'm not letting you out of my sight.'

# 51

'One question,' Annie hissed at Max in fury. 'Just one.'

'Yeah, what?' he said, tight-lipped.

'Why are you so damned *nice* to Daniella, when you're such a complete *shit* to me?'

They were in the Burlington Arcade in Piccadilly, a nearly two-hundred-year-old covered building stacked with antique emporiums, expensive perfumeries and jewellery shops. Daniella was swooning over a coral necklace in one of the brightly lit shop fronts, while Annie and her fake 'security' stood to one side. Daniella loved the Arcade with its 'beadles', liveried guards dressed in Edwardian frock coats and top hats. She thought it was so quaint, so *English,* with its strictly enforced rules of no whistling, no bikes and no spitting.

'There's a simple answer to that,' said Max under his breath. 'Daniella's a sweet young girl, and you're a fucking *tart.*'

'Annie, do you think I could buy that?' Daniella came hurrying over to them, indicating the necklace.

Max was weighed down with bags, all of them Daniella's. When Annie had asked him to carry *her* bags, he had told her to carry them her effing self and that he was *not* her bloody servant.

Annie looked at Daniella. Really, you had to

like the girl. She was so fresh and innocent with that messy fall of glossy dark hair, her air of excitement, her big dark doe-eyes. Daniella was a most unlikely Mafia queen – but that was precisely what she was now: she was the wife of the Don; she would be accorded great respect just like Annie had been when Constantine was alive.

*Poor little thing,* Annie thought.

She'd come over from Sicily to marry an unkind stranger, someone picked out and agreed upon by her parents years ago. Her wedding day had been blighted by tragedy. Annie hoped that wasn't an omen of more trouble to come.

'Daniella,' said Annie, 'you could buy this entire building if you wanted.'

The girl looked bemused. Her English wasn't great, but she seemed to understand most things. She must surely understand that she was an extremely wealthy woman now. She turned back to the shop, flashed Annie a brilliant smile, and hurried inside.

Max and Annie stood there as people walked around them.

'You know, I'd almost forgotten how thoroughly fucking *nasty* you could be,' said Annie.

'Yeah, and I'd forgotten you're a tramp. Thanks for reminding me,' said Max.

Annie stared at him. She knew his face so well, almost like her own. But inside, he was different: colder, crueller.

'I won't let you take my daughter away from me, you bastard,' she said.

'How you going to stop me?' he asked.

'Any way I can.'

'Yeah?' He leaned in, his eyes staring into hers. His voice cut into her like a whiplash. 'Don't make me laugh. Look at the state of you. You're a fucking lightweight. All you do is marry money, or steal it. Wealthy men have always floated your boat, ain't that the truth? And you don't have the backing of one any more. You're on your own.'

They were standing there among the shoppers, apparently talking amiably, while spitting insults at each other.

'You *shit*,' said Annie, enraged, charging at him for a split-second, wanting to dent that calm exterior.

'Yeah, go on then,' he said when she stopped, gathered herself. He was smiling sarcastically. 'Just try it. Hit me. See where it gets you.'

'Oh, so now you're threatening me?' Annie snorted. She shook her head and sneered at him. 'You won't lay a *finger* on me. You think I know where Layla is, you think I've hidden her away from you. Don't you? You damage me, you might lose Layla for good. Ain't that the truth?'

'Listen,' said Max, leaning in, glaring. 'If I thought for one minute that you knew where she was, I'd have knocked it out of your cheating *arse* by now.'

He was lying and she knew it. Max Carter would *never* strike a woman. It would be beneath him. Or at least the Max Carter she had known wouldn't do that. But he had changed.

'I never cheated on you,' snarled Annie. 'They told me you were dead. I *believed* you were dead.'

'You didn't even *look*, did you?'

'Look *where?*' Annie burst out. 'Where would I

have started? They said they'd kicked you down a mountain, they'd seen you die. You *know* what it's like out there; you know it would have been impossible to find anyone in those mountains. And why would they have lied to me?'

Max was staring at her, breathing hard. 'Maybe to hurt you.'

Annie looked away. 'Well fortunately they didn't,' she snapped, but that wasn't true; it had hurt her beyond belief, ripped the heart out of her.

Her angry words hung between them as Daniella came dashing back out of the shop, clutching a small burgundy-red bag.

'I got it!' she crowed, delighted. She dived into the bag and opened a velvet box to show them both her find. It *was* lovely, and would suit her olive-dark colouring perfectly. 'Do you think Lucco will like me wearing this?' she asked, and there was an edge of anxiety in her voice now.

*You're wasting your time there anyway. Lucco's a selfish, uncaring bastard,* thought Annie, trying to calm down. She had already noticed how dismissively Lucco treated his new young bride. She thought that Daniella could troop round the house naked and he'd barely even notice – or care.

'He'll love it,' she said out loud. Why load more misery onto the poor cow?

# 52

Frances Ducane was spying on Rocco and he knew he was cheating on his wife again. Within days of arriving in London, Rocco was slipping out to clubs in the evenings and then taking young men off to one of the smaller, cheaper hotels near Soho to rent a room by the hour.

*Bet his ever-loving wife doesn't know about all this,* he thought, watching them with envy and hatred in his eyes as they smiled and chatted with each other.

The latest one was handsome and blond. Tall and thin.

Once, Frances had been handsome too, but not now.

He thought of Rocco, and how much he loved and hated him.

How harsh Rocco's treatment of him had been.

How unforgivable.

Frances knew what he had to do now.

She was sorting her problems out, one by one, ticking them off her fingers. Trying to pretend that her whole world hadn't descended into madness. That Constantine wasn't dead. That Annie Carter still lived and breathed.

'It'll have to be done when I'm not there,' she said as they strolled in the sunshine. 'I don't want any comebacks. We're all out next Tuesday – you can do it then.'

But do it how? Frances had kept a few pieces in the States, but here he was spoiled for choice. He had a whole armoury of weapons to choose from, inherited from his father and all stashed down at his home in Whereys in Kent – so he'd have to start moving it all out soon now, before the new owner took possession.

New owner! The owner should have been *him*.

'Have you any preference?' he asked her politely.

'Preference? What do you mean?' She frowned at him.

'For the method. The method to use,' he said, his tongue snaking out to moisten his lips as he spoke.

He was weird. But he was also useful: she had to keep reminding herself of that.

'I don't care what method you use,' she told him. 'You choose, okay? I don't want to know. Just get it done.'

# 53

Annie, Daniella and Max didn't get back to Holland Park until late in the afternoon. Max went off to park the car, and Daniella went into the drawing room to show Aunt Gina her purchases. Tired to the bone, Annie trudged up the stairs, longing for a shower and a lie-down.

It was only when she was passing Cara's bedroom door that she heard the grunts and moans coming from inside. She paused. The door was slightly ajar. She knew she shouldn't, but she peeked inside and had to stifle a gasp.

There was a couple across the room beside the big line of fitted wardrobes, a man facing away from Annie, holding up a woman whose legs were wrapped around his waist. His trousers were down around his ankles and she could see his nude buttocks clenching and unclenching as he thrust hurriedly into the woman, each thrust pounding out a hard beat on the wardrobes behind her.

The woman was Cara.

'You hot little *bitch*,' he was groaning out, panting and pushing at her like she was a blow-up doll.

Cara's response was about the same as he'd get from a doll, come to that. She was almost grimacing, staring blank-eyed over his shoulder, as if ... as if she didn't want this but couldn't bring herself to say no.

Annie stood there, frozen in shock – and then Cara's eyes met hers through the crack in the door.

Annie stepped back, embarrassed to have been caught spying. She quickly walked on along the hall to her own room, her mind wiped clean of all but the startling realization that Cara was playing away. The man between her legs wasn't Rocco, her husband. It was Fredo, the driver.

She wasn't even surprised when there was a tap on the door an hour later. She'd been lying on the bed, half dozing, and now she got up and went and answered it. Cara stood there, her expression guarded.

'Can I come in?' she asked.

'Sure.' Annie stepped back. Cara walked into the master suite, straight over to the window seat. She sat down. Annie came over and stood there, watching her.

'Look,' said Cara, 'it's not what you think.'

Annie shrugged and folded her arms.

'Don't give me that shit,' she said flatly. 'And don't even take the trouble to explain. You don't have to. All I would suggest is, if you want to fuck the help, at least shut the door.'

Cara's eyes grew spiteful. 'And what would you know about anything? You had a great man in my father. You would never have had to look elsewhere.'

'Is that what you're doing?' Annie eyed her stepdaughter speculatively.

This was almost the longest conversation they'd ever had. And Cara had sought her out. She'd certainly never done *that* before. And thinking back ... Annie remembered Cara coming up the stairs at the Montauk house, looking shattered. And then on the day of Lucco and Daniella's wedding, Cara had been clearly unhappy, and Fredo had been watching her with a gloating gleam in his eye. If the girl was enjoying the excitement of a clandestine affair, shouldn't she at least look happy about it?

Cara stared at the floor. 'I'm not happy with Rocco. I told Papa so.'

Annie was intrigued despite her dislike. She sat down beside Cara.

'And what did Papa say?' she asked.

Now it was Cara's turn to shrug. 'Oh, nothing very much.'

'If you were unhappy, I can't believe that Constantine wouldn't have suggested something to remedy the situation.'

Cara looked up, into Annie's eyes. 'He was too preoccupied – with *you,*' she spat.

Well, she'd always known that Cara resented her. No big news there. She stood up. So much for the sisterhood.

'So what do you want me to say?' Annie asked. 'You're an adult. Adults sort their own problems out.'

Cara's mouth opened but she bit back whatever words were about to tumble out. She looked away. Then she stood up. 'Look, I just... I don't want you telling anyone, Aunt Gina or Alberto or Lucco, about this.'

'Why would I? It's your business.'

'All right then.' Cara still looked uneasy. Annie felt she wasn't getting the full story here; and looking at Cara's closed, uncommunicative face, she doubted she ever would. And, come to that, did she care? Answer: no.

# 54

There were summer storms for a few days and then the sun came out again and everyone congregated around the swimming pool in the steaming grounds behind the house to soak up this rare event.

Annie had been studiously avoiding contact with everyone, especially Max. Dolly had called and said she wanted her over at the club soonest, but that would be some convoluted business problem that Dolly couldn't sort without Annie's say-so, and she didn't want to do business right now so she was putting that off. She couldn't think straight when she was so screwed up over Layla.

She'd forced herself to make the effort to call the management team at the new Annie's nightclub in the States, and she'd been both surprised and relieved to find a very sharp-sounding individual called Sonny Gilbert in charge there. Sonny reeled off the state of preparations for the September opening, the guest list ('You're going to *love* it!' he gushed), the planned advertising campaign, and he detailed for her the lushness of the new place's interior, the colours they were using (*'So* on trend!'), the particular size of the 'Annie's' sign outside the venue.

'Massive,' Sonny told her happily. 'Huge. You're going to adore it, I promise you.'

Sonny was so enthusiastic, so patently on-the-ball, that Annie knew Nico had selected exactly the right person for the job.

'I'll send you pictures,' he enthused. 'If you'd like that, Mrs Barolli?'

Annie declined. Everything was in hand; right now, that was all she needed to know.

The day was so beautiful; the sun was blazing down. With nothing to do except worry about Layla, she thought she might have a swim in the heated pool in the grounds behind the house, try to relax if she could manage it. The trouble was, everyone else seemed to have had the same idea.

She had done a couple of lengths and was lying on a sun bed in her black bikini, which was nearly falling off her – she'd lost so much weight in the depths of her grief over Constantine and the baby.

Before very long, Cara was stretched out in a red thong and a barely there bikini top, and even Aunt Gina was out by the pool reading *The Financial Times,* sitting primly, fully dressed in her black mourning dress at a table sheltered by a parasol. Rocco dived in and shouted out: 'Christ! I thought this pool was heated? It's freezing!' before doing slow, uncoordinated laps. He was a terrible swimmer.

His wife was flicking through the pages of a magazine and paying him scant attention.

'This is England, Rocco,' she pointed out, sounding bored. 'Pools are never hot enough. Beer is warm. And it rains nearly all the time.' She glanced up at the radiant blue sky. 'Just be grateful it's not raining today. Or not *yet,* anyway.'

Lucco came out, looking svelte and toned in white shorts, and sat in splendid isolation at the other end of the pool. He was followed by Alberto, looking every bit as attractive as his darker, thinner brother; looking in fact so much like Constantine that for an instant, glancing up, Annie thought it *was* him once again, and her heart caught in her throat. Then Alberto smiled and sat down on a sun bed beside hers and the illusion was gone.

'Stepmom,' he said, dropping a quick kiss onto her cheek. 'How are you?'

'Baking nicely,' said Annie, smiling at him because you could do nothing else *but* smile at Alberto, he was so charming – and, like his brother, so deadly, she reminded herself.

Then she looked beyond him and saw Max coming out onto the terrace in black bathing trunks, carrying a newspaper and a drink. He sat down at a distance, and she just knew that he'd seen that smiling kiss she'd exchanged with her stepson. He was wearing shades so she couldn't see his eyes, but his mouth was grim.

*Fuck it,* she thought. And then she wondered why it bothered her anyway. He thought she was a slut: nothing she did would make him change that opinion.

Lucco looked up and saw Max there. He glanced at Annie.

'Do we *really* have to have the help intruding on private family time?' he asked her.

*You snobby little bastard,* she thought. But she smiled at him with her teeth gritted so hard that she felt her jaw ache. She didn't want any confrontations developing between Max and Lucco.

All she wanted was a little peace and quiet.

'Mark is my security,' she said. 'He stays with me.'

Lucco glared at Max but then shrugged and got back to his paper.

Max didn't even glance at either of them. He just stretched out on the sun bed with all the indolence of a big cat. Annie tried and failed to stop herself looking at his body, so tanned and muscular; she had to admit he looked super-fit and incredibly tough. On each of his ankles she could see a tiny circular mark, like a cigarette burn. Those hadn't been there before.

'I was upset that you left the States without even saying goodbye,' Alberto was saying.

'Hm?' Annie's attention shot back to him. She'd left the States because she was done there: finished. And Lucco had warned her off. And, she reminded herself, not even Alberto – whom she had believed to be her staunch ally – had let her know the will was being read.

'What?' he asked her, seeing her eyes fastened on his face.

'Nothing,' she said.

'It's not nothing,' he laughed lightly. 'Come on, give.'

'You didn't tell me when the will was due to be read.'

'Oh, yeah. That.' His face grew doubtful. 'Lucco didn't think we should tell you. You were so upset already, and you were really too ill to attend.'

'Then it should have been postponed,' Annie pointed out.

Alberto gazed steadily at his stepmother. 'You were married to my father, you know how it works. The Don's word is final. It always was, with Papa. Now it's the same with Lucco. The will was Lucco's call. Whatever he chose to be done about it, that would *be* done. Without question.'

'But Constantine told me I'd have the New York penthouse, and this house, and all the shares in the Times Square club instead of fifty-one per cent. He said it was in the will.'

Alberto frowned. 'I'm sorry. There was no mention of any of that. And it can't be questioned. You do see that?'

He was worried about her, concerned where this questioning might lead her if she persisted with it. She could see *that*. He didn't want her crossing swords with Lucco.

Annie shrugged and let out a sigh. Oh, what the hell? It was all academic now. Maybe she could have contested it, but that would only have brought Lucco's wrath down upon her head, and would any sane person want that? She'd been screwed over. It was best to accept it, and move on.

'How's Lucco coping with it all?' she asked Alberto, leaving the subject of the will. She could see that it made him anxious and uncomfortable.

He gave a slight shrug – it was his father's gesture, so like Constantine that again she felt her gut tighten; it was torture, but it was lovely, too, to see his movements echoed by his son.

'Okay,' said Alberto, lowering his voice slightly. 'There's been some trouble on the streets, young up-and-coming thugs trying their luck, pushing in. I've seen it happen a dozen times. Some of the Dons get sent down or they die, and for a while there's chaos. The police can't control it, but the families can. We'll get them back in line.'

'Will you though? Can Lucco hold it together like Constantine could?' she asked.

'He can. He must. Papa had the whole of Queens and the chief of police in his pocket, and now Lucco has too. Things fall apart a little under these circumstances, but they get put back in order.'

She knew what he meant. Constantine's death had left punks in the underworld with hopes of a gap they could crawl through. Now, Lucco had to close those gaps down, forcefully.

'And ... the police haven't found out anything more about your father's death?' she asked.

Alberto shook his head and suddenly his eyes were hard. 'They don't care about my father's death,' he said flatly. 'Why should they? No, we don't depend on the police to put matters right. That's for the family, not them.'

'But you don't know who was responsible...?'

'No, I don't.' Alberto's eyes met hers and for a moment he *was* Constantine. Tough. Ruthless. Ready to act. 'If I did, I would kill them with my own bare hands.'

He turned his head and saw Daniella coming out onto the terrace, and his expression changed. Suddenly, he was amiable Alberto again.

'Hello, sweetness,' he said to Daniella, who was looking horribly self-conscious in a one-piece black swimsuit. 'Sleep well?'

She flashed him a grateful smile. 'Yes, thank

you,' she said, and sat down near him and Annie.

'Gold's down,' said Aunt Gina to no one in particular, turning pink pages.

Lucco was staring across at Max. 'I suppose you're ex-army?' he asked.

*Don't rise to it,* thought Annie, but Max put aside his paper.

'That's right,' he said. 'Special Air Services.'

*Oh for God's sake.* The closest Max had ever come to the army was a brief spell of National Service, and she knew for a fact that he had spent most of *that* in the slammer for bad behaviour. If he'd ever applied to join the SAS – and he wouldn't – they'd have turned him down as too bloody rough and too downright nasty.

'So I guess you know all this karate and judo bullshit, all this unarmed combat crap?' asked Lucco derisively, making mocking little chopping motions with his hands.

Max lifted his shades and stared at Lucco.

'That's right,' he said levelly. 'You want to try it out?'

*Oh here we go,* thought Annie. *Another who-can-piss-highest-up-the-wall contest.*

Lucco stared equably back at Max.

'Not right now,' he said, and dropped his shades back into place and returned his attention to the newspaper.

'Don't fucking well *do* that,' snapped Cara, as Rocco emerged from the pool, splashing her inadvertently with water as he wrapped himself in a towel.

'Come on, sweetie, let's swim,' said Alberto, and he and Daniella went into the water at a run.

They splashed around in the pool, Daniella shrieking with laughter, Alberto trying to tickle her.

When they eventually clambered out, they were still giggling like a pair of teenagers as they dried off. And it was then that Annie saw the blue bruises on Daniella's wrists and thighs.

*That rotten little runt,* she thought.

The poor cow was out buying necklaces to make herself look good for Lucco, and he was hurting her in return. She wondered if anyone else had noticed the marks. She got up and dived into the pool, working off her anger at Lucco with fast, overarm laps. Finally, breathless, she came to rest at one end of the pool, aware that someone else had dived in and was now shooting along underwater like a torpedo, coming straight at her.

*Lucco?*

She gripped the pool's edge, thinking that if it *was* Lucco then the bastard was almost certainly going to pull her down and try to half drown her, just for a laugh. One thing Lucco loved, it was throwing a scare into people.

But the man who shot up from the water in front of her was Max. He paused there, pushing his hair back. Their thighs touched under the surface and Annie shrank away from him.

'You're still a good swimmer,' he said so that only she could hear.

'So are you.'

'Gerda been in touch yet?'

'No,' said Annie. She had to go on believing that Gerda would have the sense to do that soon.

But then ... then he'd take Layla from her. She was torn, wanting news of Layla, but dreading her return.

'Shame.'

Annie glanced around, concerned that the others would see them here talking in whispers and get the wrong idea. She caught Cara's eyes and saw the cynicism in the girl's mocking gaze. She knew what she was thinking. *Oh yeah? So it's off-limits for me to get close to the staff, but not for you?*

But that wasn't the case. She wasn't close to Max. She had not the slightest desire to alter that, either.

'So what's this business about the will?' asked Max under his breath.

He'd always had ears like a bat; she'd forgotten.

'That was a private conversation between Alberto and me,' she said angrily.

'Yeah, I noticed how cosy you were getting with Golden Boy.'

'What?'

'Alberto. The one who's the dead spit of Constantine. I *knew* Constantine, remember?'

'I don't know *what* you're talking about.'

'No?' Max looked casually at the people around the pool. 'What's this then, plan B? Lucco's too much of a slimy little worm to get close to, but Alberto ... well, he'll have his fair share of the Mafia millions, enough for you to splash out on private yachts in the Med and ski chalets in the Swiss Alps, and – let's face it – he *does* look like his father...'

Annie had to bite her lip, hard, to keep back a

flood of angry words. She felt like tearing his eyes out, but she wasn't going to give him the satisfaction of flaring up just so he could slap her down.

'Yeah, and the similarity ends there. Constantine's dead. And I don't want another man, not even one who looks like him,' she retorted.

Max's eyes were alight with spite; he could see he'd needled her and he was pleased about it. 'As to that...' he said softly.

'As to *what?*'

'Constantine's death. Daniella told me it was an explosion.'

Annie held herself rigid, tried not to react. Any time she thought back to the day of Lucco and Daniella's wedding, she felt herself break out in a cold, horrified sweat. She didn't want Max to see her losing it.

'It was,' she said. She could feel her stomach start to churn.

'And that if you'd been standing a few steps closer, it would have got you as well as him.'

'That's right.' She could see it again. Oh *shit*, she could see it. Constantine walking towards her with the parcel. *Hey, wonder what's in this one?*

*Death* was in there. His death, and very nearly hers too.

She gulped hard, turned her head away from Max's probing eyes.

'And you say he'd made provision for you in his will, but it somehow got overlooked?' said Max. 'Bet you're gutted over *that.*'

Annie turned back towards him. Once she had loved him, but now he was cruel and so predatory, endlessly picking at her – and she couldn't stand it; she felt sick, weak, shaken by events. Nico's death. Losing Constantine. Losing the baby, their precious baby...

'I don't know what you're getting at,' she said faintly, wishing he'd just leave her alone.

All around her she felt threats and danger. If there was ever a time when she *needed* a body-guard, a true and loyal protector, a shining knight in armour, it was now. And all she had was a man who despised her and called her a money-grub-bing whore.

'What I'm *getting* at is this. You think it was a hit by another of the Mafia families wanting to push in, destabilize the Barollis by taking out Constantine in the hopes that Lucco wouldn't be able to maintain control?'

'Yeah. That's *exactly* what I think.'

'Well, I'm not so sure.'

Now Annie was staring at him with puzzlement on her face. '*What?*'

'Wake up and smell the bloody coffee. This lot don't like you one little bit and they've inherited the earth now Constantine's off the scene.' His eyes were resting on Lucco. 'If *I* was looking for whoever set that death trap, I think I'd be looking a damned sight closer to home.'

# 55

The first thing Annie saw when she got to the door of the club that evening was that the 'Annie's' sign was missing. Max – or *Mark* – had driven her here and was waiting in the car for her, out in the brightly lit main road, no more shadowy side roads like last time.

She felt a shiver run up her spine as she thought of coming here with Nico, not knowing he was soon to die. Her whole life seemed to be shrouded in a cloak of doom; she couldn't shake off the feeling that at any moment some new horror was going to confront her, and she knew she wouldn't be able to cope.

'Well, you took your bloody time,' said Dolly, poodle-permed and neatly suited as always, when Annie pitched up at the bar.

It was busy, as always. T. Rex's 'Get It On' was pouring out of the sound system, the go-go dancers shaking their pretty arses up on their podiums. Annie looked up. Above the bar, there was no red neon 'Annie's' sign either.

'Oh, you've noticed,' said Dolly, following Annie's gaze.

'What is it, electrical problem? I see the sign on the front's down too.'

'*Electrical?*' Dolly gave a bark of laughter. 'Fuck me, I wouldn't bother you with something as simple as that. This is more ... a *Carter* problem.

As in, Max Carter's boys have been in and the signs have come down. They're telling me the new ones are on their way.'

'*New* ones?' Annie's jaw hit the floor.

'Palermo. That's the new name. Same as the old one, minus the Lounge part. Look, Gary's over there, you can ask him if you don't believe me.'

Oh God, she didn't want to ask him anything. But she went over there to his banquette anyway. Lanky blond Gary, Max's most feared and vicious foot soldier, was sitting there with a brightly dyed little redhead, and his pale eyes when he spotted her went from warm and full of laughter to mean and hard.

'Hi, Gary,' said Annie, having to shout to make herself heard.

The Dusty Springfield lookalike was there too, eyeing her while whispering things into the redhead's ear. The redhead looked at Annie and started to laugh.

'Not sure what I should call you now,' said Gary acidly. 'Mrs Carter? Mrs Barolli? None of the above?'

Annie felt a spurt of anger at his tone. 'Call me whatever the fuck you like. But it's Mrs Carter-Barolli actually – since you're asking.'

'Not that I give a shit either way, you understand.'

'Yeah. Think I got *that* message. What's going on with the signs?'

He shrugged lazily. 'Just Max putting stuff back the way it should be. They're *his* cunting clubs after all.'

Bloody Max. He'd driven her here and not given her a damned clue about what she was to expect. But Gary was right. The clubs had always been Max's, not hers. She had stepped in when they were crumbling and turned them around. She didn't expect to get any thanks, but she was downright offended that he hadn't even thought to mention this to her.

She was about to turn away, but she just *had* to ask. She moved closer to Gary and spoke more softly so that the two girls wouldn't hear.

'What ... what did you do with Nico?'

Gary flicked back his straight blond hair and grinned. 'Sleeping with the fishes,' he said with a cheery wink. 'As they say in Mafia circles. Which I suppose you know all about. Don't you.'

*Bastard.*

She walked away from him, back to the bar. Suddenly someone was yanking at her arm. She saw Dolly's face ahead of her, behind the bar, looking anxious. She turned.

'Look,' said Dusty, her hard eyes glaring into Annie's, 'you want to fuck off out of it. He ain't interested in you any more.'

Annie stared at the girl. Then she turned, looked behind her. Looked back at the girl. 'I'm sorry – are you talking to *me?*'

'You ought to just show a bit of dignity and eff off. You're yesterday's news. He's with me now. He don't want you.'

'Then you've got nothing to worry about, have you?' said Annie, and turned away to the bar.

Dusty pulled her back. 'What I *mean* is this: I don't want to see your scrawny carcass hanging

286

around him, you got that?'

*Scrawny carcass?*

Now that did hurt. Just a bit.

Annie shrugged. 'You got it,' she said.

'What?' Dusty looked confused. She hadn't expected it to be this easy.

Dolly was watching the exchange like a spectator at Wimbledon, her head moving between the two as volleys were exchanged. She was waiting for Annie to flatten the audacious little mare. Suddenly, the night was getting interesting.

'I said you got it. I don't want him. Trust me, he's all yours.'

'Well...' Now Dusty looked downright bewildered. She had expected a catfight. She was a tough, compact girl and she could punch her weight. That was what she had come to do. Now, all the wind had gone out of her sails.

'You're welcome to him,' said Annie.

'Right. Well ... just make sure you keep away,' said Dusty, backing off.

'Glad to.'

With another scowl at her 'adversary', Dusty went back to Gary's banquette. Annie turned and looked at Dolly.

'Well, you've mellowed a bit,' Dolly remarked. 'So, what'd he say?' she asked.

'He said he was following Max's orders,' said Annie.

'Ah.' Dolly's face was troubled. 'Listen, d'you think Max will put in his own management?'

Annie looked at Dolly. Dolly loved this job, overseeing the running of the clubs. If she lost her job, she lost her home too. She was right to

287

be worried.

'I don't know, Doll. I'll talk to him.'

Dolly's shoulders sagged with relief. Which they *wouldn't* have, if Dolly only knew how little clout Annie had with Max these days. 'Drink?' Dolly offered.

'No. Thanks. Business okay?'

'Okay in bits. Jesus, it's just the same, whether you're running a club or a knocking-shop, you get some weird punters. It ain't all beer and skittles, I can tell you. We got a nice woman comes in here, regular customer, pillar of society, married, all that, and I caught her having a three-er with one of the doormen and two of the punters out in the back alley.'

Annie's eyes widened. A three-er was one up her arse, one up the front, and giving a blow-job to another one. 'What was she, high?'

'As a kite,' Dolly sniffed. 'Don't know who slipped her the stuff, but I sacked Paul on the spot and barred the other two.' She sighed. 'Which means I got to find another doorman, and that's a shame. Paul was good at the job. You know, times have changed. You get more and more drug action now. For a minute there I thought I was back in Limehouse, running a brothel. I tell you, even *I* was shocked.'

Annie had a thought. 'I don't suppose a girl called Gerda's been in touch? She looks after Layla.'

Dolly leaned her elbows on the bar. 'Gerda? No. Why would she do that? And how is Layla? You haven't brought her over to see me yet.'

*Only because I can't.*

'Layla's fine, it's just been a bit hectic since I got back.' But what if Gerda *couldn't* get in touch? Gerda was a sensible girl – surely she would soon. But if she couldn't, if she was somehow being stopped from making contact ... oh God, that was a terrifying thought.

'You mean, with Max showing up and every-thing?' said Dolly.

'Yeah.'

'You two made up? Only Ellie told me he was mad as a cut snake about you marrying Con-stantine.'

'Yeah, everything's fine,' lied Annie. 'I'll catch you later, okay?'

She walked off, leaving Dolly staring after her. Dolly *knew* Max Carter. She knew Annie was telling porkies.

Annie came out of the club. She saw Max parked up across the road and instead of crossing over she hailed an approaching cab, got in and said: 'Limehouse, please.'

So he thought he could just barrel back in here and ride roughshod over everything she'd strived for? Well, if that was how he wanted it, then that was how it would be. But she'd be *damned* before she'd sit there meekly beside him in the pass-enger seat and, the truth was, if she'd got into that car with him again tonight, she would have tried to tear his head off his shoulders and beat him with the wet end.

*Fuck* him.

# 56

She was in the huge, well-appointed kitchen in the Holland Park house, on her own, drinking tea, when he caught up with her.

'Don't ever do that again,' he said, coming in and looking as if he was about to throttle someone, preferably *her*.

Annie, seated at the kitchen table, looked up at him coolly.

'What? Not toe the line? Not do as I'm told?' She shrugged. 'This is probably news to you, but I don't take orders, I *give* them. Like I gave orders for the clubs to be refurbed. Like I gave orders and turned them around from a loss-maker to a profitable chain. Like I gave orders to change the name to something a bit more *current,* instead of something that sounds like a sodding Fifties leftover.'

'The Palermo don't sound like a Fifties left-over. Neither does the Blue Parrot or the Shalimar. All that's bugging you is that you had *your* name plastered all over *my* clubs, and I've altered that.'

'What *else* are you going to alter?' Annie demanded as he sat down opposite her and glared at her. 'Dolly's shit-scared you're going to put in your own people. She needs that job.'

Max looked at her narrow-eyed. 'I might do that.'

Annie emptied her cup and slammed it down on the table. 'Yeah,' she said. 'You hurt Dolly and you spite *me*, right? Of all the petty, mean-minded sons of bitches, you really do take the prize.' She stood up. 'I'm going to bed.'

He stood up too, grabbed her arm, slammed her back against the larder door. Annie let out a gasp of surprise. He leaned in close. 'No, you're not.'

Now Annie was getting good and mad. 'Think you'll find I am.'

'No. We should talk about the Barolli family. About the explosion.'

'As if *you* care. In fact, if the thing had blown me to buggery too, you'd have been spared the inconvenience of coming back here and finding that your wife had crawled into bed with another man and lived to tell the tale. And that would have suited you down to the *ground,* wouldn't it?'

Max's jaw tightened as she spoke, but he didn't let go of her. 'Steve told me how Constantine helped when Layla got snatched.'

'Did he?'

'Yeah, he did. He said that if Constantine hadn't stepped in, Layla would have been done for.'

Annie looked into his eyes. 'Steve's right. That's true.'

'So what was it – a gratitude shag?'

Annie's eyes narrowed to slits. 'You don't *marry* a man out of gratitude,' she said icily.

'What then? Come on. I want to know. What was it?' He was very close now, holding her there when all she wanted to do was get away. 'Was it love?'

291

'You don't know the *meaning* of that word,' said Annie.

He was nodding his head now, eyeing her like she was something hateful. 'And you do, since you met Barolli.'

'That's right,' she snapped.

'Jesus, you are *such* a tart.'

'No, tarts charge. I give it away for free. To anyone who wants it, according to you.'

'Bitch.'

'Oh really? While we're on the subject of caring and fidelity, if you were not dead, if you were only *playing* dead, what were you doing for over two years? Taking a hike over the fucking Himalayas? Why didn't you come back sooner? Were you on a bloody world cruise or something? Come on, I'd really like to know. *I thought you were dead.* I thought that and I forced myself to move on. I had to do it. For Layla, and for myself.'

'Oh, so it was a big wrench then? Learning to live without me.'

He sounded so bitter, so disbelieving, that it just got Annie's back up more.

'Not really, no,' she lied.

'You cow,' he snarled.

'Yeah, and you're a bastard,' she shot back. 'Now are you going to let me go or do I have to scream the bloody place down? How would you explain *that* to the family, being as you're my bodyguard and you're supposed to *stop* people from doing me over, not do it your fucking self.'

Max let her go with a shove. Annie staggered and steadied herself against the polished-steel worktop. She looked at the wooden block there, stuffed with knives. Suddenly she'd had enough. She grabbed the biggest and advanced on him. He didn't flinch; didn't step back.

When she stood right in front of him holding the knife, she reversed the blade so that the point rested between her breasts. She yanked her blouse open, buttons popping off and flying in all directions with the force of it. She stared into his eyes.

'You hate me so much?' she spat out. 'Then *do* it. Kill me if it makes you happy. The way I feel right now, you'd be doing me a *favour.*'

Max was very still, just watching her. She pushed the point of the knife more firmly against her skin, and a bead of blood bloomed there.

'Enough,' he said, and wrenched it off her.

'What, don't you have the *guts?*' she challenged.

Max raised the knife until the point touched her chin. He applied the slightest pressure, forcing her head up. Their eyes locked.

'It don't take guts to kill,' he said coldly. 'It just takes rage. That's all. And if a man can't control that, then he ain't much of a man.'

He lowered the blade and slotted it smoothly back into the block. Then he turned and left the room without another word.

# 57

Annie awoke in the small hours of the night. This was nothing unusual. She slept badly, ever since Constantine's death. And as soon as she woke, the dread came flooding back, the horror of it all. Ah shit, he'd be there in the chair again, sitting there blackened, charred, unrecognizable. But ... something had awakened her, something else.

*Some movement?*

That was it. Something had moved inside the room.

She lay absolutely still, listening hard. Yeah, someone was moving across the floor ... coming towards the bed. As her eyes grew accustomed to the darkness she could see a darker outline moving towards her.

Holy *shit*, she thought, her gut tightening with fear.

Into her mind sprang what had happened to her in the hospital; someone had held a pillow over her face, and if the nurse and Nico hadn't happened to come in at that moment, she would have been suffocated.

She could hear her heart thwacking away against her ribs, could feel clammy sweat breaking out all over her body as the figure came nearer and nearer.

Finally, it was looming right over where she lay. At that moment, Annie managed to get her frozen limbs moving. She shot off the bed and sprinted across the room to the door connecting her room to Max's, and hammered on it as loudly as she could.

'*Help!*' she shouted, thinking that whoever was in here was going to pull her away, cover her mouth, and then she'd be lost. But an instant later she heard more movement and the door onto the landing opened and then slammed shut.

She turned, cringing against the connecting door. Max was pounding on it from the other side. Christ, the thing was *locked*, of course it was, on her side. She fumbled in the darkness for the key, turned it. Max dashed in.

'What the fuck's happening?' he asked.

'I don't know ... I think there was someone in here...' But now she couldn't be sure it had happened at all. She was so used to nightmares, so used to horrors dogging her sleep, that now she couldn't be sure that this hadn't been a horrible dream.

She felt him move past her, go over to the bed. He fumbled for the switch on the lamp, turned it on. Golden light flooded the room. Now Annie became aware that she was standing there, naked. At least Max had his undershorts on; she didn't even have *that*.

'Fuck's sake, put something on,' he said irritably, and flung her robe at her.

Annie caught it, slipped it on, belted it firmly.

There was movement out on the landing now, people coming. Alberto was first, shrugging on a silk dressing gown and looking anxiously at Annie standing there, sheet-white, beside the inner door.

'What's happening? Are you all right?' He hurried over to her.

There had been someone there. All right, she dreamed sometimes, ghastly dreams, but this was reality. She was *sure* someone had been coming towards her in the dark. But she didn't want to throw the whole household into uproar. And then Max's words in the pool came back to her:

*I'd look closer to home if I were you.*

Had one of the family been in here? She looked at Alberto, his eyes worried, his arms automatically going around her.

*Oh Jesus, what was happening to her? Was she losing her mind? Or could Max be right, could one of the family be trying to harm her? Could one of them actually have killed Constantine? And could they now be coming after her, too?*

'I'm fine,' she said stiffly. 'I'm sorry. I had a dream, that's all. A bad dream.'

Lucco was strolling in now, belting his robe, looking around the room, giving Max the old beady eye.

'What is this?' he asked.

'I had a dream,' said Annie. 'Sorry to wake you. It's nothing.'

'You're shaking,' said Alberto.

Annie gently detached herself. 'I'm fine now. Really. Mark's here, he'll look after me. Go on back to bed. I'm fine.'

They left the room, Lucco looking exasperated, Alberto reluctant.

The door closed behind them, and Max was still standing by the bed staring at her.

'Okay – what?' she asked.

'Nothing,' he said flatly.

'No, go on. Whatever's on your mind, say it.'

'All right. Golden Boy was first through the door. Was it him? Did you invite him in and then change your mind and start hollering the house down? Is that it? Was that little performance for my benefit, and Lucco's?'

Annie came over to the bed. She fumbled open the drawer in the bedside cabinet, pulled out a Smith & Wesson and a box of bullets. She sat down on the bed and started loading the gun. 'You know what?' she said hotly, shoving the bullets into the chambers with angry, shaky movements. 'You really are a complete *shit.*'

'What, does the truth hurt? And what the *fuck* are you doing now?' He snatched the gun off her, turned it over in his hands. 'This is *my* gun.'

'Of course it's your gun. I brought it from the villa after the hit. You remember? When I was left alone with my daughter missing and my husband was supposed to be *dead?* From now on, I'm sleeping with it under my pillow.'

He snatched the box of bullets off her and loaded them into the chambers with a far steadier hand than hers.

'No, you're bloody not, you're a lousy shot. You'd blow your effing brains out. Just what *else* have you got of mine?' he asked coldly.

'Just ... this.' She delved into the drawer and brought out the heavy gold ring with its square slab of lapis lazuli and its engraved Egyptian cartouches.

He took it, slipped it onto the smallest finger of his left hand. Snapped the gun closed, checked

297

the sights. Then he picked up the box of remaining bullets. All in a very cool and businesslike manner. Annie swore to herself then and there that she was never, ever going to let him know that she had worn his ring as a comforter, feeling that he was somehow closer to her, when she had been going through hell without him.

'There was someone in here.' Annie clutched at her head. 'There *was*. When I was in hospital in the States after Constantine ... and after I...' She gulped hard and then went on. 'After I lost the baby ... someone held a pillow over my face. Nico and the nurse came in and they ran off. I ... really think there was someone here. And before you say a word, it *wasn't* Alberto after a bunk-up. Don't you even dare *suggest* that.'

Max's eyes narrowed as they rested on her face.

'This has happened before.'

Annie nodded dumbly. Then she looked at him. Seemed to really *see* him for the first time.

'Jesus, was it *you?*' she demanded.

'What?'

'Just now. Was it you?'

Max looked at her like she'd finally gone mad.

'The door was locked,' he pointed out.

'The connecting door, yeah, but not the one into the hall. Was it you?'

Max gave a low laugh. 'You really do think you're irresistible, don't you?'

'No. I don't. But I know you're mad as hell at me and maybe you'd like to frighten me.'

'For fuck's sake, I wouldn't do a low-down thing like that.'

'How do I know that's true?' Annie was pacing

around the room now, her eyes wild. 'I don't know you any more. I don't think I *ever* knew you, not really.'

'What, and you think I'd bloody well *rape* you? Honey, I've got news for you. You're not *that* attractive right now. You're skinny and you look shot away. And more than that, you know what really gets my goat? You've behaved like a fucking *tart*.'

Annie stopped pacing and stared at him, hands on hips.

'Look,' she said shakily. 'You're my "security", ain't you? My bodyguard? Well, start fucking well *guarding*, will you? I'm telling you – someone's tried to kill me at least three times. This might have been the fourth attempt. And *next* time they might succeed, leaving your daughter without a mother. How'd you like *those* apples?'

# 58

'I checked all the locks last night,' said Max quietly to Annie next morning as they went in to breakfast.

'And?' she asked.

'They were secure. All the windows, all the doors. Impossible to get in from the outside without triggering the alarms. So,' he said, lowering his voice further as Lucco came out of the study and crossed the hall towards them, 'it was an inside job. Whoever came into your room was already inside the building.'

Lucco passed by, dressed immaculately in his morning suit, nodded to both of them, and went into the dining room while they hovered at the door.

It was really possible then. One of the family could be trying to kill her. But why, when she was no longer a danger to any of them? They had their money. Constantine's last wishes concerning her had been ignored. She hadn't dared contest the will. So why persist in trying to do her harm?

*Maybe just because they hate me,* she thought with a shudder.

Cara, Lucco and Aunt Gina certainly did. And Rocco? He seemed indifferent. Alberto ... no, she couldn't believe it of him. She had always considered Alberto to be her ally.

But ... could she be wrong about that?

Could she be wrong about *everything?*

And today they were all off to the races together, playing happy families.

Alberto was coming down the stairs, chattering to Daniella who was visibly blooming under his attention.

Annie watched Daniella, feeling pleased on her behalf. She'd helped her get dressed this morning, shown her how to use some coral-coloured lipstick, a little powder and a lot of black mascara to bring her pretty face even more vibrantly alive – and she'd shown her how to tame that frizzy black hair of hers with a smear of Estolan rubbed into the ends. Daniella wore an orange-and-black floral dress that was fitted at the bodice and waist

300

and flared out into a full skirt. The coral necklace was around her neck. Her hair was pulled neatly back in a ponytail and her olive-toned skin glowed with health. The overall effect was stupendous.

'Stepmom,' said Alberto with a smile, coming across the hall with Daniella on his arm. He kissed Annie warmly on the cheek. 'All better now? No more dreams?'

'No, I'm fine. Sorry to disturb you last night.'

'No problem. So long as you're okay. You're coming in the car with us?'

'No, she's not,' interjected Max smoothly. 'I'm driving her, we'll meet you there.'

Alberto looked from Max to Annie.

'He's very good,' he congratulated her.

'Oh, he's a marvel,' said Annie, with only a hint of the bitterness she felt coming out in her voice.

Lucco had – in the grand old tradition of his father – hired a private box at Goodwood with a spectacular view overlooking the winning post and the glorious South Downs beyond.

They had a champagne reception and canapes laced with golden imperial caviar and shavings of white truffle, then there was a four-course lunch while watching the finer details of the races on a closed-circuit TV. Alberto kept sneaking off with Daniella to place bets, mostly, Annie suspected, to cheer the poor thing up – because Lucco had invited other guests along: glossy corporate contacts who seemed to ooze wealth and bonhomie, and a stunning leggy blonde called Sophie Thomson.

Everyone knew Sophie, if only by sight. She was a regular on the catwalks of London, Paris and New York and the cover of *Vogue* and she was, Annie found, effusively charming and one hundred per cent false. She remembered walking in on Lucco making a phone call to someone called Sophie: this must be her. She was obviously besotted with that rattlesnake, and Annie thought that it was unbelievably cruel of him to parade his mistress so blatantly under Daniella's nose.

It was obvious too that Sophie, although initially jolted by the fact that he'd brought his wife along today, was made of strong stuff and, after the first shock of it, she recovered quickly and simply ignored Daniella. And it was a mark of Lucco's sadistic nature that he was visibly enjoying his wife's dismay, sipping Bollinger and watching her skirt around his spectacularly beautiful mistress with almost painful care.

'I'm betting on Surefire in the two thirty,' said Max as they stood out on the balcony, alone for the moment. He was looking at the race card. 'How about you?'

Christ, how could he behave so casually, as if everything was normal? It was anything but. Annie's head was spinning with the stress of it all. And yet here *he* was, beautifully turned out in a morning suit, looking – in fact – as if he had been *born* to wear it, with his effortless physicality and his brooding presence, and also – oh Christ, she remembered it so well – wearing that fragrant Trumper's Lemon cologne he'd always favoured.

That scent was a step back into another world for her. Such memories it evoked. Her and Max

302

in the early days, her besotted with him, him mad for her but fighting it every inch of the way. And how, for the love of God, had they come from that to *this*?

'I can't even think, let alone bet,' said Annie.

She hated being here at the races but she hadn't wanted to disappoint Alberto by refusing to come. It was too poignant a reminder of all she had lost. She should have been here with Constantine. She missed him horribly. Constantine had been a rock that she could cling to. But Max ... well, Max was a rock that she could smash against, and sink.

'You know Lucco's horse is running in the next?' she said to him, trying to take an interest, trying to pretend everything was normal and not shot to hell.

'No, what's the name?'

Annie swallowed. 'Annabella.'

He looked up from the race card, straight into her eyes.

Annie had to look away. 'It was Constantine's horse; he named it after me. Now it's Lucco's. Along with everything else.'

She hated this. She had never been in a more surreal situation, standing here with her dead first husband while attending a race meeting with the family of her dead *second* husband. She was full of anxiety about Layla's whereabouts, terrified that Nico's plan had somehow gone awry. She'd trusted Nico, she knew that Nico would have taken good care of her beloved daughter – but that didn't alter the fact that Layla was out there somewhere with Gerda, God knew where.

It killed her every day, the worry of it. But then

there was an additional turn of the screw, another torment. She so wanted to hear from Gerda, but what the hell would she do if she did? Max would take Layla away from her and he would abandon her, leave her to this pack of jackals – and they couldn't wait to tear her to pieces. She was in a state of constant fear about where the next threat was going to come from. She found herself again and again staring at their faces and wondering, *is it you who wants me dead?*

She was looking around at them now.

Aunt Gina sitting there, sipping champagne as if it was arsenic, still all in black as a mark of respect for her dead brother. Gina was old school. Annie knew she hated her for disturbing the status quo and enticing Constantine into marrying *out*. Annie knew she was jealous of Annie's relationship with Constantine, because she had been a spinster all her life and had doted on her brother with almost creepy maternal care.

And Lucco, casting sneering looks over at Annie and her 'minder' now and again. Oh, yes, Lucco hated her enough to do something about it. She was sure of that. It was Lucco who had warned her off Constantine in the first place; it had *always* been Lucco.

'He don't like you,' said Max, seeing the young Don staring at his companion.

'I don't like him either,' said Annie with a shudder.

And what about Cara? Annie watched her thoughtfully. She was looking very fine today, dressed in a powder-blue shift that hugged every curve of her body, with matching hat and shoes.

She was flirting with one of the guests, a deeply tanned and expensive-looking banker who seemed to be enjoying the experience. Lounging by the door was Fredo, on guard, watching Cara and all the other guests with a blank expression. Annie thought back to that scene she'd witnessed, Cara and Fredo humping like dogs.

And Rocco? He hadn't come today; he'd pleaded business as an excuse. He was so bland, so inoffensive. But ... there was something hidden about Rocco, something secret. Annie had always felt that. You only got a surface impression of him, you never knew what lay in his heart.

As for Alberto ... no. Of all the Barollis, she believed totally that Alberto was on her side. To him, she was family, and family was sacred in his eyes.

'Surefire?' asked Max, interrupting her thoughts.

'No, Annabella.'

'Form's not too good.'

'I don't care.'

'I'll go and sort it out.'

'Fifty to win,' said Annie, and gave him the notes. She didn't care whether she won or lost.

'Not each way?'

Annie looked him dead in the eye. 'When I commit, I commit one hundred per cent,' she said. 'I thought you knew that.'

Max nodded and she almost thought he was about to smile, but he didn't. He went off to the Tote.

# 59

Annie was standing by herself, her hands clasping the balcony rail, looking down at the multi-coloured crowds in the racecourse stands below. She could see her reflection in the glossy paint-work at the end of the balcony.

Like Gina, she was wearing plain, respectful black. But today she'd taken some trouble with her appearance; she'd washed her hair and pulled it up in a chignon, even put on a bit of make-up. She was gaining a little weight now; she didn't look too bad. There were still dark shadows under her eyes, but she wasn't stick-thin any more – although her face still had that haunted look about it.

'Mrs Barolli?'

She turned. It was Annabella's trainer Josh Parsons, a well-bred, upper-crust Englishman, tall and thin with a year-round tan, an elegant greyhound nose and piercingly kind pale blue eyes. She'd met him here last year, when she had come over with Constantine for the races. She had even visited his stables to see Annabella as a talented two-year-old out on the gallops, being put through her paces. She had taken breakfast in the hectic, messy farmhouse kitchen with Constantine, Josh, his comely blonde wife Jenny and their gaggle of very noisy children.

'Mr Parsons,' said Annie.

They shook hands.

'Josh. Please. I was hoping to catch you, but I can't stop,' he said. 'I just wanted to say, Mrs Barolli, that I was so sorry to hear about Constantine. He was such a great friend to me and we were all devastated to hear such bad news.'

'Thanks,' said Annie, feeling choked up again. She'd liked Josh Parsons and his wife, and the genuine feeling in his voice when he spoke got to her.

'It must be so hard for you,' he said.

'Yeah,' she managed.

He nodded, his face creased with sympathy.

'Sad times. I'm so sorry. But I just wanted you to know that we're very happy to have Gerda and Layla staying for as long as you like. They've both been an absolute delight and we're looking after them, you mustn't worry on that score. And if there is anything else we can do, anything at all, just name it.'

Annie stared at him.

'Mrs Barolli?' he queried at her stunned expression.

Annie got a hold of herself. Thought of how Layla had loved the yard when she'd seen it, had even craved a pony of her own when she saw the long-limbed, highly strung thoroughbreds taking to the lanes around Newbury.

'Thanks. That's ... great. Does anyone else know they're there?'

He was looking at her curiously. 'Only Nico. He said we weren't to discuss the fact that Gerda and Layla were with us with anyone except you.'

'That's good,' said Annie numbly. 'Can they

stay on for a while longer?'

He gave a laugh. 'I think you'd have to bribe Jenny with gold nuggets to let Layla go. Of course. Should I get Gerda to phone you?'

'No. Don't do that.' She didn't want Gerda tipping Max off. 'Tell her I'll contact her soon.'

'Fine. Well. Goodbye, Mrs Barolli. Wish Annabella well for the race.'

'I do. Does she have a chance?'

He gave her an ironic look. 'There's *always* a chance. I hope to see you in the winner's enclosure.'

*Not me,* thought Annie. *Lucco.*

But she didn't say it aloud. She was too stunned by the news that Layla was at the stables. She heaved a deep, secret sigh of relief. Now she knew, she could relax a little. But only a little. Because if she was so foolish as to let this slip out, then Max would know where Layla was and he would leave her to the wolves and go and snatch his daughter away from her. And she *couldn't* let that happen.

'Enjoying the races?' asked a voice behind her.

She turned. It was Lucco, smiling with apparent warmth at her. He looked at Josh.

'And you are...?' he asked.

'This is Josh Parsons, who trains Annabella. Josh, this is Lucco, Constantine's eldest son.'

'Pleasure,' said Josh and held out a hand in greeting.

Lucco looked at it as if it might be contaminated. He didn't shake it.

'You do know this is a private box? That admittance is by invitation only?'

308

'Yes, of course,' Josh replied with his usual charm and good manners, but Annie could see that he was startled to be talked to like this, and to have his greeting ignored. 'I just wanted to have a quick word with Mrs Barolli and to offer her my condolences.'

Lucco nodded. 'Well now you have. Do run along.'

With only a slight tightening of the lips, Josh nodded to Lucco, tipped his hat to Annie, and hurried off.


# 60

Annie went to move away too, disgusted at Lucco's crass behaviour. She didn't want to be out here, alone, with him. Not standing beside a balcony rail with a thirty-foot drop to the ground below. She went to pass him, but he caught her arm and held her there, trapping her between the rail and his body.

'I asked you a polite question,' he said under his breath. He was very close. She felt the pressure of his fingers bruising the flesh of her arm. 'Are you enjoying the races?'

Annie looked at him like he'd just crawled out from a sewer. Lucco gave her his most pleasant, most snakelike smile. 'You will answer me,' he told her firmly. 'You forget yourself. I am the one you must answer to now.'

'Yeah, you got some big shoes to fill,' said Annie,

unable to resist goading him, even though she knew it was crazy.

'And you've got a big *mouth*,' Lucco retorted, his black eyes gleaming with spite as he increased the pressure on her arm. 'You know what? Sometimes I think I might kiss it. I could, if I wanted. I could have you brought to me gagged and bound, but then you know that, don't you? Everything my father owned, *I* now own. So sometimes ... yes, I do think I might rather enjoy kissing your mouth. And then at other times I think I might prefer to have your lips sliced from your beautiful face as a punishment, as the Chinese emperors used to do with concubines who displeased them. I could have it done, you know. Easily.'

'I'm not your concubine, Lucco,' Annie pointed out frostily.

'Ah, but you could be,' he said.

'You like frightening women, don't you?' asked Annie conversationally, although the pain in her arm was excruciating now. She wasn't going to give the bumptious little arsehole the satisfaction of hearing her cry out, no way. 'Is that how you get your kicks with Daniella? I saw the bruises when we were out by the pool.'

He looked at her blankly. But he was forcing her back against the rail, inch by inch.

'How I conduct my private affairs has nothing to do with you,' he said coldly.

'*Affairs* is the right word,' said Annie, her eyes moving past him to settle pointedly on the glamorous Sophie, her fabulous tan and skilfully highlighted blonde mane of hair shown off to full effect by a shimmering veil of cream chiffon over a micro-mini silk ivory shift that left almost nothing to the imagination – she was bra-less, her nipples completely visible through the sheer fabric. Earlier in the afternoon, she had vanished for half an hour, and Lucco with her. When they had returned to the box, Sophie had that rumpled, flushed look that told everyone they'd just had hasty, hot and heavy sex.

'Couldn't you at least keep your playmates at a discreet distance when your wife's around? Daniella's trying to be a good wife to you, why not cut her some slack?'

He shrugged. Now she was pressed right up against the rail, it was digging into her back. 'Maybe I enjoy teasing her.'

'Yeah, because you're a cruel son of a bitch.'

'Do you think that's what my father did? Kept his playmates at a discreet distance from you?' he taunted.

'He didn't have any playmates,' said Annie. 'All he wanted was me. And all I wanted was him.'

'Ah, but are you *sure* about that?'

'I'm sure.'

'Such a pity you made a fuss last night,' said Lucco, smirking at her as he pushed in closer. 'I like you fighting me, Stepmama, I find it very ... stimulating.' He pressed nearer and now she could feel to her disgust that he had an erection.

So it had been *him*. The creep.

'So are you still playing the grieving widow? Or ready to move on yet?' he remarked, pushing so hard against her that she knew there were going to be bruises.

Christ, was he intending to shove her over the rail?

She remembered another time when he'd had her over a drop like this – and perhaps this time he wouldn't shrink from taking full advantage.

Her heart was in her mouth because Lucco really did scare her. Sometimes he acted as though the normal rules didn't apply to him at all. And she guessed they didn't. He had all of his father's power now, and none of his discretion or sound judgement. If Constantine had been a wise Caesar, Lucco was surely a deranged Caligula.

'You seem very *familiar* with your bodyguard,' he went on. 'It's like you know each other really well.'

Ha! Well, he got *that* wrong. She didn't know Max Carter at all now. He was like an alien species to her.

'Shall we slip away together?' he was murmuring now.

'What, like you did earlier, with Sophie?'

'Ah, you noticed? Were you jealous?'

Annie tried to pull away. She couldn't. 'In your *dreams,*' she spat.

'But I was quick with her,' he said soothingly. 'It'll be better with you, trust me. I'll be slower. I'll drive you wild. Now come on – you know you want to. You must be missing it now Papa's gone...'

'You little *shit.*'

'What's going on?' asked a male voice from behind them.

Lucco turned, instantly releasing Annie. Max was standing there, watching him.

312

'Nothing at all,' said Lucco. 'We're talking. Private family business. *Not* for the ears of staff.'

Max gave a taut smile.

'Excuse me...' said Lucco, and pushed past him back into the box.

Annie sagged back against the railing, rubbing gingerly at her arm.

Max looked at her. 'What was that about?' he asked.

'Nothing.' She couldn't tell Max that Lucco had all but confessed it had been him last night creeping about in her room. Max would want to kick his arse for it, and right now Annie couldn't take any more aggro.

Still, she couldn't shake the creepy feeling that if Lucco couldn't get her into bed, then he'd get her into a box – either one would do. But at least she knew now that Layla was safe. Josh and Jenny were looking after her. The relief was enormous. She hugged the knowledge to herself, held it like a warm blanket on a cold night; no way was she telling Max.

Max handed her the betting slip. Then the race was announced and everyone else crowded out onto the balcony to see it.

Surefire won by a clear head, streaking past the winning post like a chestnut thunderbolt, all the other mounts, including Lucco's prized black filly Annabella, thundering along in his slipstream. The vibrant hues of the jockeys' silks and the luxuriantly glossy coats of the horses were a kaleidoscopic blur as they shot past.

'Oh well,' said Annie, tearing up her slip and letting the pieces flutter down to the ground far below. Win or lose, she didn't much care any more.

More champagne was opened. Aunt Gina stood up with tears in her eyes and made a toast.

'To the best man in all the world – to my brother, Constantine.'

They all echoed 'to Constantine' and drank to his memory. Annie was watching Lucco. He'd been slow to lift his glass, slow to say his father's name. She could see the self-doubt in his face, and thought that maybe he was wondering if he would ever be toasted and called the best man in the world. When he glanced towards her, she gave him a knowing little smile.

Then tea was served, and the afternoon drifted on and finally dissolved into misty rain. Finally, it was time for the party to disperse and go home. It was when the cars were just turning into the drive at Holland Park, the wipers swooshing back the now heavy rain and the headlights slicing into the darkening night, that a woman flung herself sobbing and screaming onto the bonnet of Max's Jag. It was Rosa.

'Shut up,' was the first thing Lucco said when he emerged from his own car to stare at the hysterical woman. He grabbed her arm and shook her roughly. Rosa fell to her knees, gabbling a mixture of Spanish and English. 'What's going on? What's happened?'

The poor woman was incoherent.

'Fuck it, don't do that, you'll only frighten her more,' snapped Annie, moving in to push him aside. 'Rosa? What's happened? Come on, tell me.'

Finally, somehow, the woman managed to get the words out. When she did, they all stared at her in disbelief. And after a few moments, Alberto, Max and Lucco ran off inside, through the house and out to the pool. The women followed behind, more slowly, Annie and Daniella supporting Rosa in a state of near-collapse between them.

The security lights were on at the back of the house, starkly illuminating the sheeting tumble of the rain as it shattered the surface of the pool with a million hard droplets. There was a man's nude body floating face-up in the centre of the pool.

'What the f...?' shouted Lucco to the thundering heavens, and Alberto and Max dived in fully clothed and swam out to the body.

They towed Rocco to the side of the pool. Everyone was there in the pouring rain, their fine clothes being drenched; but none of them cared about that. Rosa, Annie, Daniella and Cara stood aside, and so did Lucco. Fredo emerged from the house and helped Alberto and Max to get Rocco out onto the terrace.

He was dead.

Rosa set up a fresh bout of shrieking when she saw what had been done to Rocco, and Annie put an arm around her, told her shush, everyone will hear.

'Fuck *me*,' muttered Max as he leaned over the body.

Lightning flashed, searing through the black sky and highlighting in its flickering glare the hideousness of Rocco's injuries.

Fredo was looking as though he was about to

throw up.

Rocco's eyes were wide open, staring in sightless surprise up at the tumult of the night sky. Where his genitals should have been was a neat, blood-dark hole. Someone had cut off Rocco's cock and stuffed it into his mouth.

# 61

'Is she all right?' asked Alberto as he entered the drawing room with Lucco and Max trailing behind him.

Daniella had been violently sick when she'd seen the state of Rocco's body. Now she was sitting, shivering in her sopping-wet clothes, in the drawing room. Rosa had managed to calm down enough to make up the fire. It was starting to generate a little warmth. Annie was kneeling beside the chair she had pulled up to the fire for Daniella, smoothing back the girl's drenched hair.

Alberto crossed the room to Daniella.

'Honey? You okay?' he asked her, placing a gentle hand on her neck.

She looked up at him with tear-filled eyes. 'It was horrible,' she said.

'I know, I know.'

He was smoothing her skin comfortingly, and again Annie was reminded, forcibly, of Constantine and his unexpected tenderness towards her when she had come to him in the depths of despair, pleading for his help.

She stood up. It was painful to think of that. She went and sat beside Cara, Rocco's widow, who was sitting on one of the big couches looking as if someone had knocked all the stuffing out of her. Tentatively, Annie placed a hand on hers; it was icy cold.

The men had moved quickly to deal with this. Alberto had phoned through to one of the clubs the Barollis owned in the West End. Within half an hour there was a van outside. The police weren't called and no one even suggested it. This was family business, to be kept inside the family; the power of the Mafia was at work. Everyone understood that.

The women were herded like sheep into the drawing room, which didn't sit well with Annie. When the van arrived, she was crossing the hall, helping Rosa fetch hot drinks and towels from the kitchen, and she glimpsed Steve Taylor among the big bruisers who had come to deal with the corpse. He walked straight past her and past Max as if he didn't even recognize either of them. Of course – Max would have told him what was going on with him and Annie; he would have had his orders.

She knew that the Carter firm was on a long-standing contract to provide security for most of the Mafia-owned clubs in the West End, and Steve had performed many clean-up operations in his years as a Carter foot soldier, so she really wasn't surprised to see him here tonight.

'Is there anything I can do? Anything I can get you?' Annie asked Cara now.

Cara just shook her head. She hadn't cried since they'd hauled Rocco out of the pool. But then, grief took different people different ways.

Annie had a brief mental image of Cara and Fredo in the bedroom and pushed it swiftly from her mind.

'Who would do a thing like that?' she wondered aloud, looking at Lucco. Max was leaning against the door, towelling his hair dry. There was still movement out in the hall. Annie shuddered to think of Rocco, who had seemed a kind and pleasant young man, being bundled out of here like so much dead meat.

'How the fuck should I know?' snapped Lucco. He ran his hands through his hair and glared at her.

Alberto looked round at him. 'Hey – steady,' he said.

Annie stared at Lucco. Now was the moment for the Don to take the lead, calm everyone down. They were all shocked and alarmed by what they had witnessed tonight. What it looked like... Annie didn't like to think about it, but what it *looked* like was a hit from one of the other Mafia families. Had Rocco been screwing around with the wife of another firm's *capo,* something like that? This looked like a revenge killing.

'The Mancini family aren't going to like this,' said Aunt Gina suddenly from the depths of one of the couches nearest the fire. 'Rocco was with the Barollis, under Barolli protection. And this happens.'

'Aunt, I *know* what's happened,' shouted Lucco, flinging his arms wide. 'I *know.* You think I need you to tell me that this is a fucking disaster? Don't bother.'

*He's losing it,* thought Annie.

She remembered her conversation with Alberto out by the pool. How he had said that there had been trouble on the streets, other families trying to muscle in after Constantine's death, but that Lucco could handle it.

Actually, she didn't think Lucco *could*. She didn't think Lucco knew *what* to do. And she could see the uncertainty in him now, that cool smarminess of his slipping to reveal a chink of fear.

Aunt Gina was right. There was no way the Barollis could simply dispose of Rocco's body like the Carter mob had disposed of Nico's. The Mancinis were a family of power. There would be repercussions over this. They would want the body of their youngest son shipped back to the States; they would want an explanation, and they would want someone's *blood*.

'Annie!'

It was an hour later and she was crossing the hall to go upstairs and get changed out of her wet things, grab a hot shower. The boys were gone now, the clean-up was done. Tomorrow morning, when she looked out on the terrace, she knew it would be as if Rocco's mutilated body had never been floating in the pool, his blood seeping out to tint the turquoise water around him to a muddy purple. The pool would have been drained and refilled. All would be pristine. She knew this. She'd seen it happen before. And still it made her

319

shudder, how easily the detritus of sudden, violent death could be disposed of by men experienced in the art of mayhem.

She turned. Daniella was coming out of the drawing room, hurrying after her.

'I'll come up with you,' she said through chattering teeth.

They were all shocked. But Daniella, young and tender as she was, seemed to have taken it hardest of all.

*Much harder than Rocco's wife did,* thought Annie, but that was unkind. Just because Cara wasn't wailing or screeching over her loss, that didn't mean she didn't feel it – even if she *had* been busy screwing the staff.

The two women climbed the stairs together, each feeling weary and wrung out.

'I wanted to talk to you,' said Daniella shakily.

'Oh? What about?' *Please make this quick,* she thought. *I just want a shower and then bed, that's all. I don't want to think any more.*

'Rocco. I overheard him talking on the phone before we left this morning. He said he was going to meet someone here today.'

'What?' They'd reached the landing. Annie stopped in her tracks. 'Well ... that's odd. Here? I thought he told Lucco he had a business meeting at the bank.'

'That is what he was saying,' said Daniella earnestly. 'He was ... upset. Unhappy. You know? You understand me? He said it was a nuisance and he seemed angry. But this person was saying yes, they were coming here, I think, and he put the phone down, like *that.*' Daniella made a quick movement, mimicking Rocco slamming the phone down.

*But did you get that right?* wondered Annie. Daniella's understanding of English wasn't perfect by a long shot. Had she misunderstood, or misread the signals?

Maybe.

Maybe not.

But if Daniella was right and Rocco was meeting someone here, someone he was unhappy about, then who was that person? And could he or she be the one who had killed him?

'Maybe I should not have said...' said Daniella, seeing Annie's expression change.

Annie looked at the girl, standing there with her rain-soaked hair and clothes, and her tear-streaked face. What a day the poor little bitch had had. She'd gone to the races for a happy day out, wearing a new necklace and a brand-new dress to impress her husband, and he had repaid her by flaunting his mistress under her nose. And *then* they had found this new horror waiting for them.

'No, it's okay, you've done the right thing,' Annie assured her.

Daniella saw Annie's eyes on the coral necklace.

'*This* thing,' she said, her lips clenching in sudden anger. She reached up and ripped it from her neck, breaking the clasp. Then she flung it to the floor. Chips of coral scattered, bouncing down the stairs. 'I hate it. I hate *him*.'

Annie knew Daniella was hurting. But there was nothing she could say that would help that.

'Look – Daniella – you must tell Lucco about the call when he comes up to bed, okay? And ... if you need anything, I'm right here.'

# 62

The Mancini household got the call in New Jersey at seven o'clock in the evening. Enrico was sitting on his lit back porch drinking beer and reading the day's papers. He needed glasses for that, thick glasses. Jeez, he was getting old. But not too old to see and be glad that the Vietnam thing was over now, the troops were coming out of Da Nang. He heard the phone start ringing. Then it stopped. He turned the page for the next item, and then he heard the low hurried words – and then his wife started shrieking.

He sprang from his seat, spilling his beer, throwing the glass aside. He hurried inside. His wife was screaming in a monotonous high-pitched wail. He grabbed her and demanded to know what was wrong.

She kept on screaming. He slapped her.

'Hey! What's going on?'

Had anything happened to his oldest son, Jonathan? He couldn't take that. That would kill him for sure. He had a bad heart and this would be too much for it, he knew it. Night and day the doc was after him with pills and blood-pressure checks: this would be too much.

With the shock of the slap, his wife's face

crumpled up and she started to cry hysterically.

'Rocco! It's Rocco!' she shouted.

'What about him?' Rocco? That little squirt? What had he been up to now?

'Alberto Barolli just called. He's dead, Enrico. Our son's dead.'

Enrico was stunned into silence.

His youngest son, dead?

He called for the maid and she came and led his wife away upstairs. Better call out the doc and get her something to calm her down. Better call Alberto back and find out what the *fuck* was going on here. He hurried through the room to his study, his head whirling, his heart thudding away like crazy ... all right, there was no love lost there. None at all. But this was his *son*, for Chrissakes.

Suddenly Enrico slumped down in his desk chair, feeling winded, breathless. A spasm clutched his chest and he put a hand there, thinking *no. Not now, not yet...*

And then he convulsed, and died.

# 63

Annie woke up to shouting. She sat up in bed, groggy from sleep. When she had crawled, exhausted, into bed, she didn't think she would sleep at all, but somehow she had, and now... Daniella was shouting and crying, and she could hear Lucco shouting too.

She leaned over and flicked on the bedside light.

'What the hell...?' she muttered, and was just wrapping her robe around her when the connecting door opened and Max came in wearing his robe.

'What the...?' Annie stared at him in surprise. 'That door was *locked*.'

'I took the key and put it on my side.'

She hadn't checked it before she'd got into bed. He could have burst in here at any time.

*And done what?* she wondered bitterly. He'd already made it plain that he didn't want her any more. He might have crept in here and choked the life out of her, though; but so far he'd managed to resist that temptation.

'What *is* that? I thought it was you having the fucking nightmares again, but it's in the next room,' said Max.

'That's Daniella and Lucco's room,' said Annie.

They were silent for a moment, listening. There was a shout from Daniella, and then the sound of someone or something falling, all the while overlaid by Lucco ranting like a madman. Then Daniella started to cry loudly.

'Fuck *this*,' said Max, and went out onto the landing.

Annie dashed after him and caught his arm. 'You can't interfere,' she warned. If Max did step between them, who knew what Lucco might do in retaliation?

'Like hell I can't,' said Max, and flung open the door.

All the lights were blazing in the room. Daniella

was half kneeling and half lying on the floor by the bed wearing a thin pink nightgown, sobbing her heart out and screaming with pain as she clutched at her cheek, and Lucco in his dressing gown had hold of her by the hair and was trying to pull her back to her feet, all the while swearing at her, telling her she was a stupid *cunt,* she should come to him first, she should tell him *anything* first, what did she think he was, some normal, everyday man?

'I'm the *Don,*' he roared at her. 'You come to me. You answer to *me*. You understand?'

Annie stood in the doorway, aghast. Obviously, Daniella had told Lucco about Rocco's phone call, and let slip that she had told Annie first. But for God's sake, was he nuts? Was that really something to fly into a rage about?

*No,* she thought. *It ain't. He's just taking out his panic and frustration on her because she can't fight back.*

Max shot across the room, grabbed Lucco and threw him back against the wall. Then he pinned him there, lifting him clean off his feet, and hissed out: 'Come on then, you little tit. You want the rough stuff? Try it on someone who can take it.'

For a moment, Lucco looked too shocked by Max's intervention to speak. But then he started to smile. And then he started to laugh.

'Good God, are you serious?' he managed to wheeze out, but his eyes weren't laughing. They spat venom. 'You don't know what you're taking on.'

Max gave him a shake that wiped the smile

325

clean off his face.

'Oh, I think I do,' he said. 'A chicken-livered piece of scum who thinks he can use his wife as a punchbag. Well, not in my hearing you don't.'

Annie was helping the sobbing Daniella back to her feet.

'Ma ... Mark, leave it,' she said urgently.

'What's going on in here?' asked Alberto from the doorway. He came in, his blond hair mussed up from sleep. 'I heard noises.' He looked at Max holding Lucco against the wall. He dashed into the room and grabbed Max's arm. 'Come on, enough! Haven't we all had enough trouble for one day?'

Alberto glanced at Annie and then at Daniella. Annie saw him looking at the bruises on Daniella's wrists and then at the red mark on her cheek where it was obvious that Lucco had struck her. She saw his mouth form a thin, angry line.

'What's been going on here?' he said sharply.

'Nothing,' said Daniella. She straightened, pulled away from Annie, wiped at her eyes. 'Nothing. Really. Just a...' She faltered to a halt.

'A misunderstanding?' offered Annie. Fuck's sake, *someone* had to calm this situation down, and thank God, Daniella had the sense to do it.

'*Sì,*' she said gratefully.

Max was staring into Lucco's taunting eyes, still holding him pinned there, immobile.

'Come on,' said Alberto. 'Enough now.'

Max let Lucco go. He dropped to the floor, angrily straightening the creased front of his robe.

326

'Thank you,' he said stonily. 'And now perhaps you will all just *fuck off* out of my bedroom and let my wife and me get back to bed?'

Annie exchanged an anxious glance with Daniella.

'You going to be all right in here?' she asked, not caring that Lucco could hear. *Fuck* Lucco. 'You can come in with me, if you want.'

'I'm fine. Really,' said the girl with a trembling smile.

'Yes, let's all get some sleep, shall we?' said Alberto, going back to the door. His face was thunderous. 'Goodnight, everyone,' he said, and was gone.

Daniella went into the bathroom to clean up. Annie and Max headed for the door.

'Oh – one moment,' said Lucco.

They both turned back, looked at him.

'What?' asked Annie, her voice blank with dislike.

'You're not welcome here any more. Tomorrow morning, first thing – I want you gone.'


# 64


'Oh, here we go again,' said Ellie mournfully when she found Annie standing on the doorstep at eleven o'clock next morning. Then she saw Max Carter standing behind Annie. 'Holy *shi* – hello, Mr Carter.'

'Mark Carson,' said Annie.

'What?' asked Ellie, trailing after her into the kitchen. She glanced back. Max was coming in, too. What the...?

'Max is acting as my security for the moment,' said Annie, resting her heavy holdall on the kitchen table. 'My bodyguard, right? If anyone asks, that's *anyone*, he's Mark Carson. The Carter boys already know about it.'

'Right,' said Ellie, as if she knew what the fuck Annie was talking about. *Bodyguard?* What the hell was that all about?

'Sorry about the short notice, Ellie, but I wanted somewhere Gerda could reach me.'

'Gerda?'

'Layla's nanny. So I couldn't do a hotel, it had to be somewhere Gerda had the number for. And I couldn't do that to Dolly, push her out of her flat, she loves that place, and Queenie's place is barely liveable in, and I wouldn't even *think* about my cousin Kath's, the dirty mare, and anyway there's no phone line into Queenie's and Gerda don't know the number there and she don't know Kath's number, so I thought, who'll have a room or two going begging? And I thought, I know – there's always a spare bed in a place like this...'

'You got it fixed then?' Max was looking at the freshly painted kitchen door.

Ellie smiled nervously. 'Oh, yeah. No problem.'

'Business good?'

'Brisk. Yeah. Thanks for asking.'

'We'll try not to get under your feet,' said Annie tersely, thinking that Ellie was going to start *curtsying* in a moment, and that he was big-headed enough without that.

'No problem,' said Ellie, but she was thinking that it probably *would* be a problem, because Annie Carter was a problem with a capital P, and you were pissing against the wind if you believed otherwise.

'Well, let's get you sorted out with a room,' said Ellie, trying to be cheerful about it. After all, they'd made up. She'd thought Max was going to rip Annie's head off when he met up with her, but no, look – here they were, together.

'Two rooms,' said Max coldly.

'One each,' said Annie, equally cool.

Ah. So hostilities were ongoing.

She showed them up to their rooms. Little blonde Rosie, wearing skin-tight hot pants and a sheer chiffon blouse, passed them on the stairs, and gave Max the glad eye.

'Who's *that?*' she asked Ellie when the Madam came back downstairs to the kitchen where Rosie was making tea. 'That gorgeous guy. Not a punter, is he? Not this early?'

'Him?' Ellie sniffed and sat down heavily. She reached for the biscuit tin. Fuck it, she'd sworn off the things but this called for a chocolate digestive at the very least. 'That, my girl, is a whole lot of trouble. Don't even *think* about it.'

'Well,' said Rosie wistfully, bringing two cups of tea to the table, 'a girl can dream.'

Ellie snorted and chomped down on a biscuit.

'It was dreaming about *that* one that got her into trouble in the first place,' she said, spitting crumbs.

'Yeah? What happened?'

So Ellie told her most successful working girl about Annie, about Max Carter, and how she had pinched him from her sister, and all that had happened along the way.

'But they're back together now?' asked Rosie finally, enthralled.

'Separate rooms,' said Ellie. Shit, she was on her fifth biscuit now and she didn't feel like slowing down yet.

'Ah.' Rosie gave a grin. 'But you could smell it in the air between them, couldn't you?'

'Smell *what?*' asked Ellie in exasperation. Through the open kitchen doorway she saw Chris come in the front door and she watched him wistfully as he took his seat in the hall.

'The sexual tension,' said Rosie, who in Ellie's opinion read too many Mills & Boon books when she wasn't entertaining clients, and had some very airy-fairy ideas.

Ellie tore her eyes from Chris and shook her head. Rosie and her bloody stupid romantic notions. 'I think you'll find that was pure hatred,' she said.

# 65

'Well, thanks a *bunch,*' said Annie to Max as he dumped the bags onto the floor of her room.

Oh, she knew this room. It was the same one she had stayed in when she had moved in here with Aunt Celia, when she had been in disgrace over sleeping with Max. He had been the entire source of her trouble then, and things hadn't changed a bit. He was *still* getting on her tits.

'Meaning?' asked Max, closing the door and leaning against it.

'Meaning for fuck's sake why did you have to go and do that?' she demanded, rounding on him, furious. 'You can't take on Lucco Barolli. Do that and he'll have your guts. Anywhere in the world, he'll get you. *Anywhere*. You can't needle him and think you'll be safe, ever again.'

Max shrugged. He didn't seem that perturbed. 'That little bastard needed a lesson,' he said.

'Well, let's hope he forgets that it was you who tried to give him one. Or, I tell you, you're a dead man walking.'

'I'm that anyway,' said Max.

Annie flung her bag onto the double bed and unzipped it. She paused, looked around her. The place was neat and clean, but it wasn't Holland Park, not by a long chalk. Her whole life felt like a board game. One moment up, the next down. She turned and stared at Max.

'Now what does that mean?'

'Just that I should be dead. But I'm alive. And if you think I'm going to stand aside while Junior cuts up rough with a sweet young girl like Daniella, then you don't know me at all.'

Annie paused.

'Maybe I don't,' she said. 'I don't even know why you're not dead. You never told me.'

Max came over to the bed. 'Do you even *care*?'

Yes. She did. This was the man she had once loved best in all the world, the man she had sacrificed everything for, even stopped a bullet for. So yes, she cared. But she couldn't say that aloud, there was too much anger between them right now for that.

Annie shrugged, deliberately casual. 'I'd like to know, out of interest. After all, there's nothing else pressing, is there? You got us chucked out of Holland Park, now we're dossing down in a whorehouse.'

'You're better off out of that snake pit. And anyway, this move might force someone to show their hand, come out in the open, and I'm on home territory now – *my* boys run these streets.' He gave her a glinting look. 'And as for dossing in a whorehouse – you should feel right at home here,' he said.

Annie nodded slowly. 'Say that to me just one more time and I *swear*, you're going to get your teeth back in an ashtray.'

Now he *did* smile. 'You and whose army?'

'You think I don't have clout? I've got connections.'

'Nah. Your husband had connections. Your stepson's got connections. Not you.'

'Well, he's thrown us out, thanks to you. And so my social diary's taken a bit of a dip. So go on. Just to fill in the time. Tell me what happened.'

He sat down on the bed, just a couple of feet from her; but they were miles apart.

'They threw me over the cliff edge at the villa,' he said. 'Smashed me up pretty good. But the doctors put me back together again.'

'All that time...' said Annie, feeling faintly sick.

332

The sheer cruelty of doing something like that to anybody was beyond her. She could see it in her mind's eye, so clearly: Max falling, plummeting, his body crashing onto the rocks far below.

It was a miracle that he had survived.

'But you were gone for so long,' she said.

'It took a long time for me to recover. When I came to, I didn't have a clue who I was. The doctors thought my memory would come back, but they didn't know how long it would take.'

'So for over two years you didn't even know who you were?'

He nodded.

'Then it came back in fits and starts. Almost the last piece of the puzzle to fall into place was you, and Layla. And then, when I remembered what had happened, I thought you must both be dead. I came back to London and then—'

'Then you found out I'd gone with Constantine,' filled in Annie.

'Yeah.' He stood up, looking grim. 'But then – knowing you – that shouldn't have surprised me, should it?'

'What does *that* mean, "knowing you"? I was *always* faithful to you.'

'Until a better deal came along. I'd bet you a penny to a pinch of shit, if you'd met Barolli when we were married, you'd have gone for it then and there.'

Annie gritted her teeth. How the hell could he even *suggest* that? 'I thought you were dead,' she said stonily.

'And if you'd known I was alive?'

'Then I...' Annie stuttered to a halt to stop

333

herself from saying it. What she had been *about* to say was that if Max had been alive then no one, not even Constantine, would have even come close.

But she had loved Constantine.

There was no way he was going to make her deny that love.

These were two very different men – Constantine brought up in wealth and Max in poverty. But they had both learned to carve out their niche in the world, living on their wits, and Annie admired their toughness, their resilience.

'You were about to say...?' Max prompted.

'Nothing.' Annie stood up, busied herself with emptying her holdall. 'I'd better get unpacked.'

'What, is it too painful, thinking about him? Thinking about what you've lost?' asked Max, standing up too.

Annie shook her head. She didn't know *what* to say.

Suddenly Max grabbed her and turned her to face him.

'Don't shut me out like that. Tell me what's going on in that stupid head of yours.'

'Oh, this from the man who calls me a slut and says I'll fit right in at a whorehouse? I don't *want* to talk to you; all you do is use my own words to beat me up with. And *don't* call me stupid.' Annie tried to pull away. 'And *don't*–'

'Why don't you shut the fuck up?' hissed Max, and kissed her.

Annie was paralysed with shock.

He was kissing her.

She couldn't believe it, but he was kissing her.

Instantly she pushed away, struggling to get herself free of him.

'*Bastard,*' she spat out, furious because what the hell was he playing at? He cursed her, insulted her, and then *kissed* her? Was he mad?

'What, you'd prefer it if it was Barolli?' Max's voice was harsh, cruel.

'Yeah, as it happens I *would,*' said Annie angrily.

'Well, tough. He's dead; I'm alive. Get used to it.'

'Let *go* of me,' yelled Annie, incensed. But he was still holding onto her arms, holding her there tight against him.

'You know what I really can't stand about you?' he asked her.

'That I'm a tart? Hey, I got news for you – you've already said that.'

'Nah. You know what's the worst thing? I'll tell you. It's that even though I know what you are, even though I *know* that, even when I first saw you and you looked thin and scraggy and weak – even *then* I felt it. I don't like it, but it's the truth – I can't even be in the same *room* as you without getting a hard-on.'

It was the truth. She could feel his erection pressing against her stomach but she was mad, too mad to even think of responding. 'I fucking well *hate* you,' she told him.

There was a knock at the door. They both froze.

'Fuck's *sake,*' muttered Max, and Annie wrenched herself free and went to the door and flung it open.

'*What?*' she snarled.

Ellie was standing there.

'Sorry to butt in,' she said, looking warily at Annie and beyond her to Max. 'There's a woman here to see you.'

# 66

The woman didn't look the kind who would ever willingly come knocking at the door of a back-street brothel. When Annie found her in the front parlour, she was looking around her as if she might somehow be contaminated simply by breathing the air of Limehouse.

*What the hell's she doing here?* wondered Annie.

Her skirt suit was pale camel, immaculate and obviously expensive. Her blonde hair was elegantly coiffed, her make-up was faultless, her nails too long for housework – or indeed work of any kind. Her expression was, as usual, sneering and unpleasant. Through the net curtains, Annie could see a black limo parked outside, and Fredo the uniformed driver standing alongside it.

'Good *God*,' she said with a half-smile, looking around her. 'So this is what you've come to?'

Now Annie understood Cara being here. She'd come to gloat over Annie's fall from grace.

'Take a seat,' said Annie.

She felt shaken to the core from her encounter with Max, and her mind kept replaying his admission that she still – despite all he thought of her – turned him on. Her mouth was still tingling from the force of his kiss. Her head was reeling.

But was he only trying to get back with her because of Layla? He wanted his daughter, and she believed that he was convinced – even though she had told him otherwise – that she knew where Layla was. Was he playing her like a bloody violin, to get her to spill the beans? If she *did*, then she knew he would snatch Layla from her.

But then … his physical reaction had been entirely genuine; there was no way he could have faked that. Bewildered, she pushed Max to the back of her mind and instead focused almost gratefully on Cara.

'Is it safe?' Cara sat down, looking as if she wished she'd fumigate the sofa first. Annie felt affronted on Ellie's behalf. Ellie was a dedicated cleaner-upper. The place was kept spotless and faultlessly tidy. She sat down on the sofa, too, surprised that Cara had come here and wondering why she had bothered. She noticed that Cara wasn't wearing the respectful black of mourning for her dead husband, but then she didn't kid herself that there had been any real love between them.

'Oh, yeah,' said Annie, refusing to rise to the bait.

'I suppose you feel perfectly at home here? In a whorehouse?' said Cara, her eyes wide and innocent.

'I've had worse.'

'Really? I find that hard to believe.'

'Well, I've had the *Barolli* household, and that makes this place seem like a picnic.'

'Poor little Daniella was so upset you went,' she said silkily. 'I think she felt she could depend on you for support.'

Max opened the door and came into the parlour. He leaned back against the door, arms folded. Both women looked at him in annoyance. He stood there like stone.

'Does he *have* to be here?' asked Cara.

'Yes,' said Max as Annie's mouth opened to reply. 'He does.'

He was doing a damned good job of playing bodyguard, that was for sure. But *playing* was the word. Playing at giving a toss about what happened to her, or playing dead. What game would he start playing next?

'Daniella can come here anytime,' Annie said to Cara. 'But Lucco wanted me out, so I had to respect his wishes.'

'Of course he was very upset about what happened to Rocco,' said Cara.

'Not so much upset as shit-scared, was my feeling.'

'What?' Cara's smug expression slipped a notch.

'The Mancinis are going to want answers. And can Lucco give them? I don't think so.'

Cara's face was suddenly showing signs of strain. 'They've been arguing, Alberto and Lucco. Lucco's furious because Alberto phoned Rocco's father and let him know what had happened. But Alberto said that if it was left to Lucco it would never have been done, and I think that's probably right. But now there's hell to pay. Enrico, Rocco's father, took the call ... and he had a heart attack right after that, and died.'

*Jesus.*

Cara let out a sigh. 'And now Lucco's going

338

crazy, saying Alberto shouldn't have interfered, that he's made everything worse. Lucco's saying he would have chosen the moment, spoken to one of the sons first maybe. Now, he can't. He's finding it so hard, taking over from Papa.'

'I gathered that.' Constantine could control a room with a gesture. Lucco, with all his shouting and posturing, would never master that same effortless and judicious use of almost limitless power. It was the sort of power, Annie knew, that could make a man either wise, or extremely dangerous. 'Look, I'm sorry about what happened to Enrico. And to Rocco. It was horrible. And he seemed like a nice, decent man.'

Cara looked up at her then, her pale blue eyes flashing. 'A decent man?' she said. She cast a sideways look at Max. 'You're joking.'

Annie frowned. Looked at Max. He raised his eyebrows. *How the fuck should I know?*

'Meaning?' she asked Cara.

Suddenly Cara jumped to her feet and started pacing around the room. 'Rocco betrayed me,' she snapped out.

'How did he betray you?' This sounded unlikely to Annie. What, Rocco? Play around? He really hadn't seemed the type.

'He did. In the worst possible way, the most *humiliating* way, he did.'

'How?' Annie was riveted. Cara was almost *confiding* in her: this was a first.

'Oh, it doesn't matter.'

'How did he betray you?' asked Annie, fascinated.

'With a man,' spat Cara angrily. 'Can you believe that? He cheated on me with a *man*.'

Annie's mouth worked but no sound came out. Rocco, a bisexual?

'Are you *sure?*' she asked finally.

'I had him followed. Hired a private detective to do it. I got pictures, evidence, everything.'

Annie thought about Rocco floating dead in the pool, his cock stuffed into his mouth. She looked at Cara, aghast.

'What are you looking at me like *that* for?' Cara demanded. Then her brows drew sharply together. 'You think I had something to do with Rocco's death? Forget it. I was with you all day at the races, wasn't I?'

Annie sat back, watching Cara's face closely. 'That don't mean you couldn't have got someone to do the deed.' Annie's eyes drifted to the window. Out in the road, Fredo was leaning against the limo's bonnet, smoking a cigarette.

Cara's eyes followed hers. 'What, Fredo? You're mad. He was with us.'

'Not all the time. He was down in the public area for an hour, not up in the box. He could have come back to London, done Rocco, and then come back to Goodwood.'

'Time's tight,' said Max.

Annie gave him a freezing look. *Did I ask for your opinion?*

'Did you tell Constantine about this?' she asked Cara.

'Look, I told you, it doesn't matter.' Cara looked really agitated.

'So you did tell him?'

'He wouldn't do anything.' Cara's beautiful face

340

was screwed up with anger. 'He said I'd made a mistake in marrying Rocco in the first place.'

Well, he had a point. Annie had always thought it was a mismatch. Cara had been far too strong-willed for mild, gentle Rocco.

'Do you think he was right?' she asked.

'Oh, for the love of God, what does it matter *now?* Papa's gone. Rocco's gone. It's all crazy. Except for the fact that you're out of our lives, thank God for *that.*'

'Cara – they were both murdered,' pointed out Annie, hard-eyed as she watched her stepdaughter's jerky movements.

'I know that!' shouted Cara, rounding on her. She clutched at her head and closed her eyes. 'It's a nightmare. I just don't know what's going on any more. I don't know *anything.* Except I'm glad you're here in this, this *pest-hole,* and not with us any more.'

She ran to the door and hurried out. Max and Annie heard the front door slam behind her. Annie moved to the window and saw Cara hurrying to the car, Fredo giving a smirk and opening the car door for her. Cara got in. So did Fredo. The car moved off and was gone.

Max joined Annie at the window. 'Now that's interesting,' he said.

Annie turned to him, her face angry.

'Look, do you *really* have to follow me around everywhere like a bad smell?'

Max leaned against the windowsill and gave her a slight, chilly smile.

'Actually, I think I do. *Someone's* going to make a move soon if they really want to get you.'

341

Annie stared at him, sick at the thought of his true motivation for guarding her. *Yeah, and then you could lose Layla for good.* 'What, Cara?' she sniffed. 'You're joking. She just came here to have a laugh at my expense. She might break a nail.'

He shrugged. 'Anyone can hire in labour. So we don't know, do we? She don't seem like she's got much of a grip on things. Seriously – I'd watch that family if I were you. They're poison. You know what? You could get another visit anytime, from any one of them. And if you *do* – just watch yourself.'

# 67

Rather than wait around for the axe to fall, Annie decided she'd go out – alone. She knew the risks, but she was sick of having Max around her, it was making her crazy. So she waited until he was out of sight and then shot out of the door, hailed a cab and did a circuit of the clubs to see how trade was doing.

What she hoped to find was that the places were falling to bits now that she was no longer in charge. But no such luck. All three showed every sign of thriving.

At the Blue Parrot she saw that the 'Annie's' sign was down, both above the main door and over the bar, although the place seemed packed with punters.

At the Shalimar, the situation was the same.

Christ, he'd wasted no time in obliterating her from his clubs, no time at all.

She went finally to the Palermo, and caught up with Dolly at the bar.

'All on your own?' asked Dolly in surprise, while Gary the barman hustled around her fixing drinks for a queue of customers, and 'Voodoo Chile' blasted out at full volume.

'Yeah. How's trade?'

'As you can see, bloody good,' said Dolly.

*Shit,* thought Annie.

'Get you a drink?'

'Nah, I'm fine.'

'Did you have a word with Mr Carter about the changes he's planning for the clubs?' asked Dolly, all casual, but Annie knew she was seriously worried.

She wished she could put Dolly's mind at rest. But she couldn't. Max was taking great delight in keeping her dangling, and that meant Dolly was dangling too.

'I have, but he won't tell me about them,' said Annie.

'Personally, I think he's got it all wrong,' said Dolly. 'The "Annie's" thing was good. Very current. Don't you think?'

'Doll,' said Annie wearily, 'it don't matter *that,*' she snapped her fingers, 'what I think. He'll do what he wants. I got no say in it at all.'

'Not getting on any better now?' Dolly asked.

'You must be joking.'

'Oh shit, not *you* again,' said a female voice by Annie's ear.

She turned. It was Dusty, rigged out in short

343

bubblegum pink again, her blonde hair bouf-
fanted like it hadn't gone out of style ten years
ago, her black-plastered eyes fixing Annie with
hatred.

'Yeah, me,' said Annie, eyeing this Munchkin-
sized museum piece with amusement. What was
the girl going to do, bite her in the bloody knee-
caps?

'I thought I told you I didn't want to see your
face around here no more,' said Dusty.

'Did you say that? *I* thought you said I had to
keep away from Max Carter. And as you see –
he's not here.'

'You know what I mean. You're hanging about
here waiting to see him.'

Annie straightened up.

'I don't want no trouble,' said Dolly quickly.

'Look,' said Annie, staring Dusty straight in the
eye, 'I don't want Max Carter. You're welcome to
him. But just some advice? You're acting way too
keen. No man likes that.'

'I don't want your fucking advice,' shot back
Dusty.

Annie shrugged. 'So don't take it.'

'I told you not to come back in here.'

'And yet, here I am. It's a bitch, but there it is.'

'You cheeky *cow*,' said Dusty, and barrelled
forward to grab a hank of Annie's hair and rip it
from her head.

Annie stretched out a hand and grabbed Dusty
around the neck. She didn't even squeeze. She just
held her there. Dusty, outreached, stood there
with her arms pistoning uselessly, threatening all
sorts and going steadily blue in the face while

trying – and failing – to inflict some damage.

Dolly was shouting for the bouncers, who came, grinned hugely at what was going on, grabbed Dusty and ejected her, still squirming and screaming insults, from the club.

'Christ, she's got more mouth than a cow got cunt,' said Dolly in wonder.

Annie took a deep breath as she watched Dusty being hauled away. She was tired of being the victim, the one who was picked on and sworn at. She was ready to be something else now. But what? She was no longer Constantine's wife – *or* Max's. Maybe she was ready to be her own woman again. Stroppy Annie Carter who only ever played by her own rules.

'You think she'll be waiting for me outside?' she asked Dolly with a glint of humour.

'If she *is,* I'm coming out to watch round two,' said Dolly with a laugh.

'Look, you come up the stairs *behind* the punter,' said Ellie loudly to one of the girls out in the hall. 'How many times do I have to tell you? Then, if you got a bolter on your hands, he *can't* change his mind and run out the door.'

Annie was stretched out on her bed, thinking. There had been a fracas out there a few moments ago – a punter had legged it and Ellie was giving the girl responsible an ear-bashing. But in her room it was quiet, calm. All except the noises that were coming through the wall from the bedroom next door. *Bang, bang, bang.* The headboard was striking the wall like a metronome. And *yes yes yes* was being shouted out at full volume by one of

345

Shirley's more vocal clients.

*Fucking* Max Carter, getting her thrown out. Holland Park was paradise compared to this. *And* he'd given her such a bollocking over going out alone on her tour of the clubs, the bastard, and then grilled her about Layla all over again. She'd lied to him, of course. Sworn she didn't have a clue where Layla was. Whether he'd believed her or not, she couldn't be sure.

'This Nico, you said he put Layla in a safe place with the nanny. Have you checked through his things? There might be something there, maybe a contact number.'

'I did. There wasn't,' she said flatly.

She'd already removed all Nico's papers, and she'd disposed of everything except the Times Square club contacts.

Now she turned over, hugged her pillow, tried to shut out the routine noises of the sex trade. She was used to them, she'd heard them a zillion times before. She should ignore them. But ... Max was on the *other* side of the wall, in the next bedroom. He was hearing all this too.

Her mind spun with the force of all the turmoil that she'd been through, all the wild suspicions she was entertaining about the Barollis. Were they really that low, that despicable, that they would have killed Constantine, killed Rocco, betrayed the family code of loyalty and unity?

She thought of Gina, perched everywhere, dressed in black and reading the financial pages like a malevolent old crow, squawking out now and again about the price of gold or that utilities were falling.

346

But Constantine was her *brother*.

Lucco – hateful; unstable as warmed-up gelignite and twice as destructive. To kill his father, his own flesh and blood ... no, she couldn't bring herself to believe it, not even of him.

Alberto? Unthinkable.

And Cara, she had *adored* her father.

Hadn't she?

God, she felt tired.

*So* tired of it all...

Moments later, she was asleep.

# 68

She dreamed of a hot, wild wind that swept her up amid flames into a writhing sea of pain. One moment she stood on the terrace of their Montauk home, Constantine walking towards her with a smile saying, *Hey, wonder what's in this one?*

Then he was hurtling towards her, his skin cracking open like a dry river bed, and blackening to charcoal. She felt the force of the impact, felt herself flying, flying ... and then she was in the sand, lying there, hearing nothing, not the crash of the waves, not the crackling and burning of the wreckage that she could *see* the terrace had become.

'Constantine!' she screamed, but she knew he was gone, gone into that great mystery where she couldn't follow unless she died too.

Oh, she *wanted* to die.

'Constantine!' she called again, but her voice broke and she was sobbing, standing in a dark void without him, and then ... she was awake. She shot upright in the bed, shivering, shuddering, sweating; and he was there, sitting there in the chair across the room. *Not* Constantine of the dazzling smile and overpowering charm, but the charred smoking wreck he was now.

'No...' she moaned, clutching at her head, wanting it to go away.

But it leaned forward in the chair, as if it was about to stand up, about to come towards her, and she thought that if *that* happened, if the thing came to her, tried to touch her, then she would go stark staring mad.

*Hey, wonder what's in this one?* it hissed inside her head, and she saw its mouth open in a mindless grin; bugs, dropping from inside it onto the carpet, scurrying away into the skirting board. Slowly, it started to rise from the chair.

'Annie,' said a male voice.

It had come for her.

She threw back her head and shrieked.

'Fuck's *sake,* wake up. You're dreaming. Wake up. You're all right, it's okay.'

The thing was holding her, pulling her in close. She could smell burning. She could smell *death.*

'No...' she shouted.

'Shh ... it's okay, it's just a dream.'

Now she was awake. *Really* awake. She looked around. The light was on, the thing in the chair was gone. Max was sitting on the bed, holding her. She gulped in a breath, pushed her hands

348

through her hair, closed her eyes, tried to get a grip.

'Oh *fuck,*' she wailed, slumping against his shoulder.

'You have this much?' he asked, smoothing back her hair. 'Bad dreams?'

*All the time.*

'No. Not much,' she said, bewildered by the gentleness of his touch.

'You never used to.'

'I'll be all right,' she said, starting to push away from him as she felt herself weaken, lean in. 'I'm okay.'

'No, you're bloody not,' said Max, staring into her eyes. 'You're a wreck.'

'Not your problem.'

'No – not my problem.' He looked at her a moment longer, then stood up, went to the lamp beside the bed. 'You want me to turn this off? Or you want it on for a while?'

'Just leave it on,' she said, aware now that she was naked and that he was here with her wearing a flimsy dark-blue robe. She pulled the sheets up to her chin, tried to get her mind refocused. Jesus, he was right. She *was* a wreck. She looked over at the chair. There was nothing there. Of *course* there wasn't. 'I'm fine.'

'You're not fine,' he said, turning, staring down at her. Then he said, 'Ah, fuck it,' and reached out, pulling her up onto her knees. Annie held onto the sheet.

'Max...' she said, wanting to tell him to stop, but he was here, so warm and so strong, she *knew* this man, she'd loved him, given him a child. This wasn't some impersonal stranger. This was *Max Carter.*

*But he wants to take Layla.*

She couldn't allow herself to think about that now. All she knew was that she was shattered, and he was here and she was glad of that. So this time when he kissed her she didn't pull away. She let him. She remembered his kiss, how he'd always had the power to take her breath away just by running his tongue over her lips, then settling his mouth over hers.

He did it now. Snatched the breath from her lungs so that she gave up, gave in, just clung to him and let the old sweet, sensuous feelings steal over her once again.

'Jesus, will you let *go* of that?' he muttered against her mouth, and then pulled the sheet away and stepped back just a little, enough so that he could run his eyes down over her breasts, her belly, her thighs.

Annie knelt there and let him look. She *wanted* him to look; she wanted this.

Where his eyes had moved, now his hands followed. She remembered those hands, the hands of a street fighter: blunt-tipped, broad, dusted with black hairs on the back. A tough, hard man's hands. She shuddered as they moved to cup and caress the fullness of her breasts, teasing her nipples into burning hardness with a flick of the thumbs, but she didn't try to stop him.

Now his hands were skimming down over the slight indentation of her waist, trailing with delirious slowness around her navel and then moving out to smooth over her hips before dipping inward to slip down between her thighs.

Annie gasped as his fingers curled into the dark depths of her bush and parted it to touch the hard nub of her clitoris. His fingers probed deeper, feeling how ready for him she was, sliding effortlessly inside her wetness, maddening her with long, slow, delicious strokes.

This was better, so much better, than thinking about death and having nightmares about Constantine coming back to her as a charred and hideous monster. *This* was what she needed, right now, to chase away the shadows.

Annie reached out while he was still caressing her, hearing his breathing coming harder and faster as she unfastened his robe, pushed it from his shoulders so that it fell to the floor.

He was naked too, and he was just as she remembered him. Strong, compact, with dark hair on his chest and feathering down over his well-toned stomach to where his erect penis now jutted out, hard as steel, as if straining towards her. She gasped at the beauty of it, took the hot silky shaft in her hands.

Delicately, she lowered her head and slid her tongue into the little crevice there, tasting his saltiness, then she moved her lips downwards, over the big pulsing head of it, and enfolded it in the heat and wetness of her mouth, sucking gently.

Max groaned and grabbed her hair, pulling her head back, away from him.

'Enough,' he told her hoarsely, pushing her back onto the bed. 'Lie down.'

Annie lay back, spreading her legs joyfully for him, wanting him now, the pulse of hot, hungry lust thrumming through her just like it was enveloping him. Max lay on her, the whole length of his hard body pushing hers down into the mattress, his hands holding her wrists, keeping her pinned there. He pushed his cock up into her and she cried out at how big he was, how totally he filled her.

She locked her thighs around his waist and let him have her. It was what he wanted, and she wanted it too. Every thrust was a delirious pleasure, a well-remembered delight, and she clung to him as he had her, violently, lustily; and when she felt him grow almost impossibly, hurtfully big, and when he finally came, she lay there, quiescent, feeling him relax and grow still.

At last he lay back on the bed, pulling her into the crook of his arm. They had lain like that a thousand times before, but this was new. This was *different*. She shouldn't have weakened. Shouldn't have let all those old feelings take her over. But she'd been vulnerable, shaken.

She closed her eyes, dreading the moment when she would have to think, talk about what they'd just done. Dusty had been right to be on her guard. Dusty would spit *blood* if she could see what was happening now. When she opened them again it was him, still him, Max Carter, lying there at her side, his body as beautiful and as strong and tanned as if carved from teak. She let her eyes drift down, over his flat, hard stomach, over his muscular thighs, down to his feet.

Again she found herself looking at those odd marks on his ankles, scars that were little red circles, almost like cigarette burns.

'What are those?' she asked him under her breath. 'I saw them when we were by the pool.'

'Hmm?' he opened his eyes, saw where she was looking. 'Oh.' He let out a breath. 'When those bastards chucked me down that mountain? Smashed both my ankles. The surgeons didn't think I'd walk again.'

Annie stared gravely into his eyes. She knew what that must have done to him. Max Carter was all about action, strength and physicality.

'So what happened?' she asked. 'You *are* walking.'

'Thanks to good surgery and physio.' Max remembered the physiotherapist. Marta. Jesus, that girl had put him through hell. 'And a monk called Brother Benito.'

'But the marks...'

'Bolts,' said Max. 'I had one through each ankle, then they took them out. Left scars.'

He had known hard times. She could see that. He had *suffered,* just like she had – no, worse – while they were apart. Her heart went out to him then and she thought: *Did I ever really get over him?*

No. The answer was no, she hadn't. If she was truthful with herself – and she always tried to be – just the sight of him still gave her shivers down her spine. Even when they were fighting, ripping lumps off each other, hurling insults; still there was that heat, that undeniable attraction.

She knew it. Hated it, but knew it was true.

But now ... now they were enemies, and he was going to take Layla off her the first chance he got.

One quick roll in the hay wasn't going to make any difference to that. In fact, he had probably taken advantage of her momentary fragility to soften her up for the kill.

Annie sat up. What had she been thinking? He had cursed her, called her a slut, a tart; he hated her now. If there was one thing she knew about Max Carter, it was how black-and-white his views were, how inflexible. He would never forgive her for Constantine. He just wanted Layla.

'You'd better go,' she said, and when he didn't object, when he just snatched up his robe and left her there alone, she knew she was right.

# 69

The doorbell rang very early next morning. Brasses kept very late hours, so everyone was still in bed sleeping off the gymnastics and general excesses of the night before. Annie, however, was awake, up and dressed. She thought Max was too, from the noises coming from his room through the thin partition wall.

She thought about last night, how good it had been to be with him again, skin to skin. But she had to forget that. He'd taken advantage of her, that was all, when she had been going through a low moment.

She heard his door open and his quick tread going past her room, down the stairs. She opened her door just a crack and watched him. All right, it was just a look, she wasn't going to touch ... but oh God, he was still so gorgeous. That dark hair and the way it curled just a little too long over his shirt collar ... the width of his shoulders, the narrow hips...

*Fuck it.*

She still fancied him like mad. She had to admit that. He was opening the front door, but there was no one there. She moved quietly out onto the landing. She saw him look up and down the street. The morning was bright and clear, sun glinted on his hair and made it gleam blue-black. Then she saw him start to bend down.

There was something on the doorstep.

Annie craned her neck to see around Max to what was down there, what he was about to pick up.

Her heart turned to a block of ice in her chest.

Her eyes opened wide in terror.

It was a large square box, wrapped in sky-blue paper and tied with red ribbon.

Max was going to pick it up.

Constantine had picked up one just like it.

*Hey, wonder what's in this one?*

Everything seemed to slow to a crawl. For a moment, Annie was paralysed by the sheer horror of what was unfolding in front of her eyes. Then somehow her legs obeyed the commands of her brain and she was hurtling down the stairs.

'*Don't touch it!*' she screamed at him.

She hit the bottom of the stairs at a run and lunged across the hall and grabbed Max, stopping his fingers just an inch away from the parcel.

'*Don't!*' she shouted.

355

Max was staring at her, startled.

Annie was panting, wild-eyed. 'Don't touch it,' she gasped out. 'It's a bomb!'

They stood in the back yard an hour later, all of them. The girls, Ellie, Max and Annie, who was still shaking hard from the shock of it. Annie's shrieks of warning had woken the whole household. Chris wasn't in yet – it was too early for him to start his stint on the door. And thank God for that, Annie was thinking, or else he could have picked the thing up, been blown to kingdom come.

'What the hell's going on?' Ellie had demanded, coming out onto the landing in her dressing gown.

She'd seen Annie and Max down in the hall, heard what Annie said about it being a bomb.

Holy shit, it was true; bad things followed Annie Carter around. Max had closed the door, pulled Annie away down the hall and into the kitchen.

'What time's Chris due in?' he'd asked Ellie.

'Not for another hour,' she said, half frozen with fear.

'Phone him. Tell him to stay away until we've got this sorted.'

After Ellie had contacted Chris, Max phoned Ginge; he'd been in the bomb disposal unit during the war but after that he'd drifted into the more lucrative field of safe-cracking. He was a Carter boy through and through: sound as a pound; he'd cracked open the Palermo Lounge safe once for Annie, and officiated at more heists than you could shake a stick at.

Ginge was there within fifteen minutes of Max's call. He was pushing sixty, tall, with thinning ginger-white hair, a pot belly and a long, hawkish face. He carried a Gladstone bag with him, and eyed the parcel on the doorstep as if it was a great treat, an enjoyable piece of puzzlement he couldn't wait to unravel.

'And she thinks it's a bomb, why?' he asked Max at the door, while Annie, Ellie and the girls cringed out back.

Annie had explained this to Max, even though she could barely speak because her teeth were chattering so hard with fear.

He'd nearly picked it up. She couldn't get over that. If she hadn't opened the door to secretly watch him, he *would* have.

'It's identical to one that went off before, in the States,' Max told him.

'Leave me with it then,' said Ginge, and opened his bag of tricks and set to work.

Nearly an hour later, Ginge came and knocked on the kitchen door. Max opened it.

'Was it?' Max asked.

'A bomb?' Ginge shook his head as if disappointed. 'Nah, Mr Carter. Just an empty box, tied up with paper and ribbon.'

Everyone exhaled. Sheet-white but otherwise composed, Ellie put the kettle on.

'I'll give Chris the all-clear,' she said, and then went out into the hall to phone him.

The girls started to disperse. Max slipped Ginge his payment and he departed.

'You okay now?' Rosie asked Annie as she got

up from the table.

'Yeah, I'm fine,' she lied.

She went upstairs to her room. Max followed her in, and shut the door.

Annie slumped on the bed and Max stood there leaning against the closed door, watching her.

'Someone's playing tricks on you,' he said.

Annie looked up at him with a bitter, trembling smile. 'So tell me something I *don't* know.'

'Who'd do this?'

Annie shook her head, shrugged. 'The same person who planted the *real* bomb?' she suggested.

'It was exactly the same? Tell me, about it.'

Annie folded her arms over her body as if to protect it. 'I can't,' she said through chattering teeth.

'Yeah you can. Come on. Get a grip.'

Annie glared at him. 'Oh, you think this is easy? Seeing your husband blown to smithereens and then having *this* happen?'

'Stop feeling so fucking sorry for yourself,' said Max roughly. 'Shit happens. Ride it out.'

Annie let out a shuddering breath. She dragged her hands through her hair. 'I don't know where to start...'

'The parcel. Where was it?'

'On a table. With other parcels. Presents. It was...' Her voice trailed away.

*It was the night of Lucco and Daniella's wedding. Stars bright in the Montauk sky, the chill, refreshing breeze coming off the ocean, the terrace empty of people. Just her ... and then Constantine...*

'And Barolli picked up the parcel...' Max prompted.

Annie nodded. 'Then it exploded.'

'Why'd he pick up that particular parcel?'

She forced herself to think about it. He was right. Here she was, acting like a bloody Victorian virgin when she was Annie Carter-Barolli, gang boss, Mafia queen. She *had* to get a hold of herself.

'It was the biggest and brightest, the most eye-catching. And at the front of the table.' Suddenly she looked at Max. 'It was in front of the other presents. The police in the States told me it was booby-trapped with a cluster of grenades.' She swallowed hard. 'The pins had been wired through and into the table, they told me. So that when it was picked up, it would ... explode.' Her eyes were full of tragedy. 'He would have picked that one up first anyway, wouldn't he? Later on in the evening. It's traditional, the Don hands the couple their presents.'

Max folded his arms. 'So you can rule out Lucco.'

'What?'

'Whoever planted the thing thought that Constantine would pick it up later in the evening, when the couple and the guests were there with him. Lucco would have been right there when the thing exploded. Therefore, it *couldn't* have been Lucco who planted it, or who got someone else to plant it.'

Max was right. It couldn't have been Lucco.

She tried to think. There had been so many people in and around the house that day. Usually, the place was a fortress, totally secure; but with all the people milling around, it became difficult to keep tabs on everyone. Of course checks had been made – but they'd failed.

Annie clutched at her head. 'Who's doing this? Someone left that thing on the doorstep deliberately, to scare me. *Who?*'

'That's what we're going to have to find out,' said Max. He was smiling as if this was a game, and he was enjoying it. 'You know that old saying about keeping your friends close and your enemies closer? I've been in touch with sweet young Daniella.'

'Why?'

'Oh, just fishing around. I don't know if you've noticed, but the tide of power's turning in that household.' He looked at her. 'And Daniella likes you.'

'You find that hard to understand, I suppose.'

He shrugged. 'You've been straight with her, kind. The rest of them – apart from Golden Boy – don't really want to know. I've been talking to her, she's been talking to Alberto and to that crazy bastard Lucco – and now there's been a *slight* change of plan.'

# 70

'I'm so pleased you've come back,' said Daniella, hugging Annie impulsively when she and Max checked back into the Holland Park house the next morning.

'Well, I'm pleased to *be* back,' said Annie, although that wasn't true.

At least in Limehouse she'd felt as if she was among friends. Here, she had just two – Daniella and Alberto; the rest of them were her enemies and she was sure they were trying to unhinge her.

And yet – here she was. Back again. She'd argued the point with Max, but he'd overruled her.

'Keep them up close, see how they react,' he'd said – as if dangling her like a piece of meat under their sharklike noses was nothing more than an interesting experiment. 'It's better to have them inside the tent with you pissing out, than outside pissing in.'

'Look, I *know* how they'll react. They want me dead. They'll kill me.'

'They won't kill you. You've got security. Remember?'

'Oh, yeah. Ex-SAS Mark Carson. I wouldn't put it past Lucco to check that out, you know.'

'You think I give a shit? Now, which was Nico's room?'

'Why?'

'Because I'm going to go through his things and see if there's anything there about Layla. So which is it?'

Annie told him. Christ, he really was like a dog with a bone; he wasn't going to let this go, not ever. And when he found out she'd been lying to him, keeping him in the dark, he was going to go *mental*.

'Unless you've heard anything already...?' he asked, his eyes probing her face.

'No,' she said. 'I haven't.' She hadn't even dared ring Jenny Parsons at the yard, for fear that Max might somehow hear and realize what was going on.

He went off to check Nico's room.

Now she was back in the master suite and very surprised to find herself there. She thought Lucco would have laid claim to it already, but he surprisingly hadn't.

'He's got so much on his mind,' said Daniella when Annie remarked on this, but the girl's eyes were worried and her face was still showing the bruises from Lucco's fist. 'It's been horrible here with Lucco and Alberto at each other's throats.'

'How'd you two swing this?' she asked Alberto later. 'Lucco was ready to cut my head off when I saw him last.'

'He still is,' said Alberto. 'But I had a word in the ear of Daniella's father. He's a big man, a great man back in Sicily, with important connections, and he won't take any shit. He had a word with Lucco, and suddenly anything Daniella wants, Daniella gets.'

'Except a happy marriage,' said Annie.

'Ah yeah. Except that. Miracles take a little longer.' And he smiled.

Yeah – he definitely *wasn't* the easy-going charmer you could easily take him for. And now she thought she'd been stupid to think it anyway; he'd been raised by Constantine, who had for years maintained complete order with no recourse to law. Constantine had with seemingly no effort at all held the dangerous streets of Queens in his absolute thrall; Alberto must have absorbed some of his father's cunning, if only by osmosis.

'Oh – you're back then,' said Gina, looking at her with disfavour at dinner that night.

'Daniella missed me,' said Annie sweetly.

Gina, sitting there in her usual black mourning, her handsome face as cutting as a hatchet, shot Daniella an acid look, and she blushed.

'I missed her too,' said Alberto, skilfully skinning a peach and sending a glinting, secret look to Daniella.

Cara said nothing. Lucco, sitting at the head of the table in Constantine's place, seemed not even to hear this exchange. They all looked at him. He glanced around at their expectant faces.

'What?' he asked. Then his eyes fastened on Annie. 'Oh. So I'm supposed to comment on this situation now, am I? I'm suppose to act overjoyed that my father's whore is back in residence?'

'His *wife*,' corrected Alberto mildly.

'My mother – *our* mother – was his wife,' Lucco reminded him.

'So was I,' Annie pointed out.

'Sorry, that slipped my mind.'

There was silence at the table.

'And where's the trained gorilla?' asked Lucco. 'The mighty hero, your "security"?'

'You mean Mark? He's here somewhere. Just a step away.'

'Unnecessary.' Lucco fingered the stem of his brandy balloon and stared at her with hostile eyes. 'We're your family, aren't we? According to you.'

'And families ought to stick together, especially in bad times,' said Annie smoothly.

'Sonny Gilbert phoned about the club. He wanted to talk to you,' said Alberto. 'Just to bring you up to speed with what's happening.'

'He could have talked to Lucco,' said Annie. 'After all,' she sent Lucco a sweet smile, 'we're partners in the Times Square venture, aren't we, Lucco? Although I *do* still have the controlling share.'

Lucco stared at her. 'I haven't time for bullshit like that,' he said. 'You deal with it. I'm not interested.'

Annie nodded. 'Of course, you've got so much to do. It was so tragic about poor Rocco. *And* his father, of course. Have you been in touch with the Mancinis again yet, Lucco?'

Lucco's lips tightened but his smile didn't slip an inch. He flicked a glance at Alberto.

'All that is in hand. As is tracking down whoever was responsible.'

Annie's eyes met Cara's. Cara looked away first.

'His brothers must have been upset,' said Annie.

'Yes. They were.'

'And wanting answers.'

Lucco slammed the glass down on the table so hard that Annie was surprised it didn't shatter. 'They'll *get* answers,' he said, standing up. 'When I do.'

And he left the room.

'You know, you shouldn't antagonize him,' said Alberto.

'Me?' Annie looked wide-eyed. 'I was only asking.'

'Well, I think it's very good that someone stands up to him,' said Daniella, flushing bright pink at her own boldness.

'You ought to learn some respect, my girl,' said Gina, and rose and followed Lucco.

'Nothing to say?' Annie asked Cara.

'I'm in mourning for my husband and for my father-in-law,' said Cara icily. She was staring unseeingly at her empty plate. 'I don't think I should be discussing his death or the consequences of it with you.'

'No? Only yesterday it seemed like you wanted to.'

'Well, today I don't. Got that?'

'Loud and clear,' said Annie, as Cara too left the room.

'Well,' said Annie to Alberto and Daniella. 'This is nice. Back in the bosom of my family.'

Alberto smiled and cut another slice from the peach with surgical precision. 'Isn't it?' he said.

# 71

That night, Annie was in bed in the master suite when she heard the door open and close softly. She stiffened, expecting attack; and when someone slipped into the bed with her she was halfway out the other side – before Max grabbed her around the waist and hauled her back in.

'Perks of the job,' he whispered in her ear, his breath tickling her skin and sending shivers down her spine. 'Sleeping with the boss.'

His erect cock was nudging her in the back.

God, this was a dangerous game she was playing, but it was alluring too. She had closed her mind to the possibility that she would ever see him again, yet here he was. But he wasn't here for her. All right, he was perfectly happy to use her sexually. But he was *really* here for Layla. And she had to button her lip and be *very* careful that he didn't find out that she knew already where Layla and Gerda were.

'Don't the boss have any say in this?' she objected, trying to sound coldly disapproving but failing dismally. Suddenly her blood was sizzling with desire; every pore of her skin was sensitized to him.

'No, actually – she don't,' he whispered against her breast as his tongue got busy there, lapping her, teasing her into willingness.

Annie shivered. 'But you're supposed to be

guarding me,' she murmured. 'Not *sleeping* with me.'

'I wasn't intending to do much sleeping,' he said, trailing kisses over her collarbone.

One careless little slip and he would be gone, off to get his daughter. And ... she needed him. Not only to keep her safe, but also because she had never really stopped loving him. How could she? He had been torn from her and she had turned to another man for help and had fallen under that man's spell. But in her heart, Max had always remained.

'What if I say no?' she asked, teasing, half enjoying herself now.

She'd never got over him and she knew she never would. Which was tragic, when you considered what *he* thought about *her*.

'Not an option,' he said firmly.

She turned in his arms, felt the welcoming strength of him as he pulled her in close. All right, she was fooling herself, but why shouldn't she take some comfort from this? To hold him close was magical; to let him love her was like recapturing an old and precious memory and bringing it alive again. Alive, when she had thought that death and separation were all she could expect.

'Kiss me,' she moaned, wanting to blot out her own tormenting thoughts.

He kissed her, already pushing her back onto the bed, parting her thighs and slipping inside her so easily and naturally.

Oh, this was so good.

He was just as she remembered: tender, strong, filled with desire for her. But he was just making use of her. Keeping her safe, yes – but only until he knew where Layla was. She was his key to Layla.

Annie stiffened, turned her head away when he sought her lips.

'Stop...' she said faintly.

'No,' he murmured against her neck, and finished quickly, biting her shoulder quite hard, but not hard enough to bruise or draw blood.

Oh, she remembered that. That Max was more *physical,* more brutal than Constantine. Constantine had been a smooth, accomplished, considerate lover; Max was energetic and aggressive.

It turned her on now, just as it always had. Even while she was whispering that he should stop, that she didn't want this, she did, she did.

He was using her, just like he'd use a whore. He'd called her that, and now he was using her like that too. He could already have made her pregnant again, could have just fathered another child on her, but one born not of love but of hatred.

He pulled out of her and rolled onto his back, easing her up against his chest, his breathing growing steadier. She could hear his strong, vibrant heartbeat.

Max Carter was back in her life.

She hadn't quite believed it until now.

But he wasn't back to stay. She sternly reminded herself of that. When he got Layla, he would leave her and take Layla with him. If he knew that she was fully aware of Layla's whereabouts right now, he'd probably break her neck.

Did she want that to happen? No. She didn't.

But one day soon it would, and she saw no way of preventing it.

What the fuck was she going to *do?*

# 72

Max had dropped her off at Ellie's and said he'd be back in five – he had to talk to Gary. She was trying to apologize to the shaken Madam and her girls for the whole bomb fiasco, but it looked as if what could have been a disaster had turned into a result for Ellie. Chris was there at the kitchen table with her, and he was being very attentive, Annie thought.

Then the phone rang in the hall. Rosie answered it, and called through to Annie in the kitchen.

'It's for you. Someone called Alberto.'

Annie hurried through to the hall and took the phone. 'Alberto?'

'Hi, sweetheart,' he said, sounding worried.

'What's wrong?' asked Annie, instantly alert.

'I'm glad I caught you. I didn't think this could wait until you got back. I just had a call from Jenny Parsons,' he said.

'Oh?' Annie clutched the phone harder.

'She says Layla's been taken ill. She thought it was flu, but it could be more serious than that.'

'*What?*' Annie felt sickness sweep through her guts like a tidal wave.

'Sorry. I didn't mean to frighten you, but they

say it looks quite serious and you really ought to be there with her.'

'She still at the Parsons' yard? They haven't taken her to hospital or anything?'

'Not yet, no.'

'Jesus.' Annie was thinking fast. She had to get to Layla. But she couldn't wait for Max to come back, and she didn't want to risk Max finding out where Layla was, not yet. Not *ever*, maybe. Perhaps the wisest thing to do would be to just snatch Layla herself and take off into the sunset – that was, *if* the poor little thing was well enough. 'Is there anything I can do?' asked Alberto.

'Nothing. I'll get straight over there.'

Annie put the phone down and hurried into the kitchen.

'Chris, you got your car outside?' she asked him quickly.

'Yeah, sure.'

'Can you drive me over to Newbury?'

'When?'

'Now. This minute.'

'Well ... yeah. No problem.' He was standing up.

'What's up? Trouble?' asked Ellie, watching them both anxiously.

'Not here, Ellie. Don't worry.'

'Let's go then,' said Chris.

'What about when Mr Carter gets back?' Ellie shouted after them as they went down the hall to the front door. 'What should I tell him?'

Annie didn't even break her stride.

'Tell him something came up, you don't know what,' she yelled back, and then they were out through the door and gone.

They got to the yard on the outskirts of the town by late afternoon. Horses were dozing in their boxes and the yard was quiet, swept clean, the flower baskets watered. The aura of the place was one of calm efficiency, the day's work having drawn to its close.

'You want me to come in with you?' asked Chris.

Annie shook her head. If they had to go to the hospital, it was better Chris stayed in the car at the ready. Layla could easily have deteriorated in the time it had taken them to get here.

'No, stay here, I'll be back as quick as I can.'

She hurried across the yard and into the house, calling for Josh's wife Jenny as she went.

She found her in the kitchen, dusted with flour, as were the worktops, the floor and the four excited children with her.

Layla was among them.

Annie dashed in, taking in Jenny's startled face as she ran to her daughter, bent and snatched her up.

'Baby, you okay?' she asked urgently, aware of Jenny watching her with surprise on her face.

Annie glanced up at Jenny. She was just as she remembered – slightly scruffy, with her medium-length red hair in a tangle of curls, her freckled face flushed from the Aga's heat, her pretty grey eyes wide with amazement as they stared at Annie.

'Where's Gerda?' she asked.

'Upstairs in the loo. What's up?'

'I got a call. They said Layla was ill.'

371

'*Ill?*' Jenny let out a laugh. 'God no. She's fine. We're just making jam tarts for tea, she's having a whale of a time.'

Annie looked intently at Layla's face.

'Mummy, you're squishing me,' complained Layla.

'Sorry...' said Annie faintly.

*What the hell...?*

Annie stared at Jenny. 'You didn't phone the Holland Park house?'

'Of course not!'

But Alberto had sounded so sure, so concerned...

Annie stiffened. Max had said that he expected one of the family to make their move soon. But ... oh my *God*...

No. Not Alberto. *Please* not him.

She looked around. It was a happy domestic scene in here but she had been *lured* here. By Alberto. By the man she had thought was her friend.

Chris. She had to go outside, get Chris.

Had to take whatever was happening away from Jenny and her kids, away from Layla.

'What's going on?' Jenny was asking, her eyes on Annie's wild face. 'Was someone playing some sort of joke on you? Layla's not ill, she's absolutely fine.'

'Jenny...' Annie was looking around frantically, unconsciously searching for a weapon. She turned back to Jenny and tried to speak calmly, not to frighten her or the kids. 'Jenny, I want you to do something and not to ask for explanations, okay? I want you to just *do* it. All right?'

'All ... right,' said Jenny uncertainly. Now she was looking at Annie as if she'd gone mad.

'Swear.'

'Yes. Of course. I'll do it.'

'I want you to take all the kids upstairs and get into a room with a phone and barricade yourself in there. Take Gerda in with you. Then I want you to call the police.'

'The *police?*' Jenny gaped.

'Tell them there's been an accident. A shooting. Something. *Anything.* Just get them here.'

'But that's wasting police time...' Jenny protested feebly.

Annie's expression would have stopped a ten-ton truck.

'*Jenny,*' she said, and there was fire in her voice now. This was the old Annie, Annie Carter, tough as nails and twice as nasty, and when she gave orders, people followed them. 'Get the kids upstairs. Just *do it.*'

Jenny decided not to argue. Going pale, she tore off her apron and started ushering the children out of the kitchen, up the stairs.

'But Mummy, I wanted to show you...' Layla's voice drifted back to Annie.

'Not now, petal,' Jenny said, shushing her.

Annie went to the drawers and starting throwing them open until she found a large knife. She tucked it into her coat pocket. Then she tore across the kitchen, out through the door and was across the deserted yard in a flash. She approached Chris's old Zephyr at a flat run.

'Chris!' she was shouting. 'It's a trap! It's...'

She froze mere feet from the car.

Looked for the first time and *saw*.

The Zephyr's windscreen was shattered, a thousand little chunks of glass glittering like ice, sparkling in the sun on the highly polished bonnet.

*Kicked out from inside.*

Oh no.

She forced herself to move forward, to look in the car.

Chris was slumped across the big sofa seat, one of his feet up on the dashboard. There was a damp stain on the crotch of his trousers. His eyes were closed and his face was a blotched, ugly red. His neck was a mass of livid red bruising.

Annie stepped back. The back door on her side was open. She was almost too scared to look, but she forced herself to do it. There was no one in there. Not any more. Someone had jumped into the back seat and throttled Chris from behind. He had kicked out the windscreen in his death throes. And now ... whoever had killed Chris was out here somewhere, and she was alone.

'Oh, Stepmom,' said Alberto's voice softly from behind her.

# 73

She was frozen to the spot, too terrified to even turn round. Her right hand was clenched around the knife's handle in her pocket. She was just staring at Chris, lying there dead, and into her mind, stupidly, came the thought: *How am I supposed to explain this to Ellie?*

But she wasn't going to get the chance to explain anything. Alberto had finished off Chris and now he was going to finish her. Her throat was dry, her tongue felt swollen in her mouth with the force of her terror and revulsion. Her heart was thwacking against her chest wall so hard she thought she might faint.

Alberto wasn't her friend. She told herself that and tried to make herself believe it. That night in Montauk when Constantine had been blown to bits and she had been catapulted onto the sand, he'd been leaning over her. She'd thought he was checking she was still alive. But he had been checking she was *dead*. And he must have been so angry that she wasn't. He had looked distressed – and so he had been. Distressed that she was still breathing.

She started to turn, words tumbling from her mouth.

'Why would you do this, Alberto? Why?' she gasped out, turning.

Turning.

Everything slowing down.

Waiting to see what she knew she must and what her heart told her could not be true. Alberto, waiting to kill her.

And then she could put it off no longer. She turned fully and raised her eyes and *looked*.

The man standing there was not Alberto. This man was an abomination. She stared at him in bewildered horror and fascination because *she had heard Alberto speak*. And yet Alberto was nowhere to be seen.

'What the...?' she said hoarsely.

God, he was hideous. What was most shocking about his deformity was that it was only partial. He had copper-gold straight hair, lustrous, thick; his skin was clear and unblemished. He had deep-set grey eyes, a smattering of freckles over his long, aristocratic nose, a prominent chin. He could almost be handsome, but ... *Jesus, his mouth.*

His mouth was a travesty. It looked as if someone had taken a knife to it and sliced it open at both ends. There were deep purple scars running almost to his ears on both sides of it. When he smiled – he was smiling now – the scars puckered angrily and gave him a ferocious, predatory look.

'Who...?' Annie managed to say.

'Oh, I'm nobody,' said the freak.

He was still speaking in Alberto's voice; it was pitch-perfect. That sound, so familiar, so loved, coming out of that abused purple *slit* of a mouth made Annie's blood run cold.

This was a trap and she had blundered right into it.

Max was miles away.

Chris was dead.

She was totally alone here, with this lunatic.

'It was you on the phone,' she said unsteadily.

'Not a bad little part,' he was saying, and now his voice wasn't Alberto's at all. It was radio English, cultured and with beautifully rounded vowel sounds. 'I think I played it rather well, considering. The accent was tricky but I had a tape to study so that I could get it just so. There's

a mile of difference between Bronx and Manhattan, as you know. I flatter myself that accents
are something of a speciality of mine and I do
tend to get them spot-on.'

'You killed Chris,' said Annie, still trying to take
it in.

'What, the meathead in the car? A small pre-
caution,' he returned.

The cold precision of his speech chilled her.
Her hand tightened around the knife. If he came
any closer, she was going to do it. She was
determined on that. If it was him or her, it was
going to be him.

'Why?' she demanded shakily. 'Why have you
done this? Why did you get me here?'

'Because I told him to,' said a female voice from
behind her.

She half turned and saw Cara standing there.


# 74

'Yeah, it's me,' said Cara gloatingly. 'Favourite
*only* daughter of Constantine Barolli, his best girl
... that was, until *you* came along. For God's sake,
all he had to do was take you to bed. He didn't
have to go and *marry* you.'

Annie stared at her stepdaughter. 'What, so
now you think you'll alter that?' she said, thinking fast. *Keep her talking, keep her talking...*

'Now I'm going to *definitely* alter it,' said Cara.

'Bit late,' said Anne. 'Your father's dead. Whatever happens to me, you're not going to get him back. You're never going to be his "best girl" again.'

'Yeah. But then I haven't been his best girl in a long time,' said Cara, almost wistfully. 'When I asked him to do something about Rocco, I knew then that I'd lost him. That he was too pre-occupied with you to bother about what was happening to me.'

'What did you ask him to do about Rocco?' asked Annie. *Jesus, she had to keep thinking, keep talking...*

'I wanted him dead,' said Cara bluntly. 'And Papa wouldn't do it.'

'So who did it then?' Annie saw again Rocco's poor body floating, hideously mutilated, in the Holland Park pool, the cold relentless rain sheeting down upon him.

'My friend here.' Cara was smiling slightly, looking smug.

*Jesus, she really is demented. Rotten to the core.*

The freak looked pleased with himself. He grinned. The effect was monstrous, disgusting.

'He and Rocco were lovers. I wanted Papa to kill Rocco because of it. But he wouldn't hear of it. It would upset the Mancinis. So I got Frances to do it.'

Annie was thinking frantically, making connections.

*Jesus. That was it.*

'And before that, what did you get Fredo to do?' she guessed. 'Why would you let Fredo hump you like a dog? I saw you, and you looked like you were about to throw up in disgust. You were letting him have you so he'd do other things for you. Back at the house in Montauk, I remember you coming in one night looking frantic and dishevelled. He'd just had you, isn't that right? You were giving him sexual favours in exchange for ... oh God yes! – you were letting him have sex with you because Constantine wouldn't take revenge on Rocco and you wanted *Fredo* to get revenge for you.'

'What's she talking about?' asked the freak.

'Nothing,' said Cara, but her smug smile had slipped a notch.

'How'd you get like this, Frances?' asked Annie, indicating his face. 'Someone come out of a dark alley at you? Someone like Cara's lapdog Fredo, who couldn't touch Rocco but who *could* touch *you?*'

The freak's smile was gone too. He was glancing between Annie and Cara. Finally, his eyes settled on Cara. 'But Cara didn't do this to me. It was Rocco.'

'Shut up,' said Cara to Annie.

'It was probably Fredo, her lapdog. You really think Rocco had it in him to inflict this? I don't. But Cara? Oh, yeah – *she* would.'

'*Just shut up!*' Cara shouted.

'What's she saying? Did you ... do this to me...?' Frances was asking, touching his ruined face.

Cara turned to him, seemed almost to debate the point.

'Look,' she said finally. 'All right. Fredo did it. But *not* on my say-so. I was horrified when he told me what he'd done. I wanted *Rocco* to suffer, not you, not anyone else. Just Rocco.'

*Liar,* thought Annie. She didn't think Cara

379

would care who she had pain inflicted on, just so long as someone paid in blood for her loss of dignity.

'Let's face it, Cara,' said Annie, 'you've been yanking everyone's chain and it's all gone wrong for you. You don't even know which way is up any more, do you?'

'Just *shut up*, will you?' she snarled.

'I don't know...' said Frances. He was looking at Cara as if seeing her clearly for the first time. 'I loved Rocco. Really loved him, and he just *rejected* me like I was nothing.'

'Well, he would,' said Cara. 'All Rocco ever cared about was looks. And if you didn't have *that*, what use would you be?'

'You're right,' said Frances. 'So I *wanted* to kill him, that bastard Rocco! If I hadn't got involved with him, this would never have happened to me.'

'You might want to step back from involvement with his sister, too,' suggested Annie. 'Before anything worse kicks off.'

Jesus, she was standing here with a pair of nutters who wouldn't think twice about murdering anyone who got in their way.

'What do you mean?' Frances was watching her intently. His tongue snaked out, moistening his lips.

'Don't listen to her,' said Cara. 'Shoot the bitch.'

'I *mean* that she likes to get even,' said Annie. 'And so far, she hasn't got fully even with you.'

'What?'

'You humiliated her by having an affair with her husband. Just having your face sliced in half isn't

380

enough. She had to sleep with Fredo her driver to get him to deal with the problem you created, and she won't forgive you for that.' Annie looked at him. 'You might be useful for now, but soon you won't be, and then I'd watch your back if I were you.'

Cara was staring at her stepmother with stony intensity.

'That explosion should have got you too,' she said, every word filled with hatred.

Annie swallowed hard. Spoilt little Cara. When Constantine had refused to deal with Rocco for her, he'd signed his own death warrant. Where were the police when you needed them? How long could it take for them to respond to Jenny's call?

'Well, it got your father,' she said, trying to work some spittle into her mouth and failing. 'It got him, just as you intended. How the hell could you do that?'

'Easily,' said Cara, hard-eyed. 'I got Frances the security pass to the house grounds, he got the grenades and passed them to me outside. Everyone's searched when they enter the grounds at the Montauk house, but never me, never the family. He came in as a maintenance man and while he was replacing some of the boards out on the deck, he set the booby-trap ready to explode.'

'And you wouldn't have cared if it had gone off later in the evening and killed Lucco and Daniella and a few of the other guests too, would you? Just so long as the job got done.'

'I *loved* him,' said Cara, her voice catching on a sob. 'I loved Papa. But he wouldn't do anything for me. It was always the sons. Lucco and Alberto. *Never* me. Never the girl – I didn't matter. He had Lucco to take over from him, he had Alberto in reserve. That was all that mattered. But *I* was the one with the balls and the determination. I could have been a *great* Don. But I was *just a girl.*'

Annie stared at her, feeling sick.

'That bomb *should* have killed you both. What are you, charmed or something? You lived through that, and then Frances couldn't even fucking *suffocate* you in the hospital without the cavalry charging in to save you. And then when he shot at you in London he hit Nico by mistake. That fucking Nico got the bullet, not you.'

So it had been Cara behind all that; and Frances was the one who had been staring down at her as she lay pinned beneath Nico's dead body outside the club, taking aim...

'But you know what?' Cara went on. 'It doesn't matter. Because you're dead anyway. As of *now.* Do it, Frances.'

Frances hesitated.

'I said *do it,*' yelled Cara.

This time he obeyed. He stepped forward, pulling something from beneath his coat. Annie looked and felt her bowels turn to mush. The freak was holding a crossbow. And he was pointing it straight at her heart.

# 75

'Let her have it,' said Cara, cold-eyed.

But Frances was shaking his head.

'We won't do it out here,' said Frances. He gestured with the weapon for Annie to move. 'Someone might see. Over there. There's an empty box.'

'I'm not going anywhere,' said Annie, although her voice was shaking and she was half dead with fright.

'As you wish,' he said, and raised the crossbow again to direct its bolt straight to her heart.

'Wait,' said Annie. 'All right. I'm moving. Okay?'

She started to walk towards the loose box at the end of the yard. Better to appear co-operative for the moment, if only to buy time.

*But time for what?* she wondered frantically.

Had Jenny phoned the police as instructed? She'd been worried about wasting police time. Jenny was timid, uncertain at the best of times. Perhaps she hadn't done it. But if she had, would they take her seriously, would they come? Maybe Josh or someone else, one of the stable lads, would come out into the yard? Fuck it, didn't they have security, didn't they have *anything*? It didn't look like it.

'Hurry it up,' said Cara impatiently.

*Can't wait to see me dead. And what can I do to stop her?*

She dawdled as much as she could, but now she was at the door of the box. She glanced hopefully around the yard. There was no one about. No one to help. *But she had the knife.*

She'd have to get in close, really close, to use it to any effect, and they were keeping their distance, ushering her into the box now, pulling the bottom half of the stable door closed, then the top half.

Inside the box, they were plunged into gloom. Straw whispered around their feet as they moved and its clean, grassy scent rose like a country perfume. For a moment, it was hard to see anything at all, and then Annie could see faint outlines. Could see Cara, her golden hair flowing onto her shoulders, her dreamy blue eyes suddenly manic with purpose. And the freak, still pointing the crossbow at her chest.

She was inside, she was at their mercy.

She was finished.

Frances raised the crossbow.

She had nothing left to lose. She pulled out the knife and ran at the freak, some sort of sound coming out of her mouth, some wild cry. He saw the dim wicked flash of the knife's blade coming at him and stumbled back instinctively, firing the crossbow at the same time. It shot off, missing her by a mile. Then he recovered himself and grabbed the wrist holding the knife, dropping the crossbow in the process.

Someone was screaming close by.

For a moment, Annie thought that she was making the noises herself.

The freak was grappling with her, trying to squeeze the knife out of her hand, but she was holding on, holding on for grim death, because once he got that off her, then he could use it – and if he did that she really was fucked.

He was a lot stronger than her. There was only going to be one winner in this wrestling match, she knew it. She was only surprised that Cara didn't wade in too, get her from behind.

'Holy *shit*,' she heard herself moan, as the pressure on her wrist increased to agonizing levels.

He was going to get the knife off her, he was going to kill her. Nothing she could do to stop him now. Nothing at all. She felt her grip on the knife starting to loosen.

She was going to drop it.

He was going to snatch it up, slit her throat with it.

She was done.

And then, when she felt there was no way she could fight any longer, no way she could hold onto the blade and prevent him taking it, the door crashed in, splintering off its hinges, and Alberto and Max burst into the box.


# 76


Max grabbed Frances and cuffed him hard with the barrel of the Smith & Wesson revolver he was holding. Frances fell back onto the straw. Max kicked him viciously in the ribs and then snatched up the dropped crossbow, flinging it out of the door. It clattered onto the cobbles of the yard.

'Holy shit,' said Gary Tooley, surging into the box with Steve Taylor at one shoulder and another heavy at the other.

She looked around her, dazed, shattered, thinking that she had been so sure she was going to die and now Max was here, and Alberto...

*Where was he? Where had Alberto gone...?*

She looked around. He was on his knees in the straw beside Cara. She was lying there, panting, groaning. With shocked eyes, Annie saw that there was a crossbow bolt protruding from Cara's side.

'Cara,' Alberto was saying, leaning over his sister, his face anguished.

He looked up at Annie. 'What's going on?'

Annie said wearily, 'Your dad. Rocco. It was her. It was all her. Her and this *freak*.'

'No. I don't believe it,' he moaned, and turned back to Cara.

Her eyes were open, wide with horror, and she was staring up at his face.

'He *shot* me,' she said weakly. 'She ran at him ... oh shit ... the bloody thing just went off. It should have been *her*.'

'Don't talk,' said Alberto. He turned and shouted: 'Send for an ambulance! Hurry!'

Annie saw one of the heavies run for the house.

*And where were the police?*

'Take him,' said Max, pulling Frances roughly to his feet and shoving him towards Steve and Gary. They hauled him away, bleating about he'd done nothing, it was all her, it was her who was crazy, not him.

'Shut your fucking mouth,' said Steve, dragging him off.

Then Frances was pulling a grenade from his pocket, holding it aloft. Steve and Gary stepped quickly back.

'Keep away!' yelled Frances, his eyes mad with fear and excitement. 'Keep back or I'll pull the pin.'

Annie stared at him, feeling sick. Grenades. It had been grenades that had killed Constantine, killed her child. She moved towards the door, but Max yanked her back.

Frances was backing away, heading for the drive.

'Let him go!' shouted Max to Steve as Frances retreated, still holding the grenade up.

When he was further down the drive, he turned and started to run.

Gary exchanged a look with Max, then he followed Frances.

Max looked at Annie. 'You all right?' he asked.

She nodded, barely able to speak. 'How the hell...?' she whispered.

'I was just coming into the end of the road with Steve and Gary in the car when we saw you and Chris bombing off in the Zephyr. We stopped at the knocking-shop and Rosie told us Alberto had called, she heard you on the phone to him talking about the Parsons' yard and then you left in a panic.' He paused, drew breath. 'I phoned Alberto at the Holland Park place but he said he hadn't called you. He gave me directions to the yard, and he followed on with some of his boys.'

Suddenly Annie felt so choked with emotion that she couldn't speak.

'You going to pass out?' asked Max, watching her.

She could only shake her head.

She looked down at Alberto, whose tears were falling on Cara's paper-white face.

'Hurts,' she moaned.

'I know, sweetheart. But help's coming,' he said, squeezing her hand hard in his. 'Hold on.'

*Hold on for what?* Annie wondered.

Cara was a cold-blooded killer. If she survived this, Alberto would have to learn even more harsh truths about her. Annie thought of those times Cara had come to talk to her – first after she'd spotted her with Fredo, the second time at Ellie's – and wondered what had been going on in that febrile little mind of hers. Had she been trying in some way to justify her actions to her stepmother? Annie didn't know.

One thing was certain: Cara had instigated Constantine's death, driven by jealousy and rage. And she hadn't cared who else perished along with her father; she hadn't even given it a thought so long as it wasn't *her*.

Cara would have made sure she was well out of the way of any fallout later in the evening when the explosion happened. Maybe the crazy cow had even hoped that Lucco and Alberto would perish, so that *she* could have tried to take over as head of the family.

Cara let out a wheezing breath, seemed to hold it in for a moment, and then her body relaxed and her eyes stared beyond Alberto's face with no expression at all. The life went out of them.

'Oh *Christ,*' he moaned, crouching over her and sobbing convulsively. 'Christ, no...'

Max and Annie exchanged a look. They went outside, left him to his grief. It was early evening, the yard was still, night was drawing in. For Cara, the night would be without end. Steve was over by the car, staring in at Chris's supine body. 'Shit,' he said sadly. 'Poor bastard.'

He was holding a hand to Chris's neck. Max went closer to the car, taking Annie with him. Annie turned her head away. She couldn't bear to look at Chris's dead body again; she was racked with guilt, in agony over what to say to Ellie about this. She'd be heartbroken.

'Think there's a pulse here,' said Steve.

'*What?*' Annie's head whipped round. She dashed forward and craned in. So did Max.

'You sure?' Max snapped.

'Feel.'

Max put his hand to Chris's neck – and felt a very faint but unmistakable pulse thudding beneath his fingers. It was fluttering, faltering – but it was *there*.

'Chris!' Annie said urgently. 'Can you hear me?'

There was no response.

'He's got a neck like a sodding bull,' said Steve. 'It might've saved him.'

The ambulance's siren was the most welcome sound Annie had ever heard. Max and Steve drew back while Annie stayed there, holding Chris's hand, willing him to stay alive.

'Come on, you bastard, don't make me have to explain this to Ellie, will you?' she muttered to him. 'Come *on*.'

And then the ambulance men were there, pushing her back, away from him, and she could only watch, and hope.

# 77

With Chris gone and Cara's body taken away, Annie started to walk up towards the house. Now she had something almost equally bad to face. Somehow, she had to get Layla out of here without Max seeing her.

'Sneaking off?' asked Max, catching up with her, tucking the gun away out of sight in his coat.

'Just going to check on Jenny,' she said. *Shit. Now what was she going to do?*

'And Layla?' he asked.

Annie stopped walking as they reached the little picket gate in front of the elegant red-brick Georgian building. The wisteria that clothed the front of the lovely place in a sea of drooping lavender-coloured racemes was scenting the dusky air.

Annie braced herself and stared into his eyes.

'You're not taking her away from me,' she said firmly.

'Oh?' He put his hands on his hips and stared right back at her. 'How d'you think you'd stop me, if I wanted to do that?'

'Mummy!'

*Too late.*

The front door under the fanlight was open and Layla came rushing out down the pathway towards her. Gerda and Jenny and the kids were clustered in the open doorway.

Annie snatched up her daughter and held her squirming little body close. Her eyes met Max's over Layla's silky, sweet-smelling head. She pulled her in close, hugged her hard.

'Ow! Too tight, Mommy!' Layla complained.

Max was silent, watching the little girl, drinking in the sight of her. His Layla, his little star. She had a slight American accent, but otherwise she seemed so much the same. Grown, yes – but the same. His Layla. He'd thought he would never see her again. Now, here she was. But...

'What the hell's *this?*' he asked, as he saw that the small finger on Layla's hand was missing.

'I'll tell you later,' lied Annie, just wanting to get Layla away from him, away to safety.

She saw Layla's head turn, saw her big, dark-green eyes light upon Max's face, saw her eyes widen, her gaze sharpen.

*Shit, does she still know him? She last saw him when she was three years old, can she still recognize him...?*

Slowly, Layla stretched out towards him.

'Layla? Baby?' said Max softly, moving in closer.

He took hold of her hand, brought it to his lips, kissed it gently.

'Layla?' he said again.

'Da...' Layla started.

*It's true. She knows him still. I've lost her.*

391

Layla was stretching her open arms out towards Max now, away from Annie. He took his daughter into his arms and held her tight, too overcome to speak. Annie stood there and watched them, father and daughter, a perfect scene – but one that did not include her.

This was it.

He'd won.

He always did.

'Is everything all right?' Jenny called out nervously 'I didn't call the police.'

'Fine,' said Max, kissing Layla's head and hugging her tight. 'Everything's fine.'

Defeated, heartbroken, Annie walked away.

# 78

She found Alberto sitting on a low wall at the end of the drive, his head in his hands. She sat down beside him, saying nothing. He glanced up, saw her there. His face was wet with tears, she saw, feeling a tug of deep compassion.

How was it possible, she wondered, that Alberto could have a brother like weak, oily, grasping Lucco, and a sister like Cara, who would have done anything, even murder, to satisfy her lust for vengeance? Oh, he was no saint. He could be tough and, if necessary, he could be vicious. He had to be: he was Constantine's child.

'I'm so sorry,' she said at last.

He swallowed, swiped a hand across his eyes.

'Just tell me. Tell me what the hell was going on in there.'

Annie told him about Frances, and about Cara, and about all that she had done.

By the end of it, Alberto was off the wall and walking nervily back and forth in front of her.

'I can't believe it,' he said over and over.

'Believe it. It's true,' said Annie wearily, feeling so tired, so heart-sore that she barely had the strength to speak now.

She could understand Alberto's pain. She'd loathed Cara, but she wouldn't ever have wished her dead. And she had her own griefs to deal with. What she couldn't get out of her head was the way Layla had looked at Max, the way she had been so eager to get into his arms. Now he had her, and he would keep her. She knew that. God knew he'd threatened it; and what Max Carter threatened, he usually delivered.

'I don't know what to do any more,' said Alberto miserably.

*Same here,* thought Annie.

'We have to go to the hospital,' said Annie. 'There'll be forms, things like that...' *We'll have to register the death,* she thought, but couldn't say out loud. He should have gone in the ambulance, but she thought he was too stunned to know *what* he was doing right now.

'I don't know how I'm going to get through this,' he told her simply.

*Me neither.* 'One step at a time,' she said out loud.

No matter what crap life chucked at you, was there anything else to it but that? You had to go on. There was nothing else you could do.

# 79

'The whole world's going fucking crazy,' Lucco was ranting.

Annie was sitting in the drawing room of the Holland Park house. Max was standing behind her chair, arms folded. She really didn't know why he hadn't taken off already with Layla, but he hadn't. It was only a matter of time. But for now, Layla was upstairs being tucked into bed by Gerda.

Soon, he'd take her. So somehow she still had the chance to do it, to snatch her away.

But ... she thought of Layla's face lighting up with such sweet delight as she saw him there at the stables. Her daughter would be devastated if she was parted from him again. She knew it. So what should she be truly considering here? Her own happiness – or Layla's?

It had been a hell of an evening. She'd phoned Ellie to tell her about Chris, and Ellie was far from pleased with her.

'You know what, Annie Carter or Barolli or whatever the fuck you're called? You're a nutter. If Chris hadn't been with you, this wouldn't have happened.'

Which was nothing more than the truth.

Ellie had taken the hospital details from Annie and then slammed the phone down in disgust.

'What the hell were you doing there, what was

394

going on?' Lucco was now raging, standing in front of her. He looked almost deranged.

Annie snapped back to the present. She looked at Daniella, sitting beside the fire, and Alberto standing there leaning against the mantelpiece, looking crushed, and Aunt Gina, her face a mask of silent sorrow, huddled in a low chair near the hearth.

'I–' Annie started.

'You know what?' Lucco interrupted. 'This family was *fine* until you showed up.'

'Now hold on–'

'It's the truth! But you came along and everything went sour.'

Annie shook her head. She wasn't about to be intimidated by this little creep.

'That's not true. *I* didn't make Cara do what she did.'

'Didn't you?' Lucco's black eyes widened and his mouth twisted in a sneer.

'You think I wanted your father dead?' she snapped. 'I *loved* him.'

'And don't you think it was because he was so *obsessed* with you that she became desperate, became *crazy?*'

'I think craziness runs through this family like a disease,' said Annie, standing up.

'You *what?*'

'Hey,' said Max, stepping forward when Lucco lunged towards Annie. 'You want to calm down?'

'No, I *don't* want to calm down. My sister's just died. And *she'*, he glared at Annie, 'is telling me nothing but rotten stinking lies about her.'

Annie heaved a sigh. 'She admitted it, Lucco.

She admitted everything. She started off wanting to get a little revenge on Rocco for embarrassing her, and it just snowballed. It got beyond her control. And finally it killed her.'

'Don't you think I have troubles enough, uh?' he was raging on, pacing around now, shooting her angry looks. 'The Mancinis are furious about Rocco. I'm having to move heaven and earth to placate them.' He sent a venomous glance at Alberto. 'And *you* didn't help, calling them without my permission, you fucking *fool*.'

Alberto looked hurt. 'I was trying to lessen your load,' he said. 'That's all.'

'Oh, that's all? Well, you didn't. Now the streets are full of punks wanting to take me on, break the family's hold, now they think Papa's out of the way and I'll be a softer target.'

*They got that right*, thought Annie. *You are.*

'Lucco,' said Daniella tremblingly, 'none of this is Annie's fault. Or Alberto's. He's right, he was trying to help...'

'And what the fuck do you know?' he demanded, rounding on her.

Daniella shrank back in her chair.

'Lucco,' said Alberto softly, disgustedly. 'For Christ's sake. For all that she was, for all that she did...' He paused, his eyes full of pain as he remembered how Constantine, his beloved father, had perished at his own daughter's hands. He swallowed hard and went on: 'Our sister died today. Our *sister*.'

'Don't you think I know that? My heart bleeds for it; don't you think I'm aware that Cara's gone, and Papa's gone...' His voice trailed away.

For a moment, he just stood there, clutching his brow, all control deserting him.

*He can't hold it together,* thought Annie. *No way. He's too weak, too volatile. That oily charm's a veneer, and it's pretty thin.*

'I'm going up to my room,' said Aunt Gina, rising stiffly. She shot a basilisk stare at Lucco. 'This can't go on. You do know that?' she said.

He said nothing.

Aunt Gina stalked from the room.

There was a silence. It was Alberto who broke it.

'There are things we have to arrange,' he said firmly but gently to his elder brother.

*'Don't tell me what to do!'* yelled Lucco.

'Well *someone* has to think straight around here,' said Alberto.

'And you think I don't?' Lucco asked him.

'Lucco,' said Alberto. 'You have to show strength now, show everyone that you can hold the family steady. It's a sad day, an awful day, but you have to be strong. You have to conduct yourself like a Don. Like Papa would. We have to go home, and you have to bring order to those bastards who want to chance their arm. Calm the Mancinis down, make everything right.'

'But I'm not *him,*' said Lucco, and, for a moment, Annie thought he was going to burst into tears and throw a tantrum like a petulant child. 'I can *never* be him.'

Daniella stood up, disturbed by all this. 'I'm going up to bed,' she said faintly.

'Are you all right?' asked Alberto.

'Of *course* she's all right,' shouted Lucco. 'She's

*my* goddamned wife, not yours. Will you kindly remember that?'

Now Annie saw that Alberto's face was set with anger. For a moment it was truly as if Constantine was standing there.

'I can remember whose wife she is,' he said. 'Can you? And can you be *man* enough to treat her with the respect she deserves?'

Now Lucco looked beyond furious. He looked as if he was about to launch himself at Alberto. Quickly, Daniella stepped between them. 'Don't,' she said, putting her hands to her face in distress. *'Don't.'*

Both men subsided.

Annie sat there and thought: *My God, what's going on here?*

Suddenly she could see it. Alberto playing with Daniella in the pool, fussing over her at the races, leaving the room white-faced with rage when Lucco hit her.

'We should just calm down,' said Max to all of them. 'It's been a pig of a day and we're all fucked. Let's get to bed.'

This time, Lucco didn't argue. He left the room first, looking as if all the fight had gone out of him. Alberto and Daniella followed. The door closed. Annie and Max were left alone in the drawing room.

'Now that's interesting,' said Max.

'What is?'

'Alberto and Daniella.'

'You noticed.'

'Hard not to.'

'Nothing can come of it,' said Annie, thinking

of Max's own disastrous marriage to her sister Ruthie.

'Maybe not,' said Max. 'Come on, let's get over to the hospital. See how Chris is doing.'

They went out of the drawing room and across the vast hall. Alberto and Aunt Gina were at the top of the stairs, talking quietly. They saw Annie and Max down below, and Alberto quickly said goodnight to his aunt and went along the landing to his own room.

# 80

'I don't fucking well *believe* you,' said Ellie, charging at Annie like an enraged animal when they showed up outside Chris's ward. 'You know what? Trouble follows you around, Annie Carter. Chris was damned near killed today, and all because he was with *you*.'

Max stepped forward. 'Chris is alive. Be grateful.'

Ellie's mouth opened, but she thought about the wisdom of mouthing off at Max Carter and decided against it.

*While she thinks nothing of tearing lumps out of me,* thought Annie.

'Can we see him?' she asked Ellie.

Ellie gave her one last, disgusted look. 'Yeah. He's in here, come on.'

Chris was laid out in bed in a pair of neon-striped pyjamas. His neck was bandaged. As he heard them coming, he opened his eyes. His left eye was red where the blood vessels had burst.

'They've told me his eye's going to clear,' said Ellie, bustling forward like a mother hen and taking Chris's huge hand in both of hers. 'They said it was lucky he lifted weights; it made his neck muscles dense and that saved him, that's what the doctor said.'

'Hi,' said Chris hoarsely.

'And he can't talk, he's *not* to talk, they said that too.'

They sat down. Chris's eye caught Annie's.

'Not your fault, Mrs C,' he managed to say.

Ellie's lips tightened to a thin line and she glared across at Annie.

*Of course it's your damned fault,* her angry eyes said. *Ain't everything?*

Annie sat there feeling like shit. She did blame herself.

*All my fault,* thought Annie. Yeah, Ellie's right.

'Don't try to talk,' said Max to Chris. 'Ellie's right. Just shut the fuck up, lie there and get better. That's all you got to do.'

Chris managed to raise a smile at that. He nodded and mouthed *okay.*

When Max and Annie had left the hospital, Ellie sat there still, gazing at Chris and wondering why she was such a fool and couldn't tell him how much she loved him.

Well, she knew why. She was afraid of rejection. She was fat. All right, *curvy* according to her friends. But in her own eyes she had only ever been *fat.* And Chris's late wife Aretha had been so beautiful, so tall and lithe; Aretha had carried

400

herself like a warrior queen. She'd worn clothes like they were made for her; she could turn the cheapest market tat into designer gear just by putting it onto her exquisite body.

*And then there's me,* thought Ellie as she sat there and Chris drifted off into sleep.

Fat, insecure little Ellie, always diving in the biscuit tin.

Oh, she knew she was Madam now, and she'd upped her game considerably, dressed accordingly; but in her own mind she was still the same little Ellie her mother had called *dumpling.* All the cutting remarks made to her over the years, she could remember every single one.

Her dad, when she was going out to a party aged twelve: 'Christ, she looks fat in that.'

Her first boyfriend: 'No one's ever going to call *you* Twiggy, are they?'

And so on.

She was fat dumpling little Ellie, who was – who always had been since the minute she first saw him – in love with Christopher Brown, who had nearly *died* today.

And if he had died, she would never have got the chance to say how much she loved him. And now ... his eyes were closed; he was asleep anyway.

She stood up; time to go. She looked down at him: a huge, ugly, hairy-arsed thug who stood guard on a knocking-shop door to scare away the lairy punters ... all right, he wasn't pretty. But Chris was noble, in his way. A gent. A lovely, lovely guy.

He wouldn't hear her say it anyway. It didn't

matter. So – what the fuck?

'I love you, Chris,' she said.

And then she turned and left the ward, and she didn't see Chris's eyes slowly open as her words sank in.


# 81

'You know, Ellie's right,' said Max as they were leaving the hospital. 'You certainly do attract trouble.'

Annie shot him a glare as they went out into the car park.

'Well, I attracted *you* so I suppose she got that right.'

He grabbed her wrist and yanked her to a halt, turned her in to face him. His eyes held hers.

'I thought it was mutual,' he said.

'It *was*.'

'But within a few months of my "death", you're off playing doctors and nurses with Constantine Barolli.'

Annie took a deep breath. She was tired, so tired of trying to explain, trying to make everything come out right.

'Look,' she said at last. 'You owe Constantine.'

'Yeah? Explain that.'

'He saved me. He saved Layla. He looked after us when you weren't there to do it.'

Max was silent, his eyes on her face. 'And you loved him for it,' he said.

402

'Not for that. It was never about gratitude. You were gone. I was devastated by that, but you were *gone*. And then he came along.'

'And you loved him.'

'Yeah. All right. I loved him.'

'And forgot about me.'

'I *never* forgot about you,' said Annie fiercely. 'How the hell could I do that?'

'Pretty damned easily, by the sound of it.'

Annie wrenched her wrist free and turned away. 'Oh what's the fucking *use?*' she spat, and went over to the car.

He was never going to believe her. Or forgive her. It was hopeless.


# 82


'So how are they doing?' asked Dolly, polishing glasses as Annie sat at the bar of the Palermo the following day.

It was only mid-evening and still quiet – not many punters in. The girls were already up on their podiums, swaying along to 'Get It On'.

'They?' asked Annie.

'The Yanks,' said Dolly, tutting at her ignorance. 'You said they showed up here. How you getting along with them now?'

*Worse than ever*, thought Annie. The Barollis were, so far as she could tell, in tatters. Lucco was losing it, Cara and Rocco were dead, Aunt Gina was in heavy mourning, Alberto too; the whole thing was *crazy*.

'They're all flying back to the States tomorrow,' said Annie. She hadn't told Dolly about all that had gone down with the Barollis, and she didn't want to start now. It made her feel weary, just to think of it.

'Well, you won't miss them,' said Dolly, tossing aside her cloth and coming to lean on the bar. She looked at Annie with brightly inquisitive eyes. 'So, what about you and him, then? Any news?'

Annie shook her head. Max had driven her here and dropped her off, saying he'd be back in an hour. But would he come back at all? He had Layla now; she was his for the taking. She expected ... well, what she really expected was that he wouldn't come back for her. That she'd phone the Holland Park house, and that one of the staff would answer and say, no, he wasn't there; he'd gone, and he'd taken the little girl with him.

'No news,' she said wearily. 'He's threatened to take Layla and he probably will, sooner rather than later. And he's right, there's nothing I can do to stop him. Nothing at all.'

'That don't sound like the Annie Carter I know,' said Dolly. 'Giving up? Come on.'

'Doll,' said Annie, 'if you'd been through what I've been through these past few months ... well, let's just say it's been rough. You know it has. And now...'

'What? You've lost your nerve? Lost your taste for a fight?' Dolly sniffed and straightened. 'Sorry. Don't believe you.'

Now Annie jumped down from the bar stool and stared at Dolly.

'What should I do then?' she demanded. 'What *can* I do? He's got the boys on every street corner, this whole manor's shut down tighter than a duck's arse. He's in control, not me.'

'Well,' said Dolly, 'we'll see. Won't we?'

# 83

Next day, they gathered in the hall of the Holland Park mansion to say their goodbyes. Fredo and two heavies were loading the bags into the car ready to take Alberto, Lucco, Daniella and Aunt Gina to the airport to board the private Gulfstream jet.

There was a sombre air over the whole gathering – as well there might be, Annie thought, as she came out of the breakfast room and stood there watching them. The visit to England had been intended as an interlude of light relief and as homage to Constantine's memory.

But look what had happened. Rocco and Cara were dead. The whole family was shattered, blown apart. *Just like Constantine was,* she thought. *What goes around comes around.*

Lucco was standing in the doorway, looking tetchy and tense, exchanging a word or two with Gina. As Annie closed the door to the breakfast room, he looked across at her with a deep and bitter loathing.

'Don't forget,' he said to her. 'Leave your keys with the housekeeper when you go this time. You got it?'

'Loud and clear,' said Annie.

He turned on his heel and went out of the door. Aunt Gina glanced over at her, her face without expression. Annie nodded. To her surprise, Gina nodded back, and then hurried outside.

'Stepmom,' said Alberto, and came over to her.

Annie thought he looked strained and pale, not himself. Of course he wasn't. He'd lost his sister not too long after losing his father. It was a hard and very bitter pill to swallow, a double loss, tragic.

He stopped in front of her and raised a thin smile.

'You'll come over and see us soon?' he asked as Daniella joined them.

'Very soon, I promise.' Annie assured him. 'I'll be opening the club in September, remember.'

'It'll be a big success,' he said. 'I know it will.'

'I hope so. Are you going to be all right?' asked Annie in concern.

Alberto's smile widened. 'Perfectly. There, you see? Smiling.'

*But bleeding on the inside,* she thought.

'Now stop fussing, Stepmom, and hug me,' he ordered.

Annie hugged him hard. It was like holding Constantine, and the moment was both sweet and heartbreakingly sad, because he wasn't his father, he could never be; Constantine was lost forever.

Over Alberto's shoulder she saw Max appear on the top landing, watching her. She pulled back from Alberto and looked instead at Daniella, who was smiling shyly. Annie held out a hand, and Daniella took it.

'You okay, sweetie?' she asked her.

Daniella nodded. Annie pulled her into her arms and hugged her tight. Then she pushed her back a little.

'You know what? I'm going to miss you two,' she said truthfully. She looked from Daniella to Alberto and thought that it was so sad that Daniella was tied to Lucco when it was clear that Alberto would have been the perfect match for her.

*You got that one wrong, my darling,* she thought. Even Constantine could make mistakes: that much was clear. She just hoped that Daniella didn't have to pay too hard and too long for it.

'Well, the car's waiting,' said Alberto. He kissed Annie's cheek briefly. 'We must go. See you soon, yeah?'

'You will,' Annie promised.

When they were gone, Max came down the stairs and crossed the hall to where she stood.

'That was touching,' he said.

Annie blinked. 'Don't start,' she said.

Actually, it had been *extremely* touching and she found she had tears in her eyes. She loved Alberto, he truly was like a son to her. Or, at least, given their ages, a brother. And Daniella – well, who could fail to like her? She was so sweet and innocent, and it was gut-wrenchingly sad to think that life with Lucco was going to make a hardened and bitter woman out of her.

'Where's Layla?' she asked. That was always the question she asked him every time she saw him now. She had no idea what he was still doing here. He should have left by now, taking her daughter with him.

'Playing with Gerda out the back, by the pool. Why?'

Annie shrugged. He was toying with her. Just batting her around like a cat with a mouse until he decided to act. She knew it. 'No reason.'

'He's very like Constantine,' Max went on. 'Wouldn't you say?'

Annie stiffened. There he went again, making reference to Alberto's looks and making snide insinuations.

'No, actually I *wouldn't* say that,' she told him coldly. 'Constantine will be impossible to replace. Alberto might *look* like him, but does he have the extra qualities required? I don't know.'

'He's got his hands full with that smarmy little bastard Lucco, that's for sure.'

'In what way?'

'Him and Lucco had equal shares while Constantine was the godfather. They answered directly to him and he commanded them and the troops below them; he had it all stitched up tight. But now ... well, don't tell me you haven't noticed? Lucco's unstable and ambitious, and that's not a good combination. He wants complete control.'

'But he's got that.'

'Alberto's a threat.'

'Alberto's his *brother.*'

'You think that matters? Lucco can't hold it together, but he won't share power with anyone. As the eldest son and as a mean, nasty little

408

fucker he wants it all and he don't want anyone looking smarter than he is. So Alberto had better be bloody careful,' said Max.

# 84

The tall blond one had followed him, but Frances had shaken him off. When he finally made his way back to Whereys, the first thing he saw was a For Sale sign outside. He swore and kicked it and shoved at it until it was down.

Then he went to the front door and found it boarded up. He kicked the boards until he was able to get in, not noticing that his shoe had disintegrated and that his foot was bleeding.

Sweating, panting and gasping with temper and effort, his tongue constantly snaking out to moisten his lips, he went through to the back door. That too was boarded, and he roared with rage and attacked it, wrenching at the boards, tearing at the nails, until his hands were bloody, the nails torn, the skin a mass of cuts and scrapes.

He burst through the door at last and went out to the workshop with its stupid horseshoe over the door. He yanked the thing down and hurled it out into the wilderness of the back garden. His father had never loved him. He had never loved his mother, either. After all, hadn't she always told her son that he was a secret: Daddy's dirty little secret?

'She did, she said that,' he muttered to himself.

So he and his mother had clung together, but then that had changed. She had started inviting the men in – strange, frightening men who drank – and that made him very scared. And angry too.

'He should have been there with us, but he never was,' Frances mumbled.

*And that was how it happened,* thought Frances, going into the gloomy workshop. He hadn't *meant* for it to happen, but the men had been there again, drinking, and his mother had been laughing and running in and out of the rooms with them, half dressed, and when at last they'd gone she'd said she was going for a soak.

'Frances, baby, pass me that bottle will you...?' she'd said, lolling there naked in the tub, just like she'd been naked earlier in the evening and on so many evenings before that, drinking and shrieking with laughter and falling onto the bed with the men, doing bad things there while the music played on and on and he clamped his hands over his ears to try to shut it all out.

He wanted it to *stop*.

So he picked up the half-full gin bottle like she asked, and smashed her over the head with it.

He hadn't *meant* to.

He had just been upset, scared. And angry. One quick *whack* with the bottle – he put all his strength behind it – had felt like a moment of blissful release. She'd screamed once, then he hit her again with it. And then she'd gone quiet and she'd sunk under the water a bit.

He'd gone out the back and flung the bottle away, way out into the Hollywood Hills, never to be found. He'd felt bad then, because he'd done that, hit Mommy. He thought he ought to go back in, so he did; he went to the bathroom and her head was above the water now, but there was blood on her face and in the tub but she was quiet. Then he'd got scared again because Daddy wasn't there, he was *never* there, and so Frances had phoned for help, for an ambulance.

Now he stood in his father's workshop. He dumped the grenade back in the box with the others, then for long moments he just stood there, stock-still, like a robot with a short-circuit while his mind replayed that night in all its horror.

Finally, he stirred, and remembered what he'd come in here for. He started looking around.

*Ah yeah. There* it was. He pulled out an orange plastic can from the heaps of detritus.

Now he had it.

Gasoline.

He splashed it all around the lower storey of the house, found matches in the kitchen drawer, then retreated to the ruined front door. He wasn't a fool, he wasn't *mad,* not like dear old dad, no way. He knew you had to keep back. He lit a match, and tossed it inside.

*Whooomphh!*

Oh, he loved that sound, the cleansing sound of destruction. He stepped back, onto the path, driven there by the suddenly erupting ferocity of the heat. He smiled and watched his father's home start to burn, and then he turned and walked down the path to the gate. The lanky blond-haired man was standing there. He hadn't lost him after all.

'Hey, freak,' said Gary Tooley, and started towards him.

This time, Frances didn't bother to run. Now would be a good time to finish it, after all. Neat. Sort of *fitting*.

He stood there, and waited for whatever came next.


# 85

Annie was sitting at Constantine's desk in his study, just soaking up the atmosphere, feeling him close to her somehow ... but not close enough. He was gone. She was trying to convince herself otherwise by sitting here brooding like this, but that was the truth of the matter. He was gone, and he would never return.

He didn't visit her in nightmares any more. She was puzzled by that. She had grown so used to those horrors unravelling in her sleeping brain, so used to seeing him as a spectre, a hideously deformed and threatening thing that came to terrorize her in the night, that she had believed she would feel this way forever.

But ... no. Slowly the dreams had receded and now she didn't get them at all.

He was gone.

The door opened and Max stepped inside the room, closing it softly behind him.

*And maybe that's down to him,* Annie thought, watching him as he crossed the room to where she sat.

Max had taken to sharing her bed most nights now, and she didn't mean to, but nearly every morning she woke up clinging to him as a child clings to a favourite toy.

But Max was no real comfort to her. Rather, he was a threat. To him, the sex meant nothing. He was going to take Layla from her one day.

He came to the desk and sat down in one of the chairs on the opposite side.

For her, it was so different. She loved him. She always had, always would.

But he couldn't let go of the hurt she'd caused him. And when Max was hurt, he lashed out. He sought revenge. And there could be no surer way to hurt her than to tear Layla from her side.

'Thought I'd find you in here. All packed up? Ready to go?'

Tomorrow, she would fly out on Concorde to check that Sonny had put the last touches to the club to have it ready for the opening. She still had to accept the fact that Lucco was co-owner – there was no way around that; but she was still majority shareholder, so fuck him. She'd booked tickets for herself, Layla and Gerda, but she had no confidence that Max would let Layla go with her.

But if he *did,* here was the plan. After the opening, she was just going to take off in the States with Layla; they would lose themselves somewhere out there. It was a big country. He wouldn't have the boys there to keep tabs on her. She could lose him, she knew she could do it. Start a new life for her and Layla somewhere, maybe California. Who knew?

'Yep, we're all packed up. Me and Layla and Gerda.'

'Good. Only I saw the tickets on your dressing table, and you forgot to include me.'

'What?' Annie stared at him.

'I'm sure it was an oversight. I'll book mine this afternoon.'

'*What?*'

Max looked at her in mock exasperation.

'What do you mean, "what?"? I'm your fucking minder, remember? Where you go, I go.'

'But I didn't think you'd want to.' Her heart was hammering and her mouth was dry as ashes. So much for her plan. He meant it: he was coming with her. 'Look, you don't have to,' she said hurriedly.

'I'm coming,' he said.

'But you've got the manor to run. The boys...'

'The boys have been running the damned manor without me; they can carry on doing it. No problem. So I'm coming with you.'

'But you–'

'No buts.' He stood up, leaned over the desk and kissed her hard on the lips. 'You and me, *kemo sabe*. We go together.'

Yep. There went her plan, right out the window. So ... she'd have to think of another one.

# 86

'Shit, will you look at this?' said the fireman to his pal.

There had been a call-out from a nearby neighbour earlier in the evening, saying there was a fire at an unoccupied house called Whereys, down the lane. Now it was gone eleven, and the arc lights were glaring all around the sodden, smouldering wreckage of what had once been an expensive and elegant Victorian rectory. The huge cluster of barley-twist chimney pots was still standing, but little else remained.

The crew were still damping-down, spraying the shell of the interior, when one of them all but fell over the dead body in the hall. They called the chief, and he came and looked down at the blackened, curled-up remnants of what had once been a human being.

'Poor bastard,' he said. 'Thought the neighbours said no one was here?'

'Chief!' One of the crew had been out at the back, making sure the fire had not spread to the outbuildings. 'You'd better come and see this...'

The chief fire officer followed his colleague out to the workshop behind the gutted property. It was intact; the flames hadn't reached it. And just as well. 'If this lot had gone up...' said the chief, looking around in wonder at the armoury inside the workshop. There were guns, knives, Samurai swords, but worse – there were also grenades and a box full of detonators.

'Yeah. Would have made the mess the house is in look like nothing.'

The chief chewed his lip. An unexplained corpse. A cache of arms.

'Better call in the police,' he said.

# 87

'Hiya, babe, you all right?' asked Dolly.

It was later the same day and Max had dropped her off at the Palermo. He'd already shown her the Blue Parrot and the Shalimar – all three clubs had taken back their old names; the red neon 'Annie's' signs had been pulled down.

Max was back in charge here now. He was making it plain, stamping his authority on the situation once again. Gary and Steve seemed happy to move aside and let him take over. Once the baddest of bad boys, she knew he'd been shocked to find that the Carter firm under Annie's guidance had become a practically legitimate security operation stretching out from the city to cover most of Essex.

Annie wondered if he'd ever go back to the old ways, the days of heists and the hard game. She hoped not. Sooner or later, some keen copper was going to nail him, and then he'd go down for a long stretch. The thought of him caged up was painful to her. And what did that make her, she wondered? But she knew. She was a soft bloody fool where he was concerned, she always had been.

He kept dropping her off here and there, fielding her anxious enquiries about wasn't he coming in with her, what was *he* going to do? And when he half smiled at her, she knew that he could read her mind – that she was wondering was this going to be the time he took Layla from her, when her back was turned?

Annie tried to get her mind off the subject. In the States, she would work things out. Alberto would help her. She could still win this.

*Yeah, and when you do, you'll lose the man you love – and you'll lose Layla her father, too.*

The club was busy with punters, go-go dancers and the pounding hypnotic beat of George Harrison singing 'My Sweet Lord'. Dolly was sitting at the bar while the barman rushed back and forth taking orders when Annie pushed through the throng and joined her there.

'I'm fine,' said Annie. 'You?'

'Yep, fine and dandy.' Dolly was sitting on a bar stool swinging one elegantly shod foot along to the music. She was sipping a gin and tonic. 'Drink?'

Annie shook her head. 'How's it going now the old names are back over the door?' she asked her.

Dolly shrugged. 'Takings ain't dipped,' she said. 'That's the main thing. I'd say, no change.'

'Jesus, just look what the cat's dragged in,' said a male voice behind her.

Annie swivelled on her stool and looked round. Squat, dark-haired Steve Taylor and gangly blond Gary Tooley stood there like a wall of mean muscle. Dusty was with them, scowling at her with her boot-black eyes.

'Hi, Steve,' said Annie. 'And Gary. Always a pleasure.'

'Smooth *cow*,' muttered Dusty.

'Hey!' said Dolly to her. 'I don't want any trouble, you hear me?'

Dusty subsided.

Annie turned back to Dolly, rolling her eyes.

'You know what?' Gary was saying loudly enough to be heard over the roar of George Harrison's guitar. 'If she was *my* old lady, I'd have fucking well drowned her by now.'

Annie sat there. She was getting tired of this. At least Steve was sharp enough to keep his mouth shut, but Gary just always had to get a little poke in: he couldn't resist it. She turned and stared at him.

'And do you know what, Gary?' she returned. 'If I was your old lady, I'd drown *myself*.'

'See? She's full of it,' said Dusty, glaring at her.

'Not that I would ever have got myself tucked up with a long streak of piss like you in the first place,' said Annie.

Gary's lips tightened into a furious line.

'Enough!' said Dolly, slithering down from the bar stool and thumping the bar with one fist. 'Now come on, boys and girls. If you can't play nice, just fuck off out of it.'

Annie glanced back at her best mate and smiled. Now that was Dolly. Telling it exactly like it was, without fear or favour.

Gary gave both women a sneering look. 'I

wouldn't fucking well lower myself,' he said.

'Good,' shot back Dolly. She clicked her fingers at the barman and he hurried over. 'Drinks and a meal on the house for Mr Taylor and Mr Tooley, okay?'

Gary didn't even thank her. He just gave the barman their order, said 'We'll be over there,' and went off with Steve into the crowds to find his usual banquette.

'He's a bloody fool,' said Dolly, hoisting herself back up onto her stool with difficulty. 'Steve's the clever one. Daft not to see how the wind's blowing before you start shooting your mouth off.'

'Oh, I think they both know which way the wind's blowing,' said Annie sadly.

'What, he still mad at you?'

'In spades.'

Dolly nodded and sipped her G & T. 'And he still hasn't said anything about the club management...?'

'Not a word.'

Annie wished she could reassure Dolly. She was her oldest friend; she was an absolute diamond, solid as a rock and generous to a fault. Ellie was right when she said that Dolly would happily give away her arse and shit out of her armpit. But there was nothing she could say; the last thing she wanted was to give Dolly false hope.

Dolly stared gloomily into her drink.

'D'you know how Chris is getting on now?' asked Annie. 'I thought of phoning Ellie or popping over there, but I'm not her favourite person right now. She blames me for what happened to him. I think she'd lamp me.'

Dolly brightened. 'I spoke to her this afternoon. He's doing well, he's home now. Been given the all-clear.'

*Thank God for that.* Annie breathed a sigh of pure relief.

'And I mentioned how sorry you were about what happened. Not that it was your fault. But I said it, and Ells sort of warmed up a bit, and the bottom line is, I don't think she'll lamp you if you want to go over there and make up.'

'Snooty *cow,*' she heard from behind her.

She turned a little. Dusty hadn't followed Steve and Gary over to the banquette. She was leaning on the bar behind Annie, ears flapping as she listened in to their conversation.

'Still here?' Annie asked mildly.

'Yeah,' said Dusty. 'And I thought I told you I didn't want to see you in here any more.'

Annie glanced back at Dolly, whose eyes were wide with amazement at the sheer brass neck of the girl.

'So you did,' said Annie. 'But this'll be the last time, I promise.'

Dolly's mouth dropped open.

Dusty eyed Annie suspiciously.

'Yeah, I give up,' said Annie. 'I'm leaving to-morrow, and I won't be back for a while.'

Dusty's face was a picture of uncertainty. She'd had a ruck with Annie Carter last time, and come off worst. Was the bitch finally getting the mess-age?

'Well ... good,' said Dusty. 'If you bloody mean it this time.'

'I do. I'm leaving for the States tomorrow.'

'Good.' Dusty gave her one last derisory stare and started to walk away from the bar to join Gary and Steve.

'Oh!' Annie called after her. 'Did I mention? Max is coming with me...'

# 88

'Should I throw my hat in first?' asked Annie.

She was standing on the doorstep of the knocking-shop in Limehouse. She was still half laughing to herself about Dusty getting carted out of the Palermo by the bouncers, still shrieking at the top of her voice: *I'll get you, Annie Carter!* Dolly had nearly fallen off her bar stool she was laughing so hard. Max had come back to the club to find both of them in the flat upstairs in a state close to hysterics, and had driven Annie on over to Ellie's place. Now he was waiting in the car.

Ellie had answered the door and now she stood there looking at Annie. Looking beyond her, Annie could see a couple of the girls – pretty little blonde Rosie and sharp-faced dark-haired Sharlene – clustered on the stairs ready to take in the action.

Ellie looked very stern. Then her face crumpled and she almost smiled.

'Oh for fuck's sake,' she muttered. 'I s'pose you'd better come in.'

Annie stepped inside the door and flicked a smile at the two girls on the stairs. They retreated upstairs, cheated of a fight. Annie followed Ellie along the hall to the kitchen, and there was Chris sitting at the kitchen table, drinking tea.

'Hey!' Annie was delighted to see him. 'For God's sakes! You're not back at work already?'

He shrugged his massive shoulders and gave a sheepish smile.

'It's better than staying home with me old mum fussing around me,' he grumbled.

His voice was still hoarse, she noted. But he was suited and booted, ready for the day's activities. Above the line of his clean white collar and neatly tied navy-blue tie, there was yellowing bruising.

Annie sat down at the table. 'You sure you're well enough?' she asked. Her eyes flickered from his – one eye still bloodshot, she noted – to his neck and then back again.

'I feel okay,' he said with a thin smile. 'Fucking lucky to be alive, I reckon. I just *sound* bad now.'

Annie sat back as Ellie poured out tea for her and placed it in front of her on the table.

'I'm so bloody sorry, Chris. To get you into a situation like that.'

'Christ, it wasn't your fault. You couldn't have known. Any rate, it was the most excitement I've had in a long time. Better than turfing out lairy old punters with their kecks round their ankles.'

'So, what you been up to?' asked Ellie stiffly. Annie could see she wasn't completely forgiven, not yet. Ellie sat down, sipped her tea.

*No biscuits,* thought Annie. That was a first.

'Dolly told me you're off to New York tomorrow,' said Ellie. 'That right?'

Annie nodded.

'What about Mr Carter?'

'He's coming too.' Again Annie got a flash of Dusty being bodily hauled out of the club door with her knickers on public display, and had to suppress a smile.

'You two made it up?' Chris asked.

'I dunno. I can't say. Not yet.' The whole thing with her and Max was far too complex to start explaining to Chris and Ellie. She didn't want to go there. She was going to have to fly by the seat of her pants on this one; she was going to have to wing it. And it could turn out bad, or good. She had no idea.

'There was talk about him wanting to take Layla off you,' said Ellie.

'We haven't discussed that,' said Annie, drinking her tea.

But he was going to try it. One day soon, for sure. She was just going to have to get in first – and the club's opening night would be the perfect time to do it. Lots of people about, plenty of confusion. She'd pack a bag beforehand, and they'd slip away. Just her and Layla. Forget Gerda. She was going to have to move fast, and she couldn't carry any passengers this time.

'But you're taking Layla with you tomorrow?' quizzed Ellie.

'Yeah. *And* Max – he wants to stick close to her.'

'See?' Ellie gave Chris a look. 'Told you. He's going to just whip that kid away, first chance he gets.'

Annie finished her tea, very afraid that Ellie was

423

right. He was just biding his time, waiting for the right moment. Well, so was she. She would beat him. She was determined on that. Tomorrow, New York. After that ... who knew?

'So what do you think?' Ellie asked Chris after Annie had departed. 'Maybe they'll get back together.'

She sat across the table from him and thought, *I love you.* 'Want a biscuit with that? Or I got some cake...?' Her mum had fed her cake whenever she was low or ill.

'Actually, no.'

Chris looked down at his cup of tea and then up at Ellie, all dolled up in her Madam's uniform of neat burgundy-red skirt suit, her dark hair flicked up on her shoulders, her plump, pale-skinned face full of concern for him. She wasn't anything like his late wife. Nothing at all. But she was a good woman, and pretty, and she cared about him, and she had said in the hospital that she loved him. He had been mulling it over ever since, thinking: *What should I do about that? Anything? Nothing?*

'Actually,' he said at last, 'I wanted to ask you something.'

'Go on then.' Ellie took a quick swig of tea.

'Would you come out to dinner with me one night?'

Ellie choked. She spluttered, went puce in the face. Chris leaned over and patted her briskly on the back.

'*What?*' she wheezed when she could speak.

'Dinner. You know. Two people sitting at a table in a restaurant, eating stuff.'

'Oh.' She was staring at him.

'If you don't want to...' he said.

'No! Yes! Of course I bloody well want to,' she babbled. My God! He was asking her out on a date.

'Well, good.' Chris gave a slight smile and stood up. 'I'd better get on the door.'

'Yeah. Absolutely,' she said, grinning like a fool.

She watched him walk along the hall and take up his usual position on his seat just inside the door. She clutched her empty mug and beamed with happiness. *Thank you, God,* she thought. And then the doorbell rang; the first punter of the day.

She stood up, straightened her attire, and walked out into the hall with her wide professional smile firmly in place as Chris answered the door.

# New York

# 89

'So what do you think?' asked Annie, coming out of the bedroom.

They had taken a suite at the Waldorf Astoria – she and Max, Layla and Gerda. They'd been touring the city, playing tourist, but now was the club's opening night.

Max was standing at the window, staring out at New York by night, all lit up like a Christmas tree. 'Did you know,' he said, pointing to the shining Art Deco crown of the Chrysler building, 'that's over a thousand feet high and it's got seventy-seven storeys. Ain't that amazing?'

He turned and looked at her. Annie was wearing a floor-length, slim-fitting Givenchy gown made entirely of black sequins that winked and glittered as she moved. It exposed one bare shoulder in the Grecian style and had a long slit up one thigh.

'Yeah, that is amazing,' she said, gliding across the floor towards him. 'And it's got stainless-steel gargoyles, did you know *that?*'

'Jesus.' Max was staring at her.

'What?'

'That's one hot dress.'

'You like it?'

He reached for her. 'I'd like you better out of it,' he said.

Annie skipped nervously out of reach. 'No time for that.' She glanced at the clock on the wall.

'We have to go. Right now. I've tucked in Layla, Gerda's right here, all's well and we have to *go*.'

*And it's best I don't let you touch me, not tonight. Because I'm all packed up and ready to leave.*

'I'm just going to say goodnight to her.'

Max walked off to Layla's room. Reluctantly, Annie followed. Gerda was there, just finishing off a story, and their little girl was nodding off sleepily, her dark hair spread over the pillow, her rosebud lips parted as she drifted into dreamland.

'Sweetheart?' Max sat down on the bed.

Gerda left the room and Annie stood in the doorway, not wanting to look at this charming scene of father and daughter, but unable to tear herself away.

Layla's eyes opened and lit up, tired though she was, at the sight of Max.

'You sleep well now, okay?' He leaned forward and kissed her soft brow. 'I love you, baby.'

'I love you too, Daddy,' she murmured, her eyes flickering shut.

Max stood up and moved back to the door. Annie stepped back, watching him with troubled eyes as he closed it softly.

She had the plan in place. She'd packed a small bag for her and Layla and hidden it away well out of sight along with the internal air tickets that would take them west to California. Although Alberto, Lucco and Daniella had been invited tonight, and Alberto was almost certain to be there, she was only going to be able to see him briefly, amid the crush of crowds. She knew she wasn't going to be able to check in with Alberto properly. As for Daniella, Lucco might not go and he might block her attendance tonight too. She would have liked to have been able to meet up for drinks and a proper chat with Daniella, and she was sad that she wouldn't be able to, but this was what she had to do.

She was going to slip away during the opening party, shoot back here, collect Layla, and head for the airport.

It was all planned out.

What she didn't want now was Max kissing her, touching her, weakening her resolve. She had doubts enough in her mind. She already felt she'd be cheating Layla of a life with Max. They had reformed their close bond with alarming speed; it was always Max that Layla ran to now, rather than Annie. But ... she couldn't let him snatch her daughter away. She just couldn't.

'We could spare half an hour,' said Max, watching her.

Annie was checking her reflection in the mirror. She wore her hair in a thick ponytail that hung down over her bare shoulder. Big diamond earrings – a gift from Constantine – adorned her ears, and she wore her signature red lipstick and a slick of black mascara.

'No – we couldn't. You know, you don't look too bad yourself,' said Annie. It was an understatement. He was wearing a sharp black suit, white shirt and black bow tie. With his swarthy piratical looks and his dark, curling, overlong hair, he looked like what he essentially was: a gangster. A dangerous man.

*Ah, the lure of bad boys,* she thought regretfully.

Tonight, she was going to leave him.

Handsome as he was, and much as she loved him, she had to strike first.

Her heart was breaking; but in her mind, she was already gone.

There was a queue of cars offloading celebs onto the red carpet outside the club. Everyone who was anyone was at the opening, and there was a crush of people there to spot the stars, being held back by barriers, big bullish bouncers and a couple of police. The press were out in force, snapping away as each car unloaded its passengers and they strolled up the red carpet, doling out professional smiles to one side and the other as flashbulbs popped constantly in a dazzling strobelike effect.

The noise when they stepped out of the car was like a great gushing roar of sound. Celebs were moving ahead of them up the carpet towards the entrance with the big ritzy 'Annie's' sign proudly displayed above it. Far ahead, she saw Alberto chatting to a woman in a gold dress. She hoped to catch Daniella here tonight, too, but she wasn't optimistic about that.

Up ahead were Candice Bergen and Ryan O'Neal, Jacqueline Bisset and Topol, and the crowds were surging forward, trying to catch a glimpse of them, maybe even get an autograph.

*Are those barriers going to hold?* thought Annie in sudden concern.

The security staff were lining up along each side of the carpet as more and more cars unloaded.

'The red carpet's always a great leveller,' said Annie under her breath to Max as they were suddenly the focus of the crowd's and the photographers' attention. Just as suddenly, seeing no famous face to admire, the attention of the masses moved on, looked for the next limo, the next star about to appear.

'Jesus, would you like to have to go through this every time you stepped out the door?' he asked, tucking her arm in his.

'No,' she said with a shudder.

Max was looking ahead at the club's big, glitzy 'Annie's' façade. 'It's bigger than I expected.'

Annie's gaze followed his. She'd been planning for this since before Constantine's death. She felt her eyes sting with tears. She had to swallow hard past a sudden lump in her throat. *He* was supposed to have been here with her tonight to celebrate this, but he wasn't. They should have been here, together – and she should have already given birth to his child.

They had talked about it. Constantine had been concerned – should she really be undertaking so vast a project, so huge an organizational challenge, with the baby coming? But she had insisted she would manage. She had help. Money bought that, lots of it.

But now ... now she didn't have him. *Or* the baby.

Life had been turned on its head for her yet again.

Instead, she was here with Max.

The barriers were rocking and security were moving in closer to the crowds, holding out their hands, telling them to move back, move back.

Annie looked ahead. Alberto had disappeared inside the building, and she saw Topol and Candice hovering just inside the door. She was glad when she and Max reached it, too. More roars were erupting from the crowd as new limos pulled up at the kerb.

Then suddenly the crowd on the left surged hard forward, and a barrier fell. People stumbled forward, security started shouting. Someone bumped hard against Annie and let out a shriek. Annie fell forward on the steps and she felt Max jerk her back, trying to correct her fall.

Suddenly all was confusion. There was a blurring of noise, brilliant light and people jostling close up against her. Then she was upright again and against the wall of the club. When she straightened up she saw Alberto nearby with a big meaty minder at his shoulder. Alberto was shouting something and the minder was haring off into the crowd.

There was a smell of cordite, the sounds of screams and people started shouting about a gun and scattering in all directions.

A *gun?*

Annie reached out for Alberto but couldn't touch him; there was a mob of heaving bodies between them. She looked for Max. He was right there with her, against the club wall.

Alberto was pushing through the panicking crowds towards her.

'What's going on?' she shouted at him, but her voice was drowned out.

'Is he all right?' Alberto yelled back. His face was white and strained.

*What?*

Alberto surged in close, grabbed her. 'What's

happening?' she asked, bewildered.

'Someone took a shot at you,' said Alberto.

'Someone *what?*'

'I saw it. He came out from the left-hand barrier and aimed at you. Mark knocked you out of the way.'

Annie looked at Max. 'Did you see the man? What did he look like?' she demanded.

'Like he was about to kill you,' said Max with a tight smile that somehow turned into a grimace.

'What...?' Annie drew closer to him. The sleeve of his left arm was glossy, wet. She looked down and felt her heart stop in her chest; there was blood staining his pristine white shirt cuff and it was dripping down over his fingers, falling onto the carpet, which showed not a mark. 'Oh Jesus...' she gasped.

She turned and shouted at Alberto: 'Get an ambulance! He's hurt.'

Alberto dived off into the crowds. Annie moved in tight to Max. She suddenly realized that he was supporting himself against the wall, trying not to fold to the ground.

'Don't you *dare* die on me,' she muttered, holding him tight.

'Already died once,' he gasped through teeth gritted with pain. 'Can't do it again.'

He started to sag.

'Shit! Max!' she cried out.

But his eyes were closing; slowly, he sank to the ground and she could only wait for help to come. He'd taken a bullet meant for her. She started to shiver with reaction. She crouched there beside him, and waited.

# 90

'You were lucky,' the doctor was saying to Max as he lay in the hospital bed next morning with his arm in bandages and a sling. 'It winged you, that's all.'

*That's all.*

Max glanced at Annie, sitting there watching this exchange. She dredged a smile up from somewhere, but God, she felt wrecked. She'd spent the whole night at the hospital waiting for news of his condition. At about three a.m. – the time at which she and Layla should have been taking off on the red-eye flight to California – this same, briskly smiling Jewish doctor had come out to her in a bloodstained green gown and told her that it was a flesh wound, nothing more; the bullet had torn through the outer edge of the deltoid muscle so there had been a fair bit of blood loss, but he'd be fine.

At about two, she'd phoned Gerda to tell her what was happening and not to worry Layla with the details. She'd phoned Sonny at the club and he told *her* not to worry: everything was fine their end, there was no such thing as bad publicity and a botched shooting at the opening night wasn't going to put off the doughty New Yorkers. And was it true, Sonny asked in high excitement, that the bullet was intended for her?

'Yeah,' she said. 'It's true.'

'So all you need to do today is rest up,' the doctor told Max. 'Go home tomorrow, okay?'

'Thanks, doc,' said Max.

The doctor left the room. Annie stood up too. She was still wearing the black-sequined gown, her hairdo had come unravelled, her make-up was smeared all over her face, and she felt as though she needed a bath and a few hours' sleep as a matter of urgency.

'You scared me half to bloody death there,' she said accusingly.

'I scared *myself*,' said Max. 'That bastard came out of the crowd so fast. I just had time to knock you flat and then the cunt shot me.'

She looked down at him. Even pale and in a hospital bed, he was just too damned handsome. 'Well, we're evens now,' she said. 'I stopped a bullet for you once, remember? Now you've done the same for me.'

'Yeah.' He closed his eyes wearily.

'So all bets are off,' she said, still staring down at him. At his broad chest with its curling dark hairs ... just the night before last she had slept cradled against that chest, feeling so secure, feeling that the nightmares and dramas of the past few months were a world away.

*But that wasn't the case. Someone was still trying to kill her.*

His eyes opened as she turned and moved towards the door.

'And you missed your flight,' he said.

Annie froze. She swivelled and stared at him.

'The bag in Layla's room at the back of the wardrobe? Found it. Thought you were planning something, and you were.'

Annie's mouth tightened. 'You're not going to take her away from me.'

He stared at her for long moments. 'Couldn't wait to get away, right?'

*Is that what he thinks?* she wondered, and stepped back towards the bed.

Then he yawned heavily. 'We'll talk about it later.' His eyes were flickering closed. 'You could have gone, couldn't you? Left me here being patched up by the medics. You could have done it. Perfect chance. But you didn't.'

Annie was still staring at him.

His eyes were closed now.

*Fuck it.* He was right. She could have gone, if she'd been hard enough. Determined enough. She could still do it. But she was weak where he was concerned. She'd missed that chance, and ... shit, she didn't want another one. She didn't want to lose Layla but she didn't want to lose *him,* either.

She was stuck in limbo.

He had all the power.

All she could do was wait, and see what he would do next.

When she got out into the waiting room, Alberto was sitting there, with one of the Barolli foot soldiers lounging against the wall keeping watch. Alberto stood up when he saw her walking towards him. They embraced; he kissed her cheek.

'How is he?' he asked as she slumped into a chair and he sat back down too.

'He's fine. Just a flesh wound,' she said, wiping

a tired, trembling hand over her brow. She looked at Alberto. 'That bullet was meant to kill me, wasn't it?' she asked.

Alberto nodded. She thought that he looked pale, not the all-American Golden Boy any more. His face was grave and etched with heavy lines that she hadn't noticed before.

'Did they catch him? The man who did it?'

Alberto nodded again; his face was closed, shuttered.

'Can you tell me about it?' she asked.

'If I must. Our people caught him. They made him talk.'

She wasn't about to ask how. She swallowed and said: 'And he said...?'

'Fabio Cantuzzi's boys hired him from out of town for ten thousand dollars. The news on the streets is that Lucco's letting the Cantuzzi family in on deals through the back door, and Cantuzzi did this for Lucco as a favour.'

Annie sat there staring at the floor. She had thought she knew the depths of Lucco's hatred. But to kill her? That was taking it to a whole new level.

'The Cantuzzis have been a thorn in the side of the family for a while,' said Alberto. 'Now Lucco's colluding with them.'

Annie's eyes drifted up from the floor and over to the bulky minder standing there watching over Alberto.

*Oh shit,* she thought. *Max was right about all this. Lucco wants to take over the whole outfit, absolutely. He doesn't want Alberto sitting there in reserve. Alberto's a threat to him. He doesn't want me breath-*

*ing. He hates me.*

'What are you going to do?' she asked him.

'Right now? I don't know,' he admitted.

The move against her had been a slip on Lucco's part, she could see that. He had let his emotions rule him, just as he always did, and that was dangerous. Cantuzzi's hired enforcer had squealed and now Alberto had valuable information. But what would he do with it?

She couldn't say it. She couldn't bring herself to say out loud, *How long before he tries to kill you too, Alberto?*

# 91

Lucco Barolli was out on New York Sound on his boat with two old friends: Jonathan Mancini – his late brother-in-law Rocco's elder brother – and Gianni Ecco, one of the *capos* from his district. He'd grown up with both of them, loved them. They were comrades in arms.

He had expressed his extreme sympathy to Jonathan over Rocco's grisly demise and his father's untimely end.

'He was in my care,' Lucco said as the powerful and expensive boat – Jonathan's boat, a recent gift from a penitent Lucco – cruised out into deeper water, Gianni at the helm. 'I feel responsible.'

He poured beers for them all and sat back on the deck and looked out over the sunlit autumn waters and thought it was good to be alive.

440

Things hadn't worked out entirely to his satisfaction yet, but sometimes what could you do? You hit snags. But there were always solutions. He'd paid the Mancinis ten times over to compensate for their distress.

Jonathan nodded, his face solemn. 'He was a good boy,' he said.

'The best,' said Lucco, although he personally thought Rocco had been soft and weak-minded.

'And my father is so much missed.'

'I'm sure.'

'My mother's heartbroken,' said Jonathan.

'Hey – anything else I can do, anything at all, you know that.' *Like I haven't done enough?*

'How can you bring back a son? How can you bring back a beloved father?'

Well, you couldn't. But Lucco could sweeten the loss with handouts and deals, settle the family down that way. He'd done all that. Time to move on.

'Seeing my mother in black? It breaks my heart,' said Jonathan.

*When will this fucker stop milking it?* wondered Lucco in irritation. He'd done everything he could do to make it better. *Fuck* Alberto for making that call so quickly. He could have smoothed it over somehow, made it less of a shock to that old fart Enrico. But now it was too late. Rocco had got himself done, and Enrico had dropped off the twig with his bad heart at hearing the news. And Jonathan was hardly the loser in all this. He was the Don now, like Lucco, he was in charge. Maybe Lucco had even done him a favour.

Gianni cut the engines to a muted roar. Suddenly they could hear the lap of the waves and the gulls crying overhead.

'The voices of sailors lost at sea,' said Jonathan, watching them wheel. 'You believe that?'

Lucco didn't. Dead was dead. No need to get all poetic about it.

'This was a good idea of yours,' said Lucco. 'A bit of relaxation, and no prying ears to try to listen in while we talk. Fucking FBI, they're all over this goddamned city like a rash.'

Gianni was stepping down from the helmsman's seat and Lucco saw him take a pistol out from the locker under the wheel. Lucco's mouth dropped open.

'Gianni?' he said, as his old friend Gianni Ecco took aim at his head.

Lucco turned away, yelling 'No, wait!'

The first shot took him high up in the shoulder. Blood sprayed and Lucco let out an ear-piercing scream. The shot spun him around and he slumped back against the plastic-covered padded seats, gazing up at Gianni – his friend, for fuck's sake! – and then at Jonathan, who was smiling down at him in what looked like satisfaction.

'Wait,' he said again, feeling the strength going from his legs as shock set in.

'Wait for what, you little pisser? You want to take any more bites out of my family?' demanded Jonathan, spitting angrily at Lucco's face.

'But I ... it wasn't my fault...'

'You were *responsible* for my brother's safety. You said it yourself. You know, my mother don't look so hot in black, Lucco. I wonder how your sweet young *wife* will look in it, arsehole?'

442

'Wait,' said Lucco, his voice fading as blood loss drained his strength away.

'Wait for what?' asked Jonathan. He nodded to Gianni.

Gianni stepped forward and aimed again.

Desperately, Lucco scrambled up and hurled himself off the back of the boat and into the sea.

'*Shit!*' yelled Jonathan, throwing himself against the rail and staring down at the churning waters.

Lucco's dark head bobbed up. Gianni took aim, but Jonathan caught his arm, snatched the gun from his hand.

Gianni looked at Jonathan's set, stony face and shrugged.

'What the hell, Jono? We're miles out, there's no shipping here to speak of. He's weak already. Let the son of a bitch drown.'

Jonathan shook his head. Lucco was staring up at them, pleading, gasping in salt water and air in equal measures, struggling for life. But all Jonathan could see was his mother's suffering, stricken face when she realized that both her son and the man she loved were dead.

He slapped the gun back in Gianni's hand and ran to the wheel, throwing the engine hard astern. The powerful motors roared and they heard Lucco's choking scream as he was sucked beneath the boat to hit the propellers.

There was a hard, shocking judder that shook the vessel from stem to stern. Jonathan had to snatch at a seat as he almost fell with the impact. Then he stopped the engines and ran back to where Gianni stood, peering into the water.

'Can you see him?' Jonathan demanded.

'No.' Gianni's sharp eyes were scanning the waters at the back of the boat. All was calm now. Lucco was gone.

'Look!' said Jonathan, pointing to the port side.

Lucco was there. He was floating face down in the water, with a red umbilical cord of intestine snaking through the water and connecting him to the underside of the boat. Blood seeped from his body. He was dead.

'Propeller ripped his guts out,' said Gianni, crossing himself.

Jonathan, grim-faced, went to get the boat hook. 'Let's haul him in.'

Gianni said nothing. He got out the ropes, the tarpaulin sheet and the concrete blocks that would carry Lucco Barolli to the seabed and keep him there.

Much later that same day, Sophie Thomson was sitting in the bar at the Plaza Hotel. She was drawing many admiring glances as she sat there sipping the dregs of a dry martini with her incredibly long legs twining around her bar stool and her blonde hair piled loosely up on her head to accentuate the willowy perfection of her swan-like neck.

*Where was he?*

She glanced at her watch for the tenth time.

Lucco was never late, or at least not as late as *this*. He should have been here at seven and now it was gone eight. She felt humiliated. Nobody stood her up, not even Lucco fucking Barolli. She was sick of this. Come to that, she was more than a little sick of *him*.

'Get you another?' asked the bartender as she put the empty glass down.

'No,' she said. 'Don't think so, thanks.'

Sophie stood up, gathered up her bag, and left.

# 92

Over a week after the opening night of Annie's, Annie was invited over to Alberto's place on the Upper East Side for dinner at eight. Drinks at seven thirty.

'And bring your security too. Mark Carson, wasn't that his name?' Alberto said over the phone.

'It was. It is.'

'How is he?'

'Better. Thanks, we'll be there.'

'Look forward to it, Stepmom.'

Alberto's apartment wasn't as palatial as Constantine's had been, but it was still a million-dollar place set in the heart of Manhattan. They were greeted by servants who took their coats, gave them drinks. Heavies were hanging around both inside and outside the apartment. There was an air of business going on in the background, even while this was clearly a social occasion.

Aunt Gina was there, skulking in a corner beside the fire. Saying nothing to Annie except a terse greeting.

*Nothing new there.*

Daniella was there too, dashing over to Annie

when she came in. She looked radiant, truly lovely. She was wearing a full-length tomato-red shift dress that suited her colouring beautifully. Her wayward dark hair was scooped up in a topknot. She looked ravishing.

'Hi! How are you?' she said, hugging Annie then Max, being careful of his arm. 'Is it painful? I heard all about what happened.'

'It's fine.'

Annie glanced around. Not that she cared, but if the creep was oiling his way around here somewhere, she'd like to be forewarned... 'I don't see Lucco. Is he here?'

'No, he's off somewhere doing something, who knows? You've got a drink? Come and try some of these little appetizers...'

'Mr Barolli will see you now,' one of the heavies whispered in Annie's ear ten minutes later. 'If you will both follow me...'

Annie exchanged a look with Max. He still had his arm in a sling, but it was healing well and there were no complications. He raised his eyebrows at her and followed.

The heavy took them to a door, knocked on it, then opened it. Annie and Max passed inside.

'Stepmom!' Alberto rose from behind the desk, a smile lighting his face as he saw her there. Annie saw two more hard-eyed watchers were in there with him, just leaning against the wall, looking at his guests, not at him.

Alberto hugged Annie.

'Did you see Daniella out there?' he asked.

'Yeah, we did,' said Annie. 'What's Lucco up to? She says he's not around at the moment.'

'Who knows?' Alberto sat back down with a shrug. 'He'll come back when he's ready, I suppose. If he wants to.' His face clouded then. 'For the funeral, maybe.'

*Cara's funeral,* Annie thought. So easily, it could have been her own instead.

'Well, of course he'll *want* to be there,' said Annie. She looked into her stepson's suddenly hard blue eyes and paused. 'That is, if he's welcome.'

She thought again of what Alberto had said to her when they met at the hospital. *This can't go on. Aunt Gina's right.*

'And there's Daniella,' said Annie.

'Ah yeah. So there is.'

She was still staring into Alberto's eyes. Now she was remembering other things. How she and Max both believed he was in love with his sister-in-law, and hated Lucco's treatment of Daniella. And how all the Barolli clan had known about Enrico Mancini's bad heart, and that it had been Alberto who'd made the call to the Mancini family about Rocco, precipitating Enrico's fatal heart attack and landing Lucco even more squarely in the shit than he already was. Lucco had tried to have her killed. Soon, she felt sure, Lucco would have been gunning for Alberto too.

'You can always take over, for the moment,' she said, her eyes holding Alberto's.

'So I can,' said Alberto, and gestured for them both to sit down.

He moved around the desk and sat down too.

'I wanted to talk to you about the will,' said Alberto.

'The…?' Annie looked at him in confusion.

'Papa's will. If you are happy to discuss this in front of Mark…?'

'Perfectly happy,' said Annie, puzzled. What the hell was there to discuss? All that was done and dusted.

'Then let's cut straight to the chase, shall we?' Alberto flashed her a smile. 'My darling stepmom, you were worked over in that will. It was a whitewash and I want to make amends. I want to gift you several things. The Holland Park house is to be yours, and Papa's penthouse here. Also, the club shares – Papa owned forty-nine per cent, the rest were yours. I want you to have them all, and be sole owner.'

Annie's mouth had dropped open as he spoke. She stared at him for several moments, then she said: 'Can you do that? The penthouse was sold…'

'I can do whatever I like,' he said, smiling. 'As you so rightly said … I've taken over.'

'For the moment,' she said.

'Ah yeah. That's right.'

*And it's going to be a fucking long moment, right?* she thought. *This 'moment' really could last a lifetime.*

Again, she wondered what had become of Lucco. Her gut instinct told her he wasn't coming back. But meanwhile, she had regained her home. Homes, plural. One in London, one in New York. And she had her business, too; full ownership, not partial.

There was a light tap at the door and Daniella slipped inside.

'Have you told her?' she asked as she crossed the room.

'Yeah. I have,' said Alberto.

Daniella moved around the desk and stood to the right and slightly behind Alberto's chair. Both Annie and Max did a double-take when she reached down a hand. Alberto grasped it, brought it to his lips in a brief kiss, and held onto it.

*Holy shit.*

'I don't know what to say,' said Annie.

'Just say thanks and then leave it at that,' said Alberto. 'You gave Papa a great deal of happiness. You didn't deserve to be kicked out in the cold like that.'

'Then ... thanks,' she said, breaking into a grin as her eyes met Daniella's. Now she knew what that radiance meant. This was a girl in love, and it was reciprocated.

'It'll all be sorted out with the lawyers. Everything legal and above board. Okay? No funny business. Your ownership will be indisputable.'

They talked on, but for Annie everything after that was a daze. Once again she was a rich woman, and totally independent; she loved it. For the first time since Constantine's death, she was able to breathe easily, to relax a little. And that was all thanks to Alberto.

'Well, dinner's going to be served soon, if you'll excuse us for a moment...?' said Alberto. 'I have some more friends waiting to see me before we sit down to eat.'

Annie and Max stood up and went to the door.

'Oh – and Max...?' Alberto called from behind them.

449

Max *almost* turned around. He checked himself in the nick of time.

'You're good, you know,' said Alberto admiringly. 'Very good.'

Annie turned back and now so did Max. They looked at Alberto. He shrugged apologetically.

'What can I say? I've got a very good – almost photographic – memory. Not something I talk about much, but it's there. I saw you, Mr Max Carter, at an art exhibition in London in the Sixties. You were involved in a fight. You're not Mark Carson. I recognized you the moment we met in Holland Park.'

'You mean you knew and you didn't say?' demanded Annie.

'Hey, you must have had your reasons, Stepmom. Although I *was* concerned you might have committed bigamy. But I figured it was none of my business, and maybe one day you'd tell me what the hell was going on.'

Annie had to smile then. 'I didn't mean to commit bigamy, Alberto. And I will tell you what's going on,' she said. 'Soon, okay?'

'Clever little bastard,' said Max under his breath.

As they went out, two men went in. The door was closing behind them ... but as it did, Annie looked back. She saw one of the men approach Alberto, who greeted him with a hug and a warm smile. Then the man bent and kissed Alberto's hand.

He was still Constantine's charming and polite youngest son. But now he would be Constantine's successor – and, as Annie looked back at him, she thought that he had never in his entire life looked more like his father.

Outside Alberto's study they walked straight into Aunt Gina. She gave a brief nod, and made as if to pass on. Annie caught her arm. Gina looked down at Annie's hand, then up at her face.

'And I suppose you don't know where Lucco is, either?' she asked, watching the older woman's eyes.

Gina shook her head.

'Constantine used to talk to me about *omertà,* the Sicilian code of silence,' said Annie. 'That's what's happening here. Right?'

Gina said nothing.

'You know what's happened, so does Alberto. But nothing's going to be said.'

Gina still said nothing.

Annie knew that she was right. She couldn't shake the feeling that it was Aunt Gina who had been pulling strings here. She remembered Aunt Gina whispering on the stairs at Holland Park with Alberto. Aunt Gina had decided – she was sure of it – that Lucco's destabilizing influence had to end. No doubt about it, the women of the Barolli family were every bit as dangerous as the men. Cara had spent her time plotting over real and imagined hurts, and Gina ... well, who knew?

'You won't even tell me what's been going on? Not even me, a member of the family?'

Aunt Gina's lip curled slightly. Annie knew that Gina had never accepted her for one minute as a family member. To Gina, she would always be an incomer, an outsider. Gina had never liked her;

and – to be fair – she had never liked Gina, either.

'We both loved Constantine,' said Annie.

Gina gently pulled her arm away from Annie's grasp. Their eyes locked.

Finally, Gina said: 'You're right. We did. And for that at least I wish you good luck, Annie Carter,' she said, and moved on.

'It's Carter-Barolli,' said Annie faintly, but Gina was already gone, into the study where Alberto was taking on his father's mantle of power.

# 93

Next day, Annie and Max left Layla with Gerda at the hotel and went to St John's Cemetery in Queens. Annie placed a large bouquet of red roses on Constantine's hugely elaborate grave and stood there for long moments, thinking about the man she'd loved, married and lost.

There was a cold easterly wind blowing today, ripping the leaves from the trees. Autumn had arrived and soon it would be winter. Annie stuffed her hands into the pockets of her black cashmere coat and shivered at the thought of Constantine lying alone beneath the cold earth.

Soon there would be another family funeral, another grave alongside this one when Cara was laid to rest; Rocco, however, was home in New Jersey, being buried by his own family there. Even in death, Cara and Rocco were apart. Constantine had been so right about that; they should never have been together in the first place.

'So what now?' said Max when she'd been standing there in silence for a while.

Annie looked around at him. She was Annie Carter-Barolli, Madam, gang boss, Mafia queen. Once she had stood hard-eyed and stared out at the world, living by her own motto of 'dig deep and stand alone'. Once she had never cried, never weakened. But she felt real tears in her eyes now and a hard lump in her throat as she stood there beside Constantine's grave. She had to blink hard to focus on Max's face.

'What?' she asked blankly.

'Where do we go from here?' asked Max.

'Well, I ... you're going back to London?' *And you're going to take Layla with you, I know it*. She wiped irritably at her face as a tear spilled over.

'So ... are you planning to stay here?' he asked.

Annie looked at him. Max Carter. She'd loved him just about forever, and had been through hell for it. Now he was pussy-footing around, playing mind games with her. She walked a few paces away from the grave, feeling the anger building up in her gut, feeling the exasperation, the sheer *powerlessness* of this situation.

She was in love with this man. But he was going to hurt her. That much was certain.

'Look.' Suddenly she turned and walked back to him, stood there, confronted him. 'For fuck's sake! This is doing my head in. Why are you dragging this out? You said you were going to take Layla away from me: why haven't you done it yet?'

'What?' Max's face was inscrutable.

'You heard!'

Max stuck his hand in the pocket of his over-coat and stared at her.

'When am *I* going to snatch Layla?' he said. 'Hey – *I* wasn't the one who booked tickets on a night flight to California.'

'I did that because I *had* to,' Annie burst out, flinging her arms wide in exasperation. 'I couldn't go on with it, wondering and waiting and thinking, he's going to take her, any minute now I'll turn round and neither of them will be there and what the fuck will I do then? I had to do *something*.'

'Yeah, you've always been good at doing *something*,' he said sarcastically. 'Usually the *wrong* thing.'

Annie squared up to him. 'Oh really? Like what?' she demanded.

'Where do I start?' He turned away as if in deep thought, then spun back towards her. 'Oh yeah. *I* know. Marrying Constantine and making a biga-mist of yourself when you still had a husband, how about *that?*'

'Are you ever going to let that go? For the love of God, I believed you were dead!'

'Nice to think you sat around mourning me for … oh, how long was it? A few months. Fuck it, I was barely *cold*.'

'You weren't cold at all. You weren't even *dead*.'

'Oh, and that would have kept you happy, would it? If I really had been?'

Annie's jaw dropped.

'How can you *say* that?' she spat out. 'Look, I

was in a hole. I had to act. You weren't there. I had to think of Layla.'

'Oh, the self-sacrificing mother,' he mocked. 'Prostituting herself to give her kid a roof over her head.'

'I never prostituted myself. I *married* Constantine. I *loved* Constantine.'

'Yeah, so you keep saying.' For fuck's sake, did she have to keep ramming *that* down his throat? She was standing here in tears beside the grave of her second husband, and yet he had no way of knowing if she had ever shed so much as a single tear over the loss of *him*.

'I'm just telling the damned truth.' Annie was trembling with rage as they stood nose to nose, glaring at each other. She pointed back to the grave. 'The *truth* is you owe him. You owe him for keeping us safe when you weren't there to do it.'

'I know that.'

Annie stepped back. 'What?'

'I said, I know that.' Max drew in a calming breath. 'For God's sake, what do you think I am, some sort of cunt? I know all that he's done. That makes me feel a fucking sight worse, not better.'

Annie shook her head. 'I don't understand you,' she said mournfully.

'That's obvious,' said Max, and turned away from her. She was just dashing after him when he turned back. 'Look,' he said, grabbing her with his good arm. 'Layla needs us both.'

'I know that,' said Annie. 'I've been going through seven kinds of hell thinking of taking her away from you. I know how much she loves you.'

'Then we'll *both* go back to London and make

a life there with her.'

Annie felt the pit of her stomach sink at his words. For Layla, he was willing to tolerate her. That's what he was saying. He would spend the rest of his life beating her over the head with her 'lapse', as he saw it, and they would grow old and miserable and bitter together, but Layla would have her mum and dad there, both of them.

She shook her head furiously. 'No! I couldn't stand that.'

With Constantine, she had known what it was to be loved. Once, with Max, she had known the same sweet, incredible intensity of feeling. She couldn't just live a half-life, going through the motions of a marriage for the sake of her child, however much she loved her.

'What? You couldn't stand living with me again? After him?' His face was blank, masklike.

'I couldn't stand us living a lie, even if it was for Layla's sake!'

'Is that what it would be? A lie?'

'Yeah! It would! Because you can't let this go, because you *don't love me*.'

Max's brows drew together as he stared hard at her.

'What are you talking about?' he demanded, shaking her slightly. 'You think I don't love you? You really think I'd have been so fucking cut up about you running off with Constantine if I didn't love you? You really think I'd have thrown myself in front of a *bullet* if I didn't love you?'

Annie stood there, frozen in shock.

'Well say something, if it's only "bollocks",' he snapped. 'I love you, you stupid mare. If you don't love me, then fine. I understand. You've moved on. So we'll be bloody civilized about it, all right? We'll live apart but we'll sort out something so that we both see Layla. It's not a problem.'

Annie was silent, staring at his face.

'For fuck's *sake,*' growled Max.

'It *is* a problem,' she said at last.

'What?'

'Living apart but both seeing Layla.'

'I might've known you'd be bloody antsy about it...'

'I'm not being antsy. I'm being honest. I can't live apart from you because I don't want to. I love you. I've never stopped loving you, not for one moment.'

Max was very still, not even breathing.

Finally, he gulped in air. 'But you married Constantine.'

'I loved Constantine. But I never forgot you, and I never stopped loving you. And the minute I saw you there in the Palermo, and you called me a slut, I thought, that bastard, how dare he say that to me? I was so mad I wanted to kick your teeth straight down your throat. But, you know what? Fool that I am, I fell in love with you all over again, right then.'

He said nothing.

The wind gusted icily across the graveyard. Annie wrenched a shaking hand through her hair, pushing it back from her face. 'Please say something,' she moaned.

Now Max started to smile. 'Like what?'

'Like you love me.'

'I just said that.'

'Well, for God's sake – just say it again, will you?'

For a long moment, he was still, just staring at her. Then, using his one good arm, he pulled her in tight against the front of his body. 'I love you, Annie Carter,' he said, and kissed her hard and long.

'It's Carter-Barolli,' she corrected him when she came up for air.

'No it ain't. Not any more,' said Max, and he put his arm around her and they walked back to the limo.

Just once, he glanced back. He knew he'd never come here again. He could see the blood-red roses lying there, starkly beautiful beneath the headstone and against the windswept greenery. His friend and colleague Constantine Barolli. Without him, would Annie have been able to save Layla? Would Annie herself have survived? He didn't think so.

*You owe him,* she'd said.

And she was right of course. Constantine had trod on his territory, claimed what was Max's for his own ... but now Constantine was gone. And it was time to let the grudge go, or let it eat him alive and ruin what was going to be a good life with her and their child.

He couldn't afford to let that happen. Not after they'd been through so much, not after they'd come so far and, against all the odds, found each other again.

He looked back at the grave and thought, *All right, you old bastard. Thanks, okay? Thanks, pal. Rest easy there. Rest in peace.*

And then he put his arm around his wife, kissed her, and together they walked away from the grave of Constantine Barolli.

## Epilogue

Brother Benito had been expecting them; he'd received the letter two weeks ago at the monastery, and ever since then he'd been happily anticipating their arrival. Max hadn't specified an *exact* date, but Benito held himself in readiness.

On the day when it finally happened, he'd been to prayers, had breakfast, gone out into the garden to dig the soil over for next season's crops. Then he washed, had a small lunch with the brothers, and took his Bible out to his favourite shady spot in the garden to sit quietly and read and contemplate.

When the call went up from one of the younger monks, he left his seat and went smiling to the gate just as their car pulled up outside. Max Carter got out from the driver's side. From the passenger's side there emerged a tall, slender woman dressed in a plain white shift dress. Her long straight dark hair was being blown about in the wind, but she didn't fuss with it. Benito saw that Max and the woman were arguing.

'All right,' Max was saying. 'I'll give you Dolly Farrell, okay? She can stay, she's done a good job. But the signs stay too.'

'Max...' the woman said, her tone exasperated.

459

'Don't "Max" me. I've met you halfway, that's fair. Wouldn't you say?'

'No. Actually, I wouldn't.'

A little girl of about five years old tumbled out from the car, and quickly took the woman's hand, looking uncertainly ahead to where the grizzled old monk stood waiting.

'Max! My friend!' called out Benito.

Max and the woman looked ahead to where Benito was waiting beside the gate. Max gave a grin and raised his hand in greeting. The three of them walked up the dusty pink track towards him, Max with his arm casually thrown across the woman's shoulders. When they reached Benito, Max stepped forward and gave him a hug, slapping him on the back.

'You old bastard!' He laughed as Benito embraced him.

'That *can't* be the way to talk to a monk,' said Annie, scandalized.

Max glanced back at her. Layla was hiding behind her skirts now, overcome with shyness.

'He's very difficult to offend,' said Max, grinning. 'I told him to fuck off lots of times, and he never did.'

Annie's eyes met Benito's and she relaxed slightly. He really didn't look too bothered by this irreverent behaviour. 'This is Layla,' she said, indicating the little girl.

'She's adorable,' said Benito.

'This is Brother Benito, the man who saved my life,' said Max to Annie, drawing her closer. 'This is Annie Carter,' said Max proudly to Benito. 'This is my wife.'

Benito smiled and shook her hand. 'She's beautiful,' he said to Max.

'Don't tell her that, she's vain enough as it is.' Max's eyes were teasing as they caught Annie's.

*Not a serious argument then,* he thought. These two looked to be very much in love. He guessed they sparred a lot, but always made up.

'Come in, come in. I want to know everything about how you found your family again...'

Benito led the way into the monastery grounds, thinking that this was perfect; that he was so happy for his friend. Things had gone full circle for Max Carter and it had all worked out well.

'I have whisky,' Benito said to Max, who burst out laughing. He remembered all too well that grim time in hospital, when Benito and his cheap, disgusting whisky were all that kept him sane.

'*Whisky...?*' asked Annie, puzzled.

'I'll explain,' Max was saying as the monastery gates closed behind them. 'I'll explain everything, okay?'

'Okay,' she said, and smiled.

The publishers hope that this book has given you enjoyable reading. Large Print Books are especially designed to be as easy to see and hold as possible. If you wish a complete list of our books please ask at your local library or write directly to:

**Magna Large Print Books**
Magna House, Long Preston,
Skipton, North Yorkshire.
BD23 4ND

This Large Print Book for the partially sighted, who cannot read normal print, is published under the auspices of

## THE ULVERSCROFT FOUNDATION

# Swansea Libraries

| | | | | | | | |
|---|---|---|---|---|---|---|---|
| 1 | | 25 | | 49 | | 73 | |
| | | 26 | | 50 | | 74 | |
| | | 27 | | 51 | | 75 | |
| | | | 4/19 | 52 | | 76 | |
| | | | | 53 | 1/20 | 77 | |
| | | | | 54 | | 78 | |
| | | | | 55 | | 79 | |
| | | | | 56 | | 80 | |
| | | | | | | 81 | |
| | | | | | | 82 | |
| | | | | | | 83 | |
| | | | | | | 84 | |
| | | | | | | 85 | |
| | | | | | | 86 | |

uned

wasanaethau Cyn
â chi fel cwsmer
ddim i gartrefi pol

gion cyllidebol Cyng
o gynnal y gwasana
aeth hwn yn cael ei d
ghoriad agored ynghyl
unity
rvices